SCHROEDER

Scribner's Best of the Fiction Workshops

 1997

Guest Editor
Alice Hoffman

Series Editors
John Kulka and Natalie Danford

SCRIBNER PAPERBACK FICTION
PUBLISHED BY SIMON & SCHUSTER

For Paolo
N. D.

SCRIBNER PAPERBACK FICTION
Simon & Schuster Inc.
Rockefeller Center
1230 Avenue of the Americas
New York, NY 10020

Text is set in Baskerville
Designed by Brooke Zimmer
Manufactured in the United States of America

1   3   5   7   9   10   8   6   4   2

Library of Congress Cataloging-in-Publication Data
Scribner's best of the fiction workshops 1997 / guest editor, Alice Hoffman.
    —Scribner pbk. ed.
    p.   cm. — (Scribner's best of the fiction workshops; 1)
    1. American fiction—20th century. 2. Canadian fiction—20th century.
3. Short stories, American. 4. Short stories, Canadian. I. Hoffman, Alice. II. Series.
                PS659.S38   1997
        813' .5408—dc21   96-47122
                    CIP

ISBN 0-684-83314-X

Copyright and permission information continued on page 400.

CONTENTS

PREFACE

It wasn't so long ago—Hemingway's generation—when the only school a writer attended was the school of hard knocks. That's not to say writers of an earlier era went without instruction or encouragement—think for example of how Hemingway benefited from the counsel of Gertrude Stein and Ezra Pound. But such literary alliances were fragile, and were partly forged by luck and circumstance. Today aspiring writers look to hone their craft in the more cordial environs of the classroom and may opt to enroll in one of the many American and Canadian universities offering graduate degrees in creative writing. A quick glance at the biographical notes of the recent *Granta* issue "The Best of the Young American Novelists" confirms that members of the newest generation of writers are more likely than not to have attended one of these workshops; in fact, some of the contributors to the special *Granta* issue are now themselves teachers of creative writing.

Creative writing courses began to appear on the curricula of American colleges and universities as early as the turn of the century, but it took nearly another forty years before the first program was officially founded at the University of Iowa in 1939. The real flowering of the workshops, however, began in the aftermath of the Second World War when the GI Bill and federal funding forever changed the nature of higher education in this country. Independently of one another these programs came into existence, each of them developing its own identity and legacies. In 1967 the Associated Writing Programs, a not-for-profit organization, was founded by fifteen writers representing thirteen programs, to act as a link between the workshops and "to encourage the teaching of literature as a living art."

The full story of how writing got into the classroom would be a narrative of many intersecting historical and economic developments. Perhaps a more philosophical explanation lies within the legacy of American individualism—in the Emersonian belief that any individual with enough talent, given the opportunity, can achieve greatness. Shakespeare, as Emerson wrote, was not always Shakespeare but was once a young man pursuing a dream. Critics of the workshops—and there have been notable ones over the years—will point out the contradiction in such a legacy—that individuals are now collectively pursuing their dreams in the classroom. But at our century's end such criticism no longer carries the weight it once did. The long list of prominent postwar writers who have emerged from the Iowa workshop alone—Wallace Stegner, Flannery O'Connor, Raymond Carver, John Gardner, Gail Godwin, to name just a few— is proof that workshops foster talent and don't crush individual spirit.

In collecting the best short fiction from the workshops in an annual anthology, we aim to introduce to a larger audience the exciting new voices coming from these programs, and to provide workshop writers with a publishing venue. We envision this series as a benchmark and showcase for emerging writers. And we hope succeeding volumes— so many privileged glimpses into the future—will generate continuing excitement and enthusiasm.

Over one hundred graduate workshops were invited to submit their two best stories from the '95–'96 school year. We left it up to the program directors to choose the academic year's best work in any way they deemed appropriate. It is tempting to draw overarching conclusions about the future state of American writing after reading about two hundred nominations: tempting, but almost impossible to do so accurately. Nevertheless, we can share some general observations about the stories we received. An old truism states that it is always easier to point out what is missing than to describe what is present. We found that no less apt in this case; while we delighted in the generally high quality of the stories, we were surprised at how few ethnically and racially specific characters we saw and—given the residential patterns of North America—how few stories had suburban settings.

The voices and themes in the stories themselves were quite varied, with only one motif recurring with great frequency: the tale of a protagonist who returns to his or her hometown after receiving an undergraduate or graduate degree, heavily in debt and unable to find work. We have no way of knowing whether this reflects autobiography or all aspiring writers' fear that their parents' dour recital of the phrase "starving artist" will come true.

Considering the volume of work received, the consensus among the readers—ourselves and guest editor Alice Hoffman—was almost uncanny. In retrospect, the final shape of the book now seems inevitable. Alice Hoffman, herself a graduate of the Stanford University program, was cooperative, patient, and consistently enthusiastic about this project from the start. It is hard to imagine a more generous guest editor or more insightful reader.

Alice's agent Elaine Markson was also an indispensable part of the process, as was her assistant Pari Berk. We would like to express our gratitude to all the program directors, professors, and administrators, and of course students, who worked so hard to make this project possible. Charles Baxter, Andrew Levy, Dave Fenza of the AWP, and Donald Justice all contributed information about the history of the workshops. We extend heartfelt thanks to BJ Gabriel, who took special interest in this project and brought it to the attention of the right people. Our editor, Penny Kaganoff, not only guided us every step of the way, but was an integral part of the entire process. Her endless patience and willingness to help out with both details and larger questions have had a great impact. We would also like to thank Penny's assistant, Diana Newman, Jeff Wilson of the Simon & Schuster contracts department, and our very supportive families.

—JOHN KULKA *and* NATALIE DANFORD

If you are a director of a graduate creative writing program in the United States or Canada that was not included in this edition, please send a brief note with your name, university, address, and phone number to
Penny Kaganoff, Simon & Schuster,
1230 Avenue of the Americas,
New York, NY 10020.

INTRODUCTION

by ALICE HOFFMAN

In 1973, when I was twenty-one, I went to California to learn to be a writer. I was a cosmetology school drop-out who had managed to graduate from college in part due to the leniency of the sixties. At that point, I had never met a writer, had never heard of William Faulkner, and certainly had no idea that stories had to be typed and double-spaced before they were submitted to magazines. In short, I knew nothing, other than the fact that I was addicted to books, and that fiction—both the reading of it and the writing of it—had some-how saved my life.

I went out to Stanford University. I'd never heard of the school at the time—although I was heartened to learn it was a short drive from San Francisco. It was still the sixties, though the calendar dictated otherwise, and there was a great sense of hope in the creative writing department at Stanford. We felt that anything could happen—and why shouldn't we? Ray Carver was in Palo Alto then, as was Scott Turow and Bill Kittredge. Leading the seminar that year was Albert Guerard, the eminent writer and teacher, who had worked with so many writers at Harvard and Stanford, including John Updike and John Hawkes. Through his brilliant critiques and enormous generos-ity, Professor Guerard was the mentor who changed many of our lives. He was responsible for helping his students to make that all-important leap: to believe that you are, indeed, a writer.

There have always been critics who dismiss creative writing pro-grams, and we know their complaints: There are too many programs, producing too many MAs and MFAs, for whom there will never be jobs enough at prep schools, let alone at universities. Students who attend writing programs are being taught by rote, becoming clones who can only create in the style of the school they attend: Western realists from Iowa, fabulists from Johns Hopkins and Brown. And anyway, such critics go on, real writers write, don't they? They don't sit in a classroom. They aren't taught.

I could not disagree more with such complaints. For those who say that writing cannot be taught, I say it is talent that cannot be taught. Technique and pacing can be, as can discipline and the importance of a cold eye when assessing one's own work. What students learn at writing programs is as varied as the programs themselves: To value the company of your fellow writers. To trust yourself above all others. To avoid temptation and get back to work. To revise. To revise again. And then, when you're sick to death of your story and can't even remember why you thought it was worth writing in the first place, to revise once more.

A writer, after all, needs three basic ingredients when starting out: Time, talent, and hope. Time is an amazingly difficult commodity to come by out in the real world—lack of it is the beast that chews up writers and spits them out as assistants to editors and agents, professions that circle around writing, and provide a guaranteed paycheck. Although it isn't impossible to maintain a full-time job and write, it's extremely difficult. A year or two in which to write, often paid for by fellowship, scholarship, or a university-related job, is a gift few authors can repay. Would it have been possible for me to complete my first novel, *Property Of,* had I not attended a writing program? Perhaps, but it would have taken five or ten years rather than one, and even then, would anyone have read it?

This is another truth about writing programs—a degree certainly doesn't guarantee publication, but one can be assured that a manuscript from a graduate of a writing program is taken more seriously than one that appears from out of the blue. In my own case, it was Albert Guerard who sent one of my stories to an ex-student of his who was the editor of *Fiction* magazine in New York. When that story was published, Ted Solotaroff, the highly regarded editor who was the hero of many fledgling writers, spotted it, requested another story for his wonderful *American Review,* then asked for a novel. Knowing full well this might be my only chance to publish, I swore I was almost finished with a novel, then promptly sat down and began one. Although Solotaroff ultimately decided against taking *Property Of,* he sent me on to my agent, who sold the book to Farrar, Straus and Giroux. Would this have happened had I been working at a beauty parlor on Long

Island? Doubtful, I think. Laughable, perhaps. I'd be there still, and don't think I don't know it. But I'd be dreaming of fiction as I manicured your nails.

Talent is clearly something a writer has to bring to the program, but hope can be given and taken away. Hope, after all, is the oddest piece of a writer's constitution, and perhaps the most important. Unlike the case for brain surgeons, or even maintenance workers, there is no clear-cut evidence that the world will be improved because you wrote your story. Writers have to convince themselves that what they're doing matters. Most of us who have been to graduate programs know at least one writer—often among the best in the class—who gave up, for reasons no one could ever quite understand. Was it because of financial pressure? Self-doubt? Was the criticism this writer encountered too harsh? More cruelty than criticism, in fact? One professor at a writing program, when approached by the editors of this anthology, refused to submit her students' work: She did not wish to give them false hope for what might never come to pass. One imagines she was referring to success, or good fortune, or perhaps even a well-wrought story. But without hope, no words are ever written; it is hope that begins them and hope that gets them done.

One hundred and ninety-four stories were submitted to the editors of this anthology from creative writing departments throughout the United States and Canada. Forty were then sent on to me. An interesting fact about these forty submissions: Twenty-nine were written by women, sixteen of which have been included in this collection. That so many more writers were women may simply have been based on the statistics of this past year's attendance at writing programs. Certainly, when I went out to Stanford in 1973 the reverse was true. The stars were men; the heroes, men. In fact, I was quite unsure I had anything to write about. I did not know War. I did not hunt or fish or climb mountains. The greatest truths seemed closed to me; the literary door shut.

Perhaps one of the biggest favors Professor Guerard did for me was to introduce me to the writing of Grace Paley. It was at the instant when I finished her great story "In Time Which Made a Monkey of Us All" that I knew a woman's voice could ring as clearly as a man's, and that my concerns were humanity's concerns. I must say it now gives me great pleasure to discover, in reading for this anthology, the clear and beautiful voices of so many women. As for the preponderance of women writers this year, perhaps it is only that some of the men starting out have the ghosts of Faulkner and Hemingway and Carver to wrestle with, while the women, with fewer models, are freer to experiment and find their own singular and distinctive styles.

The submissions to the editors were not as culturally diverse as I would have imagined, but they were astoundingly diverse in terms of style and tone. As you will see, the range is nothing less than amazing. The writing programs represented are equally varied. Many writers here have attended the most prestigious of the writing programs—Brown and Iowa, for instance—but there are smaller, newer programs represented as well—Saint Mary's College of California and McNeese State University, for example. (Stanford is no longer a degree program, and instead grants ten two-year fellowships for fiction writers each year, many to writers who have already completed an MA or MFA.) There are writers here from several state schools, including Florida State, Louisiana State, and SUNY at Stony Brook. Two programs—University of Michigan and Concordia University—are represented by more than one writer.

Although the stories you are about to read were crafted while the authors were students in graduate writing programs, don't think this is novice work. Some of these stories will have you sitting up at night, turning pages, well aware that the fiction you are reading is cause for celebration. "Chemistry," for instance, is so gorgeous and fluid, so achingly alive, you will remember what it's like to read something brand-new, as if with her unique use of language the author has managed to crack open the world, like an egg. In "Escape," a tale of love and entrapment, we experience a girl's passion for her jailed boyfriend—to whom she may be nothing more than a useful commodity. The prose here is cool and elegant; this is real life, real people, told with a sophistication that is startling. In "Molested," a single mother of a retarded girl fights the odds of poverty and abuse in a story so well-told, so compelling, you can see the neighborhood of desperation right before your eyes, as well as the narrator's flaming red hair.

The three stories mentioned above are all about survival of one sort or another, and this, I think, makes perfect sense given the world these writers have inherited. There is plenty at stake in the stories in this collection, and even more to lose. On the whole these selections avoid the self-involvement of youth; as a matter of fact, if presented with any of these stories in the pages of a literary magazine, I doubt a reader would guess the writer was enrolled in a writing program.

Whatever Generation X was or is, I saw no sign of the self-interest usually attributed to this group. Although several of the stories deal with the perils of adolescence, often the territory of beginning writers, they do so with wisdom and wit. "Skin," for instance, is a delicate account of a daughter's abandonment, just when she needs her mother most. In the vibrant, charming "A Few Fish and Anonymous Spaniards," a girl on vacation on the north shore of Long Island experiences the sort of family life where nervous breakdowns and voodoo are equally possible. In "Jericho," a heart-breaking story of leave-taking, it is the daughter who is the caretaker of the father, and in "Now You See Her," a moral tale about fathers and sons, it is the father as well as his boy who learns life's lessons. The aforementioned "Chemistry" and "Escape" do nothing less than take the world of adolescence and turn our expectations around with a vengeance.

Within this collection, there are several stories that address domestic life with astounding maturity and depth, from an extremely adult point of view. The lyrical "Cartography," with its focus on a mother and two daughters, is told with assurance and experience. The stirring "Consolation," which recounts the tale of a woman living in the Philippines and her ability to both accept her fate and yearn for more, is so humane and thoughtful it may bring you to tears. In "Climbers," the domestic life encountered is completely colored by a brother's mental illness, and its effects on the family member left to cope as she tries to put back the pieces of a life.

You will find in these pages stories of both hometowns and far-off places. "Living Near Canada" is a plain-spoken and riveting account of a small New York town where nothing seems to turn out right, not even youth or love. "Kerr's Fault," the tale of an adopted hometown in the American West, gives us an antihero who isn't a cowboy but a history teacher. In "The Distance Between Prague and New Orleans," an American movie star discovers the identity he wishes for in a Jewish cemetery, and tries to make sense out of a world that moves far too quickly. "Finding Land" is a witty digest of two displaced American wives trying their best to navigate Japanese society.

Some of these stories focus on the dangerous and the dark: "The One Life" examines heroin use among the young, beautiful, and desperate in San Francisco. "Watertables" is a curious meditation on what is real and what is only imagined, set against bean fields and blistering heat. "First Grade," an elegantly wrought tragedy, shows us how a group of children try to make sense out of the hand of fate and the extreme brevity of life. There are also stories that are funny and sly. The wisecracking and warm "Tallulah at Your Feet," for instance, a chronicle of early adult angst suffered by a dog-walker in Boston, told with unusual style and charm. "Bloodlines," for another, an enormously good-humored and delicious tale that concerns the love of a good bull and of Ireland.

It is possible to group these stories into categories, but in fact, each is unique. I think of this collection as a series of doors, each a portal into a separate universe. There is world upon world between these covers. Surely, those who complain that writing program alumni are all cookie-cutter alike, all mining the same tired territory, will have to admit this sort of criticism doesn't apply here. Take "The Priest," a recipe for sin and redemption that charts an impossible love affair, and set this story next to "Lady Slipper," a clear-eyed account of an upper-crust life gone bad, stylistically and thematically as different from "The Priest" as day from night. Now set both of these against "Jericho," the emotional and realistic account of a girl leaving home for college, and you will experience some of the range of this collection.

If you think there's no hope for the future of fiction, if you think it's all been written and nothing will ever surprise you again, then read "Mrs. Sarah Quash," a fabulous modern fairy tale that revamps the animal groom motif, giving us an animal bride we won't soon forget. This daring and original story works completely on its own terms; it is not like any other you will read in this collection, or anywhere else for that matter.

The voices within are strikingly fresh, and that is why it has been such a pleasure to work on this anthology. Discovery is always exciting, and you are about to discover, as I did, some uniquely talented writers. These are the voices of the future, after all, and some of them will knock you flat and renew your faith in fiction. Oddly enough, the one element that connects these stories, so very different from one another in nearly every way, is hope: in the future, in the possibility of redemption, in survival against all odds. Several of the stories included in this anthology announce the debuts of important careers. These writers will be back, of that you can be certain. Frankly, dear reader, what's in these pages is only the start.

Margaret Price
University of Michigan

JERICHO

My sister Katie came to pick me up, and for a second I didn't recognize her. All her hair was gone. Since that morning it had been shaved to half an inch, a fuzzy blond layer that showed the bulge of her forehead and the pointed bone at the back of her head. She leaned against our dad's gray Volvo station wagon, thumbs in her front pockets, squinting against the sun, and when she saw me coming she raised both hands and waved. The car keys jangled importantly. She was sixteen.

"Hey, kiddo," I said.

"Hey, adult-o."

She'd dyed her hair as well as cut it, I saw; it used to be dark blond, the color of dead grass, but now had become the glossy whitish shade of a doll's. I looked over her shoulder into the car. The back was packed with duffel bags, fishing rods, a cooler. "I didn't get Dad yet," she said.

The air inside the car seemed liquid with heat. It was the last Friday in August, and we were going up to our family cottage in northern Michigan for the weekend.

When Katie and I were little we used to go for weeks at a time in the summer, but as we'd gotten older the visits had become shorter and farther between. No one said it out loud, but we were going this weekend, in a burst of togetherness, because it was my last weekend at home. On Wednesday I was leaving for California to go to college. This weekend was a punctuation mark we all felt, without discussing it, we were required to put on the summer.

"So, haircut," I said when we were headed across town to Dad's office.

Katie put a hand on her head. "What do you think?"

"I think you look like a duckling," I said.

Still driving, Katie put her left foot on the accelerator, turned in her seat, and poked the right in my direction, trying to kick me. The car speeded up and slowed down in bursts, and we swerved slightly over the center line.

"Watch it," I said.

She kept twisting in her seat, looking at me instead of the road. "Take it back!" she said. She was grinning, but the car was dodging like a toy. Across the way, a blue sedan jigged to avoid us.

"Careful!" I grabbed the wheel and straightened the car. Someone honked at us. "Don't be stupid," I said.

"If you can't say something nice," Katie said, deepening her voice to match our dad's, "don't say anything at all."

You look like a saint, I could have said; you look like a martyr, not in real life, but the way they paint them, patient and beautiful. I didn't, though. Katie's boyfriend Art had once told me I was mean. *Bitch,* he'd said, with a sort of wonderment in his voice, as though he'd just identified a new species of mammal. And since I didn't want to tell Katie how beautiful she was, even with half an inch of hair, since I couldn't bring myself to tell her that it didn't matter whether she curled her hair or dyed it black or cut it off, maybe he was right.

"Okay," I said. "Think of all the money you'll save on shampoo."

We traveled halfway around the circular drive in front of Dad's office building and pulled up in front of the smooth, white, privately maintained sidewalk to wait. He was vice-president of a public relations company called Premier Images. The building was a squat glass cylinder, set outside town in a dead-end court called Industrial Plaza. The front of the building was striped with bars of reflected sunlight; the inside was hidden as though the windows were covered with black paint.

"What do you think Dad'll say?" I asked.

"He won't like it," Katie said, "so he won't say anything."

She put her feet on the dashboard, on either side of the steering wheel. Her skirt slid up above her knees and she plucked at it, fanning herself. She gave a deep sigh and sank even lower in her seat. "Pain in the ass, pain in the ass," she said, making it into a little song. "This is going to be a pain in the ass."

I was energetic, full of the edgy good cheer that comes at the outset of a vacation. But I wished Dad would come out. I wanted to be moving. "What's the matter with you?"

"I'm just not in the mood for a big family deal right now," she said. "That's all."

"What big family deal?"

"The whole weekend."

"It's going to be fine," I said.

"Just like Christmas."

Christmas was the last time we'd been up to Jericho. During the bright, short days Katie and I had walked miles through the woods, battling the empty feeling of having nowhere to go, while Dad slept off what he'd drunk the night before. In the evenings we crouched by the fire in the living room, playing Monopoly and Sorry with cracked, faded boards and yellowing dice. We loaded wood on the fire hour after hour, poked the embers into bits and added more wood, but we were always cold. When it was time to go home on Sunday I'd cleaned everything up, loaded the car, and left a note for the caretaker. I drove the whole way home, all five hours in one shot. Katie lay in the back seat and slept. Dad rode silent in front, his hair oily and his eyes red.

"You're getting yourself upset on purpose," I said. "You're making it bad before it even gets bad."

"You're right, I'm an asshole," Katie said. "It's going to be terrific. It's going to be a fun-fest."

Then the sunlight slid and lurched on the outside of the building and Dad came out in his suit and aviator sunglasses, a square black briefcase in his hand. His hair was thick and gray; the knot of his tie was small and tight. He saw us and grinned. He had a strange grin: it always looked a little too knowing, almost evil, even when he meant it to be kind.

Just before he reached the car I said, "You have to have some faith in people, Katie."

"I don't have any faith," she said.

My parents bought the house in Jericho when they were newlyweds; they closed the sale on the day the first man walked on the moon. Five years later my mother died, but Dad and Katie and I kept going up for Christmas, for weekends and sometimes weeks in the summer. I couldn't remember a time when I didn't know what Jericho looked like, but it was a town I barely knew at all. In the dark gold late afternoon when we reached the intersection of two-lane highway and dirt road that was downtown Jericho, when I saw the general store on one corner and across from it the blue house with the hand-lettered sign in its window that said "Camelot Beauty Salon," the bolt of recognition I felt seemed deceptive. Jericho had the intensely familiar look of invented landscapes in dreams.

We stopped outside the general store, and when the engine died we all hesitated, like mourners observing a moment of silence. Then we clunked open the doors and put our feet on the pebbly dirt parking lot.

"Smarty!" said Mr. Monroe, the store owner, when he saw me walk in. "And Cutie!" he said when Katie walked in right after me. "You girls want a Tootsie Roll?"

Mr. Monroe liked Katie and me because he'd known us since we were little, or else because we were girls. With Dad, he took on the silent, not-quite-respectful formality reserved for people who came from the softer, warmer parts of Michigan. Dad's quick-grinning city charm didn't work in Jericho. I could see, as he tried to begin a jolly, masculine conversation with Mr. Monroe, how plump and flushed his face appeared, how flimsy and expensive his white button-down shirt and gray dress pants were. Eventually he picked up a plastic shopping basket and retreated down the aisle that held bread, paper products, and pet food.

"Let me look at you two," Mr. Monroe said. I'd grown taller than him in the last year, and he sat down on his stool behind the counter, as if to justify having to look up at me. "Look how grown-up you girls are. I bet you're about ready to go off to college, Smarty."

"Next week," I said. "I'm going to California."

"A week!" he said. "All by yourself!"

"Right."

"And this one!" He turned to Katie, who was inspecting the shelf of rental movies. "You're going to be taking care of your dad, aren't you? Oh, you're going to be ruling the roost from now on. I know you, Cutie."

Katie turned from the movies. "Not likely," she said, and although neither of us smiled, Mr. Monroe gave a delighted laugh.

Some of Mr. Monroe's energy seemed to come with us as we drove away from the store. Dad unrolled his window and tapped the ledge with his hand. Katie, in the front seat, turned on the radio and twisted the dial through miles of static before she found an unexpected burst of hard rock. When we reached the end of our driveway and turned up it for the twisting quarter-mile ride to the house itself, I gave a spontaneous cheer: "We made it!" Our house was a big white square, an ex-farmhouse surrounded by acres of unfarmed land. It hadn't been painted in my lifetime, but as we pulled into the driveway the late-afternoon sun reflected off its chipped face, so that the siding and the porch and even the rumpled patch of grass around it glowed dark gold.

A red plastic snow shovel lay across the front step like a hex. I remembered sticking it in the snow by the door last Christmas. Dad was rummaging through his keys. He scraped the key into the lock, and before I could think more about what the untouched shovel meant, the door opened with a bursting sound and we stepped inside.

The living room smelled of dust and the cold remains of burned logs. Beside the door stood a collapsed pair of dark-red rubber overshoes with a gray wool sock draped over the top of each to dry. One of the windows that looked onto the back porch was gone, its glass neatly punched out and flung across the floor. Leaves had blown in through the gap, piled by the wind against the walls and in corners. The evergreen wreath above the table had died and dropped all its needles; only a black skeleton of twined-together branches remained on the wall. Although it was still hot outside the house felt chilly, filled with dead air and motionless debris.

"What the hell is this?" Dad said. "Where's Lawrence?" Lawrence was a local kid who took care of the house when we were gone. He checked the furnace, did some cleaning and yard work, shoveled snow off the porch roof. He and Katie had a vague, off-and-on relationship during the few days a year they saw each other.

"I guess he hasn't been here," I said.

"Well, where is he?" Dad strode noisily through the kitchen, then up the narrow wood stairs, as though Lawrence might be hiding somewhere in the house.

"Alaska," Katie said.

"What?" Dad shouted from upstairs. His voice clanged and echoed, and I could tell he was in the bathroom.

I gave Katie a look; she shrugged.

Dad came pounding back down the stairs. He arrived in the middle of the living room and said, "Alaska."

"He said he was thinking about it."

"I see," Dad said. "And when did you come by this information?"

Katie took several steps backward, toward the fireplace. She stood up straighter, put both hands on her hips with the thumbs turned forward, and I felt a flash of recognition: it was our mother's gesture, something I hadn't known I remembered. "Last Christmas," she said. "It wasn't like he was being serious, though."

"It looks damn serious to me," Dad said. He took two more steps toward Katie, putting himself in arm's reach of her. "We could have been vandalized, you know. There could have been a fire. Anything."

Katie picked up the iron fireplace shovel and started poking the cold, half-burned hunks of wood. "Well, didn't you ever *call* him?" she said. "He's your caretaker, not mine."

"I might have called him," Dad said, "if I thought there was any reason to call. For example, had I known of his decision to move to Alaska. That would have been a reason." He looked at the shovel, and I could see him wanting to grab it from her.

"Hey," I said. "Hey. So it's a mess. We can clean it up. Okay? We'll get it cleaned up."

They stared at me as though I were a ghost. Then Dad yanked open the cellar door. Cobwebs, undisturbed for months, swung gently out toward his face. "I'm going to check the pipes," he said. "We'll be damn lucky if this whole house hasn't fallen apart." He stomped down the stairs, and the door eased shut behind him.

"And now," Katie said, "for the prick of the year award. The nominees are. Dad."

I looked at the missing window. There was no bird outside on the back porch; either it had been picked up by a raccoon or fox or had lived through the collision. In the kitchen I found packing tape and a plastic bag and taped a patch over the gap. I trimmed the edges with scissors and added an extra layer of tape for strength. Then I got a broom and started sweeping the needles and leaves and glass from the floor.

"You missed a spot," Katie said from the couch, watching me. She lay on her back, waving her legs in the air; her red flowered skirt fell around her waist and showed her underpants, which were striped.

"You could get your butt up," I said.

"I didn't think he was serious," she said. "Lawrence. I didn't know he'd just take off like that."

"Did he really go to Alaska?" I asked.

"I guess. I haven't heard from him." Katie grasped her toes and straightened her knees, stretching. Her legs were long and white, the thighs marked with blue veins blurred like the lines on a hockey rink. Her calves were thin and stalky as a ten-year-old's. "I guess he's gone," she said.

Dad came up from the cellar and went into the kitchen without speaking. Katie sat up and pulled her skirt down. I heard the refrigerator door clank with the bottles stored in its door. There was a long wait, and then he came out to the living room with a second beer in his hand. He made a slow tour of the room, pausing by the patched window and inspecting it. There were oily streaks of dirt across his white shirt and on the knees of his slacks. He dropped into the armchair and finished his beer.

"Well," he said, "we were lucky. It's nothing we can't fix." He stretched his arms over his head and let out a long, groaning sigh. And then his smile came out and glittered at us, shone like something polished, wiping away the past half hour. "You know what I think?" he said. "I think we're going to have a *great* weekend. Aren't we?"

"Yeah," I said.

After dinner I went quietly into Dad's room and gathered up his soiled clothes from the floor. Using the downstairs bathtub, I soaked them in a solution of baking soda and cold water, then scrubbed along the bias with an old toothbrush. I wrung them out in a towel and left them hanging from the shower rod, translucent with water.

I woke up feeling buried, it was so dark. I reached to my right, where Katie's bed was, but couldn't reach it. My arm chilled quickly, and I pulled it back in. Our room was upstairs, on the northeast corner, and it was always cold. The sheets seemed slightly damp; each of my toes felt icy and distinct. I thought of how I'd rolled down the car window that afternoon, how Katie had fanned her skirt back and forth in the heat; it seemed like something that had happened weeks ago.

Then, from downstairs, I heard the collection of small sounds that must have woken me up: quiet footsteps, a creaking of wood floor, the clink and clunk of a glass being filled and set down.

I sat up and snapped on the bedside lamp, as though abolishing a nightmare. Katie didn't budge; she slept sprawled on her stomach, face turned on the pillow toward me. She had one fist tucked under her chin and a preoccupied frown on her face, as though whatever she dreamt required effort. I listened and waited. Still asleep, Katie raised her eyebrows. I watched her for a few minutes more. Then I slid out of bed and went downstairs.

Dad sat in the orange light of a standing lamp, wearing his bathrobe and reading a heavy hardback novel. At his elbow, on the small end table, sat a squat glass and a fifth-size bottle of Dewar's. The bottle was indeterminately emptied; not more than half, not much less. He smiled at me, but it didn't glitter as easily as it did in the daytime. His face looked colorless and sparse, the way some women look when they've washed off their makeup.

"I saw you cleaned my clothes," he said. "Thank you."

"You're welcome." I sat on the couch across from him, although already I wanted to go back upstairs. There was no reason for me to check whether he was awake, whether he was drinking; it had been obvious from the sounds, as self-evident as a color. But I had to come down and look. Dad sat across from me like a mirage in the orange light, perfectly clear and about to vanish.

"You won't have to be doing that much longer," he said. "What day are we taking you to the airport? Thursday?" *To the airport*, he said, as though that were the end point of my journey.

"Wednesday." I thought of the footlocker and suitcase in my room back at home, already packed with clean clothes, my jewelry rolled in Kleenexes and stored in a box that I taped shut, my favorite coffee mug swaddled in a sweater and laid among the clothes in the trunk. Wednesday, nine thirty-five A.M.

"You've gotten so grown up," Dad said. "I wasn't even watching." Then his mouth broadened and turned down at the corners, and tears shone in his eyes. "I'm so proud of you. You're such a good girl."

"Thanks, Dad." I pulled my knees up to my chest and hugged them. I was wearing sweat pants and a T-shirt, and my arms were dotted with goose bumps.

"You're going to have such a great time," he said. "You're going to do just great." He sniffed and wiped his eyes with his fingers. "It's going to be so quiet around the house. Who's going to get on my case about doing my back exercises? Who's going to throw out that junk that goes bad in the refrigerator?"

"Katie will," I said.

He stood up and came toward me. As he crossed the floor I saw him lurch and step quickly to his left for balance. Then his hand came down on top of my head, grasping my skull as though he were palming a basketball, fingers spread over the crown. I sat still and let him right himself.

"It's going to be so quiet," he said.

"Do you not want me to go?" I asked. His hand was heavy, leaning on me, fingers spread. It kept me from looking up.

"Not at all," he said. "I want you to be happy. There's nothing I want more than that. I want you to go and be happy."

I reached up and took his hand off my head, turned it and looked at his watch. It was a broad black diver's watch, shock-proof, with a dial that glowed faintly green to show the numbers. "Dad," I said, "it's two-thirty. You should go to bed."

"See what I mean?" he said. "Who's going to tell me when to go to bed?"

I waited until I heard the squeak of his bedsprings. Then I picked up the glass from the end table, took it into the kitchen, washed it clean, and left it upside-down in the dish drainer. The bottle stood uncapped; the alcohol had begun to evaporate, and the living room smelled faintly of Scotch whiskey. I twisted the cap back on the bottle and replaced it in the kitchen cupboard. Upstairs, I found Katie still asleep, on her back now, one arm over her eyes. I turned the light off.

There were no more sounds from downstairs. Only two more nights to go, I thought. But I hadn't made it through *any* nights yet; it was still the same day that we'd arrived. Five nights total, I thought. Five nights until they take me—as Dad said—to the airport.

"Not likely," Katie said; the clarity of her voice made me gasp.

I knew she was asleep; I could tell from the pitch of her voice, distinct but somehow flattened, hollow, like the voice of a simultaneous translator. But I said her name anyway, and stared across at her bed in the dark, and waited to see if she could hear me from where she was.

Saturday, while Dad slept, we worked on the house. We filled the woodbox from the load of stovelengths that had been delivered and dumped messily beside the front porch, then stacked the extra in the woodshed. We swept the back porch. We paced across the backyard, a large piece of cleared land somewhere between a lawn and a field, collecting fallen sticks and branches. Katie mowed the grass with Dad's rider mower and I followed her, raking. We rolled the piles of leaves and cut grass into three mud-colored tarps, which we tied shut like fat bags of laundry. Then we hesitated. Usually we left the leaves bagged on the back porch for Lawrence to take care of.

Katie put her hands on her hips, thumbs forward. "Let's take them to the Christmas tree dump," she said.

We hauled the wet, bulging tarps to the station wagon one at a time, developing the fits of giggles that come over you when you're carrying something awkward and heavy in tandem. We drove a mile down the road to the turnout with a ditch behind it. In the bottom of the ditch lay a dozen Christmas-tree carcasses, some burned, some just dead and skeletal. We shook the tarps out, snapping them to get the last sticky leaves off.

When we went back to the car neither of us got in. We hesitated with our hands on the doors, looking at each other over the hot gray roof.

Wind blew southwest past us, following the curves of the road. It made Katie's hair lie down in sections, like wheat, and gave quick, crooked glimpses of her scalp. Her face was flushed and beaded with sweat along the hairline and beside her nose. Flecks of dark-brown leaves were stuck in her hair, and her upper lip was smudged with dirt.

"Let's go swimming," she said.

I looked at my wrist, but I wasn't wearing my watch. "We should get back."

"A short swim," she said. "Come on. You deserve a break today."

The wind slowed, and the sun came down in pulses. I remembered that I hadn't showered that day. My body felt filmed over with layers of sleep and sweat and leaf slime.

"Okay," I said.

Katie drove to a spot in the river seven miles outside town and parked on the bridge. The water was about thirty feet across here, with broad, flat rocks on either side. A woman lay on one of the rocks, sunning herself in a leopard-print bikini while two small kids, naked, played industriously in the shallow rapids near her. In the deep hole below the bridge two older boys were swimming, shouting to each other. One of them dove down, and I saw that he was wearing cut-off jeans, wrinkled and black with water, so baggy they seemed on the verge of slipping off. His white back wavered down through the green water, blurring as he went deeper.

Beside me, Katie climbed the bridge rail and swung her legs over, perching on it as though it were a low fence. The drop from bridge to water was about twenty-five feet, I thought, although I didn't know for sure. It was far enough that, if you dropped a pebble, you would have time for a breath before it hit; it was far enough that if you jumped, you'd be able to think on the way down.

The boys caught sight of us and paused, watching, treading water. "Hi," Katie called.

"Hi," they said back, together. They were about fifteen, I saw, with very white chests and very tan arms. "You going to jump?" one of them asked.

"Maybe." Katie looked over her shoulder at me, grinning. It was Dad's grin—wicked, ingratiating. "Should I?"

I stepped back and folded my arms. "I don't want to have to pull you out of that river," I said. In fact, I wasn't sure I could. I thought about what they taught us in health class during the two-week unit on water safety: how a drowning person will grab anything solid that comes near, including another human body, will try to climb up it as though it were a ladder.

"But you would, wouldn't you?" she said.

The boys were waiting, staring upward. The two toddlers in the shallows had turned to watch. Only the leopard-print woman was oblivious, baking in the sun with her arm across her eyes. Katie looked back at me. Then she gave a shove with her hands and sailed off the bridge rail like a child jumping out of a swing. For just a second I saw her falling, arms tight against her sides, growing smaller. Then she punched into the surface of the water and disappeared, and a moment later popped up in a fizz of bubbles and waves.

"It's great!" she cried. Her hair looked just the same, white-blond, short and stalky, but her face was shining and polished with water. She waved both arms at me and laughed. Her green T-shirt swirled around her body like algae. One of the boys stuck his arm out of the water and gave her a high five.

"You do it," she shouted to me, and then the three of them were treading water, watching and waiting. The toddlers were knee-deep now, walking slowly into deeper water toward us; their mother sat up and called them sharply, and they turned back.

I nudged my sneakers off and climbed the bridge rail. My hands and knees were trembling. I didn't sit down, as Katie had; I knew if I stopped moving I'd never get started again. I put my right foot on the topmost rail, brought my left foot up to join it, balanced for a second with my arms out, then stepped off the bridge and dropped. At the deepest point of the fall my feet settled on round, slimy rocks. I opened my eyes and saw six legs, bending and kicking with the graceful sluggishness of water, waving to me from above.

We stayed at the swimming hole all afternoon. Katie talked to the boys, squeaked with laughter, flirted; I lay on the rocks with my eyes shut and listened to their voices, hearing patterns of sound but no words. I felt loose and detached, half-asleep in the sun. This was the way I'd feel, I imagined, when the plane took off from Detroit and began its trip across the country. Eventually the boys went home, and sometime after that the leopard-print woman disappeared. The sunlight moved off the water and began to crawl up the rocks on the opposite shore.

When Katie and I got in the car there was only a little dampness left in the seams of our shorts, and when we turned west toward home, the sun blasted straight into our eyes.

The house was lit up just as it had been yesterday afternoon, the walls glowing, the windows opaque with light. We went inside.

"Where were you?" Dad said.

He stood in the big room with one hand on the table and the other in his pocket. He stood very still except for the hand on the table, whose fingers were tapping, drumming in a quick four-beat pattern, index to pinkie, over and over. His nails, neatly squared and filed by his barber, clip-clopped like tiny hooves.

"Do you know what time it is?" he said.

I made the useless gesture with my wrist again, consulting its bare skin for the time. Dad stepped up to me and put his wrist in my face. His wide black watch bumped my nose. I pulled back so I could read it, but he pushed it forward again, keeping it against my face.

"I'm sorry," I said.

His voice was like rocks, like footsteps, like an engine. "Let me tell you what I found when I got up today. I found no car. I found no note telling me where you were. I found a sink full of dirty dishes in the kitchen. I found a house still full of crap and a window still broken and no one here to help me out, no one to consider me."

I took one step forward, holding the paper-wrapped window like a serving plate. "We got a new one," I said. "We had to wait for Mr. Monroe to cut it."

Dad took the package from my hand and slapped it flat on the table. The glass exploded musically inside the paper. He threw the paper on the floor between us; it tore open and pieces bounced and slid away. Katie dropped her shoes and ran upstairs.

"You don't give a damn about this house," Dad said to me. "Don't even bother to pretend."

My father had never hit me, never even spanked me when I was little. But when I turned to follow Katie upstairs I had a flash of fear, the quick irrational fear you feel reaching into a turned-off Disposall. For a second I could imagine just how it would be, the swing from behind, the slap on the ear that would send me sideways into a wall. I turned the corner to the staircase, proving the fear wrong.

"You were right," Katie said. She crouched in the kid-sized chair by the south window, hands gripping her ankles, knees jutting toward her chin. "This is a great vacation. This is the best vacation I can remember."

"Shut up," I said.

I found my watch on the bedside table. It was a quarter to six. I put it on and listened to the outraged footsteps downstairs, water running in the sink, muttering. The cabinet squeaked, the bottle and glass clinked together, clunked down. I wondered if he was on a new bottle yet. He didn't sit down; he kept walking. I heard his shoes crunching over the broken glass.

At twelve minutes past seven he opened the front door and went out. I put my hand in my damp shorts pocket and gripped the car keys. They were cool and sharp. A few minutes later, he came back in. Then, almost immediately, he left again. This time he didn't come back.

At eight thirty-five Katie climbed under the covers. "Are you going to bed?" I asked.

"There's nothing else to do," she said.

At nine o'clock exactly, I went out to get him.

I found him about three miles from the house, wandering up the road in the direction of Jericho General, carrying the whiskey bottle in his left hand. I passed him and drove about a hundred yards further on to a turnout, where I parked and got out. When I slammed the car door, the dark seemed to push against my face like wind. I'd forgotten to bring a flashlight. I moved blindly out of the turnout until I felt the flat dirt of the road under my feet. Then I turned left and started walking back to Dad.

My eyes cleared as I walked. It was a hazy night with no stars. The moon was yellow and smudged with clouds, and the clouds were moving so that the moon appeared to be falling through the sky without changing position. I began to see that the trees were darker than the sky, and then I could pick out the irregular shape of their canopies and the thick stripes of their trunks close to the road. I held my hands in front of me; they were visible now. I looked for Dad against the dark mouth of road ahead, but I heard him before I saw him. There was a crashing of ferns and branches; he'd blundered off the road.

I found him cursing, standing in the soft sand on the shoulder, struggling back out of the woods.

"Hi, Dad," I said.

"Well, hi," he said. His voice was courteous, slightly surprised, as though I'd come unexpectedly to pick him up at work. The words were clear enough, but they had the unfocused clarity of a sleeptalker's.

I put my hand out. "Let's go home," I said.

"That's where I was going."

"Good." I helped him through the sand and we turned back up the road. Dad lurched a couple of times, then put an arm around my shoulders. "You're such a good girl, Elizabeth," he said. I looked ahead for the car; I thought it was about sixty yards away.

His knees kept bumping into mine, bending and shimmying as though he'd just run miles and miles. "I'm sorry about this," he said. He gave a low laugh. "God, I'm really sorry." Then one of his knees folded suddenly outward, and I caught him by the arm.

Ahead I could see the wider pocket of darkness where the turnout was. I kept my eyes on it, but it seemed to bob in front of us, keeping its distance like a mirage. For a second I had the awful thought that we might have passed the car already. I kept stepping and pulling Dad, and then we were getting closer to the turnout, and then I could see our car, a whitish lump by the side of the road. I tried to move faster. We were about twenty feet from it when Dad tripped on something and fell down. I heard his head strike the dirt with a low crunch, and the sound of shattering glass as the bottle in his hand broke. He gave a cry of surprise and rolled onto his back, hands searching for his head, face screwed up like a petulant baby's. The trees swished with wind, and then the swishing got louder, and it was a car coming up the road toward us.

"Get up, Dad." I still had hold of his hand; I yanked on it, but he flopped at arm's length like a limp fish. The pitch of the engine rose, straining up the hill from the direction of Jericho General. I knew what we must look like. "Dad! Get up!" A glow appeared over the rise, intensified, and the headlights broke into sight. I pulled on Dad's arm once more; he was weighted to the ground, a sack, a dead thing. As the lights crawled over us the car slowed down. I looked away into the woods. The car pulled even and hesitated. Then it rolled on.

I kicked Dad on the butt. I was so angry my vision jittered up and down. I was crying, my teeth were clenched, I wanted to kill him. "Get up," I said. "Get your fat ass off the ground. Get in the fucking car."

He whined something, but climbed to his feet. I walked him to the passenger-side door, opened it, and shoved him in. For a moment I was strong enough to achieve anything; right then I could have lifted him, I think, I could have thrown him. I drove home fast, seeing each curve before it appeared. "Oh, no," Dad groaned soon after we started. "Oh, shit." Then he retched and threw up in his lap and on the floor. We still had about two miles to go, and I opened my window. When we got to the house, I grabbed his arm and pulled him out of the car. His knees sagged. "I don't want to go in," he whimpered.

"Shut up," I said.

"Why do you hate me?" he said as I elbowed open the front door.

When he saw the living room he started for the couch. His pants and shoes were patched with vomit. "Get in the bathroom," I said. He was dragging on me now, barely walking at all. His hand, clutching my shoulder near the neck, was slimy; his fingers were icy cold. We stumbled into the downstairs bathroom. I let go of him, made him hold on to the towel rack, and snapped the light on. He was fumbling with his fly with one hand, unable to find the zipper. He let go of the rack and swayed in place while he tried to get his fly undone; I caught him as he started to tip over and held him upright again.

"Dad, sit down," I said.

"I have to piss," he said. I watched him struggle with the zipper for a full minute. Then I unbuttoned and unzipped his shorts for him. He took his penis out and peed, on himself, on the floor, on my shoes. I shoved him toward the toilet, but he kept peeing on the floor. When he was done, he slumped down in the puddle he'd just made and rested his head on the side of the tub.

I was crying again. The strength I'd felt had drained away. I closed the toilet's lid and sat on it, my shoes and legs wet. Then Dad stirred and emitted a huge burp. I held his head over the bathtub and he vomited again, brown and dotted with grains of rice, smelling of digestion and rot and Scotch whiskey. When he stopped I tried to get him in the bathtub, but he was too heavy. I pulled on his shoulders. His eyes were closed; he didn't move.

"You fucker," I said. "Get in the bathtub."

He woke up for a second. With me still pulling on him, he crawled over the tub's porcelain lip and collapsed on his side. I turned his head so he lay facedown. Then I stayed up with him while he slept and woke and vomited and slept again. While I waited I went out to the car, wiped off the seat, removed the rubber footwell and hosed it off. I wiped up the bathroom floor and mopped it with Mr. Clean. I swept up the glass that lay on the living room floor, wrapped it in newspaper, and put it in the garbage. The rider mower still stood on the back lawn, and I rolled it into the shed. I sat on the toilet lid between each job and watched him sleep.

It was after one o'clock when he began to look around and talk a little. He seemed dazed. He sat up, slipped in the tub, lay back down and moaned. I turned the bathtub faucets on warm and closed the drain. I took his shoes off. He looked up at me as the water soaked into him; I saw him start to recognize me.

"Take a bath," I said. Then I went upstairs.

The bedroom door was shut, and I pushed it open cautiously, admitting a slice of light from the hallway. Katie was sitting up in bed, knees bent and covers pulled to her waist.

"Don't go," she said.

"What?" I unbuttoned my jeans and stepped out of them. I sat

33

down to pull my sneakers off and then wondered if I was going to be able to get back up.

"Don't go," she said again.

"Katie," I said, "it's late. I'm really tired. I don't want to talk."

"*I* want to talk." She held the quilt in both hands, like reins. "Tomorrow morning's going to come and everything's going to seem like it's okay again. It'll be light out and we'll all be drinking coffee and it's going to seem like everything's okay. Or at least not as bad as it seems right now."

"Right," I said. "That's why I want to talk tomorrow." I pulled my shirt off over my head and unhooked my bra. I stood and shoved all the clothes into the garbage can. Tomorrow I might fish them out and wash them, I thought; for now I wanted them to stay there. "I'm going to take a shower," I said.

"Don't you go to California. Don't you do it," Katie said. "Don't leave me here."

She stared at me, and I remembered the way she looked sitting on the bridge rail, balanced, looking back at me over her shoulder and wearing Dad's smile. *But you would, wouldn't you?* The house was so quiet I thought I could hear the sound of pine needles drying on the floor below the naked wreath, the sound of twigs detaching from trees and dropping onto the back yard, the sound of dust falling endlessly through the air.

Then a shiver caught me as I stood in my underwear, shook me unexpectedly and broke the moment.

"I'm just going to take a shower," I said. "We can talk about it tomorrow."

The sound of water falling into the tub was like an explosion, and every squeak and rub of my feet across the porcelain seemed louder than a voice. But when I came back to our bedroom, the light was off and Katie lay flat and silent.

"Katie," I whispered. "I know you're faking."

She didn't answer.

"Come on," I said. I put a hand on her shoulder and patted her through the quilt. "Come on, Katie. It's going to be all right."

And it would be, I knew. Tomorrow would come and it would be light again and things would look different. Dad would be red-eyed and quiet, but he would be there; and Katie would be sullen, but she would be there; and we would drive home, and in four days I would fly to California and I'd be home for vacations and in two more years she could leave too, and none of it was going to be so terrible. It was only the warped, early dark of two A.M. that made such things seem past bearing. It was only at this particular hour that what I was going to do seemed unforgivable.

I had never felt so tired, but I didn't let myself fall asleep right away. I waited for a while, listening to the quiet of Katie lying awake, and then the quiet of her sleeping. I wanted to see if she would talk in her sleep. I wanted to hear her sleep-voice one last time, hear her send one more message through the dark with perfect vocal clarity and a blurred, misfired meaning.

Michael Knight

University of Virginia

NOW YOU SEE HER

$\mathbf{X}$avier tells me he is upstairs doing his homework, but I know that he is watching our new neighbor. Grace Poole lives in the townhouse just across a narrow alley from our own. I was taking trash to the alley on Monday, when I noticed my son at our second story window, his face close enough to the glass to breathe mist onto it. I followed his eyes across the way, and there was Grace Poole, standing naked in her kitchen, sipping from a coffee mug. She gave no indication that she saw me or that she saw my son, perfectly still, entranced, huffing brief ghosts of longing against the pane. Today is Friday, and I've been watching her myself ever since. I have the benefit of binoculars.

I believe that I should be angry at him, should sneak up the stairs, right now, kick his door open, and demand to know what he thinks he's doing. But I'm not angry. X—he has started calling himself X— is thirteen. I remember thirteen and being full of that strange water, drawn and released by the sight of a woman, tides and moon. X was in such a hurry to get to his window after school, that he didn't even stop to wonder why his old man is home this early in the day. How can I be mad at him? Grace is, at this moment, swimming closer to me through the binocular lenses.

I have often thought about having the talk with my son, about what I would tell him. The birds and the bees, the facts of life. For a man who spent his days talking, my own father, a professor of literature, was surprisingly inarticulate. He was maroon-faced and shifty and read me a poem about love. He tried to establish a connection.

"Do you know what I mean, Byron?" he said. "You know already, right?"

"Sure. I've got it covered," I said. I was twelve and only four years from discovering that I had nothing at all covered.

X has never seemed the right age for that sort of talk. Nine and ten, still too much a boy. Eleven, the year his mother died. My wife, Sarah. I couldn't get my head around anything that year, except the fact that she was gone. Her absence was everywhere. Dust on the piano keys. Dirty dishes in the sink. A coolness beneath my covers, in place of her body heat. Twelve, our move to the city, to Alexandria, at the beginning of the school year. That seemed weight enough for both our shoulders. I sold the piano. X had a short-lived fling with smoking cigarettes. Now, thirteen and suddenly he is too old for all that.

It could be that I am avoiding the issue. Nine months ago, I went to the library and made copies of the male and female anatomy, those full body biology textbook shots, intending to make my presentation to him. I wanted to keep it clinical, the way I would have shown a customer at my veterinary clinic that their dog was having pregnancy complications. My intention was to leave love out of it. On my way home, I saw a terrifying vision of what I would do when the conversation turned to actual procedure. I pictured myself placing the male copy on top of the female copy, between my hands, and rubbing my palms together. I broke out in a humiliated sweat. I jerked the car over to the curb and slipped the pages into a gutter. X probably knows the basics already. What he doesn't know—the smooth way morning light looks on a woman's skin, the way her hair can play between bare shoulder blades—Grace across the way, with her potted daisies on the windowsill, will surely teach him.

To the uninitiated, it would appear that Grace Poole has renounced clothing altogether. She has dark curly hair, all of it, and wild eyebrows and is so pale as to be distracting. It's true that she walks from room to room naked. Sleeps and feeds her dog, watches television and eats breakfast without clothes. Grace spends almost all of her time at home, clothesless. These things I have learned in the four days since I discovered my son's little secret. And his homework fetish began almost two weeks ago, just about the time our new neighbor arrived.

When she does go out, Grace makes the act of getting dressed something almost unbearably alluring. The slow taking away of my guilty pleasure. She makes her body a secret again, dressing slowly, as if she regretted having to do it at all. A reverse strip tease; I imagine balloons inflating around her as she pulls pins out of them. The sight of her rolling panty hose over lightly muscled calves and dimpled knees, tugging them over the crescent folds where her supple thighs meet her bottom, shifting her hips side to side, or standing in the middle of the room, slipping her arms into the sleeves of a clean shirt, buttoning it over her breasts, breaks my heart. I have not seen a naked woman since my wife was alive.

Now, Grace is talking on the telephone. She has six phones, each one a different color, lined up on a card table against her downstairs window. My first thought was phone sex, but that would be too perfect. She is standing behind the table, arms crossed beneath her breasts, lifting her brown nipples, pinning the phone against her shoulder with her cheek. I can just make out the blue earpiece in all that hair. Her eyes are almost the same color. The wall behind her is lined with cardboard boxes, stacked three high, each one imprinted with the same logo—a rust-colored rooster—and writing in Spanish. I hear my son trotting down the stairwell and just have time to drop the shade in my study and stash the binoculars between the chair and my lower back before he opens the door. I can't get my hands on any documents to look busy, so I stare at the ceiling and pretend that I was daydreaming. Watching Grace seems like daydreaming sometimes, languorous as jasmine.

"Shouldn't you be working, Dad?" X says. "Somebody's got to put food on the table around here." He is standing just inside the room, still in his school uniform, gray slacks and blue shirt, now untucked. X is blond and tan and brown-eyed. He looks exactly like his mother. I try to find traces of myself in him when he doesn't know I'm watching. While he sleeps, his cheeks flushed with dreaming. At dinner, sitting in front of the television, holding his plate near his chin, his eyes half closing when he lifts a mouthful. Usually, I don't find anything, and when I do, those things are fleeting, an expression, a gesture, gone almost as soon as I've seen them. The sight of him, of his mother in him, makes me feel guilty about watching Grace. He is smiling strangely, and I can't tell if he is onto me.

"I thought maybe we could do something together after school," I lie. "I didn't know you'd have so much homework."

I say homework in italics, hoping to catch him off guard, to put him on the defensive for a change. He leans into the door frame, shoves a hand into his pocket. I can hear the muffled thump of a tennis ball on the public courts across the street.

"Yeah, well." He shrugs and looks in the direction of the tennis sounds.

"Besides, I'm on emergency call tonight. I thought an afternoon off would do me some good." This is the truth. I have become part of an arrangement of the three local vets, where one of us stays on call twenty-four hours on alternating nights. The other offices transfer their emergency patients after business hours. "So, what do you say? Should we go down to the mall and look at that CD player you want?"

He brightens visibly.

"Cool," he says. "Let me change clothes and we're gone."

He pivots on a heel and goes stomping back upstairs.

After my wife died, I moved my son from our farm in Loudon County to this place, a brick townhouse in Alexandria, anonymous among the rows of similar buildings. Ours wasn't a working farm, just some land, the old farmhouse and the sagging barns behind it and a grain silo, that Sarah called the Leaning Tower of Loudon. My practice has boomed since our move to the city. My clientele, though, has changed from horses and hearty dogs to mostly cats and those dogs that need constant grooming. Poodles and such, city dogs. I never would have thought that grooming would become a vital part of my practice, but I've recently hired an assistant, Sissy, for just that purpose. Sissy is young and attractive and people like her, and the owners of my new patients seem to find something charming, something quaint, in having a country doctor for their pets. I make my manner brusque and forceful and have lately found myself speaking in colloquialisms to fit the part that has been given me. They often ask why a veterinarian, a natural lover of animals, does not have a pet of his own. I mention lack of space and the inclemency of keeping animals confined to the city. A happy dog is a running dog, I say. I made that up. And they nod and look at the floor, guilty in their minds of animal cruelty. They like my subtle scolding.

What I don't tell them is that I once saw a Siberian husky called Bear run over by a lumber truck, flatbed strapped with skinned trees. This was before X was born, and Sarah and I loved that dog as if he were our child. She would put a plate for him under the dinner table so he could have his meals with us. On cold nights, he slept in the bed between us, his head on a polyester pillow that Sarah bought because it turned out he was allergic to down. All of us slept on polyester pillows. I still do. To console her on the evening of the accident, I had to promise that we would never have another pet. I'm not certain how serious she was about the promise, whether it was just one of those things people did at a time of tragedy, self-denial as punishment for some implicit fault in the affair, but our farm was without animals until her death.

X found a cat curled up in the grain silo the month after Sarah's funeral and I gave in to his pleading and let us keep it. The cat was never fond of me, ignored my attempts at affection, hissing at my touch and rushing to X for protection. The cat wouldn't eat until the kitchen lights were off and I had gone up to bed. Late one night, I went down to the kitchen for a snack and flipped the light switch and surprised him at his bowl. He skittered across the linoleum, out of the little pet door and our lives. We never saw him again. I tried fish, after the cat, for X's sake but could never remember to feed them or change their water and when I did remember, I thought of Sarah and the promise that I made.

Grace Poole and her shar-pei, Candle, are new patients of mine. I have never found any truth in the idea that people and their pets come to look alike over time. Candle is all wrinkles and short, wiry hair and full of high-strung motion. They have only been in once, for a flea dip and groom, but Sissy noticed something about Grace immediately. Sissy is nineteen and always teasing me about not dating. While Grace was filling out her paperwork, she pulled me aside and said, "Bingo. That's the one. Ask her out, Dr. Shaw. We'll double. You can set me up with that pretty son of yours."

She also teases X, when he sometimes comes in to earn his allowance after school. Both of us, X and I, clearly enjoy it.

"Can't. She's my new neighbor," I said. "If it didn't work out, I would always be running into her at the mailbox."

"If you don't get a date soon, the customers are going to think you're gay. Think about what that would do to business," she said.

After X left for school today, I called the office, told Sissy and my other assistant, Roy, to take the day off and spent the morning watching Grace. From the window in my study, I can see into her kitchen and living room, but when she went to the second floor, I had to dash up to X's room and crouch on his bed, where I imagine he must watch her. Our separation on the stairwell was torturous. The dog followed her everywhere. I wondered what my son thinks when he does his spying. I crossed my arms on the sill, the way he does, and pressed my forehead to the cool glass. I pulled his blanket over my shoulders. She must seem to him unreal, a gift so lucky, so fantastic, he can hardly believe in her. I pictured him saying honest prayers that she wouldn't go away. The image so perfect and fragile that to touch her, to even imagine touching her, might make her come apart in wisps of smoke. X's return from school confined me to the study, and now I have lied my way into having to leave the house altogether, but I don't mind really.

One thing has impressed me about X since my discovery. He hasn't brought anyone over to watch with him. When I was his age, the first thing I would have done was have a dozen friends lined up at the window eating popcorn or something. Having a secret to share made me feel important. But not X. He doesn't want to share her. He doesn't want to spoil whatever it is he's feeling up there. I hope he doesn't know that he's splitting time with his father.

It is almost five o'clock by the time we leave. X is very careful when dressing for the mall. He has selected a plain white T-shirt from The Gap, Levi's jeans and brand-new Nike high-tops. Close to two hundred dollars for the whole outfit. I had no idea. His mother did all his shopping. I have suits that cost less, and, except for the shoes, he looks like a fifties hoodlum. I half expect him to roll a pack of cigarettes in his shirt sleeve.

We drive awhile, all interstate and highway on the way to the mall, and X is quiet, maybe thinking about his CD player, maybe thinking about Grace. The breeze from the open window whips his hair. I let myself think about Grace, too. I'm not sure how I will react when I see her again in person. In the flesh, so to speak. Our meeting, as neighbors, as doctor/patient, is inevitable. I wonder sometimes if she knows that she is being watched, if the absence of curtains on her windows is deliberate, and not, as I tell myself, just because she's new to town. I don't think she knows that her vet lives next door—the last four days, I've been getting my mail under cover of darkness—but I wonder if she can feel our eyes on her, if the two of us are giving off some kind of lonely vibe. X is staring, blank-eyed, in front of us. Our thoughts of Grace fill the car as palpably as the quick air.

"How about you roll that window up and let's get some A-C going," I say.

He rolls his eyes at me but does as I ask. He turns on the radio, and I turn it down a little. X does a sigh, one that is full of implications.

"Dad, I need to ask a favor," he says. "There's this girl I want to ask out, and I was wondering if you'd drive us to the movies. Her parents could drive, but they're real old, and they want to drive too much, you know. They're happy-assed about stuff like that. They get off on participating."

At first, I'm panicked. He's going to ask Grace to the movies. But that's absurd and besides, Grace has her driver's license. At the same time, I'm unreasonably happy that he's asked me to be their chauffeur. I struggle to withhold a barrage of questions. I turn the radio back up.

"Sounds like fun," I say.

He nods and grows remote again. A woman in an antique convertible, a Desoto or something, passes us on X's side. It has fins and everything, makes her look like a movie star. Both of us turn to look.

I say, "How would you feel about your old man getting a date soon?"

"Cool," he says.

"That wouldn't bother you?" I'm surprised.

"No way," he says.

"Understand that I loved your mother. I will always love your mother," I say.

"Mom's dead," he says. "She'd understand." X is a man of few words, the strong silent type. Add a scuffed leather motorcycle jacket to his outfit, and he could double for Marlon Brando in *The Wild Ones*, someone I once wanted to be.

X's mother died of an infection resulting from her tubal ligation. Almost an unheard-of cause of death, the doctors said, but this I already knew. Even vets know a thing or two about people medicine. Sarah was alive in the hospital less than a week. I had always wanted a big family, wanted the constant clamor of children in our house, but there were medical reasons for the operation, and Sarah softened things by saying how much the idea of raising an only child appealed to her. We could spoil him rotten, give him whatever he wanted. She wouldn't have to divide her love, she said. Two ways was enough.

I have never actually admitted the possibility of dating again, though I have begun to entertain it more and more recently. Particularly with Sissy's insistence and the arrival of Grace Poole. The reawakening of those boyhood desires. Naked is, after all, still naked, even to a thirty-six-year-old widower.

The mall is massive and intimidating, but X moves through it easily, as if it were his natural habitat. He wanted me to give him the credit card and wait in the car. He told me he was a smart shopper. I told him that was quite possibly the most hysterical thing I had ever heard. He grabs my arm and jerks me along when I stop at the map to look for the stereo store. He knows where he is going and remains, always, about three paces ahead of me. In front of a store called Southern Culture, he freezes and raises his hand to me, fist clenched, like a soldier walking point. He is so definite in his motion that I go still as well. I think he must have seen that in a Vietnam movie.

"Wait here," he says.

I do as I am told. X weaves through the steady flow of shoppers, across the wide aisle, to three girls who look about his age. They are standing in front of a pet store, one of those places where the animals are caged behind a glass wall. The girls look happy to see X. He gives them all a smile and pushes his fingers through his hair, his mother's hair, weightless and golden. They laugh at something he says and one of the girls, the prettiest, lays a hand on his shoulder. X doesn't acknowledge the hand, lets her leave it there, waits for them to finish laughing. He's doing an eyebrow raise, as if surprised that they could find him so funny, so charming. My son is a natural. He would prob-ably do better with Grace Poole than I would. X looks over his shoul-der at me, casually, sees me watching and gives me a dirty look. I spin around to face the shop window.

Southern Culture specializes in reproduction antebellum antiques. Polymers where there should be pine. Porch jockeys with machine-induced paint chips. In the window directly in front of me is an awkward-looking fake antique telephone, black with brass cradle and receiver, the works. I don't think there were telegraphs before the Civil War, much less telephones, but seeing it there makes me wonder what Grace Poole could be up to with all those phones. Her conver-sations only last a minute or two and she takes notes while she is talk-ing. I never heard of a phone sex girl taking notes, except maybe to get credit card numbers, and she does too much writing for that to be the explanation.

X returns and leads me to the stereo store. He has a short discus-sion with the salesgirl, who is very attractive and all business. She is wearing a tan, ankle-length skirt, slit open to the knee. She is impressed with my son's knowledge of electronics and shows me the model that he wants. It holds ten CDs and is apparently the only type made on earth that can continue playing while the carriage is ejected and still rotating. On sale for $1,300.00, speakers and receiver not included. I ask if that's a feature he absolutely must have.

"It's the best, Dad," he says. "Think of it as a long-term invest-ment."

X has one arm crossed at his stomach, cupping the elbow of the other arm in his palm. He is stroking his chin, one foot forward, weight back, as if regarding a masterpiece of art.

"Tell me again," I say. "Whose child are you?"

The salesgirl looks from X to the CD player and back to X.

"He'll definitely be getting his money's worth, Dad," she says.

"It is, unfortunately, and I'm sure much to both of your disappointments, not his money," I say.

We settle on something more reasonable.

In the car, X is again silent. I have embarrassed him both in front of his friends by staring and in front of the salesperson by being cheap. Six hundred dollars isn't cheap in my estimation, but clearly X is disappointed. I resent his sullenness—and try to get him talking again.

"What about Grace Poole?" I say. "Our new neighbor."

He tenses a little but doesn't look at me.

"What about her?" he says.

"You know, for my date," I say. "We could double. Miss Poole and I could go to the movies with you and your girlfriend."

X turns his head slowly to look at me. He is angry. Before the last words are out of my mouth, I understand that it was the wrong thing to say, that I said it to provoke him. He gives me a mean, shallow laugh.

"She's so out of your league," he says.

Three months after Sarah died, I broke X's wrist. We were on the lawn playing football and he was running wildly by me, at the point in our game when I would let him go past me, through the pair of apple trees we used as a goal line. Let him do his touchdown dance, spike the ball, spread his arms like wings and prance in a circle. I ran after him and caught him from behind, wrapping him up, jarring the ball loose, driving him down. His arm went out to brace himself and the wrist snapped audibly—he asked me later if I had heard it—a sound like it too was surprised to find me on his back, the ground coming up so fast. X carried his cast, proudly, like a club.

X won't let me help him assemble his new stereo. He doesn't even allow me to help him carry it from the car. I return to the study, lock the door behind me, and take up my binoculars. Grace is on the phone, a pink one this time, and she is wearing a cream-colored bra, but that is all, like she was just getting ready to dress when the phone rang. She scratches a pencil across a pad, tears the sheet loose and jams it down on a thin spike attached to a metal base. I can't see the dog. Grace never does get up to dress, which I am glad of, just keeps on answering the phones, first one, then another, putting one on hold and coming back to it. She is a popular lady. I can't figure out the phones.

It isn't long before my house is full of music. I go out of the study and stand at the bottom of the stairwell to let the sound come down to me more clearly. There are long windows on either side of the front door leaking weak light into the foyer. The song that X is playing sounds familiar, something from the seventies, heavy with feedback guitars, but I can't put my finger on its name. Probably, I heard it on the office radio. Sissy likes that sort of music, calls it classic. And suddenly, I'm remembering Sarah and me, trying to manhandle a piano through the front door of our farmhouse. X was maybe seven, too small to help so he supervised. The piano was on a dolly, but even so we kept banging it into walls and furniture, filling the house with resonant discord, and the air was full of the smell of hay grass—someone was always cutting hay out there, if not on our land then on the next farm down the road. Just follow the white wooden fence—a sweet smell, like the cakes Sarah would try to bake and would botch more often than not, leaving them in the oven too long or screwing up the recipe. Dessert was the most hilarious time of day in our house, cakes looking like deflated footballs, pies blackened like bituminous coal. It made me hungry, that smell. I was always hungry in Loudon County.

X was trying to talk his mother into letting him have a horse just before she died. He had nearly convinced her to break her promise. X guaranteed that he would let us choose the horse, if he was allowed to give it a name. For X, this was a major concession. I never said anything directly to him, but after he was asleep and Sarah and I were alone in bed, I would argue against this idea—not the horse itself but X choosing the name. A horse is too noble an animal. I see horses every day with ridiculous, childish names, I said. Black Beauty, Sox, Paint. I had a patient called Fanny. It's degrading to them, Sarah. She told me that if there was going to be a horse, which there probably wouldn't, it would be X's and X should name it. She would prop her back against the headboard and smoke cigarettes, tipping ashes into a ceramic bowl on her lap. Smoking was her secret vice; she didn't want X to know that his mother sanctioned such a nasty habit. What are you talking about, Byron? she'd say. You're the one who's being juvenile. I wonder now what name he would have chosen. The boy who has nicknamed himself after a letter in the alphabet.

When I take up my binoculars again, Grace is nowhere to be found. Almost a half hour passes, the light fading between our homes, without a trace of her. She must have gone up for the night. She is X's until dawn. I would like to creep upstairs and stand in his doorway, the door just slightly open, and watch him watching her. Not to catch him red-handed but just to look at him, see if he is the same sort of voyeur as his father.

Grace comes running down the stairs into my line of sight. She stops in the middle of the room, breathless, harried, and stands there, one hand pushed up into that mass of brown hair, holding it back away from her forehead. Her lips are moving, but I can't see who she's talking to. She walks over to the black phone, picks it up and starts to dial, then stops and drops the receiver on the table and runs back upstairs. When she returns, the dog is in her arms, her back arched under its weight. Candle is not moving in a way that is frightening. Not loose and recently dead but stiff, body wracked with sporadic trembling. My first thought is Lyme disease, but that's unlikely. The disease is carried by ticks that don't exist in the city. I saw it dozens of times in the country.

Grace lays Candle on the table, using her elbow to move the phones. She finds a phone book and begins riffling through it, back then forward again, as if she were having trouble concentrating. I realize, suddenly, that she is looking for my number. I retrieve my own phone book from the desk drawer and look for her name, but it isn't there. That makes sense, she's new to town. Besides, I couldn't call her. She would know that I had been spying on her.

I watch her stop turning pages, watch her dial and speak into the receiver, but my phone never rings. I think, at first, that she has called another vet, that she didn't like me when I met Candle the first time. I'm crushed. But, finally, my phone rings. It is Sissy. She's manning the office line tonight.

"Get your act together," she says. "We've got an emergency call. Grace Poole. Her dog is sick. Maybe tonight's your big chance, Dr. Shaw. A woman with a sick dog. She'll be super vulnerable." She

waits a moment for me to laugh and, when I don't, becomes professional again. "The dog is paralyzed except for muscle spasms. She's
coming in."

"I know," I say.

"What?"

"Nothing," I say. "I'll be right there."

I am holding the binoculars in one hand, the phone in the other.
Grace has disappeared upstairs, momentarily, and returns carrying a
bundle of clothes. I watch her dress. She pulls on walking shorts, cut
high and flattering, and a T-shirt. She is barefoot and doesn't bother
with underwear. Candle, she gathers in her arms and burdened with
the dog, she can't open the door. It is all I can do not to go outside,
cross the little alley between us, and help her.

I wait until I hear Grace's car door close, hear the engine start.
Wait until her headlights pass my window, casting shadows, before I
get up to leave. I find X in the foyer, sitting at the bottom of the stairs.
It is almost dark and he is brushed with the last delicate light from the
street.

"I want to go," he says.

We look at each other for a long moment, neither of us speaking.
X is still wearing his mall clothes. He looks worried but never takes
his eyes away from mine. For an instant, I think I see something familiar in his face, something that I recognize. It is at those moments,
when the veneer of his confidence has cracked just a little, when he
shows, like light creeping under a doorway, in his eyes, in the set of
his mouth, traces of being a boy, that I imagine a little of myself in
him. It is at those moments when I love him most.

"Okay," I say.

My clinic is only a few blocks away, but the drive is intolerable. I force
myself to go slowly, to brake at every stop sign, to signal at every corner. X won't look at me, keeps his eyes on other people's houses, the
occasional warmth of their lighted windows. Grace is crying by the
time we reach the office, sitting Indian-style in one of the plastic waiting room chairs. There are circles of dirt on the balls of her feet, and
I can see a shadow on her thigh made by the leg of her shorts. I
remember that she isn't wearing underwear. When we come in, she

wipes her eyes and tries to fix her hair, which is wild and spiraling. She is very beautiful like that. X is wide-eyed. I think he is amazed to be seeing her in person, amazed that she exists beyond those windows.

I can't think of a suitable colloquialism, so I say, "It's going to be all right, Miss Poole."

Sissy and the dog are in the examination room waiting for me. Candle is still trembling, her I.D. tag clinking against the examination table's metal surface.

"Her temperature is high," Sissy says. "That's all I knew to do until you got here."

"Lyme disease," I say.

I look around the door to the waiting room. X is sitting about four chairs over from Grace, looking petrified, eyes glued to the floor.

"Miss Poole, has this dog been out of the city recently? Camping or something?" I say.

"Yes," she says. "About a week ago."

"Any ticks on her?"

"A few," she says. She is calming some.

"Good," I say. "I'll get her fixed up."

I wish I could stop talking like a country doctor, just for a minute. I push my fingers through Candle's fur until I find what I'm looking for, the bull's-eye reddening of a tick bite at her shoulder. I give the dog a muscle relaxant to stop the spasms and a shot of tetracycline for the Lyme's, because it won't hurt her either way. I have Sissy take a blood sample. These are the things I understand. This is the place where I know what I am doing. I stroke the dog, pulling all that loose skin out straight, then letting it wrinkle up again, until she quiets. I whisper nonsense in her ear. Pretty dog, pretty dog. Tell your mother good things about Dr. Shaw.

"That dog was messed up," Sissy says. "It's a good thing you were home and not out painting the town like you usually are."

"Hoot with the owls at midnight, and you can't fly with the eagles at dawn," I say. I smile at her.

"C'mon, Dr. Shaw," she says, rolling her eyes in the direction of the waiting room.

X and Grace are talking when I go back into the other room. They don't hear me come in. X is smiling but differently from the mall, nervous and grateful for her attention. He is tapping his feet, wringing his hands. Grace seems relaxed. It hasn't occurred to me until now to wonder how old she is. Maybe twenty-eight, twenty-nine, not too young. Somewhere between X and me but closer to me. There are a lot of things I hadn't thought to wonder about her.

"Candle is going to be good as new," I say.

They look up at me, lips parted slightly, surprised to find me there.

"That's great," X says. His enthusiasm is genuine.

"Thank you so much, Dr. Shaw," she says, standing, taking a few steps in my direction. "Sorry I got so emotional there. That isn't like me. It's Candle. Do you have pets?"

"I have X," I say. "He's sort of like a pet."

She smiles and looks back at my son who, to my surprise, is also smiling. X is watching me, not angry, but definitely watching, waiting to see what I will do.

"A very cute and charming pet he is," she says. "Does he do any tricks? Sit, X. Roll over, boy."

"Grace is in the mail-order business, Dad," he says, too eagerly. "She does clothes for this Venezuelan company. Environmentally correct sweaters and stuff."

X and Grace. They are on a first-name basis. She waves his comment away and says, "I just got the job. They're a penny-ante operation. Won't even give me a computer or an office phone. I have to do everything by hand."

"Really?" I say.

My heart starts kicking, my tongue goes gummy in my mouth. At least that explains the phones. Now, I know something else about her. What I don't know is what to talk to her about. I can't very well talk about the fact that I've been spying on her. I can't tell her that I see her in my sleep. I launch headlong into my spiel about Lyme disease. It's an inflammatory disease, I say, caused by tick-borne spirochetes. The symptoms include joint pains, fatigue, and sometimes neurological disturbances. I hear my voice, droning on like a nightmare biology teacher, but I can't shut up. Did you know that this disease was named for Lyme, Connecticut, where a particularly deadly outbreak was studied? She nods along with my words, trying to seem interested. I force myself to stop talking. I remember X and how at ease he was with those girls at the mall. I run my fingers through my hair, smile the smile and cock my hip like some kid. It doesn't feel right, feels foolish. The proper words for this moment—Grace in the washed-out light from the fluorescent bulbs, X with his hands in his pockets, his eyes full of sympathy—do not exist. I am aware that nothing can happen between us, not after what X and I have been doing the last few days, but I don't want it to be over just yet. Any moment now, I think, and she will disappear.

Julie Rold
Boston University

BLOODLINES

I

My father's father was a Bavarian immigrant who maintained through two world wars that his last name, Igelhart, was Dutch. He had settled in southern Indiana on the dirt bluffs of the Ohio River, where three-quarters of the population were German Catholic and the rest were German Protestant. My father's mother was the daughter of a butcher who had changed his name from Wieder to Wilder. Until the day he died, my great-grandfather paraded through the streets on March seventeenth of every year and declared he was from County Clare when he was sober and Galway when he was drunk, which wasn't often because he was a good Lutheran. He pronounced the latter Gal-oh-way. So did my father.

All his life, my father bragged about the complexity of his Irish-Dutch nature, claiming that his blood was a battleground for what he called his "contrary European humors." Still, he so preferred his Irish side that he had once memorized some lines of Yeats, which he found ample opportunity to recite—at the Southern States Farmers' Co-op, say, when the hog prices fell. "The blood-dimmed tide is loosed," he would note, "and everywhere the ceremony of innocence is drowned." In spite of his best efforts, he spoke with a slight southern accent.

When I was growing up, my father never asked me much, but every now and then he wanted to know, "You like Yeats, son?" Before I could answer, he would always inform me, "All Irishmen should like Yeats." The other farmers in Webster County joked around with him a lot, nicknaming him "Hoosier-boy" since he was from the wrong side of the Ohio. I was never sure what they said behind his back.

My father met my mother, the daughter of a rich Kentucky farmer, in the summer of 1955 in Memphis, listening to Elvis Presley singing at the Oyster Shell in Overton Park. As far as I can guess, they fell in love because they were nineteen and he was good-looking and she was pretty and had a big blue Chrysler. He got in it with her after the show. I don't know where they went, but I was born in April of 1956. They compromised and named me Carl Perkins Igelhart. My mother thought "Elvis" was a name for white trash. I was their only child.

My father farmed bottom land in western Kentucky that my mother's father had left her. He made a point of telling everyone that this did not bother him. "Woman's got a right to own something sure as I have," he said. He also liked to talk about how the steady Dutch part of him was responsible for keeping four hundred acres of the property in feed corn and twenty in burley tobacco. His income from crops was good enough to buy my mother a new car every year and to finance the single, abiding passion of his life, which he claimed for his Irish half, and which was made manifest in the pastures near our house, where my father had seeded high-grade bluegrass and spent his most cherished hours breeding and crossbreeding Herefords, Charlais, Red Angus, and Black Angus. He maintained that it was every farmer's duty to produce genetically superior beef cattle. What he wanted mostly, though, was to win best of show at the Kentucky State Fair.

"We Irish appreciate quality bloodlines, Carl," he would tell me, "for we are all the descendants of kings and poets."

In junior high I had to do a history project—"Tap the Roots of Your Family Tree." My grandmother rummaged through a cedar chest and presented me with a shoe box full of official-looking documents all neatly folded in half. Among them were my great-grandfather's German emigration papers. I didn't tell my father. But that was also about the time I quit helping him out with the herd. I can't remember why I stopped really, but I do recall that afterwards we both asserted I'd never had much interest in beef cattle. He claimed his greatest disappointment in life was that I did not share his fascination with genetics. He did not seem to care that I was good in school and an even better point guard. My mother did, though. She was a social woman who spent most of her time playing bridge at the country club. She gave me a kiss on the cheek and a five-dollar bill every Friday night. She bragged to all her friends about how smart I was. She looked prettier than anyone else's mother. I felt proud of that.

No one else in Webster County was interested in my father's cattle, either. But when I started high school in 1970, he got to know Roy Dunniston, the biology teacher. Mr. Dunniston had a sincere admiration for my father and his herd. Unfortunately, he also had about the tiniest eyes I had ever seen—pupils not much bigger than buckshot. The kids at school talked about how he lived with his mother and wondered if he were still a virgin. When he came out to our house, he wore an International Harvester cap and told me I could call him by his first name. I didn't tell any of my friends. Roy was careful to explain that his enthusiasm for livestock could not extend itself toward helping out with financing. I often heard him tell my father, "I sure wish I had as much money as you. I sure would like it if I could do what I liked."

With Roy's scientific expertise, my father's breeding program gained in clarity and complexity. On winter weekends, they would stay in the kitchen, mapping out charts of dominant and recessive gene traits and diagramming cattle lineages. When the weather got warmer, they would load up heifers in a truck and haul them hundreds of miles to mate with prize studs in Ohio and Missouri. The summer I was sixteen, after two years of planning and over thirty live births, they thought they had a winner: a pure-blood Black Angus bull my father named Cassius Clay. They took him to the Kentucky State Fair in August and entered him in every category—Best Flank, Best Chest, Best Hide. They got two fourth places and a fifth and failed to qualify for the championship round. They were bitter men.

"Damn judges think chest breadth is everything in an Angus," my father said when he got home. "That blue-ribbon bull measured twenty-five inches from shoulder to shoulder. Thing had so much pectoral it needed a bra."

"And they ignored the pelvis," Roy said. "Most important thing in a stud bull. All the spectators were talking about what a nice pelvis we had."

"I would have you know," my father added, "we had a half an inch over any other bull in leg length. A half an inch! Leg length is the hallmark of fine breeding. Not that those good ole boy judges would know it."

Roy's head was bobbing up and down and his little eyes were nearly crossing with disgust. "They just plain ignored it."

My father and Roy spent the next few weeks consoling themselves by writing letters of protest to county agriculture agents and the standards committee of the fair board. They drafted a petition to support the hiring of out-of-state officials. These efforts were met with scorn. About that time two of my father's heifers had deformed calves, and a Hereford bull and four steers died suddenly of bovine encephalitis. They became convinced that the gene pool in America wasn't deep enough. They conceived a bold plan. They would get new breeding stock—breeding stock so superior that even Kentucky judges would tremble to see it. They would import a bull from Ireland.

From *Beef* magazine my father had learned about an Irish breed known as Simmental. There weren't many in the United States. A sexually mature bull would cost him $20,000. He figured he could just afford it, but only if he could convince my mother to give up buying her new car that year.

When Roy learned they could charge $500 for a Simmental stud fee, he got excited. In a display of solidarity he said to my father, "If you can get her to agree to give up her car, I may even pitch in to buy one-sixteenth of that Irish bull with you."

"That's kind of you," my father told him. Roy had a high regard for his own savings, which my father had always respected.

II

At the supper table, my mother was cutting up her piece of white pork and getting ready to take a bite when my father announced:

"Camellia, I've got my mind set on importing a purebred Simmental bull from Ireland. In order for me to do this, you will have to forgo your annual purchase of a new automobile."

And then he sat down, took a drink of ice water, and wiped his lip with his thumb.

My mother and I were used to my father making speeches. She didn't listen to him most of the time, but I could tell by the way she set down her knife and fork to reach for cigarettes and her real gold lighter that he'd managed to get her attention. Her pink nails slid across its gleaming edges, and she flicked the top back and forth a few times. Finally, she asked him, "Why so far as Ireland? Just get something from Ohio."

"The best bloodlines come from Ireland," my father told her. "Blood is everything."

My mother said nothing. She had a high hairdo and an even higher bosom. The latter mass seemed to grow and then retreat as she smoked her cigarette, while the former remained motionless.

My father continued, "I've hauled dozens of heifers up to Ohio and Virginia and Pennsylvania. I've paid thousands of dollars in stud fees just to watch some premium bull sniff my heifer's rear and walk away. I need fresh stock."

"How much is it going to cost us?"

"We'll make enough in our own stud fees after the first year to cover the initial expense."

"Not if the bull's no good."

"All Irish bulls are good," my father said, winking at her. I wished I hadn't seen him do it. I took a bite of a bread roll. She started laughing, which he must have figured meant she was giving in because he said, "So you'll give up your new car?"

My mother leaned forward and gave him a kiss on the jaw. "Hell, no," she said.

My father jumped up and started to circumnavigate the dining room. As he circled us, he carried on about the necessity of scientific approaches to agriculture, about how he could put our farm on the map if he could just have a little more support from his own family, and about how an Irish bull's progeny would prove once and for all that he and Roy were right about the need for expanding the gene pool in this overly inbred state. I was shifting pieces of pork around on my plate and watching the way my mother kept her cigarette at a high, sharp angle to her face. She would never give in to him, no matter how long he talked. I was thinking about going to the kitchen for some butterscotch pie when I felt my father's hand gripping my shoulder.

"And probably the most important reason for buying this bull," I heard him saying, "is that Carl wants to."

My mother pulled the cigarette from her mouth. "Carl?" she said. "Carl doesn't give a damn about your cows."

"Carl's going to take the first calf for a Four-H project."

"He is not," she said, pointing the dead ashes on the tip at him. His fingers dug into my clavicle.

"Ask him," my father told her.

My mother's eyelashes cast needlelike shadows around her eyes as she took a drag and asked me in the same intake of smoky breath, "You want this Irish bull, Carl?"

My father let go of my shoulder and walked around the table to stand behind my mother. His face and neck were glazed with sweat. I figured he was desperate enough to do anything to get a bull, and I was expecting him to mouth "Say yes!" above the dark stack of my mother's hair. He didn't. He wouldn't look at me at all. His chin was pressed tight against his chest, and his arms were crossed over his heart. I knew he was prepared to hate me for the rest of my life if I said no to my mother's question. I could feel sweat rolling from the back of my knees down along my calves. My hands quivered with anger in the folds of the linen napkin lying against my thighs. All of a sudden, I wanted to tell him about those German emigration papers. But I kept my eyes on the blunt toe of my court shoes and was surprised at how fast I answered, "Yes, ma'am. I do."

My father didn't smile, but he gave me the slightest of nods. My mother jumped up with her cigarette in her mouth and said right into his face, "You son of a bitch." She stormed into the kitchen.

"Don't worry, son," my father said to me. "She'll forgive us. A woman always forgives."

He hooted and did a little jig by the china cabinet and said:

"We will arise and go now, and go to Innisfree, and we will get ourselves the best goddamn stud bull this state has ever seen."

III

My father and Roy began making lists of Irish breeders from advertisements in *Beef* magazine. To convince my mother of the sincerity of my interest in the bull, he decided I should write the names of different farms on slips of paper and tape them to a map of Ireland he had hung up behind the kitchen table. He was impressed every time he looked at them and would read out loud, "Ballyvaghan Farm. Donnegan Downs Farm. Lower Liscanor Farm. Fermoy Abbey Farm," trying to decide which he liked best. Roy's standards were different. He had John Deere scratch pads covered with ratios of head size to body weight, of leg length to withers girth, and he and my father would go over them again and again. My mother never said a word about being upset with me for siding with my father, but the five-dollar bills on Friday night came to a sudden stop. She told me she guessed I was getting old enough to earn money by myself.

Sometime in October my father got a phone call in answer to the letter of inquiry he'd sent to an import company in Virginia. There was an Irish Simmental that was supposed to go to a farm in Michigan. The breeder had failed to come up with the balance on his deposit after the bull had cleared U.S. quarantine. The company representative claimed that it was a fine opportunity for a fine animal. He was sired out of some place called Ballaghaderreen, and that was enough for my father. Roy took the precaution of checking out the information about his measurements and decided that he looked all right, especially considering they wouldn't have to wait for him and could deduct the Michigan fellow's down payment from their total cost. My father took cash and drove all night to Norfolk.

He came back the next evening, honking his horn all the way up the driveway. My mother had refused to listen to him talk about the bull before he left. She did tell me a few times, though, that she was sure he would get stuck with some pitiful-looking animal. Still, when we heard him come back, we both left our supper and rushed outside, stopping dead on the front porch. We couldn't see the bull, but my father's cattle trailer was looming behind his truck, ready to burst with the sheer mass of the bovine inside it. The metal castings around the wheels groaned from excess weight.

My father flicked his headlights on and off and called to us, "Let's take him down to the pasture."

So we hurried over and climbed into the cab with him. His grin was as bright as a new dime.

"Wait till you see him," he said, patting my mother's arm and then tugging on my ear. "He's got a pedigree longer than a Daughter of the Confederacy."

We were all quiet as he drove down to the field. He had put the rest of the herd in the back lot before he left. My mother and I hopped out of the truck and tried to peek at the bull through the slats, but my father said, "Stand clear. You sure don't want to get him upset while he's inside. This fellow's a real rough beast."

My father slowly unfastened the lock and undid the widgets. Then he flung open the door. The sound of hoof clanged against steel and my father scrambled over the fence just as the bull emerged.

He was enormous—broader than my mother's Chrysler Imperial. None of us could stop staring at him. His coat was the gleaming orange color of Mars in early evening skies. It seemed, though, to be little more than a thin shellac for his muscles, which ebbed and flowed beneath his outer gloss with the slow fury of an approaching thunderhead. He moved forward on powerful thighs. His hooves shone blue in their clefts as he crossed our pasture, thick with autumn dandelion fluff. In his wet nostrils was a dull gold ring.

I felt overwhelmed by a desire to touch him.

"You want to know his name?" my father asked us.

"I guess you want to tell us," my mother said. She was tapping the tip of her patent leather shoes against the fence rails.

My father pulled a pink carbon copy from his shirt pocket. "I keep this with me to show people how long his official name is," he said, pointing to the top of the paper. "You see, it begins with his great-grandsire's name and takes up two lines. But the part that's just his own is Pontius Pilate."

This tickled my mother. "That is rich," she said, giggling. "You got yourself a Christ killer."

"Now doesn't that show what you don't know," he said, without looking at her. "Pontius Pilate was a great man. In a tough time, he made a tough decision. Did what he had to do. Like all your great men."

"You mean like taking his wife's car money and buying himself an Irish bull?"

"That's right. If you want to think that way."

My mother patted the dark cliff of her hair. "Why," she said, "I'd say that makes you more like Judas."

She turned and started heading up the driveway, the gravel popping under her heels as she went. I watched her until she got to the back porch of the house and then looked back at the bull. He was standing not far from us, grinding his mouth and jaws from side to side.

"I bet part of that cud he's chewing," my father said, "came all the way from Ballaghaderreen."

He cupped his hand across the back of my head.

A sudden and powerful feeling of revulsion came over me.

"Christ, Daddy," I said, jerking away from him. "Stop it, will you? I helped you get your bull like you wanted. Why can't you just stop it?"

"What's got into you, boy?"

"You and all your Irish shit."

"Don't you cuss me, Carl Igelhart."

"You're not Irish, Daddy," I told him. "You go on and on about it, but you're not. You're not Dutch, either. You're German, I'm telling you. Now you know the truth."

I had wanted to shock him, and though I wasn't sure what kind of reaction he'd have, I sure didn't expect him just to cross his hands across the crown of his head, give two mean-sounding little snorts, and say, "What I know is that you don't know what the hell you're talking about," like he didn't care what I was saying or like he thought I was a fool. I felt hot blood pounding in the veins of my neck and forehead, and the next thing I knew I was screaming at him.

"You and your talk about bloodlines and breeding. You're a liar and you're a German son of a bitch!" and I wanted to call him every kind of rotten name I'd ever heard but I couldn't go on because I was crying so hard. I buried my face in the crook of my arm.

When I finally calmed down and looked up, my father was walking toward the hickory wood beyond the pasture, his hand trailing along the top of the fence row.

IV

For the next few weeks, my father spent all of his time down in the pastures with Pilate. We never spoke about what I'd said to him. My mother had started giving me five dollars again on the weekends. Basketball season had started. I wasn't at home very much. But when I was I would look out the windows on the landing of the second floor and see Pilate's orange bulk between the branches of the poplar trees that surrounded the house. My father would put a rope through his nose ring and lead him to the salt lick and the cow pond. He rubbed him down with repellent to keep the black flies off him. He drove him into the barn if it looked like lightning was coming. When Roy finished teaching, he would come over, and he and my father would sit on the hood of the pickup truck and watch Pilate and make plans for the next state fair.

After a few weeks, they still hadn't put the rest of the herd in with Pilate. He was off his food and had lost some weight, and my father wasn't sure that he was ready to be with the heifers. My father argued with Roy about what to feed him and how to liven him up. One evening, they came up to the house for bourbon, and I could hear them from my bedroom.

"It's obvious he doesn't like Kentucky grass," my father said.

"Then why won't he eat hay?" Roy asked.

"Because he's not used to it. The grass in Ireland is rich. Cattle there don't have to eat hay."

"Hell," said Roy. "I have never seen a bull that won't eat hay." There was a pause. "Are you saying Kentucky grass is no good?"

"I'm saying Kentucky grass is fine for Kentucky cattle. But it is obviously not good enough for a purebred Irish Simmental."

"Shit," said Roy. They were arguing about grass now and could have kept it up all night, I suspect. But then I heard Roy change the subject, saying, "I've told you what we should do. We ought to put him in with the heifers. He'll perk right up real fast."

"He's not ready."

"Of course he is. Put any bull with some heifers and it'll be hotter than a pit barbecue."

"I don't want to put that kind of pressure on him just yet," my father said.

"We can't keep him all by his lonesome forever," Roy insisted. "Not if we want to start making money from stud fees. Got to see what our own calves look like first. Got to get him used to other cattle, too, if we're going to show him."

"He needs time," my father said. "I'm telling you, he's missing Ireland."

"Shit," Roy said again. They were silent for a while.

Finally, Roy spoke first. "We'll ask the vet. If he agrees with you, I swear I won't say another thing. If he agrees with me, we'll put the herd in with him. What do you say?"

My father tried a few more arguments, saying he wasn't sure a Kentucky vet was qualified to offer medical opinions about an imported bull. In the end, though, he had to admit that Roy made sense. And when I got home from basketball practice the next day, the other cattle were with Pilate in his field. From the back porch, I could see his massive body trotting around, rubbing up against cows, and looking pretty frisky.

I was surprised to find my father in the kitchen, leaning against the stove. His chin jerked up when I walked in, and he took a couple of quick steps, stopped, and said, "Hey." We hadn't been alone together since the evening I had cursed him down by the field.

"You want some iced tea?" he asked, reaching for a blue jar. "I was just making some iced tea."

"No, sir," I said.

"Pilate's in with the rest of the cattle. You saw it?"

"I did."

"You sure you don't want some iced tea?"

"No, sir," I said. I went over to the refrigerator, and as I looked inside, I asked him, "Why aren't you down in the fields?"

He was filling up a metal pan with water. "Because I'm making this iced tea," he said. I grabbed a platter of picnic ham and sat down at the table. He twined a tea bag string around his finger.

"I wanted," he finally said with his back to me, "to leave Pilate alone for a while. Let him have some privacy."

He touched the pot lid several times with his fingertips. "How's that ham taste?" he asked

"Good," I said. I rolled a slice and held it out to him. "You want some?"

"Thank you," he said. "I will."

V

I was asleep the next morning when I heard my name and then saw gray bands of daylight around the edges of the window curtains. A voice from the doorway said, "Carl!" It was my father. "You awake?" he asked.

"Yeah," I said, sitting up in bed. He turned on a lamp. He had on his padded farm jacket and yellow work gloves. The corners of his eyes were pale. "I need you to get dressed," he said. "I need your help."

"What's wrong?" I asked.

"Hurry down to the pasture." Then I heard his boots on the stairs.

I can't recall much about getting down to the field. As I left my room, my mother was standing at the top of the landing. Her hand seemed blue as it fluttered near the neck of her bathrobe. I heard her say, "He told me to call the vet," and then I was outside. There had been a hard freeze, and the gravel was silent from the cold. There was a falcon on a telephone pole. I didn't run. I spotted my father's bare head beyond the fence row, and I kept my eyes fixed on it until I was beside him. And then all I could see was the still mass of Pilate at our feet. His body looked brown in the frost. The gold ring was streaked with ice.

I reached out and splayed my hand right in the middle of his back. I didn't move it. His flesh was as cold and solid as a mound of earth in midwinter. I heard my father saying, "I found him dead. Just found him dead right here," and then sometime later, "I need you to drive the rest of the herd into the back lot."

And I did. I don't know how long it took me. When I finished the vet and Roy were there. The vet was saying something about the bovine encephalitis the Hereford bull had died from a few months back. He wasn't sure, though. It was hard to tell with these European breeds. They could do an autopsy. He'd send a truck out to collect the body, he said, and he took his leave. The next thing I noticed clearly were red splotches on Roy's forehead as he pulled off his International Harvester cap and slapped it again and again across the top of the fence.

"Goddamn Irish bull," he yelled at my father. "Shit. Goddamn expensive bull. I knew we shouldn't have gotten him."

"You wanted him as much as I did," my father said. "I told you it was too much to put him with heifers."

"There was something wrong with him," Roy said. "Something real wrong."

"Stop it, Roy. You said he was fine yesterday."

"I was just telling you that, trying to put a good slant on things. I tell you, there was something wrong with that bull. Only tried it with two heifers."

"Shit," my father said, and he snorted the way he had the night I'd yelled at him. My heart gave a hard thud in my chest as he said to Roy, "You've never had half as many women in your life."

The red splotches on Roy's forehead spread down over his nose and cheeks, and he began to blink rapidly. He took quick breaths, obviously desperate to keep calm, tried several times to speak in a normal voice, couldn't, and ended up shrieking, "That bull of yours is damn queer."

"What are you saying?"

"I'm saying he was queer! When you were up at the house, he was only humping steers. Mounting one right after the other. Couldn't keep him down."

My father staggered back against the fence, cradling his head in his palms. His fingers pressed so hard against his skull that his knuckles went white. His lips and nostrils were pinched tight with rage. In as quiet a voice as I had ever heard from him, he said:

"You're the goddamn queer. You hear me? You're the queer, Roy. How many fellas you give it to, huh? More than he ever did."

I bent over double with a pain in my gut, squatting against the frozen field. I looked up to see Roy's chin hanging down in the cold air. His cap was crushed in his fist. He ran to the pasture gate and rattled the latch until it swung open. He jumped in his truck and sped off down the driveway.

My father was hunched up against a fence pole. We stared at each other a long time over a patch of cold bluegrass. His eyes were wet and his cheeks were scored by long, pale ruts. My throat burned. I watched him press his fingertips up under the bones of his brows as if he were trying to get hold of eyeballs. I wanted to run to the house, but instead I found myself next to him, holding on to his wrist, telling him, "I heard the old, old men say, 'All that's beautiful drifts away, like the waters.'"

He didn't respond. I wondered if he'd heard me and was about to repeat myself when he told me, "That's pretty. You make that up yourself?"

"No, sir," I said. "It's Yeats."

"Since when did you start liking him?"

"Long time, I guess," I said, looking away. "You said all Irishmen should like Yeats."

My father passed the back of his hand under his eyes. He stood up quickly, cleared his throat, and spit onto the gleaming pasture.

"That bull was too fine an animal for this poor earth."

I spit, too. "He sure was."

My father reached out for my elbow and pulled me up. "You know why Pilate died, Carl?" he asked. "I'll tell you why. He was miserable here in Kentucky."

"You think so?"

"I do," he said, nodding his head. "That bull died for love of Ireland."

"You might be right," I said.

We walked back to the house in silence.

It was full daylight now. The gravel was damp and loose. We were almost at the back porch when my father said, "You know what I'm thinking, Carl? I'm thinking I'm going to buy your mama a Cadillac."

"How you going to get the money?"

"I got credit," he said. "I could auction off some of the herd, I suppose." He kicked a little hole in the driveway with the toe of his boot.

As he opened the back screen door, he asked me, "You guess your mama wants a blue car?"

"I think so."

"I'd say I should get her a red one. What do you say? We don't want to spoil her too much now, do we?"

I said I agreed.

Adam Schroeder

University of British Columbia

THE DISTANCE BETWEEN PRAGUE AND NEW ORLEANS

"What do you mean you won't cash my traveler's check? What is that? I'm a fucking movie star!" said Timothy.

The man with a glass eye sat unflinching in his Plexiglas booth, the long fingers of one hand softly tapping the metal counter in front of him. His one eye squinted out through his green plastic visor.

"Sir," said the little man, "passport. Or some ID."

"My passport's up in my trailer," said Timothy, patting the outer pockets of his dark suit. "I told you that a thousand times! Look at this, it's American Express, I might as well have fucking cash in my hand, here, here, look at my signature here at the top, all you gotta do is watch me signing the bottom, and look, I gotta tell ya, that should be all the ID passport you oughta need, alright? Watch me sign."

"No, sir," said the man, peering through his visor and waving a long finger. "That will make your check void. Get your passport and come back here. Close at six, open tomorrow at seven-thirty. The next person, please."

Timothy stuffed the traveler's check into the basin where the Plexiglas met the metal counter, but the little man blocked it with his hand, tearing one corner.

"Oh, now it's fucked!" said Timothy, pushing back his long bangs.

"Terrance, now my traveler's check is fucked!" Terrance shuffled forward in his brick-red trench coat, smoothing down his mustache with his index finger.

"Let's leave, Timothy. I've still got some cash. Let's go outside, I'll buy you a nice Budvar, alright, Timothy? Come on, out the door." He put his arm around Timothy and turned him as the people in line stood staring.

A little bell rang as they went out the door.

It was a gorgeous afternoon. Traffic whizzed by the shop windows, little Volkswagens, Saabs, Trabants, shards of sunlight bouncing off their windshields and glancing at angles up the sides of ornate, centuries-old buildings. Pedestrians filled the narrow sidewalks, winking and whistling at one another, and Terrance and Timothy pushed past, coming out from the shadow beneath the American Express awning to stand next to a sausage vendor in the bright sunlight. When Timothy stopped moving, Terrance reached for the buttons of Timothy's jacket.

"Leave my buttons alone!" said Timothy, batting away Terrance's hands. He reached in his shirt pocket and took out his sunglasses. "What's with everybody today? Man."

"I don't want you to overheat," said Terrance, drawing his hands back against his chest. "We should try to head back to the set, Timothy. It's nearly, it's nearly one-thirty. We have to get back to the set."

"Fuck the set. What do I need the set for? Did you see that in there? That guy had no clue, had never seen me before ever. Does Paramount have zero distribution over here or what? Fuck going back to the set, man, what good is that doing me?"

"Maybe if he doesn't recognize you that should be your reason for running back. I mean, the more you work, Timothy, the more people are going to know you. It's basic."

"No wonder we came here to shoot the freakin' movie, Terrance, I mean, what year's the script set?"

"Thirteen ninety."

"Yeah, well, it's nineteen ninety-two and they're cashing fucking traveler's checks like it was the Middle Ages. What's this guy selling here? What is this? What are you selling, hot dogs?"

"*Parek v rohliku,*" said the sausage vendor.

"Well, what I want is a hot dog, Terrance. I still don't have a freakin' cent! Aw man, Prague fuckin' sucks!"

"Here's twenty crowns, Timothy, you go ahead and buy yourself that hot dog." Terrance finished combing down his mustache, handed Timothy a few coins, and lit a cigarette. Timothy dropped the coins into the bearded vendor's hand; the hand was missing its pinkie finger. After throwing the coins into a wooden box, the vendor untied and retied his apron, faced the traffic to turn some sausages in a pan, and after a minute handed Timothy two pieces of rye bread, a puddle of grayish mustard, and a long orange sausage all resting on a piece of cardboard.

"Oh, what is this?" said Timothy. "Terrance, tell me what this is."

"Hot dog," said the vendor.

"It's time to get back to the set is what it is," said Terrance.

They started down the crowded sidewalk, moving in the direction of the Charles Bridge. Timothy balanced the sausage on a slice of mustard-soaked bread and ferried it toward his mouth, his elbows occasionally catching passersby in the shoulder.

"Prague fucking sucks," he said again.

"You say that," said Terrance, "but I still don't think it's that bad. It's still better than New York. I think maybe you hate it because you got that secret."

"I knew you would say that. I knew it," said Timothy, his mouth filled with doughy chewed bread. "Just shut up."

"Klapka is probably a good Czech name. I don't know why you don't want to use it. The world's a global village after all."

"So what?" said Timothy.

"So everybody doesn't have to anglicize their name anymore."

"I don't care if it's *anglicized* or not, I just don't want a stupid name, and Klapka is a stupid name. Carson is not a stupid name. I mean, John Wayne, he didn't change his name because *Marion* wasn't English-sounding, he changed it because it was stupid."

"Did you change it to Carson?"

"No, my grandfather or somebody did. Long time ago."

"He probably changed it because it's Jewish. People didn't want to be Jewish back then," said Terrance, throwing his cigarette down behind an elderly woman in a fur hat. "You know, I'm Jewish. Nothing to be ashamed of."

"Jesus," said Timothy, "you never think of Europe as being so hot, do you? Man, it's hot."

"I don't think we can ever understand what Jews have gone through the way Europeans do. I just don't think we can."

They rounded a corner and passed a Dixieland jazz band. A tall elderly man in tinted sunglasses, a jean jacket, and a bowler hat was swaying in front of several horn players, singing a gravelly "Chattanooga Choo Choo" through a megaphone. A plump woman strummed a banjo. As Timothy passed, the singer lowered his tinted glasses and winked at him. Several Korean tourists, their cameras around their necks, stood watching the band and clapping their hands in time.

"You could at least go by Klapka while you're here," said Terrance. "Maybe it'll grow on you." They were now in a square where a hundred tourists stood staring up at a medieval clock tower and the blue sky.

"Well, for all I know, it means asshole. What's with all these people? Find me a garbage can for this cardboard thing, man." Timothy bumped his way through the crowd, Terrance behind him. "Hey, what scene is this we're doing when we get there?"

"It's where you tell the queen to go jump in the lake, you don't want to rule."

"I said I wanted that scene fixed. Why would he suddenly start saying 'ain't'? 'Ain't fit to rule.' Guy forgot what movie he was writing."

"Unless you're using bad grammar to underline your point," said Terrance.

They stopped in a narrow alleyway off one corner of the square where a dolly loaded with silver kegs of beer was being backed out of the side entrance of one restaurant and into the side entrance of another. The passage was so narrow they had to stand waiting while the beer man, dressed in a woolen jacket and leather cap, closed his eyes and strained his neck to haul the dolly up the step into the next restaurant. Timothy ground the toe of his shoe into the space between two cobblestones. Once the kegs had disappeared through the doorway, the beer man leaned out again and gave them a jovial salute. He was missing his pinkie finger.

"Cigarette," said Timothy. They were standing at an intersection, waiting to cross over to the Charles Bridge. From where they stood they could see the swans in the river and the spindles and crosses of the castle, high above the city on the opposite shore.

"Sorry, Timothy, I'm out."

"Give me some money, will ya? I'll pick some up at that place by the barracks. I can't stand not having cash on me!"

Terrance fished in his pocket and pulled out a hundred-crown note, but as he held the note between his fingers a breeze plucked it from his hand and held it in the air, above their heads and a little in front of them.

"Oh," said Terrance.

"Wow," said Timothy. There was no one else on the sidewalk. There was no traffic either, though the signal for pedestrians to walk had still not come on. The note began to flutter down. Without looking, Terrance took a step forward to seize it, and a white BMW caught him above the knees. For an instant Timothy's and Terrance's eyes met, and for another instant Timothy saw the driver, a woman, her hair pulled back, her mouth hanging open, her nails digging into the steering wheel. Then Terrance pitched into the air and came down on the opposite sidewalk. The BMW careened off at an angle, glanced off the corner of a building, dislodging a single brick, then veered off around a corner and was gone.

The people waiting at the intersection got out of their cars and stood dumbfounded, and a hundred-crown note descended in a spiral into Timothy's open hand.

"It's funny you should have to come in this afternoon. There's not many other officers who speak English, and, you know, I was supposed to have this afternoon off but my dentist got sick. So it's purely by chance I'm here to take your testimony."

"I've been having good luck all day," said Timothy.

They sat in the spacious police station just below the castle, high enough up on the hill that, looking out Captain Mejzlik's window,

Timothy could see the countless angled rooftops stretching far across the city, and the towers of churches and cathedrals sprouting up like flowers from a lawn.

"How do you like Praha?" asked Captain Mejzlik. He wore a gray suit, had his feet up on his desk, and constantly fingered the bright yellow tassel of the antique sword on his wall.

"It's fine," said Timothy. A series of air bubbles rose in the water cooler in the corner, making a sound like moving bowels. Timothy shifted in his chair. "It's okay. I have another week of shooting. But I don't know how long that'll take now."

"Mr. Singer was an actor as well?"

"He was my assistant. He organized everything I did, everything, I mean, I don't even know what day it is today. I'd have to ask Terrance."

"They can get you another assistant."

"I guess, but, Jesus, that's not exactly the point, you know?"

"Certainly," said Captain Mejzlik, twisting the yellow tassel around his index finger and then his thumb. "Are you from San Francisco?"

"Sort of."

"New Orleans?"

"No, I'm from Los Angeles, out on the west coast. Below San Francisco. Where are you from?"

"Oh, I'm from Zelivskeho," said Captain Mejzlik. He gestured toward the window. "Over there. An old neighborhood. We all know each other."

"Sounds great," said Timothy. "Look, my concern really at this point is to nab this lady who hit him, the lady in the car, it's probably got like a scratch down the, down the right side, that's my concern, okay?"

"Of course it is," said Captain Mejzlik, pulling his feet down and taking a file from his top drawer. "How long was Mr. Singer your assistant for?"

"The last three movies. About two years."

"Do you know the phone numbers of his family? We should contact someone right away."

"No, I don't, you know, really I have no idea."

"You do not know his family?"

"Listen, I just worked with the guy on a few projects. His mom and dad and stuff never came up. He made reservations for me at restaurants and stuff like that."

Mejzlik rose to his feet and went to the door, resting his hand on the knob. He seemed out of breath. "So if you work with someone you don't have a responsibility to know their family?"

"Listen, *I* don't know how to get ahold of his family, but we can just call Jerome up at the set and he can probably tell you."

Captain Mejzlik turned the knob and pulled the metal door open. "Pitr," he said. Timothy remained in his swivel chair and examined his fingernails. A young man strode in, dressed in a gray suit similar to Captain Mejzlik's, only with high black boots and a bow tie as well. His reddish hair was combed sideways across his head. He stood at attention in the center of the room as Captain Mejzlik shut the door again.

"Now pay attention to this, please, Mr. Carson. Watch the difference between the Czech Republic and New Orleans."

Timothy swung his legs back and forth in the chair, the heels of his shoes brushing across the pink carpet.

"Pitr, your mother's name is Lida. What is my mother's name?"

"Lujza Mejzlikova."

"My father?"

"Jan Mejzlik."

"And your father is Vaclav Malek."

"Just as you, Captain, have a brother named Vaclav."

"Indeed I do, and you a brother named Antonin."

Timothy lifted himself from the chair and went to stand beside the window. He looked down toward the Charles Bridge and tried to pinpoint where they had been standing when it happened. But he couldn't see the intersection because of an ornate tower at the foot of the bridge, resplendent with flags and saints. Even now Terrance was in a hospital somewhere in a metal box. It had been a busy day for them both, a long day, and the sun, slowly descending toward the distant hilltops, was only beginning to set. A greenish moss grew on the windowsill.

"My wife?"

"Lucka, of course!"

"Forgive me, that was an easy one. How about her brother?"

"Plitcha . . . Plitcha Sinderka."

"Yes, Plitcha Sinderka. Decent fellow."

The police drove Timothy up a series of winding lanes to the castle. Stopped at a corner he saw again the elderly jazz singer, leaning in a doorway reading a newspaper, and as they rolled away the man again dropped his glasses and threw Timothy a wink. Then he pulled his newspaper back up in front of his face.

The officer driving had seen it as well. As he changed gears and they went up the hill he glanced at Timothy, gesturing back over his shoulder with his thumb. One of his eyes was blue and the other green.

"You have to watch out for men like that. We don't know what to do with them."

"You speak very good English," said Timothy.

"As does everyone in Prague."

"Captain Mejzlik was telling me he was the only policeman around who could speak any English."

"Everyone tells lies," said the officer.

They pulled up in front of the entrance to the castle, where a throng of tourists stood watching the sunset, showing each other postcards, and drinking bottles of lemonade. Timothy nodded to the officer as he pulled the door handle. "Bye," he said. "Thanks a lot." He got out and shut the door.

The officer leaned over and rolled down the passenger window. "I'm sorry about your friend," he said. "But, you know, you must sacrifice something to get anywhere. As a famous person you must understand this. Good-bye." He threw his hand back onto the steering wheel, put the car into neutral and silently rolled away down the hill.

Timothy smoothed down his suit jacket and went up the half-dozen steps to the castle gate. A teenaged girl with braces and knee socks came up to him. "A-aren't you Timothy Carson?" she said. He stopped in mid-step and turned to her, smoothing back his bangs.

"Why, yes, I am," he said. "Who might you be?"

Everyone had turned to look. "M-Melinda Spoor," she said. "I thought it was great in *Nation of Anger* when you threw that garbage can through the principal's window. It-it was so funny."

"Thank you, Melinda," said Timothy. "Thanks a lot." He started back up the steps and suddenly turned and threw his hand over his head, offering an all-encompassing wave to the crowd. Someone took a picture. Then he turned again and went into the castle.

In the first courtyard another group of tourists stood clustered in one corner as the changing of the guard came to an end. A dozen men in blue uniforms and tall black hats, antique rifles over their shoulders, goose-stepped back into their barracks through a small doorway beside the main gate, their faces fixed in dramatic grimaces. A door shut behind them and there was scattered applause. Timothy strode across the courtyard and through the small crowd, pushing past them to reach another gate leading to another courtyard farther inside the castle walls. A small woman with a headset, olive-skinned, with a gauze of dark hair across her cheeks, stood guarding the gate with a clipboard in her hand. She was speaking into the headset's tiny microphone as Timothy shouldered toward her.

"Do not let the caterers go. I have not had my supper. No, do not let them go." She glanced up, saw Timothy there, and flicked the microphone under her chin. In the failing light, both their faces seemed green. "Oh, Terrance, my God!" she said. "Where have they taken Timothy? Which hospital? This is the worst thing that could have happened, my God, we have not known what to do, Mr. Bendiner has been on the telephone all afternoon since we found out and they are trying to get Christian Slater for the part now, but, Terrance, we have not known what to do because you are the only one with all the numbers for Timothy's family and all of that so we have not been able to contact them all day since we found out, Terrance, where have you been? You must go in and see Mr. Bendiner now because he has said to someone that if Christian Slater does not come we might as well all go back to the United States right now, though I don't quite understand as to why I must go, for as you know I am from Prague."

"Minka," said Timothy, "you're fucked. *Terrance* died. A car hit *Terrance* when we were down at the bridge. Terrance died. He died today. My name's Timothy Carson." He held out his hand and she shook it limply.

"Mr. Carson," said Minka, "they had told us that it was Timothy."

"Did they do any shooting today?"

"They made a change in the schedule and did the scene where the queen smashes her mirror."

"I should go see Jerome."

"No, please, let someone else tell him first. He's been very angry at Christian Slater."

Timothy pushed past her and down a narrow corridor between two of the high castle walls, where technicians wearing tool belts bumped into one another, carrying huge coils of cable over their shoulders. Some nodded to Timothy as he passed. He was looking at their hands: callused for the most part, some wearing Band-Aids and some with black nails, but not one worker missing his pinkie finger. Near the end of the passage he stopped a man with a huge black mustache, stooped under the weight of a prop door across his back. He too had all of his fingers.

"Excuse me," Timothy said slowly. "Where do you come from?"

"What do you mean? I'm from L.A. just like you. In fact my apartment was right under yours out in Laurel Canyon. You had that girlfriend who did aerobics every day in the middle of the night. Must have been four years ago."

"That's what I thought," said Timothy. "That's why I asked."

"Excuse me," said the man, and moved off with his door.

At the end of the corridor the wall to one side had fallen away, and Timothy stopped to look out over darkening Prague as streetlights and the lamps in houses began to flicker on. There was no way to see the intersection. Instead he saw the BMW ricocheting down the motorways of the Czech Republic, the hands of the driver still digging into her leather steering wheel and the car speeding across the border into Germany, into France, across the Pyrenees into Spain. Into vast, anonymous Europe.

In the wide, cobblestoned courtyard at the center of the castle sat catering trucks, massively tall light standards, and long metal trailers to accommodate the producers and cast. Moths bumped against their windows. Climbing the aluminum steps of the largest trailer, backed into the farthest corner, Timothy rapped quickly at the metal door and went in, letting the door bang shut behind him. There was a single light on above the kitchen sink. On the leather sofa lay Jerome Bendiner, his head propped against one arm and his bare feet dangling over the other. He had a bald head and trousers held up with suspenders. There was a blue washcloth across his eyes.

"Tell me who's there," said Jerome.

"The walking wounded," said Timothy. Jerome did not stir.

"Are you hurt badly?"

"It killed Terrance. The car never touched me. Sorry today's shooting never happened."

"Old Terrance, he shouldn't have gone out on a day like today. He never ate his breakfast and he told me he hardly slept at all, he was up half the night. Old Terrance, that's a problem. That's a bitch."

Timothy went to Jerome's fridge and pulled out a bottle of Budvar. The orange and white label was wet and slid off in his hand. Jerome was rearranging the washcloth over his eyes.

"Jerome, do you want a beer?"

"No thanks, no. Shoot, Terrance and I were going to play a game of golf when we got back. I don't know, did you know Terrance played golf? We were looking out at that park over behind the castle, and Terrance he says if the hillside wasn't so steep it'd be good for a round of golf. Neither one of us had any clubs."

"I didn't know you knew Terrance." Timothy was looking through the drawers for a bottle opener.

"Oh, yeah. Shoot, for years. He was around back when I was putting together *Our September* and some other thing, some thing that didn't pay off. A lot of the little ladies they thought Terrance was pretty charming, you know, but somehow, somehow he never made it very far in the industry." Jerome rolled onto his side to face Timothy, pulling the washcloth up onto the side of his head. "My secretary, she liked Terrance. I invited her along when I was nominated for that Oscar and she wanted to know could she bring Terrance along. But we didn't have room. My wife Marnie invited him to Michael's bar mitzvah, to my eldest son Michael's bar mitzvah. He bought Michael a catcher's mitt, I think. I don't know how he knew old Michael wanted one. Michael was up there doing his recitation and I could see Terrance's lips moving the whole time; he still knew the whole thing from the looks of it. Old Terrance."

Timothy pulled at his beer. "I didn't know you were Jewish, Jerome."

"Yeah, and why not?"

Timothy was silent. He toyed with the cord for the venetian blinds, pulling them up the window and letting them slide back down again.

"A good part of Hollywood was started up by a bunch of Jewish guys," said Jerome. "Whole movie industry. It was just a nice place in the desert before that. Vacation spot, like Palm Springs. They put their heads together and got it all going, and now look at the money coming out of it, out of this big machine this bunch of guys just put together. Multibillions every year. I mean, you're in L.A. and you're in the industry, you might *as well* be Jewish, even if you weren't to start with."

"You think so, Jerome?"

"Sure, sure."

"Minka told me you thought I was dead."

"She's got it wrong. I already talked on the phone for an hour with Terrance's sister in Red Hook."

"I'm going to grab some dinner and then pack it in, Jerome." Timothy set his empty bottle on top of the fridge, where a little army of them already stood.

"Why don't you take off tomorrow too. We didn't make any headway with the bloody scenes with Helen. I think that you could probably use the rest."

"I think *you* could use the rest, Jerome."

Minka sat down next to Timothy with her plate of scrambled eggs. She filled her mouth with food and kicked the leg of his folding chair playfully as she chewed.

"What are you sitting out here for?" she said.

Timothy was eating toast. He chewed and swallowed. "Waiting for the changing of the guard."

Minka nodded. "I like to watch it. Of course, they are dressed as fools, but it makes me feel a little safe, in some way. Perhaps because it is the nice little Czech army."

"And not the Russians."

"Not the Russians or the Germans."

"How can *you* remember the Germans, Minka?"

"Not me, my parents can. My mother always talks about it."

The courtyard was empty, the gate still locked, the cobblestones glistening with dew. The door in the gatehouse opened and one of the blue-coated guards came out. He waved to Minka with a rag and she waved back, then he sat against the wall and began polishing his boots.

"During the war my mother's family helped a refugee to hide. He was Jewish, I think, a businessman. His family had escaped long before, but for some reason he wanted to stay behind. I think he worked with my grandfather. My grandfather wanted to help him escape into the countryside, but for some reason he refused to leave Prague. Even though the Germans rolled their tanks in the street every day and he had to wear a star on his clothes, he would not try to get away. Then the Nazis began to arrest all of the Jews and they came to where he lived and he said he actually shot one of the Nazis, shot one while they were arresting him, and he got away and came to our house. And in a few days they came to our house looking for him, and over the years they came many times, tapping on the walls and breaking through the floor looking for him. They expected him to hide there because those are difficult places. But he was really in the bottom of the china cabinet. Every day he would get out and stretch for a few minutes, then he would go back in. He was rolled up in there like a little ball. Then one day my mother and my grandparents came home and he was lying out on the floor, all stretched out, and he had shot himself in the head. My mother says that my grandmother was sure the Nazis had come in and found him and shot him to make it look as though he shot himself, but if you see any movies with Nazis in them like I have seen then you know they would not leave him there but they would take him back to their officer and say 'Sir, we have killed this Jew,' and the officer would say 'Excellent job, men, Heil Hitler!' So my grandfather never believed that the Nazis had killed him, he told my mother that probably the man had come out of the china cabinet for his stretching and then probably could not bring himself to go back in. But then my grandparents were in just as much danger with the man's corpse in the house, so they waited until the middle of the night and dragged him to a street corner a mile away. Then they ran back to their house. And the Nazis still came back, but with the man out of the house it was almost funny to watch them knocking on things and looking under the bed, and once my mother burst out laughing."

"Your eggs are cold, Minka."

"Oh, that's alright," she said, and scooped a forkful into her mouth. The first guard had finished polishing his boots and now stood in a line beside the gate with a few others. An officer with a cup of coffee in his hand came out of the gatehouse and blew a whistle, and at once the guards began to do jumping jacks.

"What do you remember about the Russians?"

Minka scraped up the rest of the egg with her fork. She smiled at Timothy. "I remember when they left. I was watching out a window with my brothers and about one hundred of their soldiers were marching in the square, down by the clock tower, you know where I mean? All of these soldiers and all so quiet."

"Was there fighting?"

"No. The radio had been shut down but then it came back on for a moment and said 'Independence! Revolution!' or some such thing like that, so my brothers and I went down to a bar and by this time it was the evening and the soldiers were all just standing around in the street with their guns. Anything could have happened at that time. We walked by the soldiers and went and had a glass of beer, and the people in the bar began dancing and singing, and at midnight the soldiers came in and had drinks too, and everyone patted them on the back. One of the Russians was very drunk and started to kiss me. He was showing his gun to everyone and just before we went home one of my brother's friends was shot by his girlfriend."

The guards stood at attention as the officer opened the gate. A tour bus was visible at the bottom of the steps.

"I should get to work," said Minka, rising. "Give me your dish."

Timothy handed her his plate and she disappeared into the castle. He stood up and stretched his arms high above his head, then bent down to touch his toes. Then up to stretch his arms again.

He crossed the courtyard, went through the gate and down the steps to where a tour guide was pointing out the features of the castle's outside wall to her tour group. The bus pulled away from the sidewalk, revealing the jazz singer of the day before, leaning against a lamppost on the opposite side of the street, eating a roll. As he caught sight of Timothy he took off his bowler hat and shook it in the air, chewing his roll all the while. He had a head of thick black hair.

Timothy smiled and crossed the street to meet him. As he approached, the man did not stop shaking the hat but merely lowered it, until he was shaking it in front of his chest.

"Timothy Carson," said the man, "the famous movie star."

"Maybe in the States," said Timothy.

"Oh, we know you here," said the man, replacing his hat. "Here we know you." He brought his hand down and Timothy saw that it consisted of a thumb and three fingers. The knuckle of his former pinkie finger was wrapped in gauze. Timothy stared at it.

"People love my finger. It never did heal properly," said the man, blowing on the bandage. He put his hand on Timothy's shoulder. "My name is Karel. Come now, I want to discuss your films."

"*Sabotage*," said Karel, "was a great film. Your best, I think. You played the part very well. It is a memorable performance in a great film."

"I'd have to agree with you," said Timothy.

"But *Murdering Mr. Hobbs* was your worst film."

"I don't want to talk about *Murdering Mr. Hobbs*."

"Yes, *Murdering Mr. Hobbs* was your biggest mistake, I think. I suppose it was supposed to be a screwball comedy or the like, like that film at the summer camp, what was that? *Meatballs*."

"*Meatballs*," repeated Timothy, his face deep in a glass of beer.

"Yes, but *Meatballs* had Bill Murray, it was a smallish part, I know, but he brought the film a sort of kinetic energy. Now *Murdering Mr. Hobbs* you were the straight man, and that would have been fine had they cast a Bill Murray, or even a Nicolas Cage, next to you. But there was no one, it was a cast only of straight men, and as a consequence any potential for humor in the film died a quick and pitiful death."

Timothy set his glass down on the wooden table and licked his lips. "And everyone says Ivan Reitman is a genius anyway."

"That they do," said Karel, nodding, "that they do."

"*Ghostbusters*."

"Yes, *Ghostbusters*," said Karel. "With the marshmallow man." He took a pack of cigarettes out of his pocket and passed one to Timothy.

"Or *Stripes*. Ivan Reitman is a genius."

"*Stripes*, my God, yes!"

"Or *Dave*, did you see that one? It had Kevin Kline in it."

"*Dave*, that is the film where Kevin Kline works for an employment agency and he is able to impersonate the president and seduce the president's wife. He convinces everyone he is something he is not."

"Well, yeah, but," Timothy sucked on his cigarette, "he was a good-hearted guy to start with. He didn't do anything wrong."

"But he kept himself a secret, and that can make people assume the worst about whatever he is hiding." Karel took a long drink from his glass of beer, set it down, took off his tinted glasses and began to clean them on his shirttail. He had massive gray bags under his eyes. "For example, Mr. Carson, in the nineteen-eighties myself and every member of our little music group was arrested and imprisoned several times. It was because we were regularly meeting in private. The police didn't like it."

"They assumed the worst of your secret," said Timothy, tapping ash into his empty beer glass.

"Of course they did. They assumed we were planning a secret militia there in the kitchen of Vilem's house. You might have seen Vilem with us yesterday, when you passed by. He plays the trombone. We were there at his house, playing 'Swinging on a Star,' I think, and a few men come in the door and begin to arrest us. We insisted, I'm sure you can imagine, that we are only musicians practicing, and they even said that this was a good attempt to deceive them but certainly not good enough. As they put me in the back of a car I was told it was the worst rendition of 'Swinging on a Star' any of them had ever heard."

Timothy leaned back in his chair and put his hands behind his head. Except for him and Karel and a couple of middle-aged ladies sitting at the bar sipping coffee, the tavern was empty. The waitress diligently polished each of the liquor bottles on the wall and sang softly to herself. It was a very clean establishment.

"You too, Mr. Carson, would have had to be careful here back in those years," said Karel. "If the authorities had watched *Murdering*

Mr. Hobbs they would have said to themselves 'This is not a film. What are those hooligans planning? Arrest them in case it is all just cover for the making of another film. An even worse one.' " Karel laughed, tipping his head back, then he abruptly stopped, picked up their empty glasses and went to the bar. When he returned Timothy had his head in his hands.

"Don't blame me for *Murdering Mr. Hobbs*. My agent thought I should try comedy and he said the director was so into coke I wouldn't even have to audition. I have to confess to you, Karel. I wasn't supposed to be the straight man. They thought I could really be funny."

Karel pushed a full beer under his chin. "Then it is time to stop hiding from yourself. You are not in the least bit funny."

The waitress came over to them and put her hand on Timothy's shoulder. She had a long, thin arm and wore a white T-shirt.

"I knew it," she said. "I knew it. You are Timothy Carson."

Karel said he wanted to show Timothy some sights. They wandered back over the Charles Bridge and stood waiting at the intersection where Terrance had been killed, stood waiting for the signal to walk right at the spot where Terrance's body had landed.

"An American friend of mine was killed right here," said Timothy.

"When was that? With the Communists?"

"It was yesterday."

"What, that fellow you were walking with?"

"Yeah, that was him."

"Here and then so quickly gone. At least you have not forgotten him."

The signal changed and they walked across. A breeze blew up from the river.

"Where are we going?"

"I want to take you to the Jewish cemetery in Josefov," said Karel. "It is breathtaking. Twenty thousand graves."

"Are you Jewish, Karel?"

"No. Are you?"

"I don't know. I've been told I have a Jewish name."

"Carson is not a Jewish name."

"Klapka is my name."

It was still mid-morning and the streets were empty. They passed only one vendor, standing beside a small steaming pot and a large cardboard sign reading "GROG."

As they walked through the square where Timothy had first seen Karel, the clock tower began to strike the hour. A few teenagers in shorts stood under it snapping pictures. As the bells tolled, ceramic skeletons on either side of the clock face, connected to the gears of the clock by pulleys and cables, began to dance eerily, though they did not really dance so much as stand in one spot, shaking their bones.

"Let's see if the rabbi is at home."

Timothy stood under a great flowering tree as Karel tapped discreetly at the iron side door of an old brick house. It was the house of the caretaker of the Jewish cemetery in Josefov, the oldest neighborhood of Prague. The upper part of the house was a Jewish heritage center; downstairs lived the caretaker.

The cemetery itself did not cover much ground; perhaps a single city block. But from the low front wall right against the street to the lichen-covered wall at the back, nothing could be seen but gravestones. They were stacked against one another, fifteen and twenty thick, so that had the gravestones been a uniform height they might have resembled a single paved surface. But many had crumbled into piles of rubble. Some were tall and broad, and others simply short, squat posts; all that they had strictly in common was the rough gray rock they were hewn from. Timothy leaned over the front wall to read the letters on the nearest gravestones, but only the barest impressions lingered. The stones had been eroded into anonymity, dusted with yellow moss.

He shook his head.

"Timothy," said Karel. The door was slowly opening. Karel and Timothy ducked under the low lintel to step inside.

The rabbi's quarters were surprisingly bright. Fluorescent lights lined the low cement walls, revealing stacks and stacks of ancient-looking books and a collection of tattered wooden furniture. Two horseflies followed them in from outside and alighted on a pot of jam sitting on the desk. Their host shut the door and nodded at them. He was of medium height and dressed all in black, with a broad-brimmed black hat on his head and a long black coat brushing the carpet. He had a reddish beard and long sidelocks dangling down beside his ears. He silently gestured for them to sit. Timothy's chair creaked audibly, as though in pain.

"David Hayim," Karel said to Timothy, his broad bandaged hand indicating the rabbi, who nodded quickly.

"*Zdravstvuite,*" said David Hayim to Timothy.

"He speaks English," said Karel.

"Oh. Do you?" said David Hayim. "I see."

"My name's Timothy Carson. I'm American. I'm an actor."

"Are you? It's very interesting." The rabbi turned one of the chairs around and straddled it, leaning his chest against the wooden back.

"I wanted him to see the graves," said Karel.

"Yes, they are very nice, very nice," said David Hayim. "You could make a movie about them. Might be a fun time."

"You could make twenty thousand movies," said Karel. "Every single one of those graves—and how the occupant came to be in there—could each be the subject of a feature film."

"It sure could," said Timothy. "Those would be films."

"But don't dig any up, alright?" David Hayim leaned forward and gave Timothy a playful slap on the knee. He suddenly pointed at Karel. "What kind of host am I? Do you want biscuits?"

"No thanks, Rabbi," said Karel.

"We just ate," said Timothy.

"Glass of tea?"

"No thanks."

"Carrots?"

"We're fine," said Timothy. "Thank you."

"Fruit juice?"

"No."

"Okay," said David Hayim. He snapped his fingers. "What kind of movie are you in?"

"We're making a movie up at the castle. It's a fantasy film. It's about this prince who gives up his throne to wander the countryside. He fights a dragon."

"And an evil person takes the throne and the people suffer and the prince returns a hero to fight the villain and become king. I see," said the rabbi.

"You know the story," said Timothy.

The rabbi waved his hand. "Everyone knows that story."

"You could make it part of your film series based on the Josefov cemetery," said Karel. "You could have the prince be buried here at the end. You could end the film with a shot of his grave here now, and modern people walking by with shopping bags and things. Show his place in history, even though now his stone has been worn blank."

"Karel," said Timothy, "that could really work."

"He would have to be a Jewish prince," said the rabbi.

"That could really work," said Timothy.

"What other movies have you been acting in?" said David Hayim.

"*Sabotage,* Rabbi," said Karel. "Timothy was in *Sabotage.*"

"*Sabotage?*" said the rabbi. "That is a great film. I enjoyed that. I see. But you know who is great? Karel. You should hear him." David Hayim waggled his fingers in the air, as though he were playing a clarinet. He gave Karel a broad smile.

"I have heard him," said Timothy. "He's great."

The rabbi nodded and smiled. With two fingers he tapped a rapid beat on the back of his chair.

"Rabbi," said Timothy, "you must know a lot about the Jews."

David Hayim raised his eyebrows and continued tapping out a beat. Karel looked at his wristwatch and rose from his chair.

"I'm afraid it's time I met the others. Vilem has a new song. Do you want to stay here with the rabbi?"

"I'd like to," said Timothy. "Is that okay?"

"Oh. Oh, of course," said the rabbi. "Please."

"Thanks for showing me around, Karel. I'll probably see you this afternoon somewhere."

"It will be a pleasure," said Karel. He rubbed the back of his neck and went out, ducking his head beneath the door frame.

"Rabbi," said Timothy, leaning forward on his elbows, "is there such a Jewish name as Klapka?"

"Klapka? Yes. Maybe. Certainly. It could be a Jewish name."

"What do you mean?"

"Well. You see, it's like the name Kafka. You know the Czech writer Kafka."

"No."

"The Czech writer Kafka was a Jew, and so many people think of Kafka as a Jewish name. You see. But it is just a Czech name. He happened to have that name and he happened to be a Jew."

"How's that possible?"

"Oh, well. Over the years many Jews have changed their Hebrew names, or they have been married with Christians. Now one's name does not mean so much. You see? Especially in America. Many, many Jews who arrived in America changed their names. In America a man could be a Jew and be named Ronald Reagan."

"My name is really Klapka. Timothy Klapka."

"It is? Ha ha ha." David Hayim's mouth fell open as he laughed, exposing his broad white teeth.

"What? What?"

"I am sorry. It is just funny. The name sounds funny. It is a good name. Is it Jewish?"

"That's what I'm asking you!"

"Oh. I see. Alright then, it's Jewish if you want it to be. Do you want it to be Jewish?"

"Sort of," said Timothy.

"Why is that?"

"Well, Carson doesn't mean anything," said Timothy. "Klapka, you know, it's got guts."

"Would it still have the guts if it were not a Jewish name?" The rabbi frowned deliberately, as though to underline the gravity of the question, and batted at a horsefly that was trying to land on his hat.

"Not so many guts." Timothy nodded. "Jewish is gutsy."

"And a Jew is what you want to be."

"I think so, yeah. It's part of who I am."

The rabbi stretched out his legs. He wore argyle socks. "You should come to synagogue, then, Mr. Klapka. Before long we can have a bar mitzvah for you. In a few months."

"Oh, I'm circumcised already," said Timothy.

"That's wonderful news." The rabbi stared at Timothy, blinking his eyes rapidly, and pulled at his lower lip with his thumb and forefinger. Then he pushed against the chair and stood up. "I must make some tea." He glanced at Timothy and quickly walked out of the room.

Timothy sat on his chair with his hands on his knees and forced his mouth into a wry smile. He felt somehow ashamed, as though he had just made a pass at the rabbi; he felt excited, tingling, and yet ashamed. He imagined Terrance somewhere in the room, laughing to himself.

"Rabbi, do you have a telephone?" He got up and followed David Hayim. The rabbi was putting a huge brass kettle down on top of his wood stove.

"No, I have no telephone. There is a phone outside on the street."

Timothy felt in his pockets for change. "What does it take, a crown or something?"

"It needs a phone card. Here, take mine." The rabbi unbuttoned his coat and took a blue plastic phone card out of the pocket of his white shirt. He handed it to Timothy.

"How does it work?"

"Here, I'll come with you," said David Hayim.

Outside the wind was blowing blossoms from the flowering tree out across the cemetery. Caught in eddies of the wind, pink and red petals circled around the gravestones, spiraling down only to be caught up again by the breeze. As Timothy and David Hayim crossed the street to the telephone box, a cascade of petals blew up into their faces, settling on Timothy's shoulders and catching in the rabbi's beard. The street was empty and the sun threw shadows from the line of trees across the pavement, up their clothes and onto their heads. Timothy picked up the telephone receiver.

"Here, here, first." The rabbi took the phone card from Timothy and slid it into the top of the keypad. Some numbers came up on a tiny display screen. "Okay, it's okay. I hope you are not phoning San Francisco."

"I'm just phoning up to the castle." Timothy typed in a number.

"Oh, the castle. Very smart. How do you know the phone number there?"

"It's the number of my producer's cellular." It began ringing at the other end.

"Oh, a cellular. I see. Very smart. You are a smart actor."

"Thanks."

"Hello?" It was a woman's voice on the line.

"Hello, Jerome," said Timothy.

"This is not Jerome. This is Kathy speaking. This is a private business line for Mr. Bendiner's private calls. Who is this speaking, please?"

"Just let me speak with Jerome, Kathy. Tell him it's Timothy."

David Hayim leaned his head against the side of the phone box, pressing the brim of his hat into his face.

"Timothy who?"

"Just tell him I'm on the line, Kathy! Jesus Christ, would you just go tell him?"

"He may be indisposed, sir. I'll have to see if I can find him."

"Oh, could you? That'd be *great.*"

Kathy was not listening. Timothy set the receiver on his shoulder. "Hey, Rabbi."

"Yes?" David Hayim's voice was muffled behind his hat.

"Later on, can we see if there's any other Klapkas that live in Prague? I'd like to see if they're Jewish and maybe if they're my relatives. Sound alright?"

"We'll see," said David Hayim.

"Hello?" Jerome's voice spoke into Timothy's shoulder. He put the phone back to his ear.

"Hey, Jerome? It's Timothy."

"Timothy, this day is like a, is like a nightmare. Helen cut her damn hand on the mirror yesterday and now she got blood on that lace get-up we got over in England. I'd like to stop this movie now and start over."

"Hey, Jerome, tell the marketing guys I'm going to want a change. On the posters and stuff I don't want it to say Carson anymore. I want it to say Klapka."

"What the hell?"

"It's my real name, Jerome. It's a Jewish name. Like Bendiner."

"This is a godawful waste of time. Why make a joke about this?"

The pink and red blossoms blew in a dustdevil across the pavement. The rabbi began snapping his fingers.

"Look, Jerome, just fire me if it turns out this is a joke, don't pay me anything. I'm not jerking you around, I really want my name to say Timothy Klapka."

"That's stupid. So on the TV we'll have our ad going and the voice'll say 'starring Timothy Klapka and Helen Smithee,' and the people at home'll say 'Who the fuck is that? Hey, when's Timothy Carson's new film coming out? I love that guy.' No way, Timothy. Not on any picture of mine."

"Look, fuck you, Jerome. I'll do what I want, alright? I'm not gonna get fucked around, that's bullshit, Jerome, you can shove your movie right where I know you like it, I don't need that crap. I'm gonna stay in Prague anyway. You know, there's more important things than your fucking movie."

Suddenly the rabbi's hand shot out and grabbed the phone away from Timothy's ear. His head was still pressed against the side of the phone box.

"Hello, Jerome?" said the rabbi.

"Who the fuck is this?"

"This is Reb David Hayim speaking. I am a friend of Mr. Carson's. I wanted you to know, sir, that he hasn't any intention of staying in Prague and would like to return home as soon as possible. He will cooperate in the completion of your film as much as he can and would like to know if there is anything he can do now to help you."

"Where are you calling me from? Tell Timothy to get up here now."

"We are calling from Josefov. Thank you." The rabbi hung up the receiver. "You are to go back. Your boss says so."

"What are you talking about?" said Timothy. "I'm not going back to that idiot."

"Yes, you will," said David Hayim, staring straight into Timothy's eyes. His sidelocks fluttered up in the wind. He still leaned against the side of the phone box. "You have escaped. You cannot stay here. Go back to America. Do not come back here and expect us to have the memories for you. I have enough to remember. Go on, enjoy America. Have a good time." He patted Timothy on the arm. "My samovar will boil."

Timothy stood with his arms hanging at his sides as the rabbi walked back through the hail of pink blossoms and disappeared down the side of his house. Timothy looked out across the graves. He felt them mocking him. He felt all of history regarding him with disgust.

After a moment the rabbi came back out of his house, crossed the street and stopped in front of Timothy. Timothy folded his arms. The rabbi pulled his card out of the telephone, nodded to Timothy, and turned back to his house.

Timothy put his hands into his pockets and started down the street, toward the clock tower, toward the Charles Bridge, toward the castle. In a house nearby someone began to play trombone.

Kim Garcia
Florida State University

THE PRIEST

Invocation

"Isn't it interesting we keep running into each other," he says, sloshing his wine in its plastic goblet. He must have a low threshold for interesting, I think.

"Like bad pennies," I say, and try to slip past, but there's a crowd and I'm wedged by the cheese table. Stuck fast in this go-nowhere conversation.

He starts to say one thing, and then a second thing. His mouth is open, and he still hasn't said anything.

"Getting any of that worldly experience you were after?" I ask. First he says yes, then no, then that that wasn't what he meant really.

A gap in the crowd opens to his left. I look at my watch like I've just remembered that I have to wash my hair.

"When do you go back to seminary?" I ask over my shoulder.

"I don't know," he says.

"Well, call me right before you leave."

I'm hearing his name all the time now. He refuses the draft, he starts a chapter of Amnesty International, he studies philosophy, he probably doesn't eat meat. There's a rumor that he's given up the priesthood for a woman. He's brilliant at philosophy. He helps the librarians at the reserve desk clear the tables before he goes home, his inner ear ringing with Aquinas, whom he will quote flawlessly. Women get gushy talking about him. Guys get quiet and respectful like they're talking about their dead brothers. I'm one of the unconverted, so he's knocking on my door regularly, trying to bring me the good news.

He sits backwards in my desk chair while I lie on my bed trying to read, and makes guesses about me and where I've been and what I want. I tell him where he's wrong. Tell him every ugly story about me that I know. He nods his head like that's just what he said.

One day he brings both palms down on the back of the chair like something is final. He looks me in the eye.

"I like you," he says.

"That's great," I say vaguely, "I like you too."

"No," he says, "I *really* like you."

"Uh-huh." I wait for what comes next. He stands up, points a finger at me, and says, just before leaving, "Put that under your pillow and think about it."

I lie on my bed amazed. Amazed that anyone could be such a twit, such a geek, such an idiot. Like he thinks stupidity is a strategy. Like this works.

"You know," my roommate says to this, "all you do is talk about him."

Opening Hymn

I'm sitting in the coffee shop off-campus, waiting for my priest. I'm too nervous to drink coffee. He might be late, even though he isn't late, but he might be. I'm drinking cocoa instead, a child's drink. It's too sweet. Or the chocolate is rancid, or maybe it's just me. Someone has hung a gray utility bucket under a swallow's nest on the shop's porch. An ugly, practical, human solution, awkward and kind. The mother bird flies in to a line of open, anxious mouths. The floor is clean.

I could be doing other things, waiting for other men. This waiting is blind and furless. If he's late it might be a sign. I might cry. That's how new it is.

The man buying his coffee says, "The worst thing you can do is get to Europe without your coffee. I spent three months in Greece drinking Turkish coffee." He explains how he packs his coffee beans inside a French machine now. The girl behind the counter looks impressed.

A family comes in. The baby is asleep, fat legs loose on her father's hip, one half of the face flattened against his arm. A thousand disasters could be, at this very moment, tracking her exact location, zeroing in like so many heat-seeking missiles. And she sleeps. It's unbearable.

He is walking up the street, sloshing in shoes a size too big for him. He's on a tight budget. He bought them big in case he needed room to grow. When he sees me sitting near the window, he starts waving his arm round and round like he's working with semaphores, like he's an off-center windmill. Like a fool.

I'd wave back except that I'm worried it will distract him. Maybe he won't pay attention to where he's going. Walk right into the street. He's like that when he gets excited. He's half-baked. And what if a car were to jump the curb? Or something to drop out of the window where they're doing construction?

I go to the door. I go down the step. I start down the street, anything to shorten the distance that he spends out on the street, alone, sloshing, unbearably happy. I grab his skinny, soap-smelling neck, kiss his mouth. We were, for a moment, so close to disaster.

Sin

My priest is educating me on the nature of God. He is reading St. Paul. "It's wonderful," I say. "Love, joy, gentleness, self-control." I lean over the table in the commons and whisper because I get it and it's wonderful. "It's the description of the perfect lover," I say. The compound of his face dissolves and reconfigures. He is tempted. Then he shuts St. Paul and kisses me. Love, joy, gentleness, self-control.

We are all of us, St. Augustine says, pages of a book that speaks of nothing but God, Alpha and Omega, world without end. The words are fruitful, they multiply. They turn and twist as we ourselves do, are pressed down and run over, light on light. Every taste of his skin is begotten, not made.

"When I'm with you," he says, close to tears, "I feel like I'm losing my faith." He's not blaming me, he says. It's not my fault, he says. "I'm sinning," and just that word wrings his body, twists it. I start crying because he's suffering, because we're breaking up.

"Sin," he says, "is a good thing twisted just a little or slightly out of step."

"Then maybe you can take a sin and twist it into a good thing," I say. I can see sin turning and turning again, spiraling like a staircase, like a strand of DNA. I look around and see sin writhing and curling into good.

"It's not like that," he says. "Sin's not like that."

The semester is ending. He is going back to seminary. We argue like the first man and woman, leaving Paradise, no going back and everything lost:

"You tempted me," he says.

I answer, "You have misnamed everything."

Maybe this is how angels fall, slicing themselves on silver linings, wings thickening into ugly, rubbery leather, skinned raw and red. Every word forks. What once intoxicated simply stains. An old wine skin, the new wine stings in my cuts. I crack and burst.

I hate smoking, so I take up smoking. I sit on the radiator in my bedroom collecting a pile of white ash in the lid off a jar of applesauce. My mouth tastes like ash. My clothes smell like ash. I'm bad at smoking and it never gives me a high. I am dull and stolid. Only the smoke rises.

This gesture has my own shape to it. There is nothing else about this that I recognize. He leaves a hole. I know exactly where it is, here, where a rib should be.

I don't know how to lose this priest because I didn't want him, didn't know how to want him. The words my father gave me could not ask for this kind of man, unless they were twisted, skewed, unsprung, just that necessary fraction, that nth of a degree.

This blessing is a broken bone, an ember on the tongue. I don't call it a blessing. I call it by the old names, ill-fitting and undersized. I call it "dumped" and "typical" and "fuck him." But there is a hole in my side where a new creation has been torn out of me. Jagged and unstitched, gaping and unclean.

Two weeks later he's sitting in my room when I open the door. Cross-legged on my bed.

"Give me back my key."

"Try and find it," he strains an old joke.

"No thanks," I say and start unpacking my books, ignoring him. He's just dirty laundry on my bed. He's the ink-stained bedspread. He's the chocolate bar wrapper I left there.

"I think we should get married," he says, like water passes under a bridge in one quick flush.

"Well," I say, "maybe you ought to pray about it for a really long time."

He's still sitting there.

"Someplace else," I say.

Loaves

In the movie the woman has a cyanide tablet in her tooth. At the right time, when the pain is unbearable, she shuts her mouth hard, she bursts the tablet and dies quickly.

I'm watching a lot of movies. *The Conformist, Aguirre: The Wrath of God, The Spy Who Came In from the Cold.* I never want to leave the movies this summer. I stay in the college auditorium all day, work at night.

He kills her in the snow, he falls gently over the wall, he is pulling the curtain on her sedan chair back slowly with one hand. She is walking into the forest. She smiles, she is bleeding on the snow.

All summer he wants to marry me. He calls me from San Francisco where he works in a bakery. He calls me each night, tells me about waiting for the bread to rise, about the city, blue-gray in the early morning. Waiting for the loaves to rise, just waiting.

People come in tired and pale, drink coffee, eat warm muffins, wait for the bread. Head to the Chicano market. Gays from Castro in leather or jeans and hiking boots. They think he's cute, make jokes about buns. The same joke over and over. It gets old, but he's selling bread—he smiles like it's fresh.

He toasts seeds and nuts in the back. He says he has plans.

"I make a pretty good loaf of bread now," he says. "I could make raisin bread for breakfast every morning." Dropping it into the line between us like it won't matter, like it was part of my plans, like he's just adding to them.

Chicanos come in on the way to the market. Called cholos for their black cholo pants, or maybe the pants are named for the guys. They wear plaid flannel shirts buttoned to the top button, heavy crosses over the shirt. Their hair is as shiny and black as the shoes they wear with white socks. It's a uniform. One day while waiting on the bread he tells a cholo about the seminary. Next day they all know.

"Father," they call him, "Father, I'll take some white bread."

"Father, where's the cookies today?"

He has to figure out what people want. Sometimes he's wrong.

"Today I had to toss thirty rosemary baguettes." He sounds tired.

The walls of the bakery are pumpkin yellow. The floor is red tile. His hands smell like the fennel rolls he's been kneading.

"I wish you could smell them," he says over the phone. "It would cheer you up."

"I'm not sad," I say. "I'm fine."

I have no plans. I go see movies. *Children of Paradise, Three Brothers, War and Peace.* She throws open the French door. She's lost in the crowd. He leans his head against the tree. She slides down a hill of wheat, fills her skirt with grain. Stories are the paradise I must lose.

She is breathing the water. He pulls back the curtain. She is in the snow. They are by the sea. He leans over her hand, and he is singing. Blood pools in a plate. The rope tightens around the neck. Stories are the paradise I must lose.

"What?" my mother says. "What? You're going to marry a Catholic in a bakery?" And then, "Where's the sense in that?" Then, "Well, I guess you'll do what you want. That's the way you girls are. You do whatever the hell you want."

She is running down the hall. She is lying on the bed. She is strapped to the gurney like she might break out. She is bleeding from the mouth. She is still.

My sister calls. "You're getting married? I thought you had plans." No, not plans. Just stories. I can't say that.

"All I ask," says my sister, "is are you sure?" That's all everyone asks, and I wish they'd stop. I want to be drunk with love, pissing drunk, and passed out. Wake me up when it's done, like a surgery or an amputation. Sure is for people with four stomachs who can digest everything down to pure, white milk. They don't know how they do it, they just do it. I want to be plastered in bliss, but I settle for beer.

I call him up and say yes, my stomach a yeasty mixture of beer and doubt. I would be drunk with love, but I'm too cowardly for it. I would be blinded in bliss.

He calls in the middle of the night to tell me he's thinking of me, that the bread is rising in San Francisco, he's going to go knead the rolls. He's not sure why he likes it, he says, but he does. People need bread, he says, and that's a sure thing.

Husband and Wife

The man behind the pawnshop counter weighs our rings in his scale. My ring has someone else's initials engraved inside the rim. It's worn thin on one side. I tell myself a story to go with the worn ring—an old marriage. "A.C." Alice Compstock—who married young and wore this ring through six children and the Depression.

After the service we drive to the coast in his car with the new floorboard. He tells me stories about his last days at the bakery. How one of the guys from Castro Street offered to cut his hair for a wedding present. As he was cutting it, he ran his hands over the back of my husband's neck.

"Aren't you curious?" he asked. "Don't you want to be sure?" That endless question.

"I'm sure," my husband told him. And at this point in the story my husband takes his hand off the stick shift and pulls my hand out of my lap. Holds it on his thigh. I can feel the road coming up through his leg.

Then he tells me another story. How the cholos congratulated him.

"But, Father," they told him. "No offense, but if you're getting married, you've got to work out."

"No offense, Father," they'd say, "but look at you. Get some weights. Eat more."

"Well, Father," they said, looking at my picture soberly. "That's good. You won't have any trouble with her. You need a serious woman since you're an educated man."

"Sure," the others agreed. "Sure." The plain woman with the serious face made sense for their priest.

Then I told him about the movies I'd seen, right up to when he flew in to get married. Then all the stories right up until the day before. Then the rings. Then the wedding. Then now.

The bad windshield wiper thumps over the crack in the windshield. The car smells like the disintegrating foam in the paneling. The wet, black road thickens toward us, disappears under the wheels. And we've run out of past to talk about.

We park on the front yard of a beach house that has been loaned to us. We have a key, a map of the fuse box, and a bundle of wood. We stumble in the cold house. We find the bedroom and the bed. It's cold and unmade.

This marriage bed is not like other beds. It is not like any place we have ever made love. We find the sheets in the closet, mildewed, slightly damp. We begin to make the bed by the light of a bare bulb hanging from the ceiling.

The champagne of people wishing well for us, lifting us up on the hands of good intentions, has evaporated. We almost argue, already, even then, on the first night as husband and wife, fast married, hitched.

We almost argue and then stop. That would seem too unlucky, too ill-fated, too significant. We have the sheets on wrong, or maybe these are the wrong sheets. We have to start again. Nothing matches. The making of the bed is like the rock we keep pushing up the hill. At the last second the rock rolls back down, the elastic snaps back, the damp sheet tears.

We hate each other suddenly and thoroughly like spilled coffee.

The hate we feel is the exact height and breadth of this moment. Because we are life for each other now, and life is so much slower than desire, so much clumsier than possibility.

The last corner goes on. The bottom sheet finally fits. The mattress pad beneath it is bunched and wrinkled. It won't lie flat. We push at it with our hands, toward his side, toward mine. It travels but will not disappear. My husband is sweating now even in this cold room. He gives up and straightens. He looks at me.

"Maybe we better not quit our day jobs yet," he says, and we laugh. It has the relief of tears. This moment to which I am married, to which I am forever wife, embraces me who can neither have nor hold. This moment, forsaking all others.

We lie in bed, too tired to undress, holding hands, scared to make love. Sure signs of success and failure alternate like a current, like the roar and hiss of the ocean behind the wall, behind our heads. It is making its way by reversals up the beach until dawn, when it will equally surely and slowly lose the land again.

Vows

The professor at the party says, "Oh, the Child Bride."

"I'm not a bride," I say. "Not even a bridesmaid. Maybe I'm the flower girl." The idea of infidelity comes easily to me. It's like falling off a log, like dropping the other shoe. It's gravity.

"How precious," he says. He gives me a plate of chicken baked in chocolate, cold fish, croutons. "The wine is dry," he says, like it matters to me.

And I say, "Great," like it does matter to me.

"I thought I heard there was some boy I had to congratulate." He has wonderfully long fingers.

"Not that I see," I say. "But perhaps we ought to look a little closer."

We move into the hallway. He lowers his voice in tight quarters, leans over his plate of chicken, one eyebrow slightly raised. He's telling me about Pinter, and I'm watching him talk, thinking, like a slug to the stomach, how easy infidelity is. I just keep on walking the way I'm walking, keep on answering, keep on laughing. I move the chicken around my plate. I've forgotten it is for eating.

I am divided before a mirror. An unmarried self looks on the married, the married gazes back on the adulterous. I appear to be married, but I am unmarried, unbound, rattling loose inside my vows.

Adultery is to feel between me and the outer skin of marriage an itch—a bit of salt, of sand, even sugar. I will rub and stretch and scratch until this skin, this garment of fidelity, is loose over me. These are the thoughts of adultery. I might call it a desire to be truthful.

The professor leans in toward me in what is already a narrow hallway, thickened like an artery with bookshelves. He whispers an aside, as though we weren't the topic.

"You know, you don't seem entirely happy."

"I'm never entirely anything," I say.

"How deliciously complex."

So I begin in adultery because for me there is no other beginning. I begin with its first letter. That is A. Make it large. Sew it over my heart. It will speak louder than words.

A is for admit. Let's admit it. That I have already failed. That I have failed to be married. That I do not fit my vows. That I will not be ready to be married until I have been married always. That I am partial.

I shift my weight from hip to hip. I put my hair behind my ear. He's telling me story after story looking for the one that works. His glance on me is a light but focused pressure like a stethoscope. He registers every beat, every breath. He knows what he's listening for.

Breath is measured and cut into words, and they must be basted to us, letter by letter. I'm stitching that I am divided, that I am not yet made fast. It's slow work to stitch, to mend, to make fast what we promise. It's how I begin to be married.

. . .

I stop moving the dead chicken. I put my napkin on the bookshelf.

"Let's be honest," I blurt out. And his face, caught like a sling at the deepest arc of a great story about his ex, goes slack.

I leave my plate on the bookcase, make an ungraceful exit, leave someone else to clean up what I left uneaten. Collect it cold and congealed, scrape it into the trash.

In the car driving home, I listen to the engine pinging unevenly, wondering when it's going to break down. My new husband has a heart murmur, a pinging, that I can hear when I lie on his chest, and we've stopped talking. After four or five steady beats, it falters and for a few seconds is silent. Then it stumbles over itself in beginning again, several beats together. The sound of a body falling down carpeted stairs. Each time I hold my breath, each time it starts again. I care too much about this everyday thing. This imperfect, uneven thing which will persist in beating whether I listen or not.

"I've lived with it all my life," he says.

But I haven't.

Marriage is my first sampler. It's myself I'm stitching. I will begin with this first letter, this A, which I say now is for "awe" and "always" and even "apple." Which I ate, awake and aching. And I am amazed.

Benediction

I want to go into the water. He has me by one ankle. He's looking up at everything, not glossing, not editing.

"Let go of my ankle," I say. "I mean it."

"Not until you bless me," I think he says. He's lying in the sand like a broken thing. Like a weak, passing thing, but he doesn't pass. He persists. I'm stuck fast.

"What?" I say.

"Not until you kiss me," he says, and I do.

Marian Pierce
University of Iowa

FINDING LAND

It was an ordinary day until I met a woman named Linda in the snack aisle at Seibu Supermarket, where she was contemplating dried squid in a bag. "It goes well with beer," I said to her, assuming an instant bond since she was a foreigner too. In my relief at finding a countrywoman in the local supermarket, and one who, like me, was married to a Japanese, I ended up forgetting to buy milk, which only I would drink anyway, and ordering American coffee with her in a café while our groceries melted beside us in bags on the floor. She took a bite of her tiny slice of strawberry cake and said she'd been hungry since the moment she'd arrived in Japan eight weeks ago.

"It's the portions," I said consolingly. "Little portions for little people."

"And not enough frosting on the cake," she added.

We stared at each other, two large women across a toy-sized table in a room scarcely bigger than the treehouse of my childhood, in the sugar maple tree that stood in the big field where I caught butterflies, years ago, or so it seemed, in Cleveland. Afterwards I'd stuck them to a board with a pin. I was into collecting. "I'm twenty-four," I added, irrelevantly. I was large by being too tall, often thwacking my head on low doorways like a blind woman entering an unfamiliar room. A bump like the nub of a unicorn's horn grew on my head. At night my husband burned little moxibustion cones around its circumference in order to reduce the swelling, and reminded me to duck going into rooms. Linda was a modest height, though she had hips and a bosom. I hoped she'd brought enough clothes with her to last her for a couple of years.

"After a while your stomach will shrink to the size of the portions," I said.

"Not mine. I'm pregnant."

She was sure not to have brought enough clothes. But at least her children would be the size of the Japanese, though it was doubtful they'd look like them, given the color of her hair. Mine would look almost Japanese, but their height would instantly betray their difference. Their exposed ankles would always be going red in the cold, their bony arms would stick out of their sleeves. My father-in-law still couldn't get over the fact that he barely came up to my shoulders. He had mentioned basketball, which he had watched—though he much preferred baseball—on national TV. He had asked my husband if I was going to grow anymore.

"She's stopped," my husband had said. "Good thing, because we've run out of closet space." I had to sleep with my feet in the closet. Otherwise I got cranky, because I couldn't stretch out my legs on the floor of our four-mat tatami room.

Linda chewed her last bite of cake. She took ten rice crackers out of her grocery bag and ate them. I ate three, and told her I didn't want to conceive. I used birth control religiously, I said. I slept with my diaphragm by my pillow, snug in its little pink box. If I got pregnant I'd grow large in two directions, three if you counted the nascent horn. During delivery I'd be lying on the table with my legs hanging off the edge, not that I'd be able to see them. And so I was waiting. (For what, I didn't know. The shrinkage of age?)

At this point Linda said, "Deborah, let's forget about cooking dinner and go find land."

"Find land?" I was still flat on my back on the delivery table, putting my feet in stirrups, about to strike the doctor in the nose as I bent my bony knees.

"Yeah, land. Like in, space. The buffaloes and all that." She plunged her hand into her grocery bag.

Perhaps she had a deficient education in geography, not unusual for many Americans, and imagined uncharted land in Japan, vast prairies as yet unexplored. Maybe she didn't even know she was on an island in the middle of the sea. Three seas—four if you included the Seto Inland Sea. Mountains that thrust up everywhere except on the great Kanto plain, spreading under us from Tokyo to Osaka, the Osaka plain, the Niigata plain, and a few more I couldn't remember that were up north in Hokkaido. I prepared to explain a few things to Linda, feeling satisfied that there were a few things that could be explained, as there were so many that couldn't. I took out the bilingual atlas I had purchased within my first few hours on this soil.

But with nary a glance at the beautiful picture of the islands of Japan on its cover, all reds and oranges and greens in the middle of three vast blue seas and one little narrow lighter-colored one, Linda withdrew the package of dried squid from her bag. She tore it open and cautiously sniffed it. She bit down into a flat, red-brown corner. She chewed and chewed and chewed and finally swallowed. "This squid's a tough sucker," she said. She licked her finger and pressed it over the crumbs on her plate. She carefully tipped the coffee on her saucer back into her cup and drank it. The waiter, swishing a pretty checked cloth over the next table and humming a popular tune, gave us a look as Linda tore open another package with her teeth.

"Do you mind?" she asked him with a disarming smile. He blushed and folded his towel and hurried behind the counter, where he dripped coffee and rattled cups and pretended not to stare. He was probably amazed that she liked Japanese snacks. I had been accosted once with a bean cake in my hand in Roppongi Station by a Japanese TV crew, who had interviewed me about my eating habits, and then aired it as a spot on the midnight news.

"Whatever these are they're easier to chew," Linda said. "Much, much easier. And they're sugared so they'll last for our trip. Have some."

I decided not to say a word to her about the Kanto plain, or the dearth of available land. Being humbled was a constant experience of life here. One felt smaller by the day and yet larger. Linda would too. Particularly in her condition. Who was I to dash her daring with a lecture about the four islands and three seas? The waiter couldn't be expected to understand that blood stirred in strange ways here, that hunger beset one at unexpected moments. Women who had once possessed sense and a bank account suddenly threw themselves into some Japanese man's arms. They ended up sleeping with their feet in the closet. They got pregnant despite their little pink box. It could happen to me.

I put the atlas in my lap, and popped a candied azuki bean into my mouth. I turned to the twenty-three wards of Tokyo, color-coded for convenience, with place names marked in English and Japanese. In Yoyogi Park, youth with dyed orange hair teased into stiff peaks cradled ghetto blasters and danced the grass into submission, pausing to neck on park benches when they wanted to rest their feet. In Shinjuku Park, smart-suited matrons of the city walked dogs named Shiro, little toy things that went yap yap yap and wagged fluffy tails. In Ueno Park, salarymen on their lunch hour reclined on blankets under cherry trees, drinking beer, eating take-out yakitori chicken with their fingers, and serenading office ladies with warbly and mournful songs about falling cherry blossoms. Even now, in the coffee shop, shamisens were being strummed as background music to expensive coffee and strawberry cake.

The Japanese were incurable romantics. The space romance occupied was in inverse proportion to the tiny piece of land upon which they lived. They rose before dawn on New Year's Day to greet the first sunrise of the year, formed clubs to compose poetry, and sang enka—those schmalziest of tunes about loss and love best sung while wearing a kimono—at every important occasion. I closed my atlas and hummed a song about the guy rowing a boat with his girl inside, the one my husband sometimes sang to me in the bath. It went well with the background music, the plinkity plink plink of the shamisen strings. I saw my husband's long-lashed eyes flutter at me as he perched on the toilet seat because there wasn't enough room for both of us in the tub, while I, gloriously naked, drew my knees to my chest. He rested a book on them. He gazed at me across the steam. He recited haiku:

In the drained fields
how long and thin
the legs of the scarecrow

"We have provisions." Linda rummaged noisily in her grocery bag, interrupting poetry. "Yes indeed we do, even if some of them are raw. Christopher Columbus wouldn't have minded raw, so why should we? And then there's those little noodle stands everywhere." She plunked a five-hundred-yen coin down on the table. She crumpled up her napkin, threw it on her plate, and made for the door. I folded my napkin neatly, just as I'd seen the Japanese do, placed it on the table, and hastened after her bobbing grocery bag, hugging my own to my chest and making sure to nod at the waiter over the cabbage head I was going to use to make stew if I ever got back home.

"Come again," the waiter said.

I ducked my head and shot out the door. I ran to catch up to Linda. She hurried along as if she knew where she was going, walking close to the shop fronts, without a single look to either side. She swung her free arm with a great deal of vigor. "Adventure is so exciting," she said. I lengthened my stride, shooting past giggling schoolgirls with linked arms admiring their reflections in shop windows, and a man clodding slowly in his wooden sandals, on his way to the public baths with a bucket over his arm and a towel slung over his shoulder. Perhaps, I thought, my husband would choose a different kind of poetry if we fit into the bath together. His sentiment might vary if we occupied a larger space, a castle with many turrets, such as the one I'd seen on a distant velvet hilltop when we'd taken a train the length of the main island, or a farmhouse with a thatched roof standing beside terraced rice fields. I could call him at his clinic in Shibuya from some wayward station, like a wandering samurai, a ronin without lord or master, and tell him I was on a larger quest than cooking winter stew with cabbage and pumpkin.

The narrow street disappeared. A horse galloped by, waving the plume of its tail. I imagined my grocery bag flying out of my arms and coming to rest on the branch of a tree, a squirrel reaching its head inside to nibble.

"I have to go to the bathroom," Linda called over her shoulder. "Pee pee pee when you're pregnant and nothing else."

The vision of a mythical land, all green-velvet rolling hills and a many-turreted castle, vanished. I thought again of the delivery table, those stirrups just waiting for my feet. Housewives whizzed by on their errands, babies plastered to their backs. Tinkle, tinkle, tinkle, their little bicycle bells said.

"There's a bathroom in the station," I said, stepping up beside Linda. "But we have to buy a ticket first and pass through the gate."

"Hold this a minute. I'm going to get comfortable." Linda turned her back to the street, and undid the top button of her jeans. I held both bags close, and watched the sleek crowds part around us and hurry on their way up the station stairs. Japanese working women looked perfectly collected. I wondered if Linda had noticed that too. I couldn't imagine them weeping while slicing onions. They seemed entirely different from the housewives on their bicycles. They had mastered the art of fast walking on high heels. And yet, once they got married, they'd undergo a transformation. They'd quit work, or be forced to, and bear a baby within a year. They'd begin to look rumpled.

"Finished," Linda said, and twirled around twice. "Good. Looks like my zipper's gonna hold its position. Let's go!" She took her bag, and flew up the station stairs.

The train whistle blew. The announcer announced something in an amplified voice. A barrage of heels tapped the floor. The clerk at the newsstand slapped change into customers' palms along with their papers. People moved in purposeful blurs, hurrying to catch the train. What were we doing? Japan wasn't the remote Himalayas. We'd end up lost among buildings on a crowded street. We'd wander down aisles lined with discount electronic goods in Akihabara forever. We'd eat our way to the bottom of our grocery bags, and have to undo our zippers, and worst of all, we wouldn't find any land. There wasn't any, not the slightest bit of available space. I reached for the back of Linda's coat, but her forward momentum pulled it out of my grasp. She skidded to a halt at the ticket machines, and rested her free hand on the metal.

"I used my last coin to tip the waiter," she said. "That's what you get for going against custom." She took a sheet of dried seaweed out of her grocery bag and fanned herself. A Japanese woman pressed a button on the next machine, took out her ticket, and slid it between her teeth. She glanced at Linda, and then at me. She walked swiftly toward the gate, maneuvering around businessmen rushing with their coats flapping against their legs, and groups of schoolchildren with bulging black briefcases. Her slim maroon bag, embossed with the gold logo of a Ginza department store, swung gently by its handle from her ivory fingers. An edge of tissue paper swirled out of the top like a puff of whipped cream.

Linda turned a shade paler. She stared at the map above the ticket machines, at the train lines snaking in all directions. Chinese characters abounded, labelling place names unknown. "I'll have to learn how to read all those damn Chinese characters," Linda muttered. She drew her arms all the way around her bag and clasped her fingers. Her head drooped down toward her leafy lettuce.

"Where are we going anyways?" she asked in a small voice.

I swallowed the words of defeat I was about to utter, and pushed the cabbage head firmly into the depths of my grocery bag. It came to rest next to a block of Hokkaido butter.

"Getting around Japan is easier than it looks," I said. "Especially if you employ the Ouija-board method of decision making. Watch this."

Her head lifted. I crouched and sprang. My free arm extended upwards. The flat of my hand smacked the map. A mandarin orange sailed out of my bag.

"Amazing," a voice said in Japanese behind me. "She must play basket-oh baru."

I landed with a thud. "We're going to Me-something or other," I said, slipping coins into the ticket machine. "We'll change to a bullet train in Tokyo Station. It looks like it's somewhere south of here."

"Great. Terrific. That was a wonderful leap." Linda smiled at the middle-aged businessman whose gray hair was combed to cover the bald spot on his head as he placed the mandarin orange in her palm. The businessman bowed and hurried away. She tipped the orange into her grocery bag, and extended the package of dried squid.

"Trade you," she said.

I suddenly felt ridiculous carrying a grocery bag. Toshiro Mifune didn't carry a grocery bag. Instead, he swaggered around picking fights and speaking men's Japanese. Nevertheless, the grocery bag was a fact of life, and the land a mythical vision, a Me-something or other of no place and no name.

Linda shifted her bag to her hip. Something inside rattled like a saber. Whatever it was, I hoped she wouldn't eat it. "Are you ready to go? My bladder's gonna burst." She put her hand on her stomach.

"You okay? I mean, the baby and everything. Can you handle a trip?"

"I'm fine. Pregnancy is no big deal, once you get used to the little inconveniences. Besides, I've decided I don't have to wait until delivery for birth to begin. C'mon. I'd better pee before the train comes." We heard the clacking of the train wheels sounding in the distance. Linda's hair floated back like a banner. I thought of peninsulas beckoning from the sea, a butterfly on the wing, a sunset of rainbow colors throwing light in our faces. Land awaited. I faced forward. I dropped the squid in. I ran after Linda.

Later, in a lost corner of Tokyo Station, we stood holding our grocery bags, staring at the picture on a giant TV screen. A young girl strode about a stage, flinging her hair and singing off-key. "Well, will you look at that. She can't sing," Linda said, wiping off her mustache of milk. We were down to half a liter. At the rate she was going, we were going to have to find land with a cow on it. That could be a problem, unless we went to Hokkaido, which was another island entirely. I stared at the TV screen and tried to put the map out of my mind, the neat topographical picture I had of the four main islands of Japan, with lots of little ones speckled here and there like drops of cream. What we were searching for was mythical land, preferably with some kindly creatures on it, although all I could see for the moment were demons with scrunched-up faces and wicked grins. At various times throughout the morning, my neighbors had stood with their backs to the front door of our concrete apartment building that everyone called a "mansion" in Japanese-English for reasons I couldn't discern, tossing dried soybeans over their shoulders and chanting "Demons go out, gods come in!" "It's to protect their homes from bad luck," my husband said before he ran to catch his train. "It's bean-throwing day," he had added, as if that explained everything.

"She was hired for her looks," I said about the girl on the TV screen. "I guess it doesn't matter if she has talent."

"She's just a kid. What a terrible existence. She looks underfed and stressed out to me."

She turned her back to the screen, and took another sip from her carton. Citing ancient sources, my husband claimed that milk spoiled in the intestine, and drained one's life force. But here was Linda, ready to have a baby. What was she supposed to do, nurse it on green tea?

"Remind me not to let my kid go in for something like that," Linda said. "People are already telling me how beautiful mixed babies look. I want my children to have normal lives." She took the mandarin orange out of her grocery bag, and set it against the wall under the TV screen. "I knew this would come in handy. It's an offering for her. I know, it's weird, but it makes me feel better about leaving her in there. Are you ready? I'd better pee again before we go."

We found a bathroom, and then walked up the platform stairs. A conductor waved us aboard with a white-gloved hand. Linda drew a carrot from her bag as the train sped out of the station. She crunched and stared out the window. The salaryman next to us yawned above his newspaper. A cow's eyes gazed mournfully from the page. When I took the train with my husband, he read instructional tidbits to me from his Oriental medicine books about how to balance my heart meridian. In romantic moments, he held my wrist and practiced pulse diagnosis. Right now, while we were seeking land, he was at his clinic, inserting acupuncture needles into somebody's foot, or prescribing herbal medicine.

"Which way do you face when you use a Japanese-style toilet?" Linda asked.

"You go by the little feet on the floor," I said.

"Oh. I thought they were decorative. I was facing the wrong way."

The man turned the page of his paper. The cow's eyes disappeared and were replaced by the stern face of the prime minister. "He's suffering from fatigue," my husband often said when he saw his national leader on TV. "He needs a good shiatsu treatment." The prime minister seemed to be looking directly at the huge photograph of the couple languishing in hot spring waters and smiling pleasantly; it sat above the shelf where everyone kept their briefcases. "Take the

Japan National Railways to relaxation," were the words inscribed in a cloud of steam. In other advertisements, goggle-eyed scuba divers watched fish in Okinawa, and skiers in fluorescent green outfits whizzed down mountain slopes, snow flying from their heels. Couples strolled down paths lined with cherry trees, on honeymoon trips to Kyushu.

The salaryman flipped over his newspaper, without once lifting his head. Why should he care about a trip to Kyushu? He probably hadn't gone on a real vacation since his honeymoon. At most, salary-men had five or six days off at New Year's, and a few more during the Obon holiday in midsummer. Even then, they were expected to visit their ancestral villages. They didn't have the freedom to go anywhere they pleased. They were sacrifices for the economic miracle, record exports and a strong yen; their wives were too. My husband had his own acupuncture clinic, but he still couldn't go away with me for more than a few days. "Salarymen are my clients," he had said. "I have to keep *their* hours. When I went to Nepal, I lost business. But at least I found you."

"I'm going to have trouble squatting when I get bigger," Linda said. "I'll either have to find a Western-style toilet or hold it in."

"Do you have to go again?"

"Not yet."

"I think we're almost there."

I slid the atlas out of my purse, and turned it to the special maps at the back that marked where wild bladderwort grew and wisteria bloomed, where cranes migrated and white storks nested. Wildcats roamed one of the tiny Okinawan islands.

"Where did you get that? Can I see? Cool! A map of castle ruins! And here's one showing stone Buddhas!" Linda set her bag at her feet and turned pages. She took another bite of her carrot. Could I help her find what she was looking for? And what was I looking for? I didn't know. "You were looking for me," my husband had joked when I'd met him last year on a trip to the Himalayas. The recklessness of youth had inspired me to go trekking in the mountains in my sneak-ers. My trekking party ran into his at fifteen thousand feet above sea level, where our respective guides watched in alarm as he burned cones formed from mugwort leaves on my arches.

"Good thing I carry my moxibustion kit with me everywhere," he had said. "You could have lost your toes to frostbite. Don't shriek."

We'd gotten married. It was easier to get a visa if we tied the knot, and I wanted to be with him. Even so, the Japanese authorities had put me on a six-month probationary period. At the end of it, I'd get another six months, then a year's visa, then three, the visa officer had said, holding up three fingers. "Carry your passport with you everywhere," he had instructed. "In case a policeman stops you on the street."

"How did you meet your husband?" I asked Linda.

"He was attending my college in Texas. I kept inviting him over for brunch. Seduction accompli over steak and eggs. Now it's a more exotic menu. What's your story? You're kidding! Smooches in the Himalayas! A mountaintop proposal! How romantic!"

"Yes and no. It's one thing to fall in love, but another to come live in this place. Sometimes I wonder how it happened."

"Do you really?" Linda swallowed the last of her carrot. "It's easy to explain. Mine's handsome, and yours applied the heat when you needed it. Just remember your toes. No, but seriously, I know what you mean. Sometimes I wonder what I got myself into, especially since I got pregnant almost the second I got off the plane. Well, not exactly. I had to go through customs first. You're wise to wait."

"I'm scared of the whole idea," I said. "Plus I'm trying to learn how to read. So far I've memorized one hundred and fifty Chinese characters. Still, it's not enough to be able to read the newspaper. You have to know eight hundred characters, plus the two native syllabaries."

"Golly. My kid will probably learn to read before I do. Maybe something else besides procreating is in store for you. You might produce scholarly works on geography, while I become an explorer. Just don't audition to be a bombshell on TV. They go in for foreigners."

"I'm too tall to be a leading lady," I said. "I have to stoop to kiss my husband."

"Lucky man," Linda giggled. "He gets a breast-level view." She peered out the window. "Geez, this train is moving."

I joined Linda at the window, but the train moved so swiftly that all we saw were brief gleams as the sun caught windows, a blur of concrete, a factory appearing and disappearing. What would we see when we got to where we were going? None of the Japanese were watching the scenery. They read books or newspapers, or slept with their heads laid back against their seats. They stared straight ahead without looking at anything. They were lost in thought, or perhaps they thought nothing. "You maintain privacy in the crowd by keeping to yourself," my husband had said. "You'll see, you'll learn how to do it. You'll get used to it after a while." But the hush frightened me. Since I couldn't shrink to the size of the Japanese, would I become quiet instead?

"Is this your first time taking the bullet train?" the man next to us asked in English. He lowered his newspaper. We stared at him over the pages. I felt my mouth fall open. He looked like an ordinary Japanese salaryman. Not at all like someone who would strike up a conversation with two complete strangers. He caught my eye, smiled, and bowed deeply. His rounded back recalled the picture I had seen of the alluvial fans in the Nobi plain, sculpted slopes intersected by verdant valleys and flowing rivers. My heart lifted. I smiled and bowed too.

"Yes, it is our first time," Linda said, setting her bag at her feet. "And it's great, except it's really hard to see anything out the window."

"It gets easier when the train slows down near the station," the man said when he was upright again. He reached for the shelf above us, and put his newspaper into his briefcase. "Forgive me for bothering you, but I was listening to your English."

"Oh, God," I said.

"Not the words. Just the English. I'm a nosy man. My wife tells me so often. It's a good trait, I think. But not for Japanese, she says."

"I don't mind," Linda said. "You're the first Japanese who has ever started a conversation with me in public."

"They're shy people. They think you cannot speak Japanese."

"It's true," Linda said.

"Also, they think they cannot speak English. I mean, we think. Me, too, I think so. But, practice, practice. There's no other way. Speak boldly. Not like the Japanese. But I'm Japanese." He laughed. He took a handkerchief out of his pocket, and polished his glasses. His dark eyes twinkled. "When I speak English, I imagine I'm somebody new. Mr. Paul Newman, for instance."

"His aunt lives in my hometown," I said. "I saw him with her in a restaurant once." It had been a Jewish deli, of all places, Corky and Lenny's, where I'd been sitting with my grandma, who was speaking Yiddish to my mother because she didn't want me to understand what she was saying, and taking angry sips of her matzoh ball soup. She hadn't recognized Paul Newman. The last movie she had seen was *Fiddler on the Roof.* She was too busy gossiping, probably about me. What was I doing moving to Japan with a foreigner I'd met on that crazy trip? She was sure there wasn't a synagogue in the whole place.

"Yes? Truly? So you see my resemblance to Mr. Newman?" The man beamed.

"Yeah. Yeah, I do." I needed to be someone new too, I thought. Being Deborah Gusserman just wasn't enough anymore.

"Me too," Linda said. "You've got that movie star smile."

"Oh, I'm happy man. I have two fans on this train."

"We're going to a peninsula, aren't we? At least I hope I read the map right." I set down my bag, and opened my atlas.

"*Miura kaigan?* Sorry, speak English, Mr. Newman! I mean, Miura peninsula! You're going there? It's my home place! Great land! Superb territory! Best view in Nippon!" He touched his finger fondly to the map, opened his mouth, and sang in a light tenor:

> "*That mountain is high,*
> *and I can't see Miura kaigan.*
> *How I love Miura kaigan!*
> *How I hate that mountain!*"

"I translated this into English. Do you like it? It's even better in the shower, but not bad on the train, too. Oh! Look!" He stood on his tiptoes, and leaned closer to the window. All of the passengers around us stared at him in astonishment. Some bent their heads to the windows, or exchanged amused glances and a few friendly words. I ducked under the bar that ran the length of the ceiling and pressed my face to the glass. Suddenly I felt I was up in my maple tree, peering through the leaves that had turned to gold and were swirling upwards at the wind's touch. I was watching the last flight of the but-terflies. Their migration. Their escape from my net. The glass was soothing, a cool breeze against my cheeks. What did it matter what language we spoke? The best of us would be a blend, a mixture like Linda's baby, like the man beside us, who was both Mr. Newman and a Japanese. The sea stretched before us. Blue waves rolled against the shore.

"We can see the peninsula!" the man exclaimed. "And nice ocean, and some view!" He pointed out landmarks. He talked excitedly, mix-ing Japanese with English. He told us everything we could see on the peninsula, naming birds and fish and different kinds of seaweed, and then telling us where to find a rock shaped like a whale's tail on the beach. "You can sit down and have your picnic," he said. "Good things to eat in there, don't you?" He pointed to the clouds in the sky, and taught us how to say their shapes in Japanese. The train glided into the station. The doors swished open. Passengers scattered, checking watches and lighting cigarettes. Numbers flashed above us on the board. We swept up our bags, and ran down the stairs together.

"That way to the beach," the man pointed. "Only fifteen minutes by slow walking. Oh, yes! You'll see the sunset. So-o-o beautiful. So-o-o great. So-o-o spectacular. With colors like a peacock's tail." He lifted his hand in the air and spread his fingers. He turned his hand this way and that. "See? Can you imagine?"

"Yes," we said.

Denise Simard

Saint Mary's College of California

TALLULAH AT YOUR FEET

What you want, you're not really sure of at this point. But you know that it does not involve being cloistered behind a particle board wall in a place where the windows don't open and the flowers in the lobby are replaced every two weeks whether they're dead or not. At your last job—and you're beginning to think of them as gigs, four months here, almost a year there, eight long weeks as a market research assistant—but at your last job (the receptionist position at the law firm), you learned that lawyers don't really get paid, at least not in money; they get a condo in Aspen for a week in December, tickets to Tanglewood Labor Day weekend, and a table for seven at nine o'clock on Friday night at the newest Jody Adams or Todd English or whoever's bistro happens to be hot.

The last time he took you out on a Friday, or rather, you went out *together*—because you're that type o' gal—it was to the IHOP three blocks from the warehouse his band, Trip, was renting for practice space. The bars had already closed. He got the "Lumberjack" and ordered it by name. You got a bottomless cup of coffee and heartburn that kept you up half the night, giving you plenty of time to wonder if there's some sort of unpublicized correlation—along the lines of: if he's got big feet, if he's got big thumbs, it's in the way he dances—between the guy you're with and his selection of breakfast entree.

You've searched and searched but have yet to stumble across an ad that calls out to you by name, one you're truly qualified for. Your degree is in English but it might as well be in sales because nobody out there cares about "The Psychological Burdens of Secret Knowledge in *The Scarlet Letter*." The bottom line is always, *Can you think on your feet and talk your way out of a paper bag?*

Lately, you feel as if the bag is plastic and you're suffocating, but you go on the interviews anyway and sit through the chitchat and the company profile and the obligatory questions concerning your schooling, your past experience. You sit through Office Manager Jill, whose sentences end on an up note that her chin follows. "What would you say are your three biggest *accomplishments?*"

YOU THINK: I learned how to drive a stick on the Connecticut Turnpike one night en route from New York City to Boston after smoking hash in the bathroom of a Roy Rogers. I can peel an apple in one piece. I've befriended my student-loan collector.

YOU SAY: "While at the law firm, I reorganized their billing schedule, allowing their computer to generate bills on a rotating weekly basis. This past year, for Thanksgiving, I cooked and distributed thirty-six turkey dinners to the homeless. In college, I taught myself sign language to enable better communication with my boyfriend's mother."

YOU KNOW: While at the law firm, you walked four blocks to Office Max and bought the latest upgrade of Timeslips, the billing software. An accomplished meal for you is macaroni and cheese from the box with a sprinkle of cheddar baked on top. The only phrase you know in sign language is *I love you,* and you learned that from the cards the deaf and homeless distribute. On the way to this interview, you bought one for thirty-three cents and some pocket lint.

You don't get that job. But, hey, you didn't really want it, anyway.

He brings the Sunday paper home on Saturday nights. After sex, you sit at the kitchen table with the four mismatched chairs whose legs stick to the linoleum you never walk barefoot on and he eats home fries with maple syrup and you skim the paper and read him; *was* there another smell lurking beneath the damp mossiness that is his: patchouli, smoke, sweat. You wonder if he's coming home earlier or later than last week, last month; but the hours after midnight are all one. Later, much later in the morning, you'll go through the classifieds, and with a red pen, mark your intentions.

You wear the same suit to all your interviews and wonder if there's anyone on the train who notices you, week after week, wearing the same clothes. The man with the briefcase across from you looks vaguely familiar, but almost all of the men look familiar: hair clipped short, dark winter suits and tasteful ties patterned in burgundy, olive, navy, taupe. Accessories compliments of their wives, girlfriends, lovers. The men who don't have personal shoppers are easy to spot; they're the ones with the rumpled shirts, their shoes are always pointy black lace-ups with man-made uppers. Their ties are synthetic and fat or thin and leather; they never reach their belt buckles. The hair on their wrists pokes out of their sleeves because nobody is there in the morning to tell them their jackets are too small, that at the beginning of every season Filene's will have a two-for-one sportscoat sale which would be worth visiting. You wonder if they know what they're missing.

In the meantime (and somewhere in the back of your head a niggling voice that sounds like your mother's asks when does the meantime stop being the meantime and become forever?) you walk dogs. It's good money and you don't mind picking up shit. Your friend who used to have this route, the friend with the degree in Ancient Civilizations and the Phi Beta Kappa key buried in a shoe box, is off to Hilton Head to train for a bartending position at the newest hotel scheduled to open in the spring.

"Come with me," he says. He's stopped by to drop off his walking route and the keys to the dogs on his last night in town. "Waitress or something. Hilton"—he gives you a slight push, as if that's all you'll need—"Goddamn-Head. Shits and giggles. Fun in the sun."

You tell him you don't golf. You're in a high-risk category for melanoma. You fear hurricanes.

You need to figure some things out.

"You've been figuring things out for years; it doesn't matter where you do it," your friend says. "There's nothing you can't figure out with your ass in a sand chair."

The dogs are all residents of the brownstones that line Marlborough Street. Twice a day you hop the Green line down to Arlington and pick up the pack. You never see their owners—not face to face, anyhow—but you've *seen* them. Although you don't know anyone who's even engaged, the second part of the paper you scan on Sundays is the Weddings section.

Ms. A, a graduate of (Skidmore/Colby/Colgate) *with a master's from* (Columbia/Harvard/UPENN) *and Mr. B, a graduate of* (Middlebury/Bates/Bowdoin) *with a master's from* (Columbia/Harvard/UPENN) *were married at Trinity Church. Following a trip to* (St. Bart's/St. Croix/St. Kitt's) *the couple will live in a brownstone and pay someone to walk their Labrador retriever* (AKC/OFA), *Matilda.*

"Don't get mad at me," your mother says over coffee and cigarettes one morning while your towels spin in her dryer. "But what are you doing? All that money we spent—you're what—walking dogs? And even though you say you and Frank Sinatra are . . ."

"Ma, don't start," you say. "I'm happy." Even though the buzzer has not gone off, you crush out your cigarette and head for the dryer.

"You could go back to school," your mother yells down the cellar after you. "You could move back here and commute!"

"What? I can't hear you!" you yell up the stairs. You sit on an empty joint compound bucket, listen to your towels tumble, wish you'd taken your cigarette with you, and decide that you'll call Northeastern and Emerson and, what the hell, BU, and have them mail you their catalogues.

He works from four to whenever on the weekdays as a waiter in a trattoria on Hanover Street and brings dinner home with him at night. You dine haphazardly on leftovers; tripe, piccatas of chicken and veal, escarole soup, and your candlelight is the flickering blue of the television. If he's horny, when you're wiping the coffee table down or throwing out the aluminum containers, he'll surprise you with a single profiterole, a lone zeppole. He refuses to let you share it with him and instead watches you eat: the wide smile, the torpid eyes you used to think said everything his mouth *didn't*, staring, and all you see is smug; he knows you're easily bought. You make a production out of licking the cream and let him take you to bed and promise yourself that the next time, you'll remember how the sweetness curdles in your stomach and grows heavy.

"I'm thinking about going back to school," you tell him.

"Big news," he says. "Chris and McManus met this guy last night whose brother does the booking for a couple of spots off Causeway Street, and, I got a feeling about this one. He's going to come by and take a listen Saturday night."

"Two years and I'd have my degree. I did some calling around today."

"Babe," he says, and kisses you, "do you know how big this is?"

Advertising or Public Relations. That's what you'll look into because you're good at making things believable.

The dogs are all small to medium breeds and there's a Scottish terrier named Tallulah who's trouble: pooping in front of Armani Exchange, lying down one day in the middle of the street and refusing to walk. You tried nudging and poking and finally gave the walk signal to the rest of the group and they took off, the Scottie jerked into an upright position and still refused to move. You were afraid she'd strangle so you unhooked her and carried her under your arm the rest of the way home. She has this habit, this crazy compulsion to lunge after Cherokees and Broncos, Monteros and Land Cruisers. Every third car on the road has four-wheel drive, and you brace yourself for her frenzied barking and attempts to run. You try to explain this to your mother, how funny it is to be walking down the street, praying that the Pathfinder you see in the distance is going to turn at the next block. Your mother takes a long suck on her cigarette and shakes her head at you. *No,* you tell her, *you've never seen anything like it. The dog is obsessed, the dog is . . .* And you shut up. It's one of those things you have to be there for.

•   •   •

The classified section is thinning out. You now search only for jobs in public relations or advertising.

"So what do you think?" he says, tapping the paper with his fork. A splotch of syrup bleeds into an Accountemps ad. "You think that means he liked us? I mean, he was smiling, wall-to-wall, shit-eating grin on his face during that sort of reggae-ish cover of 'Blister in the Sun' we do. We were so tight! He said he'd be in touch."

"He'll call," you assure him. "What do you think about Emerson? I think I'm going to try for them. They've got one of those co-op programs, and that's where you make contacts, you . . ."

"That's great, Babe, great. Contacts are key. Hey, c'mere and listen to this."

You follow him into the living room where your mother's old sofa set and the TV—your only joint purchase—sit flanked by a small Peavey amp, a Fender Strat with a fraying strap and an Ovation with three inches of dust on the case, the one he played in college when he was going through his "Fire and Rain" phase.

He picks a few things out for you and you nod in all the right places, but secretly you think they all sound the same; you can't hear the difference. You're not sure if you ever could.

Sixty-two degrees is unseasonably warm for the third week of February, and the nine-to-five tenants of the skyscrapers are out en masse, slaphappy: sportscoats left hanging on desk chairs, sunglasses on, sipping iced coffee in the postage stamp–size park across from the BPL. You get your coffee and hitch the only dogs you have today, Tallulah and Julio, the beagle, to the wrought iron arm of a bench and sit. The rest of your clients are stuck in kennels for the week, their owners headed for the sun.

Your friend called from Hilton Head last night; things are great. Everyone working the town is under thirty. He bought a Big Bertha. There are jobs everywhere—when are you coming out?

Maybe in the summer, you tell him, to visit. You think you're going back to school.

The dogs must be paying well, he says. How're you going to afford that?

I'll probably have to move home, you say.

I hope you're majoring in communications, he says.

Tallulah is yipping and tugging and causing a scene and you're standing up to leave when you see what she's pulling toward: a man who looks like he stepped out of a J. Crew catalogue is walking toward you, waving, and the dog is frantic.

"Hey, Lula, hey, hey, how's my girl?" he says, and kneels down in front of the dog, who's berserk with joy, licking his face and trying to jump into his arms while still harnessed. "So," he says. "I guess you're the dog walker. Thought I'd come over and say hello."

"Hi."

"I see you all the time. Where's the rest of them?" He motions to Julio, who's decided to nap until you're on the move again.

You wish your hair wasn't in a ponytail because you haven't hopped in the shower yet, that you weren't wearing dungarees with a hole in the knee and your navy sweatshirt with the stretched neck and two apartments' worth of paint stains. "They're on vacation," you tell him.

"Easy, easy." He pats her head and you notice how clean his fingernails are, how smooth the skin on his hands must feel. No calluses on the pads of his fingers from guitar strings. His tie is a silk canvas with ribbons—the palest yellow, the darkest green, and ripe eggplant—tied neatly in a knot you imagine a cool blonde slipped under his Adam's apple this morning. The Scottie rolls to her side and offers her stomach. Even the biggest bitches have their moments.

"So you work around here?"

He points at the Hancock. "Up on the fortieth. I see you occasionally while I'm on my way back and forth from lunch."

"What do you do?"

"I'm at Hill Holiday. We're an ad agency."

Your laugh sounds a little off, and he smiles and tilts his head to the side like a dog, trying to get a better angle on your sudden strangeness. "I thought about going into advertising. Next fall I'm going back to school. I'm getting a master's in PR at Emerson. Tell me what I'm going to miss about the ad world."

•   •   •

He ends up walking the dogs home with you. It's Friday, he tells you, and he's had it. It'll do him good to walk in the sun. He asks and you give him the lead, and you think: if you went to his office, would he let you play with the photocopier? He's old enough to patronize you and young enough to worry that you think he's lost it. You've seen him around town sometimes: imported beer in hand, dry-cleaned Calvins, head bobbing to a band he thinks is too loud. But you're walking and he's talking, asking you a million questions about your-self, and by the second block the awkwardness of the situation has faded.

He went to Brown and you went to UConn. He's thirty-four. You're twenty-five. His wife is thirty. Tallulah is three.

"So you walk dogs and you're going back to school," he says. "What do you do for fun?"

Three interviews ago, Stacey or Tracey or maybe it was Jane, the one from Human Resources at Company X who smelled like those tiny trees you hang in your car, threw this same question across the desk at you: *What do you do for fun?* You drew a blank.

"You know what," you tell him, "I'm not sure anymore."

He laughs out loud; he has one of those smiles that are so broad the other features of the face seem to disappear. For a few moments, his eyes are erased.

"No, really. I used to go out three nights a week, I used to see every movie the day it was released. I used to . . ."

"Oh, come on. It can't be that bad. I went to the movies last Fri-day, and I'm married."

He tugs the dogs to a halt and you wait at the curb until the traf-fic slows enough to cross. A car is pulling out of its space and in the distance you see the Wagoneer speed up, its blinker on, ready for the spot.

You're expecting Tallulah to lose it: you grab hold of the lead and wait for her to start dragging Julio down the street in her frenzy over four-wheel drive. "Make sure you have it tight," you remind him.

"Got it."

The Wagoneer parks successfully, ten feet from you, and the Scot-tie dog witnessed the entire thing and retained a sense of decorum.

"There's a first," you say.

"What?"

"Your dog. You know, how she usually goes mental and pulls your arm off running after Troopers or Cherokees."

"Lula," he looks down at the Scottie, "you don't do that, do you, girl?"

"She's a head case," you say. He laughs again and you walk in silence the rest of the way, which isn't far.

"Come in for a sec. I'll give you my card."

You've been in the place before but never looked around; you were paranoid that someone would come home and find you flipping through the books in their shelves, the photo albums on their coffee table, which really isn't a table at all, but an antique chest.

"Must be nice to be able to walk to work," you say. He's off somewhere down the hallway and your words hang there. You're embarrassed to raise your voice. This is the sort of house, with its gleaming parquet floors under rich Oriental runners, where you walk into the room the person's in if you want to say something.

He comes back with a business card in his hand. "Did you say something?" he asks.

"It must be nice to be able to walk to work."

"It is. The parking situation around here is ridiculous, even with the resident stickers. Thank God the winter's almost over. My wife has a New Yorker that's just useless in the snow. My Cherokee's great for bad weather, but she won't drive it because it's a standard. Never got the hang of it."

He walks you to the door and Tallulah is under his feet the whole way; he nearly trips over her. Julio lumbers slowly by your side. You're standing there at the door and he tells you it was nice talking to you and he takes your hand, lays his card in your palm and curls your fingertips over it with his own; they're not as soft as you'd imagined them to be. Send me a resume, he tells you, still holding the fist he's formed. I'll see what I can do. You stand frozen like this for a moment, the only thing you're aware of besides the static in your ears is the maneuverings of Tallulah at your feet, pushing between the two of you. He inclines his head slightly; with your free arm you place a hand on the back of his neck; the Scottie's teeth stake their claim, nipping at the cuffs of your dungarees. When he presses you against the beveled glass of the door, she bites your ankle. Hard. Probably broke the skin. You've never kissed an ad man before. You do it for fun.

Saturday night, Frank Sinatra doesn't come home. You eat an entire bag of microwave popcorn even though the bag says "serves three." There's a black and blue mark on your ankle. In college, he begged you to get a tattoo there: a rose, a medieval cross, a butterfly, but you never did. You were afraid of pain. You never get to sleep, and Sunday at nine-thirty you throw on some sweats and head for your parents' place, where you hide out all day and read everything but the classifieds.

When it gets dark you head home and get into bed. He comes in four hours later, slides next to you still clothed and presses against you. Big news, he tells you. Trip is going to be the house band on Thursdays, Fridays, and Saturdays at The James. The band celebrated last night and he passed out at Speedy's place.

"Don't be mad," he whispers, lips wet on your neck. "Love you," he breathes into your hair.

YOU THINK: I've never bought a tie for anyone.

YOU SAY: "I'm not something you can fucking climb onto whenever you feel like it. Babe."

YOU KNOW: That the guy who orders a "Lumberjack" and asks for it by name won't see that this is his last ascent, that this tree is spiked.

On Monday you pick up the Scottie first.

"Hey, Lula. Come on, girl." When you round the corner there's a red Cherokee stopped at the light.

She barks. She yelps. Her small black body strains against the leash and for the first time you don't yank her into a sitting position but you let her pull you as she cries out after the idling vehicle. The nylon lead is chafing the skin of your hand and you don't care, you want to reach down and unhook her, let her run. She knows what she's after.

Camie Kim
Concordia University

CARTOGRAPHY

Billy lies on the living room floor on her back. She lies there sprawled, head plugged into the stereo, her shoes still on, her long hair lost in the Oriental curlicues of the carpet, staring up at the ceiling in that way that only fourteen-year-olds can. Our cat—her cat I should say—lies across Billy's stomach, purring contentedly, her half-pink nose just nudging Billy's throat. And Billy simply lies there, in ripped jeans and stained sweatshirt, her body almost as familiar as my own, and so like my own (although, granted, a more tender version). I doubt there are any other similarities, at least none that Billy or I would admit to. At her age I had neither the time nor the inclination to lie in one spot for very long. I was far too busy getting good grades, working on the school paper, playing on the field hockey team, and so on. It was, perhaps, one of the happiest periods of my life. Billy, however, is probably not happy, no, not very happy at all. In fact, she lies there as still as death on the living room floor and, for all I know, she could be dead. "Dead at fourteen": Isn't that scrawled across one of her T-shirts, one of the more optimistic ones? But then, when has my daughter, my well-dressed, well–electronically entertained daughter, ever been an optimist? All winter long she has stared up at the ceiling in that inimitable way of hers. Lesser ceilings would have caved in long ago. But this is her mother's house and that is her mother's ceiling and as such it was built expressly for the purpose of blocking Billy's view, stunting her growth, and otherwise limiting her universe. Billy shifts and sighs and the cat's purring pauses for a moment and then resumes. The cat opens her green eyes sleepily, closes them, lifts up a paw to lick it, eyes still closed, and then lowers her head back down onto her paws. Of course Billy knows that I'm standing here. Of course she doesn't budge an inch. That damn fascinating ceiling. It puts the Sistine to shame. You know, one day I truly expect to see a hole up there and even a few wisps of smoke for good effect, and my sweet Billy long gone to that paradise just on the other side—the other side of me. But perhaps I have it all wrong, perhaps it's not fair to say when Billy looks at me at all, that it's in much the same way.

"What are you doing?" I inquire loudly, leaning over her and waving my hand across her face, already exasperated by her and knowing that this is a question she hates. ("Why do we do things to our children that we would never do to anyone else?" I ask Lily, Frank's mother, this and she says gleefully, "Because we can.") To my surprise Billy answers, even pulling off the headphones. "I'm taking a break," she says, and she stretches her thin arms overhead and yawns as she says it. I catch a glittering glimpse of the braces that cost me a small fortune. "A break from what?" I say, more sarcastically than I intended. "A break from my map," she says, and I turn to look down at the large sheet of paper on the coffee table beside her. There's not much on it except a few squiggly lines running off into nowhere. "What kind of map is that?" I say, and she shoots back, sarcastically and very much intended, "Well, it's a map of my life, isn't it?" And then she sits up and tugs at the sleeves of her sweatshirt, pushing them up over her elbows. (Frank's sweatshirt and I swear she has hardly taken it off since he moved out. Bony little elbows, too, just like his.) "Look," she says, "I've got work to do," and she says this with her arms crossed and her eyes slightly rolling and this is especially infuriating because I know that she has learned both from me: the phrase and the gesture. I turn around and go back to my study. A small fortune? More like a goddamn king's ransom. "Don't you have any friends, Bill?" I say over my shoulder. "You know, other human beings who like you?" "No," she snaps, and she is already bent over her map, drawing God-knows-what with slow, meticulous strokes. Her long hair floats down toward this map of hers. Dark clouds of hair drifting over a world of crayon borders. Oh, the tenderness of that neck, so bare, so pale, that sweet little mole, my sweet silly Billy. I used to call her that all the time. My sweet silly Billy, I would coo—I could wring your scrawny little neck (oh please do, oh please do).

I fold my arms (my deliciously plump arms); I roll those eyes he once said he could drown in (yes, he really did say that). And Billy goes on drawing.

During dinner, Billy watches me eat. She sits across the table from me, hunched over her plate like some sort of teenaged gargoyle, glowering. Bastet, the cat, sits on her own chair next to Billy, also staring. "If you're not going to eat anything, why do I even bother to cook for you?" Billy shrugs her shoulders and pushes her cabbage roll from one side of the plate to the other, and then back again, Bastet's unblinking eyes following. "Yes, Billy, that's precisely why they call them cabbage *rolls*." She doesn't laugh. She doesn't even smile. Jerry giggles, at least, and says, "Good one, Mom." Billy glares at her sister but Jerry continues eating, oblivious. "I'm so sick of this rabbit food," Billy says. "Cabbage rolls are supposed to have meat in them." And then she glares at the food in front of her as if suspecting I was trying to poison her with it. "Fine," I say, "you buy yourself some meat and cook it yourself and you can eat as much of it as you want." Billy stabs a cabbage roll with her fork in response; she lifts the whole thing up and gnaws at the end of it. I don't say a word; I don't even bat an eyelash. Instead, I carefully cut a bite-sized morsel, lift it to my mouth, and chew on it delicately. What I would like to do is tip Billy's plate of food into her lap (and feed Bastet to the neighbor's dog)— but I don't. I exercise admirable restraint and go on eating. Jerry, in the meanwhile, I know, has got one of those trashy romances sitting on her lap and now and then a hand disappears as she surreptitiously turns a page. I can actually hear the page turning. Jesus, does she think I'm blind *and* deaf? And why the big hurry to get to the grand finale, anyway? As if this time things will end any differently. As if this time, in a sheepish voice, he'll say it's all been a silly mistake and she'll nod her pretty head in agreement, her calculating gaze already cast beyond his not-quite-broad-enough shoulders.

"Well, at least she's over her Ayn Rand phase," Frank says to me. "That's Billy, not Jerry," I snap back at him, "and I hardly think that a bodice-ripper would be much of an improvement, anyway. She's got a whole box of them under her bed. I don't know where she gets the money to buy so many." I shoot Frank a suspicious glance which he innocently returns. He lifts an eyebrow and tries to change the subject. "Myra, you really shouldn't be snooping around in their rooms." I ignore this. "Jesus, Frank, we've got one daughter reading *Story of O* and the other gorging on Harlequins. What am I supposed to do, start burning books?" I shake my head in disbelief. The doorbell rings. And rings again. I yell out: "Could *someone* please get that?!" Frank strokes his beard and smiles. "Why don't I take them for the weekend," he suggests, "or even for the week? They haven't been over in a while." "And your work?" I say. "You won't be able to write a thing." Frank grunts in response and stares gloomily at the salt and pepper shakers on the kitchen table, his chin sinking down to his chest. Once more, the doorbell rings. I sigh loudly and start to get up but then from down the hall we can distinctly hear Billy saying, "No thanks, we're all acolytes of Satan here." The door slams shut. Frank lifts his head up and grins at me. "A break would probably do you some good. And it wouldn't hurt them either." And then he fixes his big brown eyes on me and looks at me sadly. I know what's coming next and I steel myself for the onslaught.

It's been six years since Frank and I finally came to the conclusion—after many false stops and starts, separations and slammed doors, renewed determination and rekindled flames—that we were both miserable living together. Still, every few months Frank decides that this misery is exactly what's missing from his life and exactly what he needs to get his novel on track again. (His damn novel: Just look it up in the dictionary under "Sisyphean.") And then he pleads with me to let him move back in. Even though he only lives a twenty-minute bike ride away from us and practically spends most of his time here already, leaving a trail of half-eaten sandwiches, dirty dishes and upright toilet seats behind him and, when he's not here, phoning at all hours. Unless, of course, there's some new woman in Frank's life, in which case he'll suddenly fall off the face of the planet and Jerry and Billy will be annoyingly vague when I ask them how he's doing. But he always comes back, sooner or later, talking about how he's turned a corner and how he can see the light at the end of the tunnel and how he's determined to work flat-out on his novel until it's finished. I never have the heart to remind him of all the other times he has promised this.

Lily says I'm weak and she's right. She used to say to me: "None of this gentle weaning him off of you, Myra. Do it now and do it right. Trust me, I know, it's the kindest way." But six years later, she has all but given up. Every now and then she'll look at me and shake her head in pity (for me or for her son, I'm not quite sure), and I will say to her, "But, Lily, he needs me and I could never say no to anyone who needs me." At least not right away. So, instead, I continue to remind Frank again and again of all the fights, the nastiness, the way we both felt stifled, the way Jerry and Billy suffered, the way he could never write whenever any of us were home, how we literally had to tiptoe around him, and all his cries of creativity obstructed, all his laments of bourgeois boredom and responsibilities. But still he tries, pushing the salt and pepper shakers out of the way, tentatively stroking my hand across the table, sighing dramatically. "Maybe we should have gotten married, Myra," he says, "I mean really married, not just dancing around in our bare feet with some friends in a forest clearing on Mayne Island"—"Hornby," I correct him—"or at least we could have gone to City Hall, just the two of us, and we could have exchanged rings or something, rings with our names engraved on them." "Oh, Frank," I say, grabbing onto his hand. Bastet saunters into the kitchen just then, her head held high and her white tail pointing straight up, and makes a beeline for Frank. She jumps up into his lap and settles herself in, purring loudly. For once, I am grateful for the distraction. "Frank, you don't look so well," I tell him, and it's true, he doesn't. He's the same age as me but looks ten years older. "It's the novel," he says, "it's killing me." Bastet purrs.

Frank and I met when we were both eighteen, our first year at SFU. We were both taking the same political philosophy course and it was

1966. The last time I tried to tell the girls about this time, about how important and intense everything was, how immensely important it was to Frank and me, Jerry's eyes glazed over with boredom and Billy did a mock salute and said to me, reeling the words off, "Yes, *mother*, you all listened to Joan Baez or Pete Seeger and the Beavers or *whatever* and *The Georgia Straight* did more than just list movies and concerts and Kitsilano wasn't *crawling* with yuppies and LSD was not even against the law but using *birth control* could land you in jail and you all wanted to go back to the land or teach in free schools and none of you were into materialism or possessive relationships and all that other crap and, oh yeah, Kennedy got shot and King got shot too and Czechoslovakia got invaded and Canada made tons of money out of Vietnam and Trudeau called in the tanks—and there were you and Dad, right smack in the middle of it all, making *history*." Jerry cracked up and even I had to smile. And I almost told them about that summer before I started school, how hot it was, how I spent a weekend sitting in the backyard in the shade, drinking beer smuggled from my parents' fridge, stopping beads of sweat in their path as they rolled down my body with the cool glass of the bottle, and reading *The Feminine Mystique* and promising myself, smugly believing the promise unnecessary, that I would never end up like that: lost and defeated in some suburban wasteland, making babies, alternately worrying about the pattern of the wallpaper and how best to keep my husband's stomach content. No, I was going to go to university. I was going to be a lawyer. I was going to set up my own firm with like-minded partners and, together, step by victorious step, we would change the system from within. I was, most certainly, not going to have a child three years later—but that's what happened: first Jerry and then, two years after her, Billy. And now I can't imagine my life without them.

Frank and I were both red-diaper babies. My parents were early supporters of the CCF and Frank had grown up in a family where *Das Kapital* was the bible (his father had almost fought in the Spanish Civil War but caught pneumonia instead—or got mugged or got a job offer depending on what story he told you—and Lily helped found one of the oldest food co-ops in the city). Both of us were active in New Democratic Youth and Frank and some other students were trying to start up an SDU group on campus. Students for a Democratic University: First the university, and then the world. It seemed, at the time, a natural progression, and I was eager to help in any way possible, even when it felt like all I ever did was fetch coffee or make food and listen to them argue.

A month after we met, Frank gave me a silver peace sign on a chain. A friend of his was making these things by hand and selling them out of a café on the Avenue. Frank gave it to me while we were walking on the beach, in the rain, and I thought it was one of the loveliest gestures I had ever been on the receiving end of. I loved and cherished that little peace sign. It was such a symbol of all our dreams and for years I never took it off, not even in the shower or in bed. But later, when the girls were born, and Frank and I were finally beginning to understand that it wasn't going to work out after all—no perfect world, no perfect relationship—I started to feel self-conscious wearing it and I began hiding it under my shirts and then taking it off for certain occasions: my articling interviews, my first day in court. And then one day I looked at it and it seemed so—*sad*—so useless. I took it off altogether and hung it from the rearview mirror of my car.

Anyway, that first year of university, in that class where the professor encouraged us to "take risks, be yourself," I noticed Frank almost right away and I thought, mistakenly, that he was quiet and serious and even, perhaps, a little shy. He would sit there in class, in a dirty wool poncho, staring at the professor from behind his long hair, hinting at unplumbed depths of mystery and silence. Outside of class, he would emerge from his hair every now and then to quote stuff like, "Why have words, when their brutal precision bruises our complicated souls?" I found him fascinating. Later, when I got to know Frank better, I realized how hard this act must have been on someone as naturally vociferous as he was. At any rate, he soon gave it up and he was just as loud as the rest of us when we crashed the Faculty Club, yelling "Thought police! Thought police!" (the girls still don't believe that one). And he had read Camus in the original French, or so he claimed, and Marx, of course, in translation. And, oh, what beautiful hair he had. Hair that I would later stroke and caress, adoring it, coveting it, threatening to cut it off in the middle of the night while he was asleep and have a wig made out of it for me.

I used to tease Frank by telling him that I wanted to have his children just because of his hair. Samson, I used to call him in bed; my little Delilah, he would call me back.

This was a long, long time ago.

And now Frank is bald, or getting there; otherwise, he really hasn't changed all that much. That was the problem: I changed; he didn't.

Frank stays for dinner. Lily phones me with a new lawyer joke: "What do lawyers and sperm have in common? A one in a million chance of becoming human!" And then she cackles gleefully, and I invite her over for dinner as well. Lily is a tiny woman, barely reaching my shoulder, but about as fragile as steel, with a helmet of gray hair, and constantly on the move like the human dynamo that she is; that is, when she isn't drinking like a fish. Behind her back, the girls call her Mighty Mouse (while Frank has been known to mutter something about *der Führer*). She arrives with a salad and a bottle of wine and the first thing she spots is Billy's map still spread across the coffee table. She paces in front of it, tilting her head this way and that, peering at it quizzically. Billy explains to her patiently (when was the last time she spoke to me as patiently?) that it's a school project. "It's a map of the world, but not like the usual ones. It's supposed to be drawn from a different perspective, you know, like upside down or with Africa in the middle." Billy rolls her eyes. "And that's supposed to teach us how to look at things in a different way and change our lives forever." Lily laughs and claps her hands. "But it's a wonderful idea." And then she and Billy launch into a debate about how best to draw the map. Frank buries his nose in an old *National Geographic.* Jerry is deep into another episode of heaving bosoms and arrogant bastards. I sit on the couch and listen. Billy wants to draw the map with only the countries in the world that she would like to visit. Lily is horrified by this. "Well, that's *my* perspective, isn't it?" Billy insists. "How about," Lily suggests, "drawing it without any borders? We're all brothers and sisters, aren't we?" Billy grins. Even Jerry peers over her book and starts to giggle. Then they both break out into peals of laughter. "Oh, Lily, that's so hippy-dippy!" Frank looks up from his magazine, startled, and I use the opportunity to grab him for kitchen detail.

After dinner, Lily and I sit on the couch in my study and get slowly, pleasantly drunk. I talk about Jerry and Billy. "Lily, I swear it's a kind of lust I feel for their bodies. Is that sick? I don't know what other word to use. Sometimes I look at them and it literally takes my breath away, the perfection of them. How incredibly beautiful they are. Do you know what I mean, Lily? When Jerry was a baby and I was breastfeeding her, it was so damn, well, *arousing*. Oh, I was much too embarrassed to tell anyone about it but I was also afraid that if I told anyone it wouldn't feel that way anymore. And when Billy was a little girl, she would fling herself into my arms and literally roll her body all over mine as if my body was just as much a part of her as her own, as if there was no difference. Oh, Lily, it took my breath away, the trust of it. And now that's what I want to do. I want to fling myself onto them. I want to roll myself in them like rolling in a field of flowers. It's so greedy. It's like a hunger; no, it's a physical ache sharper than hunger. It's rapacious. Damn, there should be a word for it. Maybe there is a word. Lily, are you listening to me? Did you ever feel like this about Frank? Do you still feel that way about him? Why is there no word for this feeling? It's not like I just want to hold them, it's like I want to enclose them, surround them, take them back into me. Maternal tenderness, right. This is *fierce*. You know that fish that swallows all its baby fish in order to protect them? Like that. Like I'd rather even swallow them than breathe myself. Lily?"

Earlier, when Lily and I had retreated into my study, Bastet had sidled in before I could close the door. She had walked around my outstretched legs, not deigning even to glance at me, sniffing disdainfully at the air as if to imply that I had somehow polluted it. Bastet knows full well that she's not allowed in here, and I was about to chase her out when Lily patted her lap instead and invited her into it. Bastet didn't hesitate; she jumped up into Lily's lap with a graceful spring and just as gracefully reclined there, looking immensely smug, purring, her paws kneading Lily's denim-covered thighs while Lily stroked her sleek head, murmuring, "Oooh, but aren't you a beauty?"

Now, Lily has her own head back and her feet propped up on an open drawer of one of my filing cabinets. Her eyes are closed. She nods sleepily in easy agreement to whatever I say, humming something under her breath, her wine glass held in a hand off to the side because Bastet has completely taken over her lap. The damn cat is fast asleep. Her whole body is curved into a half-moon, the soft fur of her belly exposed, and all her paws flung out with abandon. I pour myself another glass of wine and watch Bastet dream, her long whiskers twitching in anticipation.

The next day I ask Jerry and Billy if they would like to stay at their father's for a week. I am not surprised at their eagerness to do this but I am surprised at the twinge of jealousy I feel at their excitement. I tell myself it's only natural that they would like to spend more time with their father, exclusive time with him, and I tell myself it's a healthy reaction, mine and theirs. And after all, I finally tell myself, Frank has a TV, the merits of which the girls have yet to convince me of, although, God knows, they keep trying.

The girls pack what looks to me like a year's worth of clothing, magazines, cassettes, and books. They haul out their sleeping bags and drape them over the living room furniture to air them out. They pack their pillows in garbage bags and insist on taking their clock radios as well. "You don't want us to be late for school, do you?" When I see them head toward the kitchen with an empty duffel bag, I race in after them and intervene just as they are about to zero in on the kitchen cupboards. I insist that Frank will have plenty of food for them and they back off, grumbling, but not too noisily. And then they resume their packing.

Later, Billy comes into my study with Bastet in her arms and says that she wants to take the cat with her to Frank's. Every other time the girls have gone off to their father's I have looked after Bastet. This has basically meant, for the both of us, days of circling around each other warily, Bastet coming home only to eat and then quickly escaping through her trap door with an occasional snarl thrown over her shoulder in my direction. Believe me, an enormous improvement over the first time when Billy was eight and left Bastet alone with me to go to summer camp for a couple of weeks, and the damn cat proceeded to defecate in every corner of the house. Lily, in all seriousness, suggested a cat therapist and I had to make her promise not to mention the idea to Billy because I knew it was just the kind of thing Billy would have insisted upon for weeks. Now, she stands in front of me with Bastet in her arms, passionately pleading with me like a witch and her familiar about to be consigned to the flames, while Bastet coolly examines me with eyes narrowed into green slits. (The only person actually allowed to pick up Bastet is Billy. Once, in my impatience, I scooped up the damn thing in order to move her a little more expeditiously than she was inclined and paid dearly for it with a pound of flesh.) It's oddly disconcerting, the two pairs of eyes almost level with each other and my own, looking at me. Billy, I realize with a shock, is practically as tall as me now.

"Please, Mom, just this one time, I don't want to leave Bastet alone here. I mean, if you let me take her, then you won't be bothered by her. Pleeeeease, Mom." But I shake my head and say, as patiently as I can, "Billy, you're only going away for a week and you can come back and visit Bastet whenever you want. Besides, you'll just confuse her by moving her around." "Mom, please, I promise, I won't let her out of the house." And on and on it goes. Billy keeps begging and I keep saying no but find myself, little by little, giving in. Finally, I say to her, "Let me phone your father." Billy grins; she knows that she's won.

I call Frank. "Frank, Billy wants to bring the cat. I've said no but she's threatening not to go without it." This is not entirely true. "Myra," Frank says, "let her bring Bastet. What's the big deal? We won't let her out. She'll be fine."

And then the girls are gone. I wander around the silent house, automatically picking up stray items of clothing and magazines and clumps of Bastet's fur from the carpet and then, when I realize what I am doing, I drop everything to the floor and I lie on the couch and stare at the ceiling.

Sunday morning Billy calls me, waking me up. I was up late the night before preparing a case for a Monday examination for discovery. Her voice is hoarse and unusually urgent, and at first, groggy with sleep, I don't even realize it's her. "Mom, Bastet's run off. We can't find her. We've looked everywhere. Is she back home with you?" And then I'm awake. "Billy? What do you mean Bastet's run off? Oh no, Billy, you didn't let her out, did you?" "*Mom.*" It's almost a wail. I tell her I'll look for Bastet and if I can't find her I'll come over. There's no sign of the cat near the house or up and down the block and when I get to Frank's the rain is coming down in sheets. I get out of my car and make a dash for it and the front door is pulled open even before I can get there.

Frank rents the main floor of a house from friends who live on the floor above his. It's been a long time since I was last in his place and, as always, the mess of it both astounds and reassures me. Same old Frank. Somehow, in the midst of all this chaos he manages to run his life, teaching ESL part-time, toiling away on his novel. Once, the girls showed me a personal ad they had found in *The Sun*, convinced that it was his: *Male, writer, late 30s, humorous, compassionate, seeks literary benefactress for love and inspiration.* I couldn't explain to the girls why I didn't find it funny, why I didn't even want them to show the ad to Frank. I just told them not to, and they rolled their eyes at each other, grimacing.

We look everywhere, the four of us, in the pouring rain. I keep thinking of that movie, the one my mother loved so much with Audrey Hepburn in it, and the last scene of it, the search in the alley, the cat finally emerging from a wooden crate with a weak but hopeful meow, the happy ending. But it doesn't happen that way to us. The girls and I walk up and down the street, up and down the surrounding streets, yelling Bastet's damn name over and over again. A few people pop their heads out and inquire after our search. "Basket?" they ask, puzzled: "Is that the cat's name?" Frank rides his bike along the streets farther out. He's gone for ages and comes back soaked, sniffling, and empty-handed. When we finally all return to the house we find Lily ensconced there, sitting at Frank's computer, one eye on a pot of chili, while printing out notices: HAVE YOU SEEN THIS CAT? When the rain has stopped, we all go out again, Lily leading the way, to put the notices up.

The next morning I have to leave early for work but I come back home in the afternoon to drive Billy to the SPCA. We wander among the rows of cages, looking for Bastet but not finding her, only a lookalike now and then which, surprisingly, sends my heart momentarily skittering. By the end of it, by the end of all those liquid eyes and lonely whimpers, even I am completely drained, and Billy doesn't say a word on the drive back home. Her eyes are red but I have yet to see her cry.

For weeks we keep up the search. We place an ad in the paper, and Billy recruits her friend Kate to go around with her, knocking on doors, a photo of Bastet in hand. But we never do find Bastet. She seems to have disappeared as suddenly and as inexplicably as she arrived in our lives, five years ago, when Billy discovered her under my car, a skinny thing with matted fur and the tip of an ear missing, an insistent meow, and a patrician dignity that thoroughly belied her sorry state.

Billy has almost finished her map. It looks like any other map of the world except that she's drawn it all in pencil because, as she drawls cynically, "nothing stays the same for long." And then she looks up at me, half-defiantly, half-accusingly. I suppose that Billy, with the inexorable logic of adolescence, blames me for her cat's disappearance. I suppose I should blame myself too. Like Lily says, I'm weak; I should have said no. But then Billy looks up at me again and asks me what I think of her map. She poses the question carelessly, and she doesn't appear to be waiting for my response, bent down over her map again, completely absorbed by it. But I give her the benefit of the doubt anyway. I reach down and stroke the top of her head, her soft, silken hair, and I tell her that her map looks wonderful. She brushes my hand away, without looking up, irritated: "Mom, stop that." And then I give her the benefit of the doubt again.

My parents died a few years ago, my mother first, my father a year later. Before I gave birth to my daughters, I thought that the love I felt for them, my mother and my father, was as intense a love as anyone could ever feel for anyone else. It felt like a hand squeezing my heart whenever I saw them, the way they were growing older and slower, the way my mother still worried about whether I was eating properly, and then, later, the way my father would play with my daughters, his infinite patience and gentleness. Watching the two of them with Jerry and Billy, I thought: This is how I was brought up, this is how they talked to me, touched me. It actually hurt, how grateful I felt. I wanted so much to give back to them what they had given me. I wanted so badly to make them proud of me, to please them, to be able to support and comfort them in their old age. It was embarrassing how much I loved them, when others complained of their nosy mothers or their cold fathers. What in the world did I do to deserve such wonderful parents? I would have done anything, I felt, to keep them from growing any older, to keep them happy, to keep them healthy, to just keep them.

A long time ago when the girls were very young, and when we were living in the West End and I was unemployed and not looking all that hard for work, I used to take Jerry and Billy to the downtown library most Friday afternoons as soon as Jerry had come home from school. We'd walk down Barclay and then Robson and then Billy would drag Jerry by the hand up the stairs to the mezzanine floor, ignoring my pleas to slow down. Jerry would let Billy drag her, bemused, and when they reached the top of the stairs Billy would announce their arrival with triumphant squeals. Librarians would stare at me meaningfully. I'd quickly herd them toward the children's section where Jerry would methodically go through the shelves until she had finally picked something out and then, carrying the book like an egg about to hatch, she would settle down on one of those old bean bag chairs with stuffing coming out (but from where you could never discover and there would always be stuff in her hair afterwards that I would have to carefully pick out) and there she would sit, in a corner, with her nose in the book and her feet in the air, and that would be the last I'd hear from her until it was time to go back home. Billy, on the other hand, would grab as many books as she could hold, each one infinitely more necessary than the last and, if another child had a book, that would be the one, of course, that she especially wanted. Parents would stare at me significantly. Finally, tower of books balanced precariously, she would slowly make her way over to where I sat, sunk into a bean bag chair myself, wondering what to do with my life and half-dreaming even then of going back to school, but not quite knowing how I would ever be able to get up again. Billy would show me her spoils and I would have to respond to each book with suitable admiration, reading every title out loud, exclaiming over each one. And always at the bottom of the stack or somewhere near it would be her favorite, a colorful, tattered, tiny picture book with only a few words inside in big bold print. (How she managed to do that—and why—I still don't know. Under the carpet, inside another book? She must have kept it hidden somewhere, her own private stash of library.) She'd sit in my lap then, a perfect fit, my chin perched on the top of her head, and urge me on to read: *"Fuzzy Wuzzy was a bear./Fuzzy Wuzzy had no hair./Fuzzy Wuzzy wasn't very fuzzy, was he?"*

She never laughed. She didn't find it funny, I guess, although I tried to read it as comically as possible, this minor tragedy that I would have to enact every Friday afternoon for her, and to which she would always respond with the same one-word critique: "Sad." She'd draw the word out with one long exhalation and it was always then that I wanted to gather her into my arms and wrap myself around her—but before I could she would demand another reading and, obedient, I would read the story to her again and again while she sat there, her eyes following my finger over the words and over the brightly colored pictures, solemnly staring at the denuded bear as if she could somehow, by force of will alone, cause the hair to grow back on its body. It was easy enough to imagine her wise beyond her years—at least until "Fuzzy Wuzzy" became "Hairy Jerry"—and for a long time I wasn't allowed to stop reading this story to her, even though I tried, now and then, to tempt her with more cheerful tales. Maybe I could have tried harder. But how reassuring it was, how straightforward and simple: I would read, and she would respond, always in the same way. Week after week something between us never changed; something, for a while, actually stayed the same.

Jon Billman
Eastern Washington University

KERR'S FAULT

We're on top of my aluminum trailer in Hams Fork, adjusting my satellite dish because the earthquake jounced it cockeyed and instead of the French porn channel Wayne showed me I could get, I now have snow. "I got a dad in Preston, Idaho," says Wayne, pointing to the northwest with a socket wrench, says it like he's got another in Denver and maybe one in the garage, says it like he's holding on to this dad because he might come in handy someday and you just never know. "He just bought a new compressor, a real portable job. I'm gonna hook it onto this big brush I got ordered and we'll be in business." Wayne's already in business so I know this new business is recreation, sport, diversion, maybe count me in. I am glad his talk is of art. It is late afternoon and the high desert snow is starting to turn purple, like a bruise.

"What sort of business?" I ask.

"You'll see," he says. And I know he's right.

This is the Renaissance man, the Wayne Kerr I used to know two years ago who, when I first came to Hams Fork, reached out his hand and was the only one to offer me a beer; my friend Wayne Kerr who is passed around here in conversation like so many Bible stories of miscreants and ne'er-do-wells. Like the best myth and legend, *Wayne Kerr was an artist.* Wayne believes every creature on land has a counterpart at sea. He's becoming an artist again since he met Copper, his new model and his new girlfriend.

I still teach history at the high school and it's colder than billyhell up here, but I've got a vista. My trailer sits on the windy east scarp over Hams Fork so that standing up here I am even with the water tower behind the school, across the town, along U.S. 30 just this side of one Mormon ward house and the port of entry where over-the-road drivers idle their rigs and secure trip permits before driving through the state we're in. Westbound, the cable of asphalt leaves the valley and turns into Utah.

I can look out over the shiny tops of trailer after trailer set in awkward rows of gritty Old Testament gray, sage and sooty snow lapping at rusty snow machines and four-wheel-drives as if someday the land, with a swarm of locusts and a hurricane wind, might muster up enough force to take back this godforsaken desert. No one wants to live up here. You are exposed and can almost see too much; I can look right down into the sewage treatment plant. I see the smokestacks from the coal-burning power plant that lights half of Salt Lake City. There are mine shafts all underneath my trailer and they are on fire from an explosion fifty years ago. You can smell the smoke. It's March, the temperature doesn't get above thirty in the daytime, the regional suicide rates rise, and I still have flies.

If you are not Mormon in Hams Fork, you have a past. I was married. It pushes a man against the wall to come home from work and find everything he owns in the front yard in the rain. I have lived in a car that didn't run. Slept in libraries.

My wife was pretty, but now she lives in Illinois. Right now I am content to stand up here and watch.

The water tower stands like a phallus—Be fruitful!—and is our skyline. It is white and inviting: WELCOME TO HAMS FORK. Without it Hams Fork couldn't flush. The caged ladder doesn't begin until twenty feet up a leg, I guess to keep crazies or a dizzy kid from scaling the thing to paint his girlfriend's name in Day-Glo letters, or hanging himself from a rope halfway down and really giving this town something to see when the sun comes up. I teach U.S. and Wyoming history mostly, where white men put their names on everything, shot rifles at Indians and got their pictures in the textbooks and their surnames on maps. I know it by heart and it bores the hell out of me. The aluminum is thin—no insulation—and under the wind I can hear the faint buzz of the.TV that keeps me company. I never turn it off. We don't have a town square, we have a triangle. Elevation at the triangle is 6,923 feet above sea level. Hams Fork is proud of its elevation, above most, closer to God level. The ward houses stand guard at both entrances to the valley like Monopoly hotels. The size of aircraft carriers and no crucifixes, just thin steeples, antennas. I'm fighting like king-hell to keep my job and, to tell you the truth, I'm getting my teeth kicked in.

VACANCY flashes over the Antler Motel, just behind the empty-parked Union Pacific coal train from west of here, where it sat too long in civilization and now tells a spray-paint story of Vegas or L.A.: *Westside Bombsquad, Gabriel,* city fish, black cartoon people, *Roman, Jessie,* girlfriend hearts. The big brown building southeast of the cemetery is the Afghan Apartments where a lot of Texas and California swampers live because they don't have to sign a lease. I lived there when I first moved to Hams Fork a year ago and you can hear people fighting and throwing things and crying and dreaming and screwing and laughing at all hours through the thin sheetrock walls. A lot of babies get made there. It is also where a few heads get blown off with self-inflicting shotguns. I learned this seven years ago, when I was twenty-two: nothing is easy. Once I saw a couple of gray hobos go by below me. They weren't doing anything, just drumming through on a noisy coal train. I'm watching Wayne work on my antenna because he knows what he is doing. The wind whips our hair like flags.

I've seen dogs committing intimacy. People in town below are only maybe two millimeters high. You can see the top of Wayne's house, a not-so-nice older home over on that side of the switchyard, amid where most of the community pillars and bishops live in very nice newer homes. All of them, actually. His house used to be a hospital when Hams Fork was just a coal camp without a name. Wayne needs to put a new roof on the place this summer—his shingles are spongy—though he probably won't; but if he asked me I would help him do it. I would stand shirtless on Wayne Kerr's roof in our brief summer and not be ashamed. It's close enough he could hoof it up here but he doesn't. It's got a widow's walk and a laundry chute. You cannot see Abraham Lincoln's head from here.

But we've got it, down on I-80, just east of here. Just his big traffic-stopping head, like a huge Victorian gazing ball in the world's biggest rock garden. There are toilets and a gift shop where his boots would be. Abe himself was never west of Missouri, but he gets his head in Wyoming. He looks sort of confused.

A hawk is riding a thermal above the water tower, above the little brown birds whose names I don't know, up, around, up, up, over. I came here because in the atlas this seemed the cleanest of slates and it read like starting over. Tens of thousands of years ago, way before the coal was a sulfurous swamp, Hams Fork used to be the bottom of a deep ocean. A red beacon flashes on the tower to keep airplanes from folding-in against it. Now, even in winter, dust covers everything.

"Ouch," says Wayne. The wrench slipped and he scraped his knuckle against the rotor bracket, drawing slow blood in the cold.

It hurts my hand just to look at it. "Bet that hurts," I say. Wayne just looks at me, bent over at the waist. He sorta grunts. I go back to watching, waiting. It is cloudy to the far northwest, where Idaho is.

"Let's see if that does it," says sweaty Wayne. But with my ear to the aluminum, I still hear fuzz.

Today, this is what I told my first-hour Wyoming History class: Prairie women, from the East, went crazy out here because they papered their walls with white flour sacks, the snow glared white, the sun was bright, no sunglasses. No perspective. Nothing to keep them grounded. While their husbands were out hunting jackrabbits, they went crazy in a white hell. This happened mostly in Kansas and Nebraska and the Dakotas, but it adds drama to an otherwise damn-right boring class.

Just before dark I stand up here with this monocular I ordered from a catalogue. You have to hold the thing very still because even the slightest movement distorts everything and it's more like looking through a cheap beer glass, but I watch wildlife: moose, deer, antelope, stray dogs, elk, Robin. After work, like now, I stand up here and think until my stomach hurts or my face gets too numb to feel or both. When lights go on I can see people doing warm things through the windows of the Afghans. My face is getting numb.

I'm on the Black List right after Wayne, and the commandments of town life don't pertain to me anymore. They are just holding their breath until my contract runs out in May. I'm just a little earwig in their hair, nothing like what Wayne is. A white moon is rising in the east. I wish the monocular was a telescope. No French satellite. It's getting dark. People are doing domestic things in the Afghans. Lights are coming on. I go for beer.

"A five-point-five on the old Rectum Scale!" yells Wayne, letting off steam, daring God to do better, a bigger earthquake. Still no Galaxy 4, Channel 17, but I reach Wayne another can of beer, which I guess I shake up on the climb back up the ladder. Half of it runs down his arm as foam and he swallows the other half in two gulps. I tell him I read in the paper even the oil geologists didn't know about the fault and it doesn't even have a name yet and Wayne says he's not surprised and they ought to call it something profound like "Kerr's Fault" and I agree that that sounds as good as anything. The surprise quake cracked a hatchery pool up above Lake Viva Naughton, near the epicenter, and knocked a few dishes off some shelves, sheared off a few rivets on the water tower, cracked a little pavement in the IGA parking lot, but nothing much more than give everyone something to talk about at the Busy Bee Café. And see to it that I'm not watching any French huff and puff while I'm grading bad Civil War term papers tonight. The mountains keep the vibrations in check. Wayne says he's not sure just what is the matter.

He drops a nut which bounces once on the thin roof and lands silently in a scrub pine below. "You'll never find it in the snow in the dark. I'll grab one at home and drive it over later," he says.

"No hurry. I can wait," which is difficult to say. Wayne leaves. I stay to enjoy the view for a few more minutes. Robin hikes by but Wayne does not see her. She does not see me as I stand up here, stiff as the water tower, watching. I must look two millimeters tall.

I need to tell you about Robin.

• • •

Crazy Wayne Kerr, the used-to-be-artist, he'd tell you. "The small-ness of this town has beaten me into painting goddamn landscapes for goddamn tourists," he'd say with indifference in his tar-and-nicotine-thick voice, though he makes quite a little cash from these paintings he churns out by the dozens and sells out of the office at the Antler Motel. "Now I just do crafts." Wayne says "crafts" like a filthy word, coughing it out of the back of his throat and spitting it into the wind like it might ooze through the cracks of the grace-saying fam-ily's house next door and ruin supper. Wayne makes enough to keep imported green bottles of beer with foil over the caps in the old refrig-erator in his studio and pick up a dime bag of Mexican hash when-ever he wants, which is quite frequently. He'll sometimes spend all night in the studio drinking, smoking, chewing, spitting, churning out twenty-minute landscapes with cheap Prang watercolors and a fan-brush, listening to that sixties and seventies music of his: old Stones, Doors, Creedence, Janis Joplin. He works three easels at a time: rock, rock, rock. Cloud, cloud, cloud. No trees. Lots of perspective.

The administration was not impressed with my lesson about Ben-jamin Franklin, an artist, and I was called on the rug. Again. My lec-ture in doubt included his rendezvous with concubines, illegitimate children, painting, voyeuristic tendencies. The history books fail to mention those elements that make a man real. The Mormons pre-tend they never existed.

"What will you tell them in your next Ben Franklin lecture?" they wanted to know. I answered.

"He was a man with poor vision who is engraved forever in the his-tory books but did not get his face put on a rock in South Dakota?"

"Yes," said the Mormons.

I asked him once how come he doesn't just fly this place and move to Jackson or Park City and open a real gallery. "Because the tourists there tend to have more taste," said Wayne Kerr the realist. "Because our tourists are bait fishermen's wives from Ohio. Besides, I haven't finished a real painting in twenty years."

Do the Mormons want truth? "Hell no," says Wayne.

• • •

Through the window I have seen Wayne fly off the handle and just start throwing and kicking maybe $300 worth of landscapes around the studio until he's so winded and shaky and coughy he can hardly stand, which doesn't take long. He's careful, though, careful not to hit the figures, the beautiful almost-finished oil figures he's kept hanging in gold no-glass frames next to the oil body parts on cheap gessoed paintboard scraps that form a collage in the studio as a reminder; a reminder of what he used to do, what he has done, will do again.

I could feel for Robin.

Robin is the wife Wayne's got. She used to model for Wayne's paintings before she got to be "hippy," as he calls it. Now she just teaches math at the junior high and makes little geometrical wind chimes out of monofilament and aluminum conduit that she hangs all over their back porch and eaves along the garage and which Wayne sometimes takes to the Antler with a load of landscapes and elbows his friends into buying one here and there to keep her happy, to keep her feeling useful. Angel music, she calls the tinny pings and dings that fill the air. Music for angels and the ghosts of dead Shoshone, she says. Yes, right, make sure you write this down, Wayne's wink says.

Sometimes a tourist will want one of Robin's chimes and the guys will be sitting around drinking coffee or Cokes with morning rum and they'll look at each other from the corners of their eyes and grin and look outside to check the license plates on the tourist's car. The tourist always asks How far is it to Jackson Hole from here? and Which way do I go? Never do they buy anything on a return trip; they've already spent their wad, are tired of the excitement of it all, the raree show, don't need a fish-line wind chime. Robin is pretty in the way wood smoke smells nice. She was a nurse in Vietnam. We have in common that we both teach and are friends of Wayne Kerr, but that is about it. If I could paint, I know what it would be like.

I asked that too, when I came here from the tired Midwest, because on the atlas it's only an inch, maybe an inch and a quarter away, but this place is far from Jackson Hole. TV tourism spots for Wyoming do not show Hams Fork. They show natty fly fishermen and chesty cowgirls grilling steaks and dinosaur eggs, Devils Tower, snowy peaks, never the desert. Never a local throwing chunks of sucker meat on a treble hook at a rainbow trout choking in runoff, never a strip mine or a PTA meeting. On TV this place looks like starting over. Robin's hair is the color of new motor oil and she is on the List because of what Wayne did, because of what Wayne does. In their forties, no kids. She smells like apples when she walks by at a crowded district meeting. The wind doesn't quit blowing in Hams Fork and you can hear the Kerr place all over town.

I wait an hour and call Wayne but he isn't home yet. It is dinnertime for most people here. Robin checks and says, Yes, their satellite dish is fine and sure enough their French porn channel—Galaxy 4, Channel 17—is coming in clear as sunshine, but I know she doesn't watch it and Wayne doesn't need it so wouldn't you know they're getting it loud and now. She adds that there's a new crack in the foundation along the side of the garage where the studio is and wasn't that quake something. She'll send Wayne over when he gets in. That is, if he gets in, because Wayne is probably seeing Copper over whiskey sours at the Number 9. This is the most we have ever talked and I don't say this to Robin, don't wish to make her sad. Sadder. She knows. We talk about California weather and school. Since the quake I pick up garbled AM radio over the telephone. It's not real clear but the Jazz game is on and for a minute I listen to the fantasy of professional basketball and Robin's voice.

He is painting real paintings again. "Pictures," Copper calls them in her nasal red-haired Montana accent. "Beautiful pictures," she says in a way that allows for the fact that she's in them. He's even growing his beard back, though this time it is streaked with gray. Copper is from Billings, an explosives engineer fresh out of School of Mines where, Wayne tells me, she switched from electrical engineering when she found she had a passion for blowing things up. She's with the Wyoming branch of some outfit out of Houston that puts out derrick fires with explosives. Word of mouth had it that Wayne Kerr used to do figures, nudes, and she approached him at a junior high faculty party where she was a date of one of the assistant football coaches who spent the better part of the party overshaking everyone's hand, slapping them on the back, and drawing plays on damp cocktail napkins. "I hear you're into oils," she said to Wayne, making a little "o" with her lips on "oils" and sucking the rest of the word in like good cigar smoke. They talked for an hour and a half while Robin ate celery. Copper rides a vintage motorcycle and Wayne says she's good and wild and narcissistic and that that ain't easy to please. I see here in the *Casper Star* that geologists still can't pinpoint the fault.

Okay.

So the superintendent and principal are on me. I am a good teacher and that is a problem for them. They make unannounced visits and just sit in my classroom taking notes and trying to get to me, write me up on trifles they find in dusty policy books, then put the pink slips in my permanent file. It doesn't matter that I can lecture the hell out of Thomas Jefferson, the Gettysburg Address or women's suffrage (Wyoming was the first). They are frustrated because they cannot write *Is a friend of Wayne Kerr* in my file. I buy beer. I like blue movies. They know because they watch. They see. Things are harder for Robin; she has tenure and they must ride her harder, search a little deeper, raise their voices a little more. They just won't hand me a new contract in May; they'll have a fat file of why's, and I'll be starting up again in another middle of nowhere somewhere else. Though those places are becoming fewer. It isn't easy, but there is a point you have to hit where you quit sweating. With each move I travel a little lighter. I'm just not quite sure which side of that point I'm on.

It is March and not nearly spring, not nearly warm, not nearly the May or June recess we get from winter. But Copper is out there in the night, a whiskey shadow on her old piston-knocking Indian motorcycle, though it still snows hard and the north winds from Canada and Montana still blow and howl like hell and find every bad rivet and seam on this trailer; out there in her leather jacket and faded jeans with holes and grease and tears all up and down her legs and nothing underneath, long red mane flying behind her. Up and down Main Street, Antelope Street, U.S. 30 and 189; all over Carmel County, miles of black snowdrift backdrop. She leaves a trail in the cold from the bike's hot exhaust and the breath that comes from deep inside her.

People get a little anxious this time of year. Mormons have turned to coffee. I've seen Copper open a beer bottle with her eye socket. The fire of that Indian is rhythmic and steady, like Robin's walking, something heartening. Wayne should be by soon.

They have visions and see things against their eyelids. What I am going to tell you next is in my file. They know I helped Wayne one night when he airbrushed Revelation 22:18 and left his mark on thirty-two cars of a Union Pacific coal train that took half an hour the next morning to lumber through the switchyard at the center of town: "I warn every one who hears the words of the prophecy of this book: if any one adds to them, God will add to him the plagues described in this book . . ." On the last car, the one right after "book," Wayne sprayed this cartoon Joseph Smith hammering away on a laptop computer and the Book of Mormon spitting out of a laser printer. Cartoon Joe had a little name tag above his pocket, just like the guys at the Chevron station: Joe. I just carried the big carbon dioxide tanks and paint—Wayne's got a bad back—but they knew. Copper kept watch, though it was okay because the train was parked out in the middle of Pratt Canyon, real nowhere. It started getting light and Wayne didn't get the Book of Mormon quite finished, so that it read "Book of Mor," but everyone got the idea. This made the paper in Cheyenne where the Revelation rolled through on its way to Omaha and power plants farther east. It was the first time I had felt alive and useful since the idea of being married stopped sounding like a good one. I don't feel that alive now. Wayne's an atheist, but he knows his Bible.

The *Hams Fork Gazette* front page called it "Juvenile Graffiti," but Wayne just called it Something for the boys at the bar. "In this place you've got to make your own fun," he says. This is true and I'm glad to see it and with Copper Wayne makes much more of his own fun more often. Every once in a while now you'll see one of Wayne's words roll through town: plagues, words, if, one, book, God. His new paintings are impressive.

It's alright to go to the bar more often now that I'm new history. I go with Wayne because he has never bought into living for someone else's standards and his attitude gives me a lift. He writes editorials to the *Gazette* (the *Gazoo*, he calls it) under the pen name "Stephen

Hero," Star Route, Hams Fork, Wyoming. He harangues the mayor, the town council, the school board, the Carmel County sheriff, the bishops, the superintendent, the chief of police. All for fun, he says, all for fun. I don't really give a shit about any of that, Wayne claims after really throwing the dictionary—sometimes the Bible—at them. All for fun. The thing is, though, he is always dead-on and the written replies in next week's paper never touch him. His new word, I think he coined it, is "Custerian."

I don't sleep well anymore. The alcohol helps. I get recurring nightmares. It's evening in the dream, summer and green. I'm with friends and peers and most times they have dates. We laugh and drink and make fun of the movies. Between features all the other cars leave but ours. Then the big gray speaker in the window quits working and we only can see the movie, not hear it, but we don't mind and sometimes don't even notice. Then the picture gets fuzzy and I guess I must fall asleep. When I wake up in the dream I am alone. It's cold and the windows are iced over from the inside. I try to start the car from the backseat and the starter just grinds. I get out of the backseat in just my underwear and run around in the snow. No one is here at this boarded-up theater in the middle of nowhere. The marquee out front reads CLOSED FOR SEASON. I look back toward the car and my footprints are blown over. I didn't bring a shovel. I have jumper cables but I'm alone in the world. Every dream it's a different drive-in.

I told Wayne about this dream once. He said he has a recurring nightmare that his snowblower quits working. I think he was joking, because Robin shovels their walk after it snows.

A while back we worked out a deal. I'm learning to sketch, a first step. Wayne lets me sit in the studio for twenty minutes or half an hour now and then and I sketch from what he has already done, his work with Copper and the unfinished figures and parts on the walls: arms, legs, breasts, hips, faces, sex, and shadows. In exchange for lessons and studio time, I change his oil and wash, sometimes vacuum, his truck. I'm going to run the idea by him of maybe sketching Robin sometime, maybe paint her. If I make it that far. For some Polaroids of Copper I gave Wayne two racks of Heineken.

"Persistence of the New West" he will call his next exhibit, and when he says this he looks a little younger, a little thinner, a little taller. He's even making his own paints with lead and cadmium, toxins from deep in the ground that Wayne says are truer in color and tell a more accurate story. Copper has been posing in cowboy boots and nothing else, Stetsons, lariats; she has posed with little mini-cigars and big Dutch stogies, a fringe leather vest over nothing, a buffalo hide, skis, branding irons, whiskey bottles, Susan B. Anthony dollars, a rawhide whip, nothing, flyfishing vest, chaps.

I have seen them work when Robin says they're in the studio and I walk out not wanting to disturb them and look through the curtain crack in the little foundation window. There is an energy that fills the air and ground of the studio; art and sex, yes, but also, somehow, magic. The mad, naked nude painter, Wayne Kerr. Copper, like art history book prints of Titian's Mary Magdalene looking to the sky in ecstasy, grasps her long hair around naked shoulders, breasts, sex. He puts his Rockies cap on backwards and a thick black-handled brush crossways in his teeth and bites down on it as color rushes and swirls for minutes at a time until the session is over, until he's slick with sweat, the pain is gone, the egg is out, the painting is begun; until the mouth brush is splintered, wet with tobacco spit, used. I've seen it more than once. Then he'll take her, most always from behind like a dog, and they'll scratch and howl and bite and curse, Copper's white breasts turning red with heat, Wayne's hairy waist and gut heaving with in-rut, mythical lust, really driving his back into it. He plays a lot of Mozart now. It's been a long time since Wayne has had one of his landscape-kicking fits.

The UPS driver is a Mormon. Wayne and I are convinced our packages ride around town for a few extra days but what can you do? I'm opening a package of new paints, safe paints, wash-with-water acrylics, and glance out my front window and see Robin walking. I often see her walking, hiking out her frustrations at having her name uttered in the same sentences as mine when the microphones are turned off at school board meetings and in the lounge before the 8:15 bell rings, where a clique of teachers are taking last hits on their Monday morning herb tea. She is frustrated from being looked at by housewives when she's searching—maybe humming a hymn or a folk song—through the cereal aisle, looking for Wayne's Honeycombs.

She takes long, strong strides and stares straight ahead, inhaling, exhaling hard, sweating, her breath trailing behind her, misting her long brown hair until it vaporizes and another puff of breath takes its place. She walks down a stretch of fenced-in yard where a young elkhound is thrilled to be running beside her until the end of his fence where Robin looks at him like she could be party to every dog wish if only that were in the design of things, and for twenty yards or so it is. She walks past the stockyards and rodeo grounds, up the BLM road that leads to the radio towers and relay station on top of Sarpy Ridge. The snow is deep and less sooty up there, well above me. Through my monocular I'll see her trudging through thigh-deep drifts, kicking, slapping at the white with her fists, throwing it, daring the earth to move. The snow dampens her screams of anger—anger because she is under fire for what her husband did and anger because she is not an Indian-riding redhead with big tits and shit for morals—until she gradually disappears into the blackening winter sky. By daylight the wind has wiped clean her tracks, footprints that from down here are only sixteenths of an inch, millimeters apart. Wayne says her mind deals in the concrete and they are concretely married and he still comes home most nights and still puts his dishes in the dishwasher.

Up there maybe there's less chance her prayers get trapped in the inversion of wood and coal smoke that sometimes hangs over the valley. But maybe those prayers blow to Utah. She copes. Robin is from California where they have real earthquakes.

I'm grading some horrid red-pen term papers and watching aerobics, which I can still get on ESPN, and drinking a beer. It's ten o'clock or so now, but I'll skip the news. Women. The knock at the door is Wayne in overalls. Before I answer he mounts the ladder with the new fifteen-millimeter nut he promised me this afternoon and I'm in my living room with the remote control and the window open. I set the control box to Galaxy 4, Channel 17. Fuzz, snow, snow, okay! "That's it!" Three French women have cuffed a no-clothes policeman to the radiator and are smearing him with ice cream and licking it off to some kind of psychedelic Wagnerian fugue, *dow dow dowww, whoka-neeow, whokaneeow.* Wayne tightens up the nut on the antenna, pounds across the metal roof and back down the ladder. I go outside to meet him, to thank him. He's breathing hard and looking through the window at the TV. "You know," he says, "what does this tell you about the state of our nation?"

"This is France," I say.

"That's right. Use your phone?"

Wayne checks in with Robin. I can feel her disappointment on the other end, Wayne's excitement on this end.

"You still with me here, man?" asks Wayne.

"I thought you were going to get some new equipment. From your dad?" I'm stalling for myself, but I know I'm in. Wayne doesn't even hear me. The dogs are running tonight.

This is a problem I seem to always have had: How do I know how much I have? And how do I know when I am losing it? I get up and pull my coveralls on, go out to the truck and we're off. "Hey," says Wayne. "You can hear those UFO freaks from that Albuquerque station on your phone."

We park in the sage on the other side of U.S. 30. The only traffic is an occasional semi, so there is no real effort involved in keeping unseen. It's clear and the moon makes it possible to pick up outlines well without being seen from a distance.

"Look at that honey moon," says Wayne. "Magical." It creates a shadow over everything we do. A bolt cutter makes short work of the lock on the cyclone and barbed wire gate. I muscle the ladder off the truck and drag it to the base of the tower. Wayne fixes a bandana over his face like a nineteenth-century highwayman, turns his cap around, throws a climbing rope over his shoulder and nods at many quarts of paint, the pressure regulator and tanks—twenty pounds of gas in heavy-steel cylinders, three of them—in the rusty truck-bed, nothing lightweight from the Idaho dad. I just get the ladder telescoped and steady and, like that kid on a beer buzz hell-bent to spray his girlfriend's name on the tank, bad-back Wayne is a quarter of the way up, to where the caged ladder starts, before I get to the bottom with the clumsy tanks. Over my breathing I can hear soft pings like hail on aluminum as Wayne takes to the top like a house spider. I look up and can barely make out the WELCOME I've seen a hundred times. Underneath the lettering is Wayne's canvas tonight. He drops me the rope.

My face and fingertips go numb in the sharp midnight cold. The air is thin—another hundred and fifty feet above sea level—and I'm shaky when I get to the top and get the godawful-heavy CO_2 tanks hoisted up with us. Heights are not as intimidating in the softness of moonlight. I look down. Who has not thought about what jumping into shadow would be like, before you have to be pushed, knowing from cold memory what is there in the daylight? Would you pass out in the air from fear? Would you still be alive after landing? Without the conviction to pull it off, these thoughts are pretty harmless. I lock the couplings in, adjust the regulator, and Wayne is in business at fifty psi. "I'm cold," he says. "What took you so long?" But he's been busy painting in his mind, preparing, sweat beading on his high forehead and breath freezing on his beard in the stinging wind, an athlete. His eyes are dark and intent, pen and ink Zeus eyes from junior high textbooks.

I can see the dim reflection on my trailer, across the valley. From here it looks cold and empty, like a beer can in a field, looks like it will blow away and keep blowing and not stop for barbed wire or Nebraska in the western wind. Two windows are lit at the Afghans, yellow and warm like cabin lanterns. Wayne's drafty house. Lights are on, Robin is awake, grading papers, pacing, worrying. Coyotes are singing.

The heavy, old, and leaky Paasche airbrush hisses, a high-pressure serpent in Wayne's hands. His strokes are swift and graceful. He turns his head only to spit over the edge. I watch for police cars and hit him on the back when I see the lights below. We freeze for a moment until the headlights turn away—a bread truck, a mine truck—then he starts in again, blending densities with overspray, caressing with pressure. His painting becomes a mating dance, which has been rehearsed hundreds of times in his mind. I am cold. Wayne gradually strips as he sweats and soon he's down to only dark, holey polypropylene underwear and backward Rockies cap. He pauses, wheezing, only to switch the airbrush tips I retrieve from the rucksack of tools from my back, dump the paint cup, and for me to change colors: True Blue, Grass Green, Spectrum Yellow, Ruby Red. I clean tips and hand the fresh brushes to Wayne like a caddy. It's hard for me to completely make out the painting, but it's coming alive and Wayne slows to work in detail. The half hours grow into hours, history.

"You'll see it when it's light and it's finished," Wayne tells me when I disturb him once to ask what it is. "To tell you now would be to drain my creative energy, to change what I have, risk killing fruition."

"Okay," I say. It is all I say for the next few hours. The painting is coming alive.

The moon has moved across the sky. It's getting lighter out. The hills go from midnight moonlit blue to morning bruise. I see deep concern in his face—not panic—but he picks up his pace. I trust in Wayne, though cheating time is something even Wayne Kerr cannot do.

"That's it," he says, putting his overalls back on. With the finest brush tip I pulled up here, this is what he signs in black letters too small to see from below: w. kerr. I let out the deep part of my breath that I've been holding all night. We double-check everything, drop the tanks on the rope, descend the ladder Wayne-first, and hustle to the truck. Wayne gets there before me, cranks the old V-8 over while I collapse the ladder, strap it to the truck, lift the tanks and rucksack of brushes in. The cab is warm by the time I open the door, the radio is on, Wayne is whistling.

At my trailer we open beers, unfold lawn recliners in the snow on the lane that is my front yard, and wait for sunrise to unveil the night's, the morning's work. "Apollo, get your dead ass over Sarpy Ridge!" yells Wayne that the town below might hear. It's still cold but anticipation is warming so I forget about it. Now it's like I am ice fishing, snow and cold up to my own lounging ass, but without a pole, hole, or bait. Waiting for the picture show. Wayne slips inside for more beer and some old doughnuts.

I take my cordless phone outside to call in sick from my yard so Wayne cannot hear me apologize. The phone rings in my hand like the last straw before I hit the call button. "Hello?" It is the urgent Mormon accent of my principal. "Sorry, I'm sick today," I say. "I can't come in early to meet with you." Over the phone I hear they're having hot dogs and green beans at the high school, church bake sale tonight, cattle prices are steady. "I realize it may be important. Put it on a big pink slip. I'll need a sub." The town council will discuss a pet ordinance, stray dogs. A guy over in Farson took his head off with a snow machine and a barbed wire fence. "Yes, I'm making a doctor's appointment." Convenience store in Green River held up. "Yes, lesson plans are on my desk." Game and Fish will limit deer and elk tags next fall. "(Cough) thank you, good-bye." U.S. 30 to Jackson is slick in spots. Geologists found the fault, hooked their equipment up and named it something I couldn't make out, couldn't hear clearly because of the fuzzy AM reception on this cheap telephone. It sounded like "Bring 'em asphalt," but that isn't it.

The first real daylight to come over the ridge is softened with clouds and light snow. The legs of the tower reach up into the fog and support an ethereal redhead mermaid, an enormous half-trout, tuna-can Copper. Shaking with tired and cold I raise my monocular to her to see the detail. I take a deep breath to steady myself, my vision clears. She is art. Slender, asexual amphibian hips and stiff traffic-pylon nipples. Her fluent hair is the same color as the stripe down her speckled side that makes her a *rainbow* troutwoman.

She is sitting on a rock just underneath WELCOME TO HAMS FORK. Below the rock, in flowing cursive letters: *Gateway to Zion and the GRAND TETONS.* She is holding a trident and smoking a mini-cigar. She is complete.

Hams Fork is waking up. Wives and moms are beating pancake mix, scrambling eggs, not making coffee. An occasional orange mine truck rattles along Antelope Street. A four-wheel-drive with whip antennas and a light bar is spinning up the lane, my front yard. It's Frank Grant, chief of police. Wayne waves with his beerless wedding-band hand. Frank gets out not smiling and adjusts the equipment belt under his belly. "Let's see the hands, Hero," he says. Wayne smiles a doughnutty grin, sets his beer in the snow, swallows, and lays his palms over like a magician. His hands are enameled black, green, Copper-red. My hands are mostly clean and I hold them up like a child counting to ten.

"I'm an artist, Chief," says Wayne, voice full of possibility.

· · ·

In a couple of days photographs of "Wayne's Rainbow" will hang in both bars in town, next to bowling trophies and framed black-and-white photos of rodeo cowboys on bucking horses. Pictures will be shown to me at my contract meeting. On Sunday morning, in both Mormon wards, they will talk about us: me, Copper, Joseph Smith, Robin, Jesus Christ, and Wayne Kerr. Next fall's school calendar is already printed. Copper will apply for a transfer to the city in Texas. She'll get it. She has ridden Hams Fork to exhaustion. Just up and leaving is acceptable, expected in the West.

Robin will keep walking, sweating, and making wind chimes for angels. Looking after Wayne. Loving for him.

I'll get out the atlas I keep in the bathroom with back issues of *Wild West* magazine and a Gideon Bible, though I'm beginning to see that opportunity here runs only so far that way until it turns into California. Tomorrow I will take a Big Chief tablet and a dull number-two pencil into my principal's office, shove them under his gray nose like a divorce, and say, "Excuse me. Put my recommendation here, you no-balls, Diet Coke–drinking, blacklisting, goddamned son of a bitch." And he'll do it. And I will be as alone as I have ever felt.

They will talk prophetically of select revelations, earthquakes, and visions.

Wayne will continue to shake this little town like the ball bearing in a paint can.

But if you could have been around Hams Fork a hundred and fifty years ago, and passed through the landscape as a beaver-trapping tough with Jim Bridger or Jedediah Smith, before coal barons, before Mormons, soda ash, and oil, before you could stand outside and watch satellites pass through the night sky or silhouettes kissing in warm apartment windows, when this history was wild and new, you could have just pointed and named something of permanence, a mountain, a river—at least a creek—after yourself. Or they would have named it for you, just for being here.

It was the least they could do.

Kerry Cohen
University of Oregon

SKIN

I had never before lived anywhere outside my mother's and my small apartment in Tenafly. But the summer I was to turn thirteen, I went upstate to stay with Aunt Lucy and her family. My mother had agreed to go to Florida with a man named John—the first man, she told me, she had felt important with in a long time. The day she left, we shaved my legs for the first time. We sat on the rim of the tub, both of us bent over our knees, moving the razors with slow concentration over our calves.

"Check your ankles," she said. "You don't want to miss them."

I nodded, running my fingertips along the bone to feel for hair. The smoothness of the skin on my leg felt important, like the promise of new beginnings.

Mom was in her nicest summer dress, yellow and sleeveless with tiny white flowers along the trim. Her yellow, open-toed sandals were waiting outside the bathroom door, along with her suitcase and summer handbag, the beige-weave one she saved for special occasions. She said it was important to dress appropriately for each situation. This man, she had told me, was cultured, and noticed such things. I didn't understand what being cultured meant, but I knew it had something to do with little things: a beige-weave handbag, smooth calves, and silent men.

I had met John only twice, once when he had come for dinner, and another time when he had come to pick her up for a date and had waited by the door, his hands in his pockets, till she came out. He was a conductor, and my mother said that he thought she was a talented pianist. I didn't like him at all, his manicured mustache, or the way he ate the cranberry salmon Mom had made in four huge, tidy bites. I didn't like his dark suits, and the fact that he kept the jacket and vest buttoned all the way through dinner. But still, my mother was going with him for three weeks to a nice hotel in West Palm Beach, and I would baby-sit Laura, Aunt Lucy and Uncle Bill's ten-year-old daughter.

We were still in the bathroom when Aunt Lucy pulled up in her station wagon. June had begun, and everything grew lush. Dandelions covered the small patch of grass in front of our building and leaves hugged the trees. My mother wiped her legs with a towel, then handed it to me. She peered out the window of the bathroom to watch Aunt Lucy come up the walk. Aunt Lucy wore a long dress, a sweater tied around her waist. My mother shook her head. "Look at her," she said. "Even in this heat." I stood beside her to watch until Aunt Lucy rang the doorbell.

A few years earlier, when we had gone to visit Aunt Lucy upstate, my mother told me that Aunt Lucy had never gotten a date when she and my mother were girls because Aunt Lucy had spent too much time helping their mother cook and clean, and that Uncle Bill had been my mother's date first until she decided she could do better.

"What's wrong with Uncle Bill?" I asked at the time. We were sitting on the back porch of their house, watching two squirrels chase each other up the trunk of an oak tree. Aunt Lucy and Laura were preparing lunch inside, and Uncle Bill and their son Brett were working on Brett's moped in the front. My mother had told me plenty of other times that she thought Aunt Lucy had settled for mediocrity. "I would never want her life," she said. But Aunt Lucy didn't strike me as unhappy. She seemed content to make the meals and wash the dishes, without splitting these jobs between family members like in my mother's and my home. Aunt Lucy didn't seem to consider this possibility. Her housework was common practice, like brushing her teeth. I had never heard her complain, not in the ways my mother complained. It occurred to me, sitting on the porch that day, that Aunt Lucy could be hiding her sadness, and it bothered me to think that every day so much could go unnoticed.

"Oh, come on, Jory," Mom said. "Look at him. He's a brute. The man thinks the world should bow down in his presence." I sat back in the wicker chair and sipped my iced tea considering this. It was true he was loud, but once, when I had fallen playing on the driveway with Brett, Uncle Bill had sat me on the toilet and used a cotton swab to rub hydrogen peroxide on the cut. Mom saw that I was doubtful and leaned back to let the sun tan her face. "You're just a child now, honey," she said. "You'll see when you're older. You'll want refinement, too."

Now Mom rushed me into the main room where I had put out my duffel bag the night before, and opened the door. She hugged her sister quickly, thanked her, and then pulled me to the side, her hands on my shoulders, her face bent down to mine. It was hot outside, the air heavy and damp, and I felt uncomfortable in my shorts. Up close, I could see the powder on her cheeks, the faint freckles underneath. She smelled strongly of musky cologne, her favorite, and I felt a sudden tightening in my throat.

"Three weeks, pumpkin," she said. She pressed a finger to my nose, then pulled it away. "Are you going to be a good girl?"

I nodded.

"And then I'll come back and we'll have a big birthday party. All your friends can come."

"Okay," I said. I didn't have any friends really, except a boy named Roger who lived down the street. But we only did math homework together, and then he would go home.

She leaned forward and kissed me lightly on the nose and Aunt Lucy put a hand on my shoulder and guided me to her car. Her wagon smelled unfamiliar, of moldy leather. My mother waved, standing on the balcony of our small, brick apartment building, and I waved back until she was only a tiny dot in the distance.

•   •   •

Aunt Lucy lived two hours away in a house set back in the trees, far from any other house. It was large and red, like a barn, and Laura had once told me that they had gotten the house registered as a historical building in their town. The wide lawn was neat and freshly mowed. Our apartment had no private yard, and the long corridor leading up to our front door now seemed bare and confining in comparison to the walk that ran up to theirs, which was lined with purple and yellow irises. In the backyard, I knew, they had an apple tree that Brett and I used to pick from when we played outside.

"Here we are," Aunt Lucy said as she stopped the car in the driveway. She patted my shoulder. Inside, I could hear the low murmur of a television. My mother didn't allow a television in the house. She said it ruined the brain. Instead, we would sit together in the main room and my mother would practice piano while I did my homework. Or, we took walks to get ice cream or just to move our legs.

Aunt Lucy's house was cool from air-conditioning and I felt goose bumps form on my arms. The rug in the entrance had lines from a vacuum. I followed Aunt Lucy to the den. Brett and Laura were sitting together on the couch, Laura's bare feet up near Brett. They both turned their heads to look at me. Brett was two years older than me, in high school by now, and my mother had told me he had a girlfriend at school. He looked different from the last time I had seen him, his face broader and darker, like someone I didn't know. He looked like the boys in upper grades who pushed each other playfully but aggressively in the school halls. One of these boys had reached out and patted my behind in the stairwell and though I had been frightened I found myself watching for him between classes, hopeful.

"Say hello," Aunt Lucy said.

"You're staying in my room," Laura said. She got up and pushed past us. Brett stared at me and I turned away, ashamed, though I didn't know why. "I'll show you."

"Go on upstairs and settle in," Aunt Lucy told me, "and I'll get some lunch started." I followed Laura up the carpeted stairs. Her room was decorated in pink and white with twin beds. Between the beds hung a poster of sad-eyed puppies in a wicker basket. The tape on one corner had peeled, and the poster curved forward a bit. A white dresser stood against the wall, a crowded collection of horse figurines on top. I picked up one horse and rubbed my fingers along the smooth plastic muscles. The complicated lines of its body intrigued me. It held a permanent proud stance. Laura sat on a bed, her dark pigtails bouncing. Beside her sat three stuffed bears, all wearing bows.

"This is my bed," she said, and pointed to the other one. "You can sleep there." I nodded and put my bag on the bed. Out the window I could see Uncle Bill sawing wood. He wore cutoffs and no shirt, and he stopped to wipe his forehead with his forearm, then squinted into the sun. I could see the sweat glistening on his shoulders. I wasn't used to seeing men. My own father had left before I could remember him, but every couple of years he sent a postcard from California. He was remarried now, with two small girls. I had never met them, but I imagined the family sitting by a fireplace, the two girls coloring on the floor. My mother had revealed their names to me, bitterly, after discovering their existence through her lawyer, and I wrote the names down later, along with my father's and his wife's: Gordon, Mary, Sara, Wendy. I still kept the paper locked in the jewelry box under my bed.

Laura, bouncing slightly on her bed, watched me. She pulled one of the bears onto her lap. Laura was small and dark like her mother, her skin the color of tea. She had doughy, childish limbs, the undistinguished body of a doll. We all shared the same large eyes that a boyfriend of my mother's once said made us look like we had questions for him. My mother used to tell me that Laura would be fighting off the boys someday. She said that if I stayed thin, I might too.

"Do you like peanut butter and jelly?" Laura asked. "That's what we're having for lunch."

I shrugged, then opened my bag. I had packed most of my summer clothes and one dress in case I needed to look nice. My mother had bought me my own nail polish, just the right color for my skin, and I had it safely zipped inside a pocket so it wouldn't break. Laura came over to peer inside my bag. "You can keep those in my top drawer," she said. "I cleaned it out."

"Fine," I said. Laura watched as I pulled the clothing out and refolded it before putting it in the drawer.

"How long will you be here?"

"Three weeks," I told her. "Until my mother comes back."

Laura lifted a white blouse from my bag and held it up. Then she folded it and placed it in the drawer. "My mom said your mom wants a job from the man she went to Florida with."

I grabbed the bathing suit she had taken from my bag. "He loves her," I said. "Besides, he thinks she's talented."

Laura sat on the bed, leaning back on her arms. "I wonder what it's like to be loved by a man," she said.

"My mother says it's like nothing else in the world," I told Laura. Once I saw my mother tip back her head and laugh while in John's arms. She was never like that with me. Instead, there was always something that needed to be done, always something not yet right. We spent a lot of time figuring out how to get her a man. We read fashion magazines and paid close attention to the articles on attracting and keeping men. The women in the magazines were sometimes smiling, their gazes fixed on the men who held them close or stood at a distance and assessed. All the other magazine women looked at themselves in mirrors, showing how to apply mascara or lip liner in the correct manner; they never smiled in these pictures.

"I'm going to marry a man with blue eyes and curly hair," Laura said. "He's going to bring me flowers every day."

"You can't know that," I said. I put my bag under the bed I'd be sleeping in. I didn't want Laura to touch my things.

"Why not?"

"Because you can't just decide who's going to love you. You have to work at it."

Laura frowned, her head cocked. "Three boys in my class are in love with me. They signed a card to tell me."

I shook my head and sighed. "You're just a baby," I said. "You don't know anything yet."

That night I lay in Laura's room, unable to fall asleep. I listened to Laura's steady breathing in the next bed. Outside the crickets hummed their soft song. The house was still. I got up, careful not to squeak the bed, and tiptoed into the hallway in my nightshirt. Brett's door was closed and I imagined him inside, the slow rise of his body, muscled like the horse's. I stepped quietly down the stairs and into the entrance, then unbolted the door and walked outside. The air was cool and sweet-smelling, the grass damp against my bare feet. The stars were a million faded pinpoints in the sky. Behind me the house stood silent and dark, disinterested. I lay on the grass and felt the coldness seep through my shirt. When my mother couldn't fall asleep, she would wake me up and urge me to come outside with her to name the stars. We would sit on the balcony, the rest of the world asleep, and identify the shapes we found: a rabbit with one ear, a piece of apple pie, a tree my mother had seen on the West Coast when she was a teenager. Right now she was probably dancing in the hotel lounge, or maybe not. Maybe she was sitting outside just like I was, watching the sparkling sky. I could almost see her, the crease of her skin where her leg bent, her dark hair, frizzy from the pillow.

I remembered the night she came home from a date, sat on my bed, and waited until I woke. She frowned at me, her eyes bloodshot, the moon lightening half her face. Mascara ran beneath her eyes and her shirt was only half buttoned. I sat up in bed, afraid and disoriented. "What's going on?" I asked.

"Promise me," she said, leaning forward to touch my face. Her hand was warm and dry. "You'll never leave me." I nodded and she smiled. She took her hand away and her shirt flipped back to expose half a breast. I looked at the clock; it was two in the morning. "Oh, someday you will," she said. "You'll go off to college or somewhere else and leave your poor mom alone." I looked down. I didn't know what she wanted me to say.

"I'll visit you," I said.

"Yes, but it won't be the same, you know."

"I know." A car rumbled by, its headlights scanning the wall.

"These are special times." She pointed her chin toward my pillow. "Scoot over." I moved aside and she pulled back the covers, exposing my skin to the cool air. Then she settled in, her arm around me. I leaned against her, breathing in her scent. She carried another smell too, something masculine, unfamiliar. I pushed closer against her, but she was already asleep, her eyelids fluttering, lost inside a dream.

Sometime around sunrise, I woke to the patter of Aunt Lucy's feet behind me. I opened my eyes, confused to see the gray-blue sky, the oak trees shaking their leaves. Aunt Lucy whispered my name and helped me up, taking my arm. She rubbed the skin, which was so cold it didn't feel like my own.

"You're alright," she said. "Just a little cold." She put an arm around my shoulders and led me back inside.

We ate breakfast in the kitchen that morning. The sun streamed through the windows. Pancakes, bacon, eggs, and toast. At home Mom and I had one-half cantaloupe each morning with black coffee. Mom believed that a large breakfast slowed you down. I took only a small helping, afraid of what they would think. Laura put four pancakes on her plate and doused them with syrup. Aunt Lucy got up to get everyone more juice.

"So," Uncle Bill said. "What do you and Laura plan on doing today?" He smiled at me, serving himself eggs.

"I don't know," I said. Brett kept his head down as he ate. He was in a T-shirt and sweatpants, his dark hair matted from sleep.

"I'm going to go swimming in the river," Laura said.

"Shut up." Brett looked up. "You are not. You're not allowed."

"Yes, I am. Mom said."

Aunt Lucy poured orange juice into my glass. Her sleeve, light and soft, touched my cheek. "We thought you would like to take Laura to the river, Jory. She's not allowed to go alone."

I nodded, surprised by their restrictions on Laura. My mother had sent me on errands when I was five. She believed children needed to gain a sense of independence. Uncle Bill watched me a moment, waving a fork above his half-eaten eggs. "You don't want to watch over Laura here constantly now, do you?" I raised my eyebrows, and Laura fell back into her seat, the chair scuffing the floor. "No, what you need while you're here is a project," he said. He had a voice that boomed, like a bass drum in an orchestra. He slapped the table for emphasis, and the silverware clattered against everybody's plate. Brett shuffled in his seat, looked out the window. "Every summer I have a project. Last summer it was a new door for the garage. This summer it's a toolshed." Laura kicked at the table leg, again and again.

"Laura," Aunt Lucy said, and Laura leaned back in her chair. She pushed her pancakes around in the syrup.

"How about you help me with that shed?" Uncle Bill said. His face was tanned and thick, and his mustache was graying.

"Sure, I guess," I said. I had never built anything, but I was afraid to refuse him. My mother had told me to never outright refuse a man. It makes them more persistent. Instead, she told me, you praise them, make men feel good. Men like to feel good, she said.

"Usually, I'd ask Brett to help me, but he's not interested in spending time with his dad anymore." Uncle Bill waved his fork. I looked at Brett and he sneered at me. Laura got up and pulled on my arm.

"Let's go," she said.

Aunt Lucy, who was sitting now, smoothed the corners of her place mat. "Let Jory finish her breakfast." I took a small bite of pancake and chewed slowly. Brett stood and started for the doorway.

"I didn't hear you ask if you could be excused," Uncle Bill said. He was talking to Brett, but he looked straight out, as if Brett were still in the chair. Brett stopped, traced his foot along a floor tile.

"What's the big deal?" he said softly.

"What did you say?" Uncle Bill still hadn't turned around, and Brett looked down, his face tensing and reddening.

"Bill," Aunt Lucy said. She placed a hand on his arm and looked at Brett. "You're excused, honey," she said. Brett broke off into a trot, and we all listened until the front door slammed shut. Uncle Bill looked around at the table.

"Does breakfast usually include coffee?" he said. "Or would that be asking too much?"

Aunt Lucy stood and opened the cupboard. She pulled down a can of Folgers and fumbled with the filters.

"How come Brett gets to go?" Laura said. We were all quiet.

"Brett's older," Aunt Lucy said. She reached behind the toaster to plug in the coffee machine. "He can take care of himself."

"Next summer that boy's going to find himself a job," Uncle Bill said.

Aunt Lucy took Uncle Bill's plate, wiping toast crumbs from his place mat with her other hand. "Oh, well," she said, and smiled at me. "Jory doesn't need to hear our little discussions." I looked down at my lap. The sun made a rectangle near my foot. I missed my apartment, the sound of my mother's shower—which she always let run awhile before she got in. We ate our breakfast quietly, reading sections from the newspaper or simply not talking, listening to the cars roar by. Mom liked to call me her little lady, but right now I felt very small, a child.

"Come on," Laura said. I set my fork gently on the plate and stood. I thanked them for breakfast, and followed Laura out the door.

The trail to the river was thick with leaves and roots, and I kept my eyes on the ground so as not to trip. Laura ran ahead of me, the leaves crunching under her sneakers. I held a book from my summer reading list against my chest. Next fall I would be in the eighth grade, and then I would go to high school. I saw my life as logical steps forward. My mother had been right that night she came into my bedroom after her date. It wouldn't be that long really before I left Tenafly and found a career, maybe got married and had children. Sometimes I thought about going to California and finding my father.

No one else was at the swimming hole. A long rope hung from a tree and Laura began peeling off her clothes. I sat on a rock and rolled my sleeves so that my shoulders would get sun.

"Come in with me," Laura said.

"I don't feel like it." Laura shrugged and jumped. The splash sprinkled onto the rocks. I lay back and started reading, but my eyes felt awfully tired and after a bit I closed them and listened to Laura in the water. The sun felt good on my face, like a warm hand. The summer before, Mom and I had gone to the public pool every Saturday. She bought us both Diet 7UPs and we sipped them through straws so as not to smudge the sunscreen on our lips. She bought me a bikini halfway through the year. I wasn't quite twelve, and just that spring I had begun to feel an achiness in my breasts. Cold water made my nipples sore. Mom told me I was an early bloomer, like her, that I should show it off while I could. She said she couldn't wear bikinis anymore. But I didn't want to wear a bikini at the public pool. Girls from the upper grades were there, and only the ones who already had boyfriends wore bikinis. I was embarrassed, afraid of what they might think. Mom pouted until I tried it on for her, and we stood together, looking in the full-length mirror on the back of the bathroom door. She squeezed my waist, making me jump, then lifted my tiny breasts with her palms.

"Mom," I had said, pulling myself away.

"What?" She smiled at me. She was proud. "Can I help it if you have a cute little bod?"

That day I wore the suit to the pool, but lots of people were there, and I wouldn't take my T-shirt off. Mom told me I was being selfish, that I was ungrateful after she had bought me such a nice present. The bikini was supposed to make me feel good. Then she wouldn't talk to me for most of the day. She lay back, her eyes closed, and I sat cross-legged on the lounge chair and watched the way the water split the sun. Water was dripping on me now, and I opened my eyes to see Laura standing above me.

"Hey," I said. I rubbed my eyes to focus. "What's the matter?"

Laura stared down at me. She squeezed her hair and water dripped onto the rocks. "You're not like most girls I know," she said. She waited, watching me.

"So?" I lay back and closed my eyes.

"My mom says that your mom doesn't let you do anything with your friends. She says your mom always wants you to stay with her."

"That's not true," I said. I held on to my shoulders which were warm from the sun. "I do lots of things with my friends."

"My mom says you barely have any friends."

"Your mom doesn't know anything," I said, feeling hurt. I sat up to look at her. "Besides," I said. "You're the one with no friends. You needed me to go swimming with you."

Laura bit her lip. "I have friends," she said.

"Oh, yeah?" I leaned toward her. "Where are they then? Your so-called friends are probably having fun without you right now. They're probably making fun of you." I pressed my finger into her fleshy arm for punctuation.

Laura looked down. Her lip trembled. "I want to go home now," she said.

"Tough. I want to stay." I lay back again and closed my eyes. I heard Laura settle beside me, a wet strand of her hair touching my arm.

· · ·

A few nights later, Mom called. I was in Laura's room, reading my book, and Aunt Lucy called to me from the bottom of the stairs. I ran down and picked up the phone from the counter, trying to catch my breath.

"How are you, pumpkin?" She sounded far away. There was static on the line.

"I'm fine," I said.

"Is Aunt Lucy treating you nice?"

"Yes." Outside it was already dark. I could hear frogs in the grass somewhere. Aunt Lucy was washing dishes in the next room.

"You wouldn't believe how beautiful it is here," Mom said. "It's like paradise."

"Are you coming back soon?" I asked.

"I'll be here for a few more weeks." I heard a door close on her end of the line. "You know that."

"I know."

"Are you having fun with everyone?"

"I guess."

"I love you, pumpkin. Give everyone kisses for me."

"Okay," I said, and hung up the phone. I stood in the hallway a moment, watching the dark outline of the trees. Aunt Lucy walked out from the kitchen, wiping her hands on a towel.

"How is she?" she asked.

I shrugged. "She's alright."

Aunt Lucy nodded, then she put a hand on my arm. "I could use some help making a pie." We went into the kitchen. Aunt Lucy pulled out flour and brown sugar, butter and vanilla extract. She piled measuring cups and metal bowls on the counter. Standing side by side, we measured out the ingredients. I stayed quiet, unsure what Aunt Lucy was thinking. I didn't want to believe that she had really said those things to Laura.

"Your mother," Aunt Lucy said. "She's one of a kind." She passed me the sifter for the flour, then began mixing the eggs. Butter melted slowly on a burner.

"You don't like her, do you?" I said carefully.

"She's my sister, honey. I love your mother." She beat the eggs, her expression serious. "We have our differences, that's for sure. When we were girls she used to get so mad at our mother for everything. She used to come home from school and start yelling about the way Mom did things. You know, too much this, too little that."

I looked up at Aunt Lucy. This close I could see lines in her pale cheeks. Her skin was loose and tired looking, unlike my mother's. "What did Grandma do?" I asked.

"Nothing. None of us knew what to say to your mother. Sure, we would defend ourselves a little. But, really, we didn't know what it was she wanted from us." Aunt Lucy looked into the bowl, mixing and mixing in circles. She sighed. "She loved Daddy, though. Whatever he did, she just thought he was the cat's pajamas."

"Grandpa?" I looked up at her, wiping an itch off my nose with my sleeve. Grandpa lived in a home now. He had a nurse who changed his bed pan and massaged his skin to keep his circulation up. The last time Mom had made me visit him, he looked past me with milky eyes. Mom started crying before we even got past the door to his room, and she had to go into the waiting room, where Grandpa's nurse rubbed her back and handed her tissues. I stood in the doorway, smelling the rotten odor of old age. I had a faint memory of watching Grandpa through the iron barred fence at Rockefeller Center when I was very young. He and my mother skated beneath the bright, wintry lights, one of his hands lightly touching my mother's elbow to lead. He had been graceful, and it seemed impossible that this was the same man, gaunt and immobile in his bed. I went to the bathroom and waited a moment before I went back to my mother so that she wouldn't know that I hadn't gone inside his room. In the bathroom I tried to find the image of Grandpa skating again, and it occurred to me that I had felt lonely there, standing behind the bars.

"Oh, yes," Aunt Lucy said now, smiling. "Grandpa was quite a distinguished fellow in his day. A real go-getter. People looked up to him." She looked out the window, as if he were right outside. "Your Mom wanted to be just like him. She used to follow him around the house and sit with him in his study while he read. He called her his princess. She cried when he didn't let her come on his evening outings. So often, in fact, he finally gave in and brought her along. God knows what he did with her. He was going to see his mistress more often than not."

"Grandpa had a mistress?" I asked. She sat across from me and cracked an egg into a bowl. We both watched it slide down the side, the yolk broken.

"Her name was Emma, a wisp of a woman. I saw her twice, once by mistake, walking by a café window. She was having lunch with him. The other time he introduced her at a company Christmas party. He acted as if she were just an old friend, but I saw he held a palm to her waist, thinking we wouldn't notice, or not caring if we did." Aunt Lucy's voice turned hard. She beat at the egg, her forehead tight with wrinkles.

"Grandma let him do it?" I asked softly.

"She didn't feel strong enough to leave him, honey. We were dependent on him, you know, financially. She didn't know how she would take care of us if she did. What could she do?" She looked up at me. I was unsure what she wanted me to say.

Aunt Lucy went back to beating the egg. "She endured it for seventeen years. And your mother was so angry at Grandma for not gathering the strength to change things." She sighed and stood to get the melted butter, which she poured into the eggs. "Your mother," she said. Right before Grandma died my mother refused to visit her and wouldn't let me go with Aunt Lucy. She said Grandma liked to make her feel like a failure, that she criticized her for everything, including the way I was growing up. I remembered Grandma as a heavy woman who constantly got up to make sure everyone was comfortable. In the kitchen she had an enormous glass bottle with a tiny opening at the top. The bottle was full of pennies, and I used to wonder how she would get them out. Grandma had baby-sat me once, when I was still too small to stay alone. I remembered little except that my mother hadn't returned when she was supposed to, and Grandma had been frantic. She walked the long hallway, back and forth, her strange, manly shoes clunking against the floor. I cried, but Grandma ignored me and picked up the phone. She yelled at me to be quiet so that she could call the police. I stayed very still after that, convinced that my silence would bring my mother home. When she did arrive, sometime after dawn, I was asleep on the couch, my head on Grandma's lap. I woke when Grandma lifted my head. After setting it back down she walked out the door, past my mother, without a word.

"Why did you say those things about my mother?" I said to Aunt Lucy, looking down. The flour looked soft and light as an angel.

"Oh, honey," she said. She stopped beating. "I can only imagine what Laura's been overhearing in the last few weeks. I never should have opened my mouth. I'm just upset with her, I guess. For always putting herself first. But who am I to judge?" She stood to close the blinds, then leaned across the table to wipe spilled flour into her hand.

"It's not the worst thing to do," I said. I looked into the metal bowl. The flour was a feathery pile. Without warning, a pressure rose inside my throat, and tears came to my eyes. I didn't want to be angry at my mother, because somehow, if I was angry, she would never come back. Aunt Lucy reached across the table and touched my hand. Sun moved from behind a cloud and sent a ray of light onto the kitchen floor. The clock on the oven flipped to the next minute. I didn't have to say anymore, the hand said. She knew as well as I.

Most mornings I put on my bathing suit and lay in the backyard on a towel. I closed my eyes and let the day drift past, brushing flies from my legs, applying more oil. Laura sometimes came outside and wanted to lie next to me. I told her to go play elsewhere, but she said she could tan too if she wanted, so I let her set a towel beside me if she promised not to talk.

Some mornings while I tanned, I saw Brett watching me from his window. I pretended not to notice, but bent one leg so that my thighs wouldn't spread fat on the ground. I liked to have him watching. I was the only girl in the area, and I felt important that way, grown up. I thought, maybe he loves me, and lying in the sun I imagined ways he might tell me—sneaking into Laura's room at night, pulling me aside in the hallways, leaving me a note in my book. I imagined him kissing me, his full mouth, the hair that grew on his upper lip. But once inside the house, everything went back to normal. We passed quietly in the halls, him turning a bit so as not to touch me, barely a nod exchanged.

Late afternoons and weekends, beneath the shade of a tree, Uncle Bill and I sketched out our plans for the shed. I was better at drawing than he was, so he spoke while I sketched, marking lines with measurements. We taped the sketches to the side of the house, above the sawhorse and wood, and began to nail together the boards for the shed. We worked in silence, the hammers echoing against the rest of the world. There were no other sounds for a long way, except for the robins and an occasional woodpecker tapping against a pine. I had never done physical work before and I liked it, the repetitive movements, the rhythmic sounds. I liked that it stopped me from thinking. I got tired of the way my mind usually moved up and down and in circles: There was always something I should be doing or improving or thinking further about. With the shed, there were tangible ways to make improvements. There were answers. We sawed, nailed, fit board against board, and slowly the shed materialized, standing on its own. For the first time I felt that I was creating something that made sense. Uncle Bill spoke only when necessary, to ask me to hand him a longer nail or the hammer.

"You're as smart as a boy," he told me one day. His neck was red, like a rash. I wiped back the hair that had fallen from my ponytail.

"My mom says that girls are smarter than boys." I peeked at him. He watched the hammer as he tapped, his forearm muscles broadening and contracting as he squeezed and released.

"She would say that." He laughed, a booming sound. A red-breasted robin dropped beside us and picked at the ground, looking for something. He smiled at me, his mustache spotted with sweat droplets. "You're not much like your mom, are you?"

"I don't know," I said. I watched the robin bob up and down, its red breast winking.

"No," he said. "Your mother would never be out here working."

"Maybe she would," I said, though I knew what he said was true.

"She's still your mother," he said. "I know." The sun disappeared behind a cloud and I felt the wetness beneath my arms begin to cool.

"She plays piano better than anyone."

"Hey," he said. "Calm down now. I was just kidding around." I looked down, went back to sawing, falling into the rhythm. I could feel my heart slowing to meet the strokes. I felt ashamed. He was right, of course. My mother would never do physical labor. She always called on men to do this sort of work. It was too brainless for her to bother to learn. She had more important things to think about. From the corner of my eye, I saw the robin flutter into the air.

Just before the end of three weeks, my mother called again. When I heard the phone ring I ran in from the yard. Her voice was thin and unfamiliar, and she told me she wouldn't be coming back just yet. Outside I could see Laura running back and forth, chasing a butterfly with open hands. The shed was done, set up against the side of the house. I could see the plans I had drafted, like sign boards above the shed.

"Why aren't you coming back?" I asked my mother. I looked down at my knees, which were darker than the rest of my legs. The carpet was soft and cool beneath my feet.

"John has me playing in a symphony here, honey. Isn't that great?"

"Great," I said.

"You know," she said, "not every mom can do something so well."

"I know that."

"You should be proud of your mom," she said.

"I want to go home," I said quietly.

"Oh, now," she said. "Where's my grown-up girl? Soon you'll be a thirteen-year-old young woman, you know. You better start behaving like one."

Laura was sitting on my towel, rubbing my oil on her arms. It made me angry to see her using my things like that.

"Aren't you having a nice time?" my mother said. "Spending time with your cousins?"

"No." I looked down at my feet, a strand of hair falling into my face.

"You sure know how to ruin a good time for your mom, don't you?" Her voice lowered.

"No," I said.

"Maybe we'll talk again when you're feeling a little more grown up."

"Fine," I said, and we both hung up.

I stepped back into the heat. Laura was lying back, her leg bouncing to a song she was humming. "Get off my towel," I said. She stood, cocking her head at me. I put on my T-shirt and sneakers and gathered the towel and oil into my arms.

"Where are you going?" Laura asked. I strode over the grass, past the shed and toward the road, the sun burning into my scalp. Laura ran behind me, her footsteps pattering on the ground. "Can I come?" she called out.

"No." The gravel crunched beneath my feet.

"Why not?" Laura had caught up now, and she trotted beside me to keep up.

"Go away, Laura," I said.

"You have to watch me, though," she said. I stopped and struck her hard on the arm. The slap was loud and I could feel the sting on my palm. She looked at me, her eyes wide. Then she started crying.

"Go home," I said. I dropped the towel and oil and took off down the road, nearly running, until I reached an intersection. I turned onto that street, knowing I would get myself lost, but not caring, not caring one bit. A pickup truck rumbled behind me, and when I turned to look, it slowed down, moving alongside me. A large man in a baseball cap and no shirt rested his arm in the window. He smiled through dark stubble. The wheels kicked up dust, and I felt a drop of sweat roll from beneath my breast. I remembered that I had no shorts on, only a bathing suit and T-shirt. Suddenly I felt tired.

"Hey there, sweetheart," he said. "Do you need some help?"

I shook my head and sped up a bit, trying not to look.

"Don't be afraid," he said. "No one's going to hurt you. You look lost." I heard music from his truck, heavy metal, screaming men, the kind of music my mother hated. She said that no one knew what music was anymore. Everyone was so unrefined. Her words were weighty little stones inside my head. I stopped and stood a few yards from his door. "Come on," he said. "Hop in." I looked down at my sneakers for a moment. They were covered with dust from the road. Then I walked around his truck. Spurts of gray smoke puffed out of the back like a secret code. The door squeaked when I opened it, and I lifted myself onto the seat. I was high up, sturdy. It felt good to have something so firm beneath my weight. The seats were vinyl and warm from the sun, and the cab smelled strongly of cigarettes and exhaust. My heart was beating like a hammer against my chest.

The man pulled away from the side of the road. His jeans were yellowed, and I watched as his thigh muscles jumped when he shifted gears. "So," he said. "Where to?"

"Turn around," I answered. My voice sounded squeaky, not my own.

He did a slow three-point turn, and then we were facing the other way.

"What's your name?" He turned to look at me, and I smiled, the blood hot in my face.

"Jory," I said.

"How old are you, Jory?"

"Sixteen."

He nodded, and I pointed for him to turn onto Aunt Lucy's road. The radio announcer came on to report the temperature. Ninety-five degrees.

"Sure is hot," he said.

"Yes," I said. He smiled again. He had tiny freckles scattered across his shoulders, like my mother. His skin glistened, damp with perspiration.

"You from around here? How come I've never seen you before?"

"We just moved here," I told him. "My mother and father and older brother. We just moved here from the city."

"A city girl," he said, and laughed. "I like that."

I swallowed and pressed a palm against my thigh. It was clammy and cool. He leaned forward to look at my face. We slowed down a little.

"Hey," he said. "Hey. You have no reason to be nervous. We're just talking now. That's all."

"Okay," I said. I watched as we passed Aunt Lucy's house. The shed in the front yard looked small and silly. I imagined the family inside the house, carrying out their lives like any other day.

"Mind if I smoke?" he said. I shook my head, watching as he lit the cigarette from the car lighter, his cheeks puffing in and out. His stomach bulged slightly at the waist. I saw perspiration where his skin met the jeans. A breeze came through the window and touched my face gently, then was gone. I felt light, my stomach a balloon. Fright passed through me like cold water and I lifted my legs off the seat to keep them from spreading. The vinyl peeled away like another skin.

"This is it here," I said. There was a driveway, and at the end I could see a small white house. The gray mailbox said, "Wilson."

"You sure?" he said. I nodded. Then I pressed up against the door and waited. A crow called loudly from above. "So can I see you again?" He leaned over, trying to look at my face.

"Maybe," I said. There was a cellophane wrapper on the floor of his truck, and I pushed it back and forth with my sneaker.

"Can I kiss you then?" he asked.

I took a deep breath and turned my face toward him. "Okay," I said, and he leaned forward and pressed his open lips against mine. His tongue moved inside my mouth like a fish. I tasted cigarettes. He took my hand and put it to his crotch, which was hard and very warm through his jeans. I pulled my hand away and opened the truck door. "Thank you for the ride," I said. I slammed the door and ran up the driveway of the house. He was calling my name, but I kept running, and as soon as I heard the truck pull away I hid behind a tree and tried to slow my breathing. When he was gone I began the long walk back to Aunt Lucy's house, ducking into the woods every time I heard a car on the road.

When I arrived, I saw Aunt Lucy's and Laura's figures in the kitchen window. They were working on something together, their heads bent over the kitchen table. My towel was still in the yard where I had dropped it. We were all expecting that I would leave that weekend. Aunt Lucy had made cookies for me to take back to Tenafly. I knew I could not go back inside yet, to Laura's reddened arm, Aunt Lucy's warm, understanding eyes. Instead, I went to the shed and touched the new door we had just hinged. We had celebrated the completion with lemonade, and Uncle Bill told me that I was a natural, that we should paint my name above the door to honor my hard work. I reached to touch the cool, rough wood. The robins sang their farewell chorus before they disappeared for the night. A car roared past, kicking up stones. Laura had probably told on me, and I still smelled of cigarettes and exhaust from the truck, but I felt strangely calm and untouched, as if I were someone else. My sketches were taped above the shed, like paintings hung in a house. Carefully, so they wouldn't rip, I peeled them off and tucked them under my shirt.

The following day I turned thirteen. Aunt Lucy set up the barbecue in the backyard and we sat around the picnic table while Uncle Bill cooked hamburgers. They gave me two presents: a Scrabble set from Uncle Bill and Aunt Lucy and a book on horses from Brett and Laura. After dinner Aunt Lucy brought out a chocolate cake that had a teddy bear drawn in white frosting and said "Happy Birthday Jory" around the edge. I thanked them, taking only a small piece. Then the phone rang, and Laura jumped up to get it. After a few minutes, she yelled that it was my mother, and I went in and took the phone from her hand.

"Happy birthday, pumpkin," she said. She was cheery. She seemed to have forgotten about our last talk.

"Thank you," I said.

"Did Aunt Lucy do something nice for you?"

"Yes."

"It won't be that much longer, you know. Maybe another week or so."

"Alright," I said.

"And I got a present for you. Something you'll really like."

"Okay."

"I love you, honey," she said. "Do you love your mom?"

"Sure," I said, and then we hung up. Out the window, I watched Aunt Lucy slicing Laura another piece. Brett had already left, after the hamburgers, to watch a game at his friend's house. If Aunt Lucy knew anything about the man, she didn't say, and she had not mentioned Laura's arm. Instead, she had told me that I was no longer responsible for Laura. The contract was only for three weeks, she said. She acted careful with me now. Laura avoided me, and when I was near she hung close to her mother.

The second week of August, my mother came to get me. She had been gone for a month and a week. Things had fallen apart between her and John, and though she had arrived from the airport the night before she had been too tired to drive into the country. She had spent the night in our apartment. I was in Laura's room, sitting on the bed with my packed duffel beside me, when I heard the sound of her Peugeot in the driveway. Rocks snapped beneath the tires and she cut the engine. A woodpecker clicked outside.

I heard Aunt Lucy open the door, and then Mom's voice, and I took my duffel and walked slowly down the stairs.

"There she is," my mother said when she saw me. She was tan and wearing a long white dress. Her hair was newly permanented into waves. She hugged me and I smelled her cologne, felt the familiar warmth of her chest. "Let me see you," she said, holding me out from her body. She smiled with hope at me, searching my eyes, waiting, but I had nothing to say.

"Welcome back," I said. Then we went into the kitchen where Aunt Lucy had made fresh lemonade. Laura jumped up on my mother's lap and my mother nuzzled her face into Laura's hair.

"I hope Jory wasn't any trouble," she said.

"Oh, no," Aunt Lucy said. "She's been a perfect guest." She reached over and patted my leg. "We had fun, didn't we?" I smiled. "What about you?" she said to my mother. "How was Florida?"

"Oh, well." My mother took a dainty sip of lemonade. She liked to act humble, like she didn't deserve the attention. "I played a lot while we were there. Nothing too special."

"You said it was a symphony," I said, watching my fingers as I wiped sweat from my glass. "You seemed to think it was special before." My mother glared at me, surprised, and Aunt Lucy straightened her place mat, smoothing each corner.

"Well, sure," my mother said. "It was certainly an opportunity. It was nice." She combed her fingers through Laura's hair, pulling it back from her eyes.

"Good," Aunt Lucy said. "That sounds good." I looked back and forth between them. As much as I had seen them together, it still surprised me how distanced they were from each other, like strangers. We were all quiet a moment, watching Brett send a Frisbee across the lawn. I knew later, in our apartment, my mother would cry to me about John, crawl into my bed and tell me the story of how they got together and how things slowly went wrong. My hands felt heavy in my lap.

"Well, I guess we should go," my mother said. "We've got a long drive." We stood up. Aunt Lucy hugged me, then Laura did. On the way to the car I waved to Brett. He waved, then went back to his game. My mother and I got into the car. She put on her sunglasses and pulled slowly out of the long driveway. She had her window cracked, not wide enough to muss her hair. We were quiet, like strangers on a blind date. My eyes passed over the shed, but I didn't tell my mother that I had built it. Now, as I inhaled the smells of my mother—her cologne, the sharp, menthol smell of her Peugeot—the shed seemed tiny and ridiculous. A house for no one.

"Well?" my mother said. She put a hand on my knee. It was dry and warm. "Here we are again." She smiled, watching me.

"Watch the road," I said. "You'll get us killed."

"Well," she said, turning away. She took her hand from my knee. "I guess you didn't miss your mom." I didn't say anything, watching the thick trees beside the road. We passed the Wilson house where I had been kissed for the first time by a man. I wondered if he thought about me, or if I was already a fading image in his mind, evaporating from memory.

"I guess you didn't," my mother said again. I pressed my fingers into the seat, squinting against the bright sun.

"I did," I said, to quiet her. I lifted my hand and looked down at the indentations, five small holes in the skin of the seat.

Catherine Li-Ming Seto
University of Michigan

FIRST GRADE

Joko, my older brother, was the one who'd always eat the steel wool sea urchin and *tou fat,* pubic hair (really seaweed), Ma cooked for us. He was nibbling her stardust fish on an ordinary school night, rubbing his big belly. Its remains went around the dinner table on a cobalt heirloom plate—I was exactly six then, and I remember how much I feared the carcass that was being torn apart before my eyes. The fish looked disgusting. The lips of its mucous head smooched at me. I watched it race, that fish, passing over hungry hands, being snapped up by the sterling tips of chopsticks until nothing was left but a white cage. Everyone's mouth was wiggling, everyone was working a bone. My parents always liked how Joko grew and grew. He could outshow Ma's friends' kids, who pitched fits and wouldn't eat dim sum. It killed me to think I could never eat enough for her. If I had known all the events of that year, I might not have reached over and somehow fit the head of the fish into my mouth. At first it was too sour, then too fresh; I was thinking I could feel the gill slits—I leaned close to Joko and I spewed it out between his eyeballs.

"Think that's smart, eh?" Ma said. "Spitting on your brother— what are you hoping for?"

"Dunno."

"Smart mouth too. *Saw tzai,* crazy little boy." She pinched me on the ear. "Food's not for wasting and a smart mouth will shame your ancestors, isn't that right, Father?"

"That's right," my dad muttered. His face returned to the rice bowl, hidden as always.

I honestly didn't know what I hoped for. It wasn't that I wanted to upset the routine. I was the one who got dragged off by Ma, my hands hooked on the weave of the lace, lifting the tablecloth with slow webs forming—me, the little brother, feeling magical, above my fat brother who ate around the fatty rings of a salt pork, contemplating the rings, then eating them anyway. She shut me in my room overlooking the Toronto Harbour through the biggest window of the entire apartment high-rise. The window happened to be the circle at the very top, the giant cathedral eyeball that kamikaze pilots would crash through in times of nuclear war. I stood watching the turning sky through the window, the darkening of the waters which I knew would soon be black, ominous. First grade was the year I deliberated about death and samurai. The slipping I felt, of the lights going out and my panic—my chest rose, fell, rushed through without hindsight, like a bird's heart swept through a forest. My fire trucks were very red, sitting there in the corner, drowned in carpet. For the first time, in that room, I thought to sleep forever. A five-second dream about a dream that never ended, and Joko and Ma and Pop standing on the other side of a wall. *This is death, right, this is death?*

Ma woke me up in the middle of the night. She was in her thin robe and she put something under my nose, Lucky Charms in milk and a *bao,* sweet bun. Even through the night-light I could see her Concord grape lids cast on me. Pop was always real important to her—she never took her makeup off, not even in the night. Ma was beautiful to me, even when she was angry, but then she became more of a wicked beauty, a Disney witch that I could never despise. I waited for a sigh, the smell of her half minty, mildew breath. I was sure she had found Joko's Blue Jays baseball that I rubbed Magic Marker all over. Fear worked up my face in a series of pins. But she just sat at the edge of my bed and waited for me to finish. I couldn't finish. I looked at the sweet bun and it looked too huge for words, puffy, hot and sticky. The cereal had turned to mush, the way tissue paper was in water, how I'd seen it stop up drains. If it went into my stomach it'd clog me up just the same, and I would die. I believed that if I didn't die, I'd throw up in class first thing in the morning and Mrs. Jenkins would haul me down the corridors and into the clinic. The janitor would be paged and he'd come and throw that peppermint sawdust over my desk and the rest of the day would smell like burnt rubber with candy cane.

"I'll eat this now," I said, "if I don't have to eat later."

"You'll eat this now, and later."

"Please, Mom!" I pushed the tray away, I was crying. "I'm going to die."

"*Mo Cho!* You shut your mouth—your grandfather would carve your head off if he heard you, *bot yeem!*" she called at me.

Bot yeem really means *up to no good*. Of course, it could also mean *eight salts*, which was how I interpreted it—the same way I had it in my head that what Ma called going to a meeting, *houy wouy*, was "turning walnuts." I saw Ma and Father getting dressed up in the evenings with their briefcases and going into an auditorium where people took turns turning a seven-foot walnut. I was crying so hard by then, nothing mattered—I thought I was a demon child to be labeled something as strange as eight salts. It was the quantity of it, not one but *eight* salts, one of those big words she'd saved up for the really bad times.

If it was soccer in gym class, I never threw up. Luckily, Ma didn't know it the next morning and let me skip the rice porridge. Joko left early because the trend was for fifth graders to walk and take the city bus. I got picked up by my carpool: Soo and her mom, Gina, and her older sister Adabel.

"Girls are just like boys," Soo whispered to me. "Ghosts are all the same. They're all like Lord Jesus."

I laughed in her face, then my face grew slack when she flashed me to prove it. I saw what was between her shirt and I realized she was right, girls didn't really have boobs, they were flat as pancakes.

"You're going to hell for that."

"You shut up." Her face lost color. Soo and Adabel were in the second grade and were into eight balls, Ouijas, talking to the dead, and bringing their dead green parakeet in for show-and-tell. Adabel leaned back and lifted the shoe box lid to reveal the parakeet all corseted in tissue paper, the feathers pressed flat to its skull. When we got dropped off, I grabbed the shoe box from Adabel and played tambourine with it, feeling the parakeet rattle inside. What I hoped for was the head beaten off, or the leg bent sideways, but Adabel had preserved it like a mummy, tissue paper intact.

Life was easy guarding the goalie net. I knew exactly what I had to do. It was an equation, but better, because I understood it. It was instinctive to dream about smacking the milky, wood floor when I leapt, and dream about jumping back up when I fell. This was where I felt I could live forever, framed in the light metal brackets, caught like a perch, wrestling around in those silky nets. I could move around slow, because those girls kicked all crooked, getting between the ball and getting scuffed on the shins, Mr. Lockwood calling time-out over their wails. My only hole was Gina Wang, the girl in my carpool. I had to keep my distance because we were the only ones in the first grade who had the same hair: Asian glossy like Barbie's, almost synthetic, blacker than hell. For Lunar New Year, our kindergarten teacher had made us stand together and give a report, and from then on, everyone claimed we were in love. Whenever she kicked the ball, I had to act disgusted, and the crunching up of my face made me nervous and I let the ball slip by. Once in a while, someone like Tim or Ravi would kick a swift one; those were the ones I waited for, my stomach like steel, you could stick three million fried steaks down my throat and I'd still be blocking those balls. It was always an amazing feeling to open my eyes and find my body shaped to that ball, hugging it tight to the ground. A dark hush would ensue, over too quickly, and then I'd get congratulatory cheers from Team A. It was hard to let go of that ball. Too much like love, as Ma always explained it: the way the human body is cratered for give and take.

We lined up by the door. I was flushed on the forehead and down the arms and I had decided my duty in life was that of a professional goalie. I thought I could wait until next Wednesday, and then I thought I couldn't, but one thing was for sure—when soccer day rolled around, there was no holding back, the ball up her ass if Gina was in the way again. It was the beginning of my next obsession—I'd soon crave the accessories of soccer: bright numbered jerseys, the striped cleats, and the knee-highs rimmed in red. In the gym line, I could feel my heart beat, and it told me to be fast, to move quickly, think deep. We passed the glass showcase where the best of the best of construction paper pirate masks made by the fifth graders were displayed. *To ever be that good,* I thought, *it's a dream.*

"The B Team's the best. We got Ravi, and we got Timmy." It was Missy, the popular one that everyone had a crush on. One of those peculiar rise-to-the-top situations, because she wasn't blonde with saucer eyes, but freckled, and pudgy around the legs.

"No way." The class rounded the corner, past the girls' bathroom, the doors leading outside to the playground that was drenched with sun.

"I'm smarter than you, so I know," Missy boasted through ugly baby teeth.

"I'm better at gym than you are." I arched my back, while jutting my head forward at the same time. "Next week I'm going to kick that ball really hard at you."

"You can't," she said. "Next week we're not playing soccer anymore."

"No, no, no," I corrected. "That's not what Mr. Lockwood said."

But I remembered, and my chest tightened. We were playing lame things, like DuckDuckGoose, and Parachute. We walked onto the carpeted part of the halls, passing the fourth-grade rooms, then the third-grade rooms, and I grew nauseous at the thought of no soccer. *Oh, no, I'm in trouble.* I saw my brother bent at the drinking fountain, his arms wrapped around the metal.

Crackbutt! Someone said. Crackbutt, crackbutt!

Joko didn't turn his head, his thumb was on the button and I knew he'd stopped drinking, letting the water arc onto the floor. I thought he looked pathetic, and I ignored him, blanking my mind, a warm white like a projector screen. Missy stood with her feet apart, laughing until everybody got the message that they should be laughing, that it was okay, that if they did, then they were on the same road to something. Without soccer I was in trouble, this much I knew, because even in that moment, I felt my chest shrinking again, and the largeness of everything tensing to a pinhole. Missy's name for Joko was Fried Rice Fatso. Where was Mrs. Jenkins, why wasn't the line moving? She had poked her head into Mr. Taylor's classroom and all I could see was her shapeless hip wrapped in a long skirt. Missy stood with Ravi and she was daring him to do something, maybe run across the hall and mash Joko's face into the spigot.

"Watch this, guys!" My voice was high, desperate. "I'll show you something."

I ran over to Missy and grabbed the elastic of her pants and pulled them down, *all the way down*. She wasn't human looking, standing there with so much exposed flesh, one sheet of color at the bottom half. This was not the Missy we all loved and knew. She didn't pull them up, she held her hands over her face and cried, and my heart was stricken with terror—no one would laugh now.

One glimpse at Missy and I believed this world too huge for words, Soo knew nothing about boys and girls, and adults held worldly knowledge, they knew things, and I believed my Ma: this was absolutely the worst thing I had done in my life. I was beyond the darkness feeling, I was heavier. Ma came right up onto the curb in her Cadillac and Mrs. Jenkins had me by the hand, jerking me down the sidewalk and I wanted so badly to be free of school, I tumbled head first into the navy leather seats and just lay there. My knees were on the floor and my head tried to find a hole somewhere in the slit of the cushion and seat belt.

"What's wrong with him?" Ma asked Mrs. Jenkins. And Mrs. Jenkins made small sounds: maybe Ma should've been the one who knew.

"He's usually just fine, Mrs. Chong."

"Tell Mrs. Jenkins, Kang—go ahead and tell her how good you are."

My mind was preoccupied: days without soccer, the goalie net folded and rotting in storage, of going home and watching Joko feed on apples filled with peanut butter, wet lips puckering, like that fish, *here it goes again*, the fish racing around, Joko chasing it, the smell smeared on my walls, the kamikaze pilots in samurai suits crashing into me. I said it smothered in leather. "I want to die."

"What?" Mrs. Jenkins asked. But Ma heard, because she wasn't talking anymore, it was her eyes talking, getting wide and anxious.

When we got home I got smacked across the mouth. "*Tsou jouy!* Dirty lips!" she said. "Where are you getting this from, Uncle Chu, Freddie, Yan?"

In my room, my heartbeat slowed down, but it took almost forever. Where am I getting what from? I counted what must have been ships, fading in the darkness of the river—they crossed the waters slow, like gators with their bellies exposed. I knew it would be too dark to see the farthest ship even reach the middle of the window frame, that's how fast the sun was turning. *Planes always move north around here,* that's what Pop said every time I panicked about nuclear war, *they won't ever crash through the window.* I didn't believe my dad on anything because Ma was always trying to please him—buying nightgowns that felt cool and slippery as night. She yammed it up with the maids, my brother and me, even the clerks at department stores; she got fierce and temperamental and got her way every time, but with my dad she hardly said a thing. She smiled.

I did have my own assorted clues about why Ma was afraid of my dad. There was always his girlfriend who lived in Chinatown and bad-talked about Ma. When she first pulled me aside in front of the apartment entrance, I thought she might have been a cousin of Soo's drunkard mom.

"Kang, right?" She had blue sunglasses on, and a spotted fur coat. "You're little Kang, aren't you, sweetie?"

I had folded my arms and shrugged.

"Listen, I want you to give your mommy a message for me. See, I know your daddy real well, we're the best of friends. But he's not been so nice to me lately, he's been very bad."

"What'd he do?"

"He doesn't want to be my friend anymore. So I think you'd better tell your mommy about that. I think she should know, don't you?"

"My ma's a good friend."

"Well, I don't know about that, sweetie. Your mommy can be kind of, well, scatterbrained." And that was that. *Scatterbrained?* She should've known I never talked about my dad to Ma. When I asked

Joko, he said it meant *el stupido, retard, King Dick.* Then he told me the nightmare.

"She's not Pop's friend, stupid. She's his pajamas."

I had waited for more, but he turned his back on me and stacked his comic books and trudged into the bathroom. But I figured she was getting a part of my dad that was really Ma's, or she had better pajamas than Ma, something like that.

No matter how hard I tried, Missy came back into my head. And the feeling I got was unsettling, thinking of how she stood before the class, jodhpur thighs and all. Missy was not going to be popular anymore, she'd lost something and it was true, I was a tyrannical monster by Ma's definition. As I lay in bed without dinner again, my stomach a balloon of air, a horrible thought occurred. What if the kamikaze pilots crashed through the window and they lived, struggling in their mesh wire samurai garb, glass shards speared into my fire trucks, a propeller reaching into the far end of the kitchen and pointed at my dad's throat? Would they be so sad that they'd tumble out of the window and smack the cold cement?

When I returned back to class the next day, Missy wouldn't talk to me. She turned her back to me and whispered to the other girls around her desk and they made a big show of letting me know I was not wanted, making a ring-around-the-rosy with Missy in the middle. I had been excommunicated.

"You and Buttcrack are just the same," she said. Missy looked proud, because I didn't dare say a word.

I watched Mrs. Jenkins pull the projector screen down over the blackboard, and I focused hard on the blankness. My stomach twisted and I rubbed an eraser across my desk, making cloudy trails. The other girls had become more of Missy's followers than ever before—they winced one eye shut and grinned mean and tricky as Cheshires. *Here it comes,* the world is dark, the lights are off, the blue dictionary is talking to the pink ballpoint pen on the screen, *please let me sleep forever, please.* I threw up across my desk and Timmy, who sat across from me, jumped up and howled in disgust. Mrs. Jenkins flipped on the lights, and for a moment I was where I wanted to be, caught in that pause of refocus, numb to my senses.

My dad's girlfriend was the one who picked me up. "Remember me, sweetie?"

I nodded and rolled in, my throat dry and hollow.

"Your mommy's not home so they called your daddy and your daddy called me." She lit a cigarette, and stroked my face with the sleeve of her spotted fur coat. She looked like a derelict bear, one that was a dropout from the circus—swirling the steering wheel, starting and stopping the car and cursing out pedestrians. She didn't have to tell me to keep a secret. I wasn't going to be the one who made Ma cry.

Each day was almost the same. One of the girls had told her older brother and they called to me in the hallways. They called me older names, the things I heard thrown at Joko: Chinky tiddlywink, stinky Nip, a Susie-Jap dick. The boys in my class were okay out in recess with me, because I was the best at sports and there was nothing they could do about it, but in the hallways I was left nomadic, singular. Missy carried a chip on her shoulder because the boys no longer had crushes on her, it had turned to Becky Dawson who rightfully should have been the one in the first place—she had the rosy skin and knock-out teeth, the wholesome cashmere look.

Due to popular demand, we played Parachute for three weeks in a row, each of us designated to a stripe and lifting it to make domes shaped like bras. We rippled to make waves, then lifted it high above our heads, spinning inwards and pulling the chute down. For ten whole seconds we were enclosed in the vacuum of air, most of us awed, waiting for the ceiling to drop, to darken, the nylon falling over faces. I could hardly stand it, the tightening space, my chest constricting, my heart beating furiously, watching the dizzy stripes like a monster claw descending. In Parachute, sports stars like me weren't valuable. I was one of the last to get picked for partners.

Gina's mom picked us up in the carpool from school on the half day reserved for report card marking. Adabel rode in the front seat, while her friend Trish and the rest of us crammed into the back. Every one of us was Chinese-Canadian, except for Trish, who had beautiful lemonade hair, and glasses already—she was in the second grade, mature, composed, laughing, she and Adabel proud of their library books, the good ones with the Royal Ballet pictures and the caterpillar who ate holes into everything. We—me, Gina, the first graders—we got all the leftovers, mildewed books with yellow and orange pictures, *Peter Pan* with some kid's dried-up puke (maybe mine) on the inside cover. We were impatient in the car, but thankful because it was Gina's mother's turn to drive, and not Soo's, who wore Goody curlers and smelled of sweet fish (really rum).

I think Trish said hi to me in the car. It was intimate space, and she was the weird one in the back because her mom wasn't in our carpool. I felt invaded, greedy, like I didn't want to let her in. But we let her in. Gina's mom told us she had an enormous headache, and she'd park on the other side of the street and let Trish out. Our car waited, still running, I was flipping through a book. I didn't catch the blue Chevy coming around the corner or Trish's glasses up in the air, her library books projected the other direction. I saw her body on the ground. Gina's mom jumped out of the car and ran to Trish's house, calling through the screen. Trish's mom answered the door holding a cake in her hands, and she smiled at Gina's mom and something in that calmed me, *you're overreacting again.* But then she saw her daughter, and she dropped the cake into the shrubs, and ran out into the middle of the street.

The neighbors were out now, the mothers instinctively closed in like a circle. Gina and Trish's mother, and more mothers rocked in a circle in the middle of the pavement with Trish in her mother's lap. Then Gina's mom was out of the circle somehow. She stood with her skinny arms propping the back of her head, the sun slapping a stripe up her back. In that moment, we had potential to freeze in terror, but we watched Adabel straighten up her back with excitement and lean forward on the dash. "Wow," she said. "I've never seen a live ambulance before."

We craned our heads out the windows and waited, listening for the sirens. We were anxious to get out, to move around and get a better look at Trish. Adabel couldn't stop relaying the events to us, and by the time the ambulance came, we were fighting with one another. The policeman tried telling us to go to sleep, and Lord knows I tried because he was the law. We bent our knees up and we faked it, our heads rolled back on the hot vinyl, our mouths open for air, enamored with hot darkness.

Explain to your mom why you're late, Gina's mother clutched the police report, *explain to her and tell her I'm sorry.* She parked up onto the curb and walked me to the doorman, taking his hand and putting it around mine. I hyperventilated trying to tell my mom. She didn't believe me.

"You playing hooky?" she demanded.

"It's for real," I pleaded. "The ambulance came and Adabel's friend got really hurt."

"What is wrong with you, why these lies?" Ma took me by the shoulders, shaking me. "You want me to call Gina's mom, you want me to ask her if this is for real?"

I didn't say anything. I waited for her to pick up the phone, to dial, but she never did. I got sent to bed without dinner again, which was fine because it was that same fish.

Trish died in the oxygen tent overnight. Her picture was in the local newspaper the very next day, front page, and I proved it to my mom. She started to cry, and walked into her bedroom and didn't come out for half an hour. She explained to me about the oxygen tent. I imagined the oxygen tent, a saran-wrapped dollhouse, Trish losing a breath every second until there are no more by morning. I didn't ask where Trish went, but Ma told me anyway. She told me it was dreaming forever, something I already knew.

I was famous in the first grade again. Everyone wanted a piece of me, except Missy who was even more jealous. It was good to be the one alive. They didn't much care for Trish, because in the first grade, to be dead was to awaken from it sometime later.

"*You* were in the car, did you see blood, what did her head look like?" They all said, "Geez, you're so lucky!"

"I saw it all," I boasted.

"And the blood?"

"Of course, dummy. Of course I saw the blood, it was red and all over the street." Though Trish's injury was internal, though I was fast asleep through most of it, I swore to seeing her soul asleep on the hood of the Chevy, blood gushing like a river down the pavement. Mrs. Jenkins had to pry everyone away from me and Gina. Every note intercepted was for us. My breakfast lurched from excitement, but I stomached it, thought my way through it, and to my amazement, I didn't throw up.

As the week passed, it was funny that nobody explained it to Gina and me, not a single teacher, administrator, big person there pulled us aside to ask about what this was all about, what in the hell was happening with our minds—maybe it was because they were afraid we thought we were being punished. I thought maybe they weren't as fascinated as kids.

Over dinner, Joko shredded a sweet duck and sucked his fat thumbs. "Whaddya mean?" he said. "You know what Vince said his mother said?"

"Nope."

"He says Chinese people don't know how to drive on the right side of the street."

"That's why?" I asked. "She's mad at us?"

"Of course, *duh*. Learn your history," he said, half disgusted. Some kid probably said that to him. "Everyone's mad at us Chinky-dicks."

In the middle of the night, my mother woke me. I could feel her hands over my shoulders, and I opened my eyes to her smeared makeup. Sweat was over her face, and down her neck. The window silhouetted her, and she looked witchy again, long tangled hair that matched the path of her tears, so large they made a *spat* sound when they hit my sheets.

"Kang, you awake?" She shook me harder. "It's Ma, it's me."

"I'm sleepy."

"You have to tell me, why you always get into trouble at school this year, why all this *sai*, death talk, tell me."

She scared me like this, and I started to cry along with her, whimpering like a kettle on low, resting flat on my back and searching the river for barges.

"I dreamt about you. You don't want to die, do you?"

There were actually several barges out this time of night, but no planes, no crazy kamis.

"Tell me you don't want to die," she said.

She made me think of Trish, and in the weakened state of sleep, the girl came easily before me. Trish's face was serene, without color, her fingers curled up like the feet of Adabel's parakeet. There was so much fuss, noisy cop cars, and thousands of pages that Gina's mom sat filling out. The streets got blocked, there were books hidden in the grass on the lawns. Everyone was crying. It came to me, Ma fearing being left all alone—I thought to survive to appease her, at least that'd be a good start. "I don't," I said matter-of-factly. "No way, José."

Jean C. Lee
Louisiana State University

MOLESTED

My head is upside down and I am brushing my hair. Brushing it this way makes it full, makes it float like a parachute the wind is catching up. I am brushing my hair, too, because I love it. Quite simply, my hair is beautiful. It is an abundance. Full and long and soft as silk. Rippling and wavy as a rain-fed stream. And the color: as if the sun in setting had flamed into the prairie. A cool, pure flame. Without heat. A flame you want to touch, to enter.

I didn't always love my hair, the way it called attention to me, over-shadowed me, somehow made me feel empty, as if all my body's energy were sucked up by its roots. How it tricked others, deceived even me, into seeing all of me as beautiful, but unapproachable, like an icon. How sometimes, unpredictably, it inflamed men, made them want to hurt me. Like the man in the hall of a hospital once, who simply walked up, clasped his fingers round my neck, and tried to strangle me, screaming my hair was the devil's sign. Or even the man two years ago, a man as old as my grandfather, who invited me to dinner, a business dinner, then tried to rape me. What do you expect when you look like a whore, he told me. I don't go out with men anymore, except my friends—who are mostly gay. The other men, the ones who acted badly, their behavior had nothing to do with my hair. Neither their hate nor their desire had root in me.

I've claimed myself; my hair is mine now: it shields me, it sings for me.

I finish brushing one last stroke, flip my head upright and watch. My hair floats, settles down like seeds that have burst from a milkweed pod. I pick up a comb, place a small part just above my left temple, then gather a section down to the tip of my ear, twist it back and up and fasten it with a yellow plastic comb. I do the same with the hair along the front and right of my face. A sort of forties pompadour. I secure the combs with hairpins underneath; I'm going to dance tonight.

I apply my makeup carefully. Ivory foundation, a pale, creamy ground, warmed to life by ochre, a minuscule drop of red. Soft turquoise smudged to gray frames my eyes, echoes a small flower in the background print of my blouse, echoes my irises as well; not a period, not quite an exclamation mark. And under my cheekbones, like a scimitar slicing the fleshy roundness of my cheeks, I brush a brownish peach, a peach that has been newly bruised. The mask is nearly complete. My mouth: this too-wide, too-soft scar across my face. My lips full and fleshy. Liver lips my brother called me as a child; a lover, vulva lips. I wield the lipstick like a weapon, lay the paint impasto, thick and heavy. A coral, bright and juicy as freshly cut ripe mangos. It bleeds, it declares itself. I smile widely; a gash of large white teeth, the canines pointy. I laugh, toss my head. I am happy.

Downstairs it is quiet. My daughter, Felicity, is sleeping. I hope she is sleeping; if not, the baby-sitter may have trouble. Felicity demands so much; I think it is because she has so little. She is a pretty child, sprite-like and golden-curled. People comment on her appearance. What a pretty child, they say. Cherubic. But they don't know. Her appearance belies her behavior. She is no larger than a three-year-old, but in fact has just turned seven. She barely speaks. She didn't learn to speak till she was nearly six. Not really speak, though she could get my attention. Ma Ma Ma Ma Ma Ma Ma Ma Ma, she'd shout, loud and rapid-fire as an Uzi. She is retarded. Delayed, they call it now, as if she were a bus that could catch up to schedule. She will not catch up; this is permanent. Even with three years of therapy, her speech is minimal. But she screams, she screams. Hours-long tantrums that wear me out. And despite her size, she is strong, wiry. It takes all my strength to hold her, to contain her. When she was first born, her father would display her on his forearm. My little angel, he called her. When he discovered she was damaged, he didn't want her. He left us. You can't do anything right, he told me. My little angel, he called her. I call her my changeling, my little changeling. Sometimes I watch her sleep—she is so beautiful then—and I can feel my heart bleed slowly.

I listen again. There is no sound from Felicity. Outside, the sound of tires pulling closer, slowing, stopped. An engine shutting off. I glance at my watch. Eight o'clock. Pam must be here. The baby-sitter will arrive momentarily.

Pam drives fast, deliberately; her car is hot, a yellow Trans Am, only a few years old. It's one of the few things she got out of the divorce. The house she's only allowed to live in until it's sold; the support for her kids is barely enough to feed them. The usual story, though most ex-husbands will tell it the other way around. She's always driven this way, even when the back has been packed full: groceries and kids of assorted sizes. The light is changing; Pam speeds up and makes it through the yellow. She gropes in her purse for a cigarette and punches in the lighter. Don't you worry, she says to me, exhaling a long white stream of smoke, about your baby-sitter? I know what she's getting at, but I pretend not to. Why? I ask. Well . . . She doesn't quite know how to say it. Well . . . you know. A teenage boy and all. Don't you worry? She takes a sudden turn, no blinker, one hand on the wheel, then glances over at me. I pluck my hand slowly from the sissy strap and rummage for a cigarette myself. John baby-sits a lot of the neighborhood kids, I say, his brother's kid, too. This is not exactly what I want to say. My purse is too full: lipstick, powder, blush. Finally, my cigarette case. Besides, I say, I think it's great, a teenage boy spending his evenings responsibly, earning money rather than hanging out getting into trouble. Rather than smoking dope and lusting after girls. Pam shakes her head. She doesn't believe me. His mother's dead, I say, pausing to light my cigarette. He's a pretty quiet boy and his dad's a drunk, who alternates between ignoring him and yelling at him. The kid hasn't had an easy life. I still don't have it right. I take a drag. Now, now I have it. Even if I did worry, I say—and underneath I'm beginning to—I believe it's the right thing to do. Boys have to learn to be caretakers too. They have to be supported if they're willing to step outside traditional roles. It's a small thing, but small things make a difference in the world. Pam stubs out her cigarette in the ashtray. I've been soapboxing and I'm a little embarrassed. She smiles at me. You're a dreamer, she says, but that's why we love you.

Pam wheels into the parking lot of Johnson's 40 Lanes, brakes suddenly, and backs up to claim a parking space. We're lucky to find a spot close to the building. The place is packed. Johnson's, the local hot spot, is one of those Midwest oddities: not just a bowling alley, but a sprawling complex with restaurant, travel agency, beauty and barber shops, and two full-fledged nightclubs. My friends and I have dubbed the upstairs club, which has live music five days a week, the happy hunting grounds. Singles who no longer want to be single and non-singles longing to be single again predominate. There's a lot of loud laughter. People mostly ignore the band, but the hunting is deadly serious. Women often arrive in packs. I think maybe Pam would like to go there, but I direct us to the downstairs club, a disco, where most of my gay friends hang out. We can actually dance there, only occasionally having to fend off some sloppy salesman who inadvertently wandered down hoping to trade tired lines and cheap drinks for a faceless fuck. The owner still doesn't realize this has become a gay bar. Last Halloween, he nearly had a fit; most of the guys came in drag and the owner couldn't understand why so many women were using the men's room. There are also women like me; a fag hag, my ex used to call me. There are real fag hags here, but I'm not one. I stay away from the gays who like to make women fall in love with them, who like to humiliate them. My gay friends stay away from them, too. Through the strobe lights and smoke I glimpse Michael and Jeff sitting at a table across the room. They've saved chairs for us. The music throbs upward through my feet. Come on, I say to Pam. What, she says, gesturing incomprehension. It is too loud to speak. I take Pam's elbow lightly and lead her across the room. Michael waves a waitress over and she bends down to hear us yell our orders in her ear. Pam looks a little uncomfortable. We sit and smile, waiting for our drinks; not much chance for conversation here. In pauses between songs, I manage introductions. Our drinks arrive and I take that first cold, rusty gulp of Scotch. You look wonderful, Michael yells in my ear. Carmen Miranda? Why not? I yell back and laugh. Let's go, Michael says and grabs my hand. Jeff takes the cue and leads Pam off to dance. Michael and I stride like peacocks to the dance floor. People give us space. Michael and I have been dancing partners for some time now, and we have a right to space. We perform as Michael taught me. Michael earns his rent teaching dance, but not to women like me. In dancing class, the women Michael has to teach are generally of two types; fiftyish women, brittle as sticks, who bind their faces into expressionless masks with too much pancake and mascara or youngish women with bad perms and pimply skin, youngish women whose bodies have already gone matronly, plump rolls popping from bra and panty elastic. The women adore Michael, because he is beautiful, tall and blond and lithe like the angel in the movie *Barbarella,* and because he is polite. They all want him to really teach them something, to change their lives. But all Michael can teach them is steps; they have no rhythm. Me he taught for free. The music's tempo slows and Michael steps behind me. He moves his hips close and pulls my arms out full to the side, then moves his hands in front, lightly pressing back my pelvis. Our knees are bent, legs wide apart, our necks entwined. We begin rocking, slowly, side to side. This is the Wave; done right it's like sea anemones on a coral reef, like underwater fucking. Lower and lower we go, never breaking from the singular motion, two creatures turned into one, then the ascent. We rise and break and twirl, two creatures again, a circle of balanced tension. His hand just below the small of my back, he draws me close again, chest to chest, pelvis to pelvis; we stride thigh between thigh, then he dips me slightly back, up again, and out, three spins exactly, full extension. Snap and in. The song is coming to an end. Death drop, he whispers in my ear. I smile, but inwardly shudder. Even with Michael, even with someone to whom I entrust my entire body, I am afraid. And now it comes, the straight down drop, arms fully extended, one leg bent up for balance. The strain is nearly too much, but Michael does not fail me. Just before I hit, he pulls, and up I come, white-faced, breathless. We laugh and collapse in each other's arms. When we get back to the table, Jeff tells us that Pam decided to go upstairs. I am a little disappointed, but I understand. Let's go upstairs and dance, says Michael, wake them up, give them a shock. I laugh and toss my head, my hair spraying droplets like a wet dog.

Upstairs, Pam is sitting at the bar with a fresh drink. Leaning up close to her is some slick wearing gray poly slacks that bulge at the pockets and a blue plaid, short-sleeved shirt, his stomach beginning to paunch over his belt. He looks a little like her ex, a city cop, in fact. Michael and I move onto the dance floor. We do our moves again, up and down, in and out. People begin to drift, begin to gape or look away. When we finish, nearly the entire dance floor is clear. I walk over to Pam and her new acquaintance, who excuses himself. To see a man about a horse, he says. Michael steps down the bar to order us drinks. Scotch, I tell him, double. With lots of ice. Lots and lots of ice. I want to chew the ice, let slivers hard and cold slide down my throat.

God, says Pam. You two look like you're having sex on the dance floor. I laugh. We are, I say. It's like extended foreplay. Except it's better. No birth control, no disease, no condoms to carry around. No one to kick out of bed in the morning, no regrets. Pure, clean, healthy sex. Michael brings my drink, says he's going back downstairs to find Jeff. He kisses me on the neck, and I tweak his cheek. Pam's new interest has slipped out. I wonder what horse he had to see about.

Pam and I close up the bar, back downstairs by this time and dancing to the last song. Even if she didn't bag a man, I think she has had fun. Her driving is more reckless than ever, and I worry we might get stopped. But then, she knows all the local cops. She drops me off, waits until I unlock the door, then peels off. John gets up from the couch, where he has been sleeping. Felicity woke up once, he tells me, but she went back to sleep. Good. Maybe she'll sleep through till morning. I pay him and watch him walk through the backyard and alley, until I can see he's home and in the door.

I am almost too tired to wash my face, but I can't bear the thought of waking up caked with sweat and makeup. And I smell: exertion, alcohol, stale cigarette smoke. I fill the washbasin full and find a clean washcloth. My face is full of soap when I hear a padding up the stairs. Damn, Felicity's awake. I rinse my face and turn around. Felicity stands in the bathroom doorway, her curls damp, her face still soft from sleep. Hi, baby, I say, were you a good girl? Felicity nods her head. She sways a little in her long white nightgown. John said you woke up. Did you go right back to bed? Felicity nods again vigorously and sticks her finger up her nose. I pull it out. Come on, babe, back to bed, I say. Felicity begins to rock. Mommy, she says, Mommy. What, babe? I ask. She rocks some more. I take her by the hand and begin to lead her out of the room. She shakes my hand free and says again, more insistently, Mommmmy. What, Felicity? I am losing patience. She stops rocking then and looks directly at me. John like me play his body. I don't believe what I am hearing. She keeps her eyes on me and says again, John like me play his body. I kneel. Felicity, I say calmly as I can. What do you mean? She will not understand. I try again. Where on John's body? She points to her groin. Here, she says, stabbing at her crotch, here. I draw her to me and slowly pull her nightgown up. Her panties are still on, white cotton panties with blue flowers. Slowly, I pull them down. There is no blood, but her little pink cleft is pinker than usual. I disentangle the panties from her feet—she begins to pull away; I must not frighten her—and I sniff them. I sniff her, gently burrowing my nose into that shameless cleft. With that, everything becomes clear. It is not the acrid smell of baby sweat and urine, but a deeper, musky odor like fungi, like rotting leaves. She begins to fight me as I grab her panties, gather her into my arms and carry her downstairs. A blanket. I enfold her—she is struggling like a piglet now—and carry her under one arm to the telephone. I trap her between my knees, trying to soothe her and dial the telephone at the same time. Six rings. Maybe Pam's not home. I pray. Seven, eight. Pam's voice, sleepy, Hello. I can barely choke the words out. Please, come get me, I say. Please come get me. Felicity's been molested. I need you to take us to the hospital. I can't hear you, says Pam. What are you saying? Felicity, I say. Felicity. Felicity's been molested. Oh, my God, says Pam, oh, my God. Wait there. I'll bundle up the kids. I'll be right there. Don't panic, she says, I'll be right there. I hold Felicity, I rock and hold her as if I'm holding on to life itself.

.   .   .

As we pull into the emergency entrance a cop car swerves up behind us, blue light flashing. Pam has called ahead. An orderly comes out, opens the car door and plucks Felicity from my arms. I hold emptiness. Do you have everything? he asks me. I nod mutely and hand him the panties, which I've been clutching like Kleenex. He is wearing latex gloves. I follow him inside. Felicity. He carries her to an examining room, draws the door shut. A woman touches my arm, stopping me. We'll need to ask you some questions. Felicity. I don't want to leave Felicity. I look around: the woman smiling; two cops, gruff, embarrassed. Pam has taken her boys to the waiting room and she comes to me, takes me by the elbow, sits me down. They need to ask you some questions, she says to me. I don't understand. I don't want questions. I want Felicity. I want them all to go away. The orderly comes out of the examining room. I look at him. Felicity? It's all right, he says, there's a nurse with her. We're waiting for the crisis team. We need to ask you some questions, says the blond cop, younger, red-faced. He leans down over me and I smell onions on his breath. We'll make it easy as we can, but we need to ask some questions. The questions they ask confuse me. Where was I? What was I doing? Did I know the baby-sitter? Why did I hire a boy? This isn't about me, I want to scream. This is about Felicity. But Pam strokes my hair, encouraging me, and I try to be a good girl, I try to answer their questions properly. I have no idea what I say. The other cop comes up and taps me on the shoulder. I flinch. We need you to come with us now, he says, to witness the examination.

In the examining room, the light coats everything with a pale green, sickly sheen. Felicity. Spotlighted in the center of the room. Naked, spread-eagled on a table, hands and feet captured in restraints. Struggling, but silent at this point. Across the table, a nurse stands, her hands encased in latex gloves. She is placing Felicity's nightgown in a plastic bag, labeling it. We'll have to send this in, she says, vaguely apologetic. We can give her a hospital gown to go home in. The blond cop crosses the room, takes the plastic bag, and writes something on his clipboard. The cop's face is still pink. Neither looks at me. Neither looks directly at Felicity. A second nurse enters, replaces the first. Then the doctor strides in, pulls on a pair of latex gloves, and begins to examine Felicity. He checks for bruises, cuts. There are none. The cop writes this down. The doctor asks the nurse to loosen the restraints on Felicity's ankles, and he bends her knees; with his fingers he spreads her labia. Felicity's eyes are round with fear, but she is still for once. The skin is reddened, sign of slight abrasion, he says, and the cop writes some more, his face reddening all the while. The nurse holds open another plastic bag; the doctor uses several swabs, drops them in the bag. The nurse seals it, writes, hands it to the cop. It is placed with the other bags: nightgown, panties. Speculum, the doctor says, never glancing up. As the nurse hands it to him, light glints off the steel like the flash of a drawn blade, hard and cold. He inserts the speculum and spreads it. Felicity's eyes widen; her mouth opens like a gaping wound. Silence. Then from that dark hole, as if ascending from a cave deep in the earth, issues a howl, animal-like, pure and loud. Pain. Fear. Unmitigated. Uncanny. I am seized, frozen, unable even to blink. Felicity. It doesn't appear that there was penetration, the doctor reports, swabbing her vagina, then withdrawing the speculum. Felicity's mouth remains open. The howl has ended, but I can hear it echoing about the room. The cop's face has turned white. We'll have the results of the tests tomorrow. You can take her home now, the doctor says, pulling off his gloves, leaving the room. I feel ice cracking, falling away, as I claim the blanketed bundle that now is Felicity from the nurse's arms. She is limp, boneless; her eyes stare vacantly. I have no tears to revive her.

When I put her to bed, she pushes me away.

I sleep badly, awaking at seven, my usual hour, or rather, Felicity's usual hour. It is nine now, and she is still sleeping. I am thankful for this, for these few hours of quiet if not peace. Pam is supposed to call at ten. She needs the sleep, too; we didn't get back from the hospital until after three-thirty. I kept waking up in the night, thinking I heard Felicity. But when I checked her, she was sleeping soundly. I didn't bathe her last night; it was too late and I thought it would upset her more, upset her routine. She needs routine. I didn't bathe Felicity, but I took a bath myself, hoping the water's heat would warm me, would melt what felt like slivers of ice inside of me. But as soon as the water cooled, the chill returned. Even though it's early September, the house is cold this morning. This far north it can get cold early. I turn the thermostat to seventy-four and return to my chair, next to the heating vent, wrap my fingers around my coffee mug. Maybe it's only the lack of sleep, too much Scotch last night.

Sunshine filters through the lace panels on the windows, spreading dappled patterns across the walnut-stained floor. I have been fond of this house, its comfort, its orderliness, even its small size. I rent it from a friend I've known since high school, who bought the house as an investment two years ago. She's still unmarried and lives at home. Sometime, if she ever gets married, she might want to live here. Together, we refurbished the house: stripping paint-encrusted woodwork; sanding, staining, and varnishing the battered wood floors. The house had had heavy use. The walls in the living and dining rooms were abundantly cracked and patched, as if they had survived numerous heavy objects being rammed into them. We covered them with wallpaper. In the dining room, an unpatterned textured peach, and in the living room, an exuberant pattern of pale gold iris and small blue starlike blooms over a chocolate-brown ground. The woodwork we painted creamy white. My eclectic collection of antique, modern, and just-plain-secondhand furnishings actually look good here, as if they had been planned. My women friends like to visit and sit at my old oak table sipping herbal tea, talking about their lives, their men, their lack of them. I'm happy being alone, I tell them. I've never felt better or stronger in my life. And this is true. I've gone back to college to complete my degree. It's hard sometimes—and lonely. But, I tell my friends, it's better than being lonely with someone around to remind you of it constantly. Pam laughs and tells me if I were Catholic, I might have become a nun. I think about this. Yeah, I say, except I'm not into submission and I don't want to be *anyone's* bride. The telephone rings, but it's not Pam. It's a detective; he says he'll be over this afternoon. I hear Felicity begin her morning yelps.

The detective has turned down my offer of tea. Though I'm not thirsty, I pour myself a cup. It gives me something to do with my hands. My hair is pulled back; I'm not wearing makeup. I've bathed Felicity and dressed her in clean coveralls and a sweater. The house is spotless. I don't know why, but I feel like I'm on trial. Felicity, thankfully, is playing quietly in the living room where I can keep an eye on her. She is absorbed in her game: a cat's head with a thin red plastic board that pulls out like a tongue. The tongue-board is marked in squares, on which Felicity places little plastic mice, moving them square by square to safety away from the cat's gaping mouth. The mice seldom reach the safe point, though; the tongue recoils suddenly, whipping the mice into the cat's maw. When this happens, Felicity shakes out the mice, draws the tongue out again, and begins placing the mice. She does this over and over and over. I've given her the toy to play with because I know it will keep her attention, though it disturbs me, as if I were feeding her narcotics. She gets like this watching television too, which is partly why we don't have one. The detective is asking me questions, like the cops last night. Felicity has moved three mice nearly to the safety zone when the cat's tongue snaps again. Just as suddenly, my attention is snagged by what the detective is now saying. The tests were inconclusive, he says. I talked to the boy this morning, but he denies it. He says your daughter is retarded, that she's making it up. Is that a possibility? She's not capable of that . . . yet, I say. I didn't think so, the detective says. Anyway, I'm going to try to talk to the boy again tomorrow, at school, while his dad's not around. He drums his fingers on the table. You know, he says, I've got kids myself, a little girl . . . Well, you know, I talked to your friend Pam. My wife and I have known her quite a few years. She's really fond of you and your . . . Felicity? She's concerned. He nods his head, as if he were agreeing with himself. I wonder what would be happening if Pam were not my friend. He slaps his palm on the table and pushes his chair back. Well, he says, I'll try to get back in touch sometime tomorrow. Will you be home? I nod. I don't have classes on Monday. He stands and nods again, as if he's trying to remember something. If you know any other parents this kid babysat for . . . it might be a good idea . . . it might be better if you contacted them. Less frightening. He shrugs. My body feels so heavy that, momentarily, I wonder if I can rise, see him to the door. Felicity has begun throwing the mice about the room.

·   ·   ·

The school bus came for Felicity this morning. She goes full days to school now, which makes my life a little easier. She was uncooperative this morning, though; I had trouble getting her dressed. Last night, when I tucked her in, she pushed me away again. She seems angry, refuses to be held. I tried to study this morning, but found I couldn't concentrate. It doesn't help that the material is boring: court decisions and opinions, communications law. I keep waiting for the phone to ring. Pam called yesterday, after the detective left, and we talked for a long time. She told me she called her ex to see who would be handling the case. After she told him what had happened, he was cooperative. She must have left out quite a bit of information about our night out. Her ex still doesn't like her hanging out with me, but I guess he has nothing against Felicity. Anyway, she said, I called Carl then. Actually, I called his wife and told her about it first. She had him call me back. He's a pretty good guy. I think he'll follow through. She wants me to call her when I hear anything new. I haven't called any of the other parents yet. When I told Pam about having to do that, she said she'd come over if I wanted her to, give me moral support. I told her I thought I could do it by myself, but now I'm not sure. I don't know most of these people, except to say hello when I walk down the street. The only ones I really know are John's brother and his girlfriend. They're the ones who recommended John. He baby-sits their little boy. I suppose they might already know, because of the police visiting John's house. Nevertheless, I can't imagine any decent way to broach the subject. I mean, I could call up and ask Jolene if she wants to bring Dylan over to play after school. And, oh, yes, by the way, I may be pressing charges against your boyfriend's brother for molesting my daughter. You might want to question Dylan to see if John's done anything with him. Really graceful. Something every parent wants to hear. But I know I'm going to have to do it. I pick up the phone and call Pam. Tell her I've changed my mind; I would like her to come over tonight.

Sounds—zhro-o-o-o-om, zhro-o-o-o-om, a-a-a-a-a-A-A-A-A-A-i-i-i-H, k-RHOOOM—issue from Felicity's room. Then Felicity's delighted squeals. Pam's boys have brought over their little cars and are playing race and crash. Felicity loves this, and the boys seem to like showing off for her. They even give her a couple cars of her own. Your turn now, they'll say, and Felicity, excited, will throw the car across the room. Sandy, the older boy, will laugh. No, Felicity, he'll say. You've got to keep it on the ground, like this. See? Another crash. Felicity laughs again. Cool it down a little in there, Pam yells as she mixes us drinks. This is our second round, and she makes them stiff. Margaritas. She walked in, handed me the bottles. Tequila, margarita mix. Thought this might be a good idea, she said. Hey, she yells again, more serious this time. I said keep it down in there. Giggles. But the volume is lower now. You ready? she asks. I take a sip, savoring the saltiness giving way to tart, nod my head. She unwinds the cord of the phone and places it on the table in front of me. I take a breath, exhale, begin to punch in the first series of numbers from a list in front of me. The first of four. I hear the phone ring at the other end, four, five rings. Hello? Jolene. I've been expecting you to call, she says. She doesn't sound angry. I was thinking about calling you myself. She rushes on. I don't have to say much of anything. John's brother talked to his dad; the story came out. Jolene didn't trust the father's story, she told her boyfriend. They talked to Dylan. It seems there might have been some sex play there, too. We're certainly not going to have him baby-sit again. But something should be done about this, she says matter-of-factly. I'm trying, I reply. She asks about Felicity. I explain about the tests, the doctor's statement. But is Felicity okay? she asks. I don't know, I say. I don't know. Jolene asks me to let her know if anything happens, if she can do anything. Yes, I say, nodding. Yes, I will. Pam raises her eyebrow, questioning, as I place the receiver back on the telephone. That one went fine, I say. Here, she says, shoving a pack of cigarettes closer to me. Take a break; have a smoke. As I light the cigarette, I notice that I'm trembling. Pam gets up to check on the kids, who have gotten strangely quiet, but it turns out that Sandy has taken out one of Felicity's fairy-tale books and is trying to read a story to his brother and Felicity. I don't think Sandy knows how to read that well yet; he must be doing it from memory. I'm surprised that Felicity is sitting still for it. I usually can't get further than a page before she starts squirming and grabbing for the book. The next call isn't so easy. Penny. What are you trying to do to me, she screams. Are you crazy? Wails from the bedroom. Felicity. Penny hangs up. Mommm, Sandy yells. Felicity's trying to grab the book! More wails from Felicity. Well, give it to her, Pam says. It's her book. Sandy comes out, hands on his hips. But I wasn't done with the story, he says. That's okay, Pam says, she doesn't understand. Sandy huffs a little. Yeah, he says, heading back to the bedroom. Put the toys away and start picking up the room, Pam calls after him. We're going home soon. Yeah, he says, turning into the room. Well? says Pam, lighting a cigarette. I light another one, too. That was bad, I say. I'll wait to make the other calls tomorrow. Probably best, she agrees. Sandy comes out with his jacket on, his brother trailing behind. I can't get his zipper up, Sandy complains. Felicity's tearing pages, he says to me.

When I put Felicity to bed last night, she threw the book at me. She is decidedly more hostile. The detective called after she was asleep. He's coming over after I get home from classes.

I sit in my classes, but I find myself doodling in my notebook rather than taking notes. I keep thinking about what Penny said when she called me this morning.

I'm a single mother, she says. I'm all alone, and I'm doing my best to take care of my babies. I take *good* care of them. Well, I say, I'm a single mother, too. It's hard for us all. My babies aren't like yours, she says. People warned me, but I'm good-hearted, felt sorry for your kid. I am too astounded to reply. Now I see what people meant, she continues. You keep on making trouble like this . . . I hang up the phone.

The other mothers I called weren't much better. From what I could tell, Penny had already talked to them.

I'd like to throw the book at him, the detective says. But there isn't much I can do, even if he does confess. He shakes his head. We don't have enough evidence to go to court without a confession. Even if we did go to court, say, and by an outside chance win, it still wouldn't be worth much. The boy's a first-time offender, and molestation by juveniles isn't considered a punishable crime, only a delinquent act. The court can recommend counseling, that's all. I am stunned. You mean, I say, they can't even require that he get help? I'm afraid not, says the detective, shrugging and looking at the floor. He looks up at me then. But I'm going to keep on, he says. I'm really not supposed to do this, to lean on him. But I'm going to be there every morning when he gets to school. He's going to talk. He's going to admit it. He slaps the table. At least then, the social workers would have to get involved, and they *might* feel compelled to do something. I don't know. He holds his hands up in appeal. It's all I can do. I nod my head numbly. I told him about the other mothers when he first came. Don't worry about it, he told me. People just don't know how to respond. Let me know if you have any problems, though. He gives me his card, takes it back to write a number on the blank side. This is my home phone, he says, handing it back to me. You can call me there, if you need to. As he's leaving, he tells me a social worker will be getting in touch with me. It's part of the procedure, he says. When a complaint is filed . . . He shrugs again and leaves, just as Felicity's school bus pulls up front. The driver is having trouble getting Felicity off the bus. I go to help. No, Felicity says, shaking her head as we try to pry her from the seat—No! No! No!—and she kicks me square in the shin.

The social worker doesn't even want to talk to Felicity. It's the same bitch, sorry, woman, I had to deal with two years ago, when some concerned neighbor called in to say I was abusing Felicity. Felicity was having a lot of tantrums then, more than she has now. That was when the doctors discovered she had epilepsy. The tantrums, they explained, might be connected. The medication to control the seizures might help control the tantrums, too. Anyway, it was summer, hot. All the windows were open, and there was Felicity, screaming and screaming. I couldn't keep fighting her, so I'd shut her in her room until she'd calm down. She'd bang on the walls, throw her toys around. The time the neighbor called, Felicity had smeared shit on the walls and had thrown a wooden toy at the window, breaking it. Fortunately, she wasn't cut. I was cleaning up the mess and crying when the social worker came. I didn't have time or patience for her questions, which I considered insulting. I mean, they assumed my guilt, just like the classic vaudeville joke: Are you still beating your wife? I guess I wasn't very nice. Anyway, I ended up having to be "monitored" for six months; weekly unannounced visits. The social worker never found anything incriminating. She held that against me, I think. I think she still holds it against me. She's asking me WHY I went out that night. As if that had anything to do with the situation. I suspect that, in her eyes, I have no right to enjoy myself. I don't answer her. So what exactly is the purpose of your visit? I ask. To evaluate, she says. And what is it you're evaluating? I reply. She squirms a little, manages to evade the question. I'm not supposed to be the one asking them. She launches her counterattack. This sort of incident is pretty common, she says to me. We deal with it all the time. I wonder if that's supposed to make me feel better. So what about Felicity? I say. Well, she says, starting to gather her belongings, you know, with Felicity's problems, her limitations . . . well, I doubt she'll remember much of anything. She stands, pulls on her coat. We're concerned about the boy, too, she says to me. He's at a delicate age, emotionally and sexually. This could have a damaging effect on him. She turns and leaves. I don't see her to the door. My mouth is hanging open. Who's the fucking victim, here? I want to scream. She's left her pen, a cheap blue Bic, lying on the table. I pick it up, then go to the door. Her car is just pulling out; I throw the pen, barely hitting her back fender.

By the time the detective calls, I have almost stopped crying. I got him to confess, he tells me. We're trying to push for therapy. That's all we can do now, but at least he confessed. So that's it, I think. Done. The confession is small consolation.

I dream I am dancing with Michael. But when he whispers in my ear, Death drop, I realize it is not Michael. Who? His face is masked, and I am dizzy from being whirled about. He brings my face close to the mask. I can hear him breathe, a metallic rasp, insect-like. Underneath the mask, all I see is blackness. Even the eyes. He drops me, and the fall is terrible, uncontrolled. I hit the floor like an explosion. I am lying there stunned and dizzy, when suddenly I realize I am naked. The not-Michael man has disappeared. I cannot move. In a circle all around me, people stand. I look for someone I might know. No one. Help me, I say, something's broken. They don't seem to hear me. Instead, they write something on the clipboards, which they all carry. My hair spreads around me, like a lake, rippling, red as blood. I pull the tresses toward me, to hide myself, but the hair falls away in my hands. The circle of people write again; they are wearing latex gloves. I awaken, drenched in sweat, my nightgown clammy and stuck to my skin. I hit the light on the clock next to my bed to read the digital display. Three A.M. I try to sleep, but the dampness of my bedclothes bothers me and I cannot shake the images of the dream. I toss and turn. I am finally drifting, when I hear a noise downstairs. I listen more closely. Felicity? When I throw the covers back, the air hits my still-damp nightgown. I shiver and pull on my robe. As I descend the stairs, the air gets colder. Felicity is sound asleep, snoring softly, her mouth open. I pull the covers up about her shoulders and go to get a drink of water. As I turn the corner into the kitchen, a blast of really cold air hits me. The back door is open. I try to remember; I see myself locking it last night, rechecking the lock. Maybe not. I close it tight now, pull the handle to make sure it's held.

When the alarm rings at six, I have just fallen asleep again, but I have to get up and get Felicity ready for school. Felicity has wet the bed.

In reporting class today we are analyzing interview styles and techniques. The instructor has invited Shelly, a former student who now works as a reporter at the local rag. She gives a brief rundown of preparation techniques, backgrounding, then interviews the instructor. She is not an attractive woman, blondish, slightly overweight. Her face is already beginning to paunch; she will age early. But her voice remains breathy, babyish, which I find irritating. And she is teasing, flirtatious, when she asks questions. What a cliché, I think. The interview as seduction. I have long lost interest and am beginning to lose patience, but the instructor seems to enjoy this.

After the reporter leaves, we view a videotape made last week. Four students, a panel, interviewing our instructor. I am on the panel. The videotape surprises me, or rather, my appearance surprises me. I had pulled my hair back into a chignon that day, trying to look more professional. I don't necessarily look professional; I look small, delicate, even frail. I can't get over it; I've always thought of myself as large. And my voice on the tape: soft, but strangely insistent. As I ask my questions, I pause to reflect, to choose my words, then lean forward, hands clasping, unclasping, as the question works its way out to hang in the air between us. The quietness is almost a threat. It's as if an Inquisitor has possessed the body of a child. I don't know that woman on the screen.

When class is over, the instructor signals me to stay. Despite his traditionalism, I like the man. Short and roundish, his head too large for his body, like a beach ball stuck atop, he has few pretensions. He doesn't waste time trying to assert dominance, but is straightforward and friendly. Even affectionate in an unpresuming way. Brenda Starr, girl reporter, he sometimes calls me, referring to my hair. From someone else it would be an insult. I wanted to talk to you, he says to me as I'm stuffing my notebook in my satchel. You know, when we were doing that interview, I thought you were in trouble, that you weren't doing very well. But watching it today . . . I don't know. It's strange, intense. I ended up saying things I thought I never would say. You threw me off base. I was going to suggest you take some pointers from Shelly, but I don't think so now. Whatever it is you're doing, I think you should work on it. Take control of it; make it into a conscious technique. But you're going to have to be careful with it. It'll scare some people, men especially. I look at him. I don't know what he means by that last remark.

Michael stops me in the hallway. He wants to know if I'm going out dancing this weekend. I haven't talked to him since that night, and, brokenly, I begin to tell him what has happened. Jesus, he says. Holy Jesus. You poor babies. He reaches out, brushes my hair back from my face. You poor, poor thing. I hear again that rasping underneath the voice and fight not to flinch from his touch.

Indian summer is early this year. Yet my blood quickens at the reprieve. I can almost forget what will necessarily follow: the relentless gray of late autumn, the blanketing shrouds of winter. The numbing cold, the tedium.

The sun is nearly hot today, though low and yellow. I am drying my hair in its rays, pretending to study and watching Felicity at play. She is digging holes in a patch of soft sandy earth by the front porch, burying her Weebles people, then digging them out again. I will have to check the sand when she is done, make sure she has resurrected them all. She has been doing this for almost an hour now, as if she has been mesmerized. I cannot account for her attention, but I am grateful for the quiet. I check to make sure she's still engaged, then slip inside to put some music on the stereo.

When I return to the porch, two neighbor girls, sisters, are standing on the sidewalk out front. Felicity has stopped digging and holds her spoon out, inviting them to join her. I don't like these girls, but Felicity has few playmates and I feel sorry for them. Their mother is some sort of Bible thumper; mentally unstable, according to the neighbors' reports. Who or where their father is is anybody's guess. Still, they're not appealing children, insolent and tattily dressed. Glazed, as it were, with a permanent film of dirt, like something out of a Walker Evans photograph. Underfed, too, I suspect, judging by the way they ask for food when they come to play. I have to watch them, too, the way they'll try to sneak away after trashing Felicity's room. I've even caught the younger stealing Felicity's toys. They stand there now, dirty-faced, blonde hair dull and scraggly as an abandoned doll's. The younger picks at a scab on her leg, then says to Felicity, We can't play with you, Felicity. Mama says so. Felicity, ignorant to their taunt, moves toward them, offering her spoon. Shelly told you, says the older, Mama says we can't play. Well, don't stand there then, I tell them, moving to gather up Felicity. Go on home. Go on, get out of here. They move reluctantly. Under Felicity's wails, I hear the younger one mutter. Witch, she says. Witch. Mama says so. Go on, I yell louder. Don't come round here again. Felicity is struggling so I can barely get her in the door.

Shits, I tell Pam that night on the phone. Little shits. I don't need this.

I don't need this, I tell Pam again, tapping at my nearly empty double Scotch and water. It is two weeks later, and Pam has insisted we go out. You can't stay cooped up all the time, she tells me. She's arranged for a baby-sitter at her house; Felicity and I will stay overnight. We've decided against the popular bars—too noisy—and have come to the Barrio, which on a Friday night is nearly deserted. It suits me fine: dark and worn, faded-looking, forties big bands on the jukebox, three or four serious drinkers lined up at the bar, and no one but Pam and me in the overstuffed booths. Glenn Miller has just wound up "In the Mood"—Michael and I worked out a good jitterbug routine once to that song—and a ballad begins. Bing Crosby, maybe, *I'll never smile again . . .* I hum along, mentally mouthing the lyrics. The silliness of the song strikes me—*I'll never smile again, until I smile at you*—there are worse things than losing a lover, however bad it feels at the time. Pam's drink is almost gone. I'll get this round, I say, picking up our glasses and heading toward the bar. No table service here. I've been telling Pam about how those two girls have been coming and standing in front of the house, yelling at Felicity. I keep her inside. I've also been getting hang-up calls. Worst of all, an anonymous note I found tucked in my back door. Retard and Hore it read on the outside. Scribbled inside: You will be punished. The girls' mother, perhaps? The boy? Pam thinks I ought to call Carl, but I've burned the note. I didn't even think twice about it, just took my lighter and lit the paper over the sink, washed the ash down the drain, as if I could erase the filth.

The drinks spill a little as I set them down, and I wipe at the puddle ineffectually with a cocktail napkin. Pam pulls some Kleenex out of her purse and mops up the rest. So what about Felicity? she asks me. Is this affecting her? It's hard to tell with Felicity, I say, shrugging. She seems, I don't know, hostile. But then she's always been that way at times; I could be imagining things. I stir my drink and pull out the straw, fold it up. I'm thinking of telling Pam about the noises I sometimes hear downstairs at night. But I don't know if I'm really hearing them. Felicity could be sleepwalking. She did once or twice before. I just don't know, and I think that maybe I'm getting paranoid. Pam leans back in the corner of the booth. This really bothers me, she says, interrupting my train of thought. I've never told anyone this. She is huddled into herself, staring at her glass. As she tells me her story, she doesn't once look up. She was molested, she says, when she was just about Felicity's age. Walking home. A friend of her father's. Offering her a ride. Unzipping his trousers. Forcing her head down. The discomfort. The gagging. The sense of shame. She never told anyone. She still feels the shame, I can tell. I want to reach across the table, touch her, remove it, but she huddles down further, then looks up at me, tears leaking slowly from the corners of her eyes. Pam crying. I've never seen her cry, never even imagined it. It ruined my marriage, you know, she says, blinking. I couldn't do it, you know . . . go down. She drops her gaze to the table. I'd try; I'd gag. Didn't you tell Gary? I ask. I didn't know how, she says. I failed. No, I say, shaking my head. No.

And I don't know how to tell her. It had nothing to do with that.

Even though Pam and I had been friends and neighbors for more than two years and even though Gary couldn't stand my ex, he didn't like Pam hanging with me after my divorce. I guess he thought she might get ideas. Be corrupted by the Dee-vor-cee. That's certainly how he began to treat me: not as his neighbor, not as his wife's best friend, but as some nameless woman, loose and oversexed. I never told Pam how Gary called me one night when she was gone, tricked me into coming over. He was having a stag party, it turned out, for a buddy on the force. So I walked into a room full of off-duty, foul-mouthed, beery-breathed, horny cops. I don't know what Gary expected me to do, strip perhaps. I drank half a beer to be civil and left. I was pissed. Not fifteen minutes later, a knock at my door. One of the cops, a big, beefy blond, obviously drunk, holding out a cigarette lighter that he said he thought I'd left and trying to work his way in. It's not mine, I told him, smiling. But thanks for thinking of me, I said, shutting the door in his face. I didn't respond to the continued knocking.

I never told Pam either how Gary had his girlfriend staying at the house when Pam had taken the kids to visit her parents. She was hoping some time away would mend matters. Fat chance. The girlfriend's car was parked in the driveway, facing my screened back porch, for an entire weekend. Sunday morning, I'm sitting on the porch, drinking coffee, when out they come in full embrace. Gary kisses her, grins over his shoulder at me, and waves as she drives away. I don't acknowledge him, but he crosses the yard to my porch and lets himself in the door. I just sit there. So, he says, settling into a chair, you got any more coffee? Sorry, last cup, I say, hoping he will go away. He leans back, his arms behind his head, and grins at me. You won't say anything to Pam, he says. It would only hurt her. I say nothing. He gets up finally and goes to the door, turns around. Have a good day, he says and walks off whistling. The worst thing was, he was right. I didn't tell Pam. Even if she had believed me, it would have hurt her. And it would still hurt her now. I can't tell her anything.

It wasn't your fault, I say again. You tried everything. Gary just wanted out. Yeah, I guess so, Pam says, gulping the last of her drink. Let's go home.

Felicity has taken most of the space in the twin bed we're sharing in Pam's boys' room. Half-asleep, I push her over, then notice a creeping warm liquid. She is wetting the bed. I struggle up. Come on, Felicity, I say, gathering her in my arms and carrying her to the bathroom. She seems sound asleep. I pull up her nightgown and set her on the toilet, when I notice she is jerking about. A seizure. I take her off the toilet seat and lay her on the floor, where she begins to flop like a beached fish. Sandy appears in the doorway. Is something wrong with Felicity? he asks. She's having a seizure, I tell him. Go get your mom. He returns a minute later, holding his mother's hand, eyes big and curious. Do you need me to call the doctor? says Pam. No, just get me something soft to put under her head, I say, and a towel and washcloth. I strip off Felicity's wet nightgown and lay it aside. Pam hands me a dampened washcloth and I begin to wipe the urine from Felicity's legs. Do you need to put something in her mouth? Pam asks. No, I just need to make sure she doesn't vomit while she's on her back, I reply. Felicity is still flopping. This is a long seizure. Go on, Sandy, Pam says, you don't need to watch. It's okay, I say. Sandy looks frightened. She'll be okay. The movements come slower now and finally stop. Sandy has stood as if transfixed. What'll happen now? he asks. She'll sleep, I say. She won't remember anything. I ask him to get me a blanket so I can wrap Felicity up, and he brings it to me. Do you want to take her to the hospital? Pam asks me. No, I say. There's nothing they can do right now. She'll probably sleep most of the day. I wrap her in the blanket and carry her to the bedroom.

When Pam takes us home, I discover another note stuck in the door. Retard and Hore. You better call Carl, Pam says, and makes me promise I will.

Felicity has slept most of the day and is sleeping soundly now. I've taken advantage of the quiet to get some of my reading assignments done. There was a hang-up call shortly after we returned home, so I took the phone off the hook. It's almost too quiet in here. Some music would be nice. I have selected a Stravinsky recording, the *Pulcinella* suite, and have just inserted the tape, when a knock at the front door startles me. No one stops by on Saturday night. I pull the curtain aside and peer out. Michael stands on the front porch, stomping his feet. I undo the bolt and chain. What are you doing here? I say. Is that any way to greet a friend? he asks me. It's cold out here. Can I come in? Sorry. Sure, I say, opening the door wide. Come on in. He looks tired. Is something wrong? I ask. Jeff and I had a fight, he says. I needed to talk with someone. Your phone was busy for the longest time. I figured you were home, but it worried me a little. I took it off the hook, I tell him. I've been getting hang-up calls. Looks like we've both got troubles, Michael says. He holds out a bottle of Chivas. I thought we could have a drink or two. You tell me your troubles, I'll tell you mine. And that's just what we do.

We have nearly killed the bottle of Scotch when I look at the clock. Christ, Michael, I say, it's two o'clock. Felicity will be up at seven. I have to go to bed. I'll tuck you in, he says. I'm drunk and tired and I agree. Climbing the stairs, I stumble. Michael laughs and says to me, Good thing we're not dancing tonight. We'd both be on the floor. He pulls me up clumsily. In the bedroom, he pulls my nightgown off the hook behind the door and hands it to me. Go put this on and brush your teeth, he says. I feel like a five-year-old, but it's comfortable, so I do as he tells me. I am standing back in the bedroom, in front of the dresser mirror, taking off my earrings, when Michael comes up behind me and places his hands on my shoulders. I look at us in the mirror. We look like models from a pre-Raphaelite painting, a Hunt or a Rossetti. The low light, coming from behind, haloes our hair, mine reddish, his a cool blond. He sweeps my hair back and runs his fingertips along my neck, watching my reaction in the mirror. I've slept with women before, you know, he tells me, his gaze steady. His fingers halt at my collarbone, lay there lightly, soft as the touch of a butterfly. I close my eyes. I am tempted, sorely. I know this body already, though always as if cushioned by the dance, and it's lovely—the length and tension of its muscles, its grace. It would be sweet. But sadly, I shake my head and turn to him, trace my fingers down his cheek. It would be a mistake, I say, a terrible mistake. He nods silently, then looks down. I don't want to go home, he tells me. I don't want to be alone tonight. I laugh. Well, I say, you can *sleep* with me. I'm not afraid. He nods again.

Though the bed is wide, Michael curls up close to me, for comfort. I find it comforting, too. His breath is warm and wet on the back of my neck, and I listen as his breathing slows toward sleep, settles into a soft rasp, not quite a snore.

As if through a fog, I hear Felicity calling me. Sunlight burning; it's morning. I turn groggily to find an empty furrow where Michael had lain and painfully roll out of bed. Hangover, a monster. Felicity is perched on the kitchen counter, trying to get the cereal down for breakfast. I pick her up and put her down on the floor, take a bowl and place it on the table. Sit down, Felicity, I say. I'll get you something to eat. As I go back in the kitchen to get the cereal and milk, I notice the back door is slightly ajar. Michael may have left that way. But his car was parked out front. Felicity is banging the bowl on the table. Hang on, Felicity, I say. I'm getting your food. I need an aspirin.

I finally call Carl a couple days later. I've continued getting hang-up calls, and someone has thrown eggs at the house. But that's not the worst of it. Coming home from school on Tuesday, I go to take the wash that I had hung out that morning off the line. My underwear is slashed. Slashed. Every bra, every panty. Nothing else touched. I leave it hanging on the line. When Carl comes I show it to him. He looks perplexed. I show him the note, too, and tell him about the calls, the vandalism. They might be related, he says, shrugging. I'll file a report. Not much we can do, though. It might just be kids. He scratches his head. I'll check into it. He suggests I change my phone number, get an unlisted one. The phone company can't trace the calls, because they're not long enough. You keep your place locked at night when you're home, don't you? he asks me as he's leaving. I nod my assent. Good, he says. Keep me informed if anything else happens. I say I will.

Jesus, I tell Pam later on the phone. It's just so useless. There's nothing I can do. Maybe you ought to get some protection, she tells me. What do you mean? I ask. You know, she says, a gun. A gun? I say. Christ, Pam, I couldn't do that. But later, after I've put Felicity to bed and the house is quiet, I begin to get the creeps. Maybe a gun wouldn't be such a bad idea, I think. Sure, I tell myself. As if you'd do anything with it.

I dream that night that someone is in my bedroom. I can't see him in the shadows, but I can hear the soft rasp of his breath. I wake, terrified, and the feeling doesn't go away. Someone is in the house. I keep telling myself it's only a dream and calm myself enough to go downstairs and check the house. It's silent, but the darkness threatens from every corner and nook. The moon is full tonight, and a bright patch of light cuts through the back-door window and across the floor like a path. I follow it and look out. I haven't taken down the wash, and it floats in the silver light like seaweed underwater, my underwear tattered and waving like torn sails on a sunken ship. I shiver and check the back-door lock. It's secure.

Later that night, I awake again. The dream, it must be the same dream. Someone is in my room, I'm sure. I am afraid to open my eyes, but I finally force them open and see in my doorway a shadowy, white figure, but small. Felicity. My heart is pounding. Felicity, I say. I can hardly speak. She doesn't respond, but stands there. I pull the covers off and go to her. She seems to be asleep. Come on, babe, I say to her. I take her to the bathroom, then back to her bed, where I tuck her in.

Two nights later, I am awakened by a crash, and I run downstairs. Felicity is standing in the kitchen doorway. Across the floor, glinting like stars in the moonlight, lie shards of glass. A sharp wind blows in the back-door window, shattered and empty of glass. I flick on the kitchen light. Stay there, I yell at Felicity as she starts across the kitchen floor. You'll cut your feet. I snatch her up and cut my foot instead. Shit, I say, struggling to carry her back to bed, leaving a trail of blood. Back in the kitchen, I check my foot, remove a small sliver of glass, then step carefully over the mess to reach the broom and dustpan. I sweep it up and get a garbage bag from under the sink to tape over the empty window frame. When I have finished taping the plastic, I go upstairs and wash and bandage my foot. I don't want to leave Felicity alone downstairs, so I pull a blanket off my bed, go downstairs and lie on the couch. It's cold in the house. I check Felicity to make sure she's covered, but I can't get back to sleep. I don't know what is happening, and I'm scared. I am reconsidering the gun.

The next morning, I call my friend who owns the house. I have to tell her about the window. How did it happen? she asks me. I don't know, I say, and partly that is true. I don't tell her anything about what has been going on. I don't want her to get worried—about me or about her property—yet the almost lie makes me uncomfortable. She says she'll call the glazier, have the window replaced. Will you be home today? she asks. I'll be back by three, I say. My last class ends at one. I've looked in the telephone directory and found a gun shop located on the bus route home.

Guns 'n' Games is situated between two bars, which even at this hour are doing a brisk business. The door to the right opens and the sound of country music, the smell of old tobacco smoke and stale beer issue forth like a bad memory. Two flannel-shirted, down-vested men emerge, stumbling and laughing loudly. They look at me as if I am an apparition, then continue their way to a pickup parked across the street. The metallic slam of its door propels me forward like a slap on the back, and I take a deep breath and push open the door to Guns 'n' Games. I pause just inside the door. The air is warm and dusty. To my right are bins of arrows, to my left and ahead rows of shelves displaying hunting supplies. I peer through the aisle straight ahead and to the back, where from behind a glass counter filled with guns of all shapes and sizes a man in a plaid flannel shirt stares boldly at me. As I slowly work my way toward the counter, his gaze never shifts; his face remains expressionless. I arrive finally at the counter and stand there, eyes downcast. Is there something you want? he says. It is not a friendly question. I'm looking to buy a gun, I manage to get out. It feels like a confession. I stare dumbly at the metal objects in the case, ashamed. His hands spread before me on the glass countertop. So, what kind of gun are you looking for? he asks me. I don't know, I say, then glance up at him. His eyes are stony, unreadable. I want it for protection, I say more boldly. The corners of his mouth lift slightly, just the beginning of a smile, maybe mocking. Semiautomatic or revolver? he asks. I'm not sure, I say. I've never bought a gun. I won't be intimidated, though. I put on my best reporter voice and brush my hair back from my face. Perhaps you could explain the advantages and disadvantages of each, I say. His mouth shifts closer to approximating a smile. Well, he drawls, unlocking the case and withdrawing a shiny silver handgun, this is a semiautomatic. Do you have a little one in the house? Yes, I reply. A semiautomatic is cartridge-loaded, he continues, pushing a lever, pulling back a slide on top of the gun, and extracting a rectangular metal case. It has a safety, he says, pushing the case back in the gun and moving his hand back over the top. Here, he says, handing it handle-first to me, you try it. I am a little startled, but I reach for the gun. His movements were so fast, I'm not sure what to do. Push that lever there, he says, pointing to it on the gun. I struggle a little. Like this, he says, taking the gun and showing me more slowly. He hands it back to me. I pull the lever toward me. Now what do I do? I say. He points at the top of the gun. Just pull that section, he says, slide it back toward you. I put my fingers either side and pull. Nothing happens. Try it again, he says, just pull straight back. I pull and pull. I can't do it, I say. He takes the gun from my hand then, pulls the slide back easily, extracts the cartridge, and shoves it back in. He is genuinely smiling now. That's the disadvantage, he says. Most women don't have the strength. He glances meaningfully at my hands resting on the countertop: long thin fingers, nails tapered and polished red. I draw them back toward me. Now this, he says, reaching back under the counter and pulling out another gun, is a revolver. He pulls the cartridge chamber down, twirls it. It takes six shells, .38s. You don't want anything smaller; it won't stop a man. He leans on the counter, holding the back of the gun toward me and twirls it again. You can always see whether it's loaded. He twirls it again, then pushes the chamber back into place and extends the gun toward me. Disadvantage: it doesn't have a safety. I take the gun carefully and pull the chamber down, twirl it, and push it back in place. I do it once again; it works easily. I test the trigger. I am amazed at how the gun fits so neatly in my hand, heavy, but beautifully balanced. It feels good to hold, familiar, almost like the toy six-shooter I had when I was five. I try the chamber again, then lay the weapon down. I realize that I am serious. The man must realize that, too. His attitude has switched from mocking to helpful. What about price? I ask him. He reaches under the counter again, pulls five different revolvers from the white satin bed and lines them up on the glass. He begins to explain the differences in features, metals, weight. You don't want too light a gun, he tells me, the recoil is worse. As he explains each one, he discreetly displays its price tag. I am surprised, but recover quickly. The lowest-priced is more than two hundred dollars. With the stainless steel, he continues, you don't have the upkeep, unlike the blue. The blue? I ask. He points to a black-barreled model. Blue. It must be a police term, I figure. I don't think that matters so much to me, I say. What about a safety, though? He shrugs. A revolver doesn't have one, he says. But you can get a trigger lock, or a locked case. How much do those run? I am relieved to learn a trigger lock begins at less than ten dollars. I'll have to see about a loan. He remains quiet as I pick up the various guns, then asks me, Do you have an FOIC? Pardon? I say. A firearm owners identification card, he replies. No, I say. Well, I can't sell you a gun without one, he says. Do you want to apply? I agree. He puts the guns back in the case and locks it, hands me a form. You need to fill this out. It costs ten dollars and I'll need two forms of ID, a driver's license. I nod and begin to read the form. What about the picture? I ask. He picks up a Polaroid from the counter. I can do it here, he says. The form is simple: name, address, license number, and a few check-box questions. Are you a convicted felon? No. Have you ever applied for an FOIC? No. Has your application for an FOIC ever been denied? No. Are you mentally retarded? That one stops me a moment; it's almost offensive. But I check the no box. The entire form takes only a minute. I hand it back to the man and take my wallet out of my purse, extract my license, a credit card, and a ten-dollar bill. How long will this take? I ask him. He shrugs. Two weeks, sometimes. Sometimes as much as eight. Depends. On what? I ask. Who's working, I guess, he laughs. He looks at my application. Yours shouldn't take too long, he says. Nothing to clear. He directs me behind the counter and places me against a blank spot on the wall. The camera flash blinds me momentarily. He pulls the film from the back of the camera. Let's see how this turns out, he says. We may have to do another. I go back around to the front of the counter and watch him watch the image on the film emerge. Hmm, he says approvingly. Not bad. He holds the picture out for my approval. It's not a bad picture, but that grim visage hardly looks like me, I think. Just about perfect for a gun card, though. Here's your receipt, he says to me, and I turn and head for the door. Just as I'm about to leave, he yells across the room. You might want to learn to shoot it. I turn. Where would I do that? I ask. He gives me the names of a couple rifle clubs. Thanks, I say. I'll be back. Sure thing, he replies. We'll take care of you.

By the time I get home, it's nearly three and the glazier is waiting. I let him in and watch for Felicity's school bus.

You can't do anything right, Felicity's father used to tell me, and I believed him at first. After hearing that for more than two years, though, I became angry. I'm angry now, because I'm beginning to doubt myself again. I'm listening to the tape of the interview I did last night, wondering how much I can salvage, if anything. Felicity is digging through my bag, and she's found a pack of gum. She won't leave me alone, so I give her a stick and lead her to her room to find a toy to distract her.

The interview is an assignment for reporting class. A personality profile—of someone unimportant, someone unknown, both to the audience and to the interviewer. Challenging. But I thought I had come up with a great solution. A fellow student I had worked on a presentation with once, in a philosophy class. Buber. *I and Thou*. What made the interview potentially interesting though was that this young man had started out as a professional baseball player. He was on his way to the majors, when he just dropped out, decided to go back to school and study philosophy. To me, it seemed a tremendous change, and one worth examining. He readily agreed to the interview, even offered to come to my place so I wouldn't have to get a sitter. It seemed like a good idea at the time. The tape starts out innocuously enough: questions about his childhood, where he grew up, his family, his aspirations. But about ten minutes in, it begins, subtly at first, veiled innuendoes. It degenerates quickly into a direct sexual come-on. I hear myself try to recover control, but the interview is gone, off track, hopeless. He left angry. I'll have to ask my instructor for an extension.

I am rewinding the tape when Felicity comes back in the living room and climbs up on the couch next to me. Mommmy. Just a minute, Felicity, I say, grabbing hold of her legs as she stands precariously over me. Sit down, Felicity. Mommy will take care of you in a minute. I reach with my other hand to push the recorder away so that it doesn't fall. Mommmy, Felicity insists. I try to get her to sit. Mommmmy. The gum falls out of her mouth and onto the top of my head. I try to push her away, grab her hand, but I am too late. She's pounced like a starving puppy on a piece of meat. Both hands. Lunging at the gum. Embedding it in my hair. Squealing in anger as she fights to retrieve it, entangling it all the more. I can't get her away, and I fear knocking her off the couch. We are genuinely scuffling, and she seems to have the advantage. Finally, she stops, takes one swipe at my face, opens her mouth, and lets out a howl. I set her down on the floor and raise my fingers to my hair to see if I can pull the gum out, but find only a sticky tangled lump. I leave her howling and go to get some ice. If I'm quick enough, I might still get it out.

Felicity has progressed to a full-blown tantrum, shrieking and throwing things about. I'd like to smack her, but I am so angry I don't dare go near her. She'll wear herself out eventually. Meanwhile, I concentrate on removing the gum. The ice does nothing. I read somewhere that peanut butter might work, but it doesn't. All I've succeeded in doing is making more of a mess. I'll have to cut it out. I get the barber's shears from my bedroom and return to the bathroom mirror, begin to cut away the gluey mass. When I am finished a patch big as a drinking glass tufts up like new grass from the crown of my head. Reluctantly, I pick up the shears again. Streamers of hair fall, mound and drape like fabric around my feet. A stranger stares at me from the mirror, a penitent, tears runnelling her cheeks. Downstairs, the racket has finally ceased.

The instructor granted me the extension, but it wasn't easy. I don't like to do this sort of thing, he said, staring curiously at me. It's too easy to get behind. I stare at the floor; I have nothing to hide behind anymore. Did something happen? he asks me. Is there anything wrong? It just didn't work out, the tape . . . I mumble. I'm not going to explain. It's too embarrassing. Well, let me know if there is something, he says, running his hand through his thinning hair. If I can do anything to help. I murmur my thanks and leave his office gratefully.

I'm thinking I'll call Pam, do an interview about being a cop's wife. It's cheating on the requirements, since I know her, but I don't care so much about those things anymore. I am walking toward the phone booth, when someone grabs my arm. Michael. I haven't seen him since that night. He draws me out of the stream of bodies, into an empty doorway. Holy God, he says. I almost didn't recognize you. What have you done to yourself? I cut my hair, I manage to get out, before he turns me about, inspecting me. And what happened to your ass, girl? he exclaims. It's disappeared. He whistles low, then turns me about to face him, his hands on my shoulders. Are you all right? I'm okay, I say. I've just been losing weight. I'll say, he replies. Look, he says, I'm sorry I haven't gotten in touch. I tried a couple times, but your phone was busy. I shrug. I kept the phone off the hook most of the time until the telephone company switched my number. I have a new number, I tell him, opening one of my notebooks to write it down. It's unlisted. Don't give it out, please. I tear out the page and hand it to him. I won't, he says, taking the paper and folding it. He puts his hand on my arm again. Are you sure you're okay? Yeah, Michael, I'm fine, I say. I don't like this scrutiny. I've got a class now, he apologizes. I've got to go. But give me a call later in the week. He reaches up and brushes my hair. I steel myself to remain still. Jeff and I'll come over. He'll trim your hair up properly. As I watch Michael's back receding down the hallway, I think about the shocked look on his face. The hair, of course. But also the thinness. I noticed myself the other night, standing in front of my dresser mirror. I could count my ribs all the way down the front of me, even under my breasts, which seemed to be shriveling like fruit laid out in the sun. My pelvis beginning to hollow like a bowl. But the sight didn't alarm me; in fact I felt calm, strangely satisfied. I remember, though, the dream I had that night. I am standing, bound to a post, and my hair begins to drop away like water. I hear hissing and watch the hair begin to twitch and wriggle like snakes. It's alive, I think. Then I look up. A crowd. I can't see their faces, but I know the hissing is coming from them. Like waves. I look down again; the snakes have transformed to flames, licking first at my feet. I feel no pain. The flames writhe higher; my flesh begins to melt away like wax. I can see the bones underneath. I watch calmly as smoke begins to rise. The crowd is gone, but beyond the smoke darts a shadow. I can hear the rasp of his breath as he moves completely out of sight.

A short time after I get home, I hear a knock at the door. I open it and stare confused at the social worker standing there, clipboard in hand. Can I come in? she finally asks. Silently, I open the door wider. I don't know what this is about. It doesn't take long to find out. Someone has reported me again for abuse. I checked on Felicity at school, she says. She has a rather large bruise on her leg. Yes? I say, thinking back. She probably got it during her last tantrum, but I don't offer the woman this information. This is the second report, you know, she says. She looks almost gleeful. So what does that mean? I say.

What it meant was that I was called to a conference at Felicity's school, where her teacher, the principal, and the social worker interrogated me. It also meant that I would have to put up with the bitch making unannounced "visits" again. Two months' worth. I've passed nearly a month of the sentence now, and have just ushered the bitch out the door again, when the telephone rings. Pam asks if I'm taking Felicity out for Halloween. I don't think it's a good idea, I say. Well, you're probably right, she agrees. She says she'll bring the boys by after they make the circuit in their neighborhood.

There aren't many trick-or-treaters on Halloween, but Felicity seems happy enough running around in her sheet, stuffing candy into the proffered bags. Every time there's a knock at the door, she runs to it, shrieking at the top of her lungs. It's getting wearing. Jolene came by with Dylan, but that's the only neighbor I have recognized. Pam and the boys finally show up about eight. The bowl of candy is still two-thirds full. Don't get too comfortable, Pam says to them as they head for Felicity's room. We can't stay long. Pam and I are finishing our drinks when an especially loud knock surprises us. We've shut off the porch light. A little late, isn't it? she says, glancing at her watch. I shrug and go to the door, turn on the light. Pam follows me. It's a group of older kids, junior high, high school age, loud and boisterous. As I'm filling up their bags, glad to be getting rid of the candy so it won't be around for Felicity to get into, I catch a whiff of alcohol. A couple kids are hanging back in the shadows, paranoid, I suppose. Pam peers intently over my shoulder. Did you recognize those kids?

she asks me when I've closed the door and shut off the light again. No, I say. Why? She hesitates. Oh, it's probably nothing, she says. What? I ask. Well, she says, it's just that for a minute I thought maybe one of those kids standing back was the baby-sitter. I look at her, then pull the curtain aside to look out. No one in sight. I'm probably imagining things, she reassures me. But as she's leaving, she says to call her if anything happens. We'll be fine, I say.

Felicity has finally settled into sleep; she was overexcited from all the people and activity—and, maybe, from the candy that she ate. I'm overexcited myself from trying to get her to bed and I decide to pour myself another drink, relax a little. I turn on the tap until the water runs cold, put the glass of Scotch underneath, when I hear a scuffling on the front porch. I turn the water off, listen. A thud. Glass in hand, I go to the front window, pull the curtain aside to peer out. Something's burning on the porch. I douse it with my drink, turn on the porch light to examine it closer. I wouldn't believe this if it weren't Halloween: someone's pulled the burning-bag-of-shit trick, setting it afire, hoping I'd rush to stomp it out. Sorry to disappoint you, I think, turning the light out again and peering into the night. No one in sight. When I close the door and bolt it tight, though, I think I hear muffled laughter close by.

Next morning, Felicity's sleeping late, and I take advantage of this respite to clean the mess off the porch. I grab a trash bag. The snow shovel should still be there on the porch. When I step outside, I notice the yard is draped in toilet paper, and as I'm carrying the bag of shit around to the trash can in back of the house, I glance up. Spray-painted in red on the side of the house are the words Retard and Hore, at least two feet high. As I dial Pam's number, I realize I'm shaking. What are you going to do? she asks me. I know what I'm going to do. My FOIC arrived last week, and I've been approved for a student loan.

Pam had some leftover paint, and she came over that morning and helped me paint over the graffiti. We put on two coats, but you can still see the words if you look carefully, bleeding pink through the pristine white, as if it's growing like mildew, refusing to be eradicated.

Hatred is like that, I'm learning. Or maybe it's not hatred, specifically, but blind and generalized evil hanging in the air like spores all around you, looking for a place to root, nourishing itself with the fear it generates. I refuse to be fearful, or at least refuse to show it.

The telephone company offered to switch my number again, because of the hang-up calls—actually, they had progressed to heavy breathing by that point—but I declined. Another number, another point scored. It would start all over again anyway. Now, the only time I answer the phone is for Pam and Michael, and those are pre-arranged. You can't live like this, Pam told me. I'm afraid it's no longer a matter of choice, I said to her. And, of course, there are still the anonymous notes, threatening Felicity and me. The police aren't interested anymore. Me, I'm just waiting for the next move. I know in my bones it's coming. I dream about it, that shadow. Sometimes it wakes me up at night, and I listen. I listen. I know every noise that belongs to this house, to my daughter, to me. I know all the smells. It's as if I've developed radar. I can even tell when that shadow draws *close* to the house. I could hear a doorknob turn. I'm waiting. I will know its face.

And it's the smell that wakes me tonight, like something musty. Not only the smell, I notice, but the silence, muffled, as if a blanket had been thrown over the entire house. It's here, I know, and I am ready. I edge my legs over the side of the bed and stand up, withdraw the revolver from under the bed, where I keep it at night. I withdraw the key from my lingerie drawer, where I've taped it, and turn it in the trigger lock. The lock snaps like a stick breaking, then falls away in my hand. When I reach the top of the stairs the cold hits me. A door, a window, is open. I listen, then descend the stairs. At the bottom I pause, look toward the living room. Nothing. I feel transformed, unhesitating, deadly certain. The cold is coming from the kitchen. I ease around the corner, my back to the wall, both hands gripping the revolver, not tight, but relaxed. The room appears empty, but the back door is slightly ajar. I cross the doorway to the corner of the counter, my bare feet soundless, impervious to the cold. I crouch. Outside the door, I hear a shuffling, like dead leaves blowing, but I know there's something else. I can hear the breathing. I sit, my elbows propped lightly against my knees, as if I'm balancing a camera for a long shot and I don't have a tripod. I am in position. A shadow emerges through the window and spreads across the floor. The door whines lightly open. I can hear the breathing. I take aim, squeeze the trigger. It's like dancing.

George Rogers

University of Alaska, Fairbanks

LIVING NEAR CANADA

Dad used to drive tanker. Milk tanker, that is. Twenty-two years for McCadem Dairy Products. But then, even with all those Drink Milk! commercials on, prices started dropping and McCadem told their drivers to buy their own trucks or lose their jobs. So, with a tanker running twice as much as the yearly salary of your basic milkman, and a new prison coming on line, it wasn't much of a decision for him. He went and took the civil servant's test. And, bingo, they called him up. Measured him for a uniform. Making twenty-six a year now, but he's a damn prison guard. It isn't exactly hauling milk, but at least he didn't have to leave town like a bunch of the others did. So there's one thing. The other thing is that now, on some mornings, after Dad has worked a night shift and I've been out drinking at the Z-Bar, he and I will pull into the driveway at the same time and, if the night is clear, we usually stand out on the porch awhile, listening to the morning sounds and muttering stuff about the government and the way the new prison lights make our whole frigging valley glow.

Mostly this town's just trailer parks and bankrupt dairy farms. The only bar in town is the High Falls Inn, and that's where our grandfathers drink, so we go to Doc Roc's Z-Bar in Malone. Malone is a bigger town with fewer cows. The Z-Bar is a good enough place, although occasionally I do like heading across the border, into Quebec, having a few at the Bamboo Room. It's good not knowing the language sometimes—just being able to drink your beer without a clue. I like French.

I used to push a lawn mower into Canada, but my brother does that now. There's a cemetery on the border that takes twenty hours to mow. Lot of room in that place. Lilacs and tiger lilies there, too. Working around the dead part of my family made me appreciate the live ones more. Then, like I say, my brother took over. This summer they gave him a new mower to use and everything—mixed his gas up, too. Nothing to it. But it was the same way for me, and then I went off to Plattsburgh State for a couple years until Johnny, this ox-head friend of mine, had some townie asshole knock his head open because we tried to piss in this guy's backseat—like that's a reason to jerk a lead pipe out of your trunk and split open a guy's face. A bunch of us threw that townie down in the snow and put our boots to him until a wallet and cigarettes and blood began to spill out. So I don't go there anymore because the college gave me a lot of grief about that, and now I got a job sorting and collecting junk at the recycling center here in town. I tell everybody I turn their trash into cash. But Holly's going to finish her degree. She says she'll come home and teach at Bishop Smith.

When Holly puts henna in her hair and slips in those ivory earrings of hers, it makes me want to shout and dive off bridges. She and I ice-fish in Chateaugay Lake. I had heard the lake was full of mercury, but we never worried much about all those perch and trout and salmon we'd eaten until Holly's hands and feet started going numb. She'd been seeing a doctor. And last night we were all sitting in the living room—she and I on the couch and her father in his slippers, beers beside him, shouting at the Canadiens game—when Holly asks me to hold her hand and I tell her I have been, can't you feel me? Then she says her whole left side is floating away. So I scoop her up and jog her to the car while her dad flings open doors for us and screams about the damned perch that Holly and I had caught for the aquarium—yelling about how he's going to get his chemist friend to analyze them so he can sue the Department of Environmental Conservation.

Holly's dad is a crazy French bastard. I'm not Catholic or married to his daughter, but he lets me call him Serge anyway. He walks like he's got staples in his ankles, but he's silk on skates. He coached me and Johnny for years, still says I take slapshots off the wrong foot. That bastard. If he saw you screwing off in practice, he'd send a puck toward your head. He never hurt anybody, although I don't know if he meant not to; it just worked out that way. Anyway, he'd pile half the team in his wood-paneled station wagon and motor us through snowstorms to weekend tournaments all over the North Country. In between games, he'd find a bar with a pool table and video games and throw us out a couple rolls of quarters while he and the other fathers drank.

He stayed with Holly all last night. I was sitting in the waiting area with him, looking for something to read other than goddamn coffee-stained issues of *Redbook*, when he turns and says, "You can't do much good here," then jerks out his wallet and shoves twenty dollars at me and says I should go out since it's Saturday night and all. I point out that he can't do much good either and push the money back at him.

"When I give you money, you take it," he says, shaking the bill.

"Keep your damn money," I tell him, and a nurse looks over at us. "I'm not going anywhere."

Then we see Johnny tromping down the hallway, swinging his arms and asking us what's the matter. He'd been on his way out to the Z-Bar when he'd seen us bounce over the curb and into the emergency entrance. He stands over us now, asking if there's anything he can do and smelling like a fragrance insert in a magazine, all slicked up because he's going someplace there'll be women—like it's going to make them forget he's a farmer's son. We tell him what happened to Holly, and then Serge reaches across me, waving the twenty dollars at Johnny, saying "Take your buddy out, loosen him up. Tell him she'll be fine."

I push his arm back, but by now Johnny's grabbed the money.

"Come on, asshole," Johnny says to me.

"Go on," says Serge.

• • •

I was just as glad to get out of there, because waiting for news about Holly made me feel like last year when Johnny and I went down to the winter carnival in Saranac Lake. They've got a little parade that goes down Main Street—pee-wee hockey teams and pep squads, grade-school floats on hay wagons, things like that—and an ice castle carved out of blocks that they make the prisoners cut from the lake. Main Street is narrow, so they string up orange plastic fences along the sidewalks to keep the crowds from bulging into the parade and pinching off the procession.

Snow was in the air that afternoon, and we had our backpacks crammed with brandy flasks and beer, most of them empty, and we were hanging off the balcony at the Waterhole, whistling and clapping for little girls and their batons, when Johnny falls off the bar's railing and into a snowbank and that takes the wind out of him, and I jump next, somersaulting onto his knee, and he howls, and that's when a cop starts through the crowd after us, and we scramble over the orange fence, sprinting through the center of the parade, making some kid drop his trumpet. We pass the ice castle and the boat launch, jogging out onto the lake. Cops pull up. But none of them come after us, and we can't understand why until they start making megaphone announcements about weak ice, and then a Ski-Doo comes screaming up the lake and breaks through. Everybody scrambles over to see if the guy's going to surface, and he does, clawing his way up and almost out of the water, arms and chest resting on the ice a moment before slipping back under, fighting for the surface while two guys squirm out onto the ice, throwing him the end of a pair of jumper cables, dragging him to shore. And after he's safe and someone's tossed a blanket on him, he starts hopping around and swearing about his snowsled, beating a trash barrel.

That's when we look at each other and Johnny asks, "What's that bastard's trouble? He's on shore."

So we decided to sit down and pass a flask around as they shouted more safety tips our way. And we sat there like that, talking and catching our breath, taking bets on how much we'd get fined. Then we lay back on the ice so the wind would swirl over us and wouldn't bite as much. We lay beside each other like that awhile, letting snow drift in around us.

We push our way into the Z-Bar and the Blind Pig Blues Band is squealing away. Christmas decorations in the rafters. Pool table strung with garland. Bouncers in Santa hats. The place full of broomball teams down from league-night at the arena—all seats taken and others lean against barn-board walls. Johnny orders shooters and drafts, and we start talking with everybody. They ask me where Holly is and if she's having a good Christmas break, and I tell them she's about as numb as I'm going to be in a minute. Then Johnny gives them the details while I turn to the bar for another shot and announce that the only reason anybody plays broomball is because they don't know how to goddamn skate. I get some looks from the few guys I don't know, but everybody else thinks I'm pretty funny.

By now we've got a few shooters rattling through us and we're working on fresh beers. The band breaks, and my cousin, Nick, comes up and tells me to let him know when I need my next round. He's in his broomball uniform and saying Holly will be fine.

During the summer the migrant workers would walk down here to the Z after working the spinach fields. Then some pricks kicked the hell out of them. I wasn't there when it started, but I guess it wasn't the type of fight that guys on opposite broomball teams get in. Or the way a guy from Malone will start something with a guy from Chateaugay. The migrants got jumped while they were shooting pool. Slashed with broken bottles. Chased into the street. Knocked one out with a pool cue. The owner said it was the migrants' fault, so they don't let Filipinos in anymore. Sometimes I think I'd like to get into that same kind of fight with one of those bastards who did that to those pickers. I can't imagine waking up in the middle of the street, thousands of miles from home, asphalt scraped into me. Damn, when I got there, the whole bar was emptied out on top of the guy, red-blue lights sweeping over the scene while some local son of a bitch was explaining to his high school cop-friend how the unconscious guy started the whole thing.

• • •

Holly came home from school last week, and we were driving out to the lake when she told me she'd been losing some of the feeling in her hands and feet—said the doctor had told her what she had was rare—she was losing the thin sheath of cells that surrounds her nervous system. She told me to picture a nightcrawler losing its skin, its body turning against itself. So that day I drove my little shit-box truck out on the ice because it was clear and about fifteen below and I didn't want to find out that she got frostbite because she couldn't feel it coming. The wind pushed across the ice, carrying a mist up from some open water past where we parked that turned to snow as it blew our way. But she didn't have any trouble that day. She said she was getting cold just like me, and we laughed about that when we would hold hands and jog back to the truck's heater.

I had trouble keeping the auger running in that cold. And even though the ice was only ten inches thick, we didn't get many holes drilled and baited. Damn auger. The choke on that thing has never been right, and in bad weather it just reminds you more. So while I tried to drill, Holly, in her father's wool hunting pants, followed along with a minnow bucket and skimmer, clearing the slush out of the few holes I managed to sink, bending over the holes and warming her hands underneath her armpits before threading the hooks through the minnows and running our lines out under the ice.

Trout and salmon cruise high in winter, backs almost touching the ice, so we set our lines maybe a foot under, never using any weight. We understand how they move, so me and Holly lay more fish on the ice than anybody. That's why these maniacs come skidding over to us on their frigging four-wheelers after we've had flag after flag snap up, asking us what we're using, and gawking at the frozen fish and stained ice around our holes. Most times they ask Holly because they figure a woman will give them a straight answer (plus she's damn near perfect-looking). So when I'm off checking a line, they'll dart up to her and tell her how refreshing it is to find a woman out on the ice, and say "My, what nice fish you have," and then ask her how we're catching them. And, of course, she lies like hell.

Some of the rainbows are so bright when we pull them from the water that it hurts us a little watching the colors drain out of them.

Holly and I talk about building a shanty. She says her father's got one of those kerosene heaters, and with that, and plywood, and some fiberglass insulation, there's no cold that could keep us off the lake. Holly might not be able to feel the difference, but at least I'd know she'd be warm. One of the reasons we don't build a shanty is because we aren't married yet and aren't sure what Serge would think of the idea. He's a hell of a guy and all, retired from McCadem last winter, has the walls of his home decorated with five-thousand-piece jigsaw puzzles. I've seen him put one of those together in two days, and I like to watch him, even help pick out the edge pieces sometimes, but he's damn careful about Holly, and who can blame him?—with a red-headed daughter who likes catching trout and all.

They got a buffalo mounted above the dance floor with tubes running from a smoke machine down into its nostrils, so if you tip the bartender, he'll make it snort a cloud over everybody. We've tried to steal that bastard a few times, but they got it bolted up there good. Of course, what the hell we'd do if we did yank it off the wall I don't know. You don't exactly slip out of a bar with a bison. Probably one of the first things they tell a bouncer when they hire him is to guard that buffalo. But I don't know what's so special about the damn thing—it's not like it was wild or anything. It was raised on Hesseltine's farm. They shot the thing when it came down with brucellosis. This was after months of telling everyone they were going to have a hell of a barbecue with buffalo steaks and kegs and Johnny's brother's band would come up from Syracuse. The whole deal. It still pisses me off thinking about how we never got a chance to eat that son of a bitch.

The band starts up again, and I give my last few dollars to the bartender, telling him to keep that buffalo wheezing until there's zero visibility on the dance floor. So he starts priming the smoke machine and a bunch of us start strutting to the Blind Pigs. By now smoke is curling out of the nostrils and everybody's gathered round, cheering and clapping, and the band's sax player is tooting low bison notes while the drummer's pumping out a stampede beat. The creature's really starting to steam, and by now there's probably a dozen of us leaping around the dance floor, and the band's getting louder. The whole bar is screaming at us, the beast's eyes glowing, and I can't see much with all the smoke. Then they turn the frigging strobe on, making the place look like the redneck disco barn that it is. Others join in, running onto the dance floor, pushing and blowing cigarette smoke at the animal, some lifting each other up and taking drags straight out of its nostrils. That's about when some asshole catches me in the chin with his elbow, and I swing back through the cloud and connect with somebody, and I'm not even sure who. But I'm thinking that I probably know this guy I just smacked. Then I see my cousin go down with some bastard on top of him, so I put my knee into the guy's ear, and he rolls off Nick. The crowd is soaking us with beer and shoving anybody who tries to leave the dance back into the middle of it all. Everybody's throwing their weight around now, and some bottles hit the floor, and somebody catches Johnny from behind, and he slumps toward the glass, but I catch him and stand him up. I see who hit him—some guy in a Santa hat that we graduated with, the bastard grinning like it's a damn football game or something and looking to have at somebody else, so I take a kick at him and miss his groin, but he doesn't miss me, and the next thing I know Johnny's pulling me off the floor and saying we might want to get out of here so we can pull some of this glass out of my hands.

Serge had a tooth pulled once. The wrong tooth. Dentist told him to relax and with a little nitrous he did, then the doctor hauled out a perfectly good chomper instead of the abscessed one. Serge raised hell in that little office, sending a tabletop of teeth molds and complimentary toothbrushes into the waiting room where Holly was sitting.

Serge still tells the story: "You should've seen that guy when I jumped out of the chair. He was shivering like a dog shitting razor blades. Next time you need a filling, you just tell him I sent you and see what kind of deal he gives you."

Now the entire LaRoque family—cousins, aunts, uncles, everybody—gets dental work done no charge. But if the dentist had really stopped and thought about the state of that family's teeth, he might have been better off taking the lawsuit Serge threatened. Holly's teeth are decent, though. Probably the best smile in the family—only a little crooked—kind of like how a sidewalk gets after a few winters, undulating, but fun to walk on.

They weren't going to let us in Alice Hyde even though Johnny and I told them we were there to see Holly. I said, "Go get Serge," that he'd vouch for us. But some damn receptionist was pointing to the door and saying sobering up would be the best idea, when I remembered my hands and held them up and said, "Oh, yeah, by the way, how about fixing these?" So he punches me into their computer, and we go and have a seat beside a now-sleeping Serge—his head's slumped over, glasses in his pocket.

"Hey, Serge," I say.

He reaches for his glasses, raises his head slowly, blinking a couple of times before sliding on his bifocals. Johnny comes over from the vending machine with a coffee and hands it to him. He takes it from Johnny and drinks.

"What time is it?" he says, taking another sip, and then looks at my hands. "Tough night, eh?"

"Looking like a ten-stitch Saturday, Coach," Johnny says.

"Probably ought to throw both your asses right in the goddamn clink, is what they ought to do," Serge says, then sets down his coffee and turns away from us, looking toward the emergency-room door. "I don't know," he says. "They've had her in there this whole time. Nobody's told me a damn thing. Starting to piss me off." He watches the door a minute, then stands with his coffee, reaching for his cigarettes, and walks out of the hospital and into the empty parking lot. From the lobby, we watch him smoking under a lamppost, the snow coming down around him only visible as it falls into his umbrella of light.

I never met Holly's mother, but I mowed around her. She's on the Quebec side. Maples shade the border there and that's unusual because everywhere else they've clear-cut a hundred-yard swath to show you where our country ends and the next one begins. But I suppose cemeteries don't need precise boundaries. My brother's been doing a hell of a job up there—and you've got to because everyone knows who to complain about when Uncle Albert's headstone gets stained with lawn clippings. When I was working it, I'd walk a line of graves, pulling up flags and setting aside wreaths, run the mower by the stones, then set the decorations back. Some mornings I'd find deer feeding among the plots and when I'd begin pouring the gas, they'd spook back into Canada.

When I was a kid Serge came by one day while I was mowing. He got down with a trowel and put in a little bush for his wife, then called me over to tell me not to run over it. After that he tamped the dirt down around it a little more and walked off through the maples.

Hell. Me and Johnny and Serge waited outside that emergency room until my hands were almost healed before they let me in, and then some smart-ass kid doctor starts making jokes about how I was saving money on anesthesia, and maybe more folks should stop by the Z before operations.

He tells a nurse to sew me up.

"I wouldn't have come here at all except I want to know how Holly LaRoque is doing."

The nurse tells me to keep still and forces the needle through the thick part of my palm. "We're keeping her overnight," she says.

Then Doc Hollywood struts over, hops up beside me like he's my buddy or something, watching the nurse poke away at me.

"Look," he says, "we want to keep her overnight. We'll be running tests tomorrow—probably give Burlington a call in the morning, see what they have to say."

Last summer two Pakistanis tried to take a damn cab into Quebec. Of course they got deported. I don't know why so many want to get into Canada, don't know why everybody seems to want to keep moving. But they do. Hell, if I wanted to take a cab into Canada, I could. I bet if I'd been driving those Pakistanis, I could have got them across the border, because when me and Johnny drive up to have a few at the Bamboo Room, they wave us right into their country. They know we're just from Burke. And when we come back all lit up, our headlights wagging over the road, slowly coming to rest in front of customs, the officers don't say anything to us—maybe ask us if we've got our deer yet, or if we think the fields are dry enough to start cutting corn. But that's it. In fact, I only have one friend who has trouble getting into Canada, and that's because he's a Mohawk and he shot at a couple RCMP officers one time. But, shit, they'd strung razor wire around his cousin's reservation.

"Johnny," I say, and he wakes up with a jump because I'm close enough to lick his eyeballs. He's the only one left in the waiting area now.

"Son of a bitch, back up a little, why don't you?"

So I give him some room and I hold up my new hands for him. "What do you think?" I ask.

"You look like a shark-attack victim."

"Where's Serge?" I say, looking down the corridor.

"He's with Holly."

"What'd the doctor say?"

"I don't know. He and Serge walked over to the front desk and whispered awhile. Then Serge came over, slapped my leg, and told us that we should take off because he's going to stay the night."

"What room?" I say, and start down a hallway, with Johnny following, telling me they don't need us hanging around. "I just want to look in on her."

"Come on. We'll visit her tomorrow," he says, putting his arm on my shoulder like he's trying to comfort me, but all he's really doing is trying to steer me toward the door.

I push him away.

"Look," he says, "if this was serious, they'd let you in there. They'd want everybody to see her. Don't worry about it. Let Serge watch her sleep." Then he asks to see my hands again, and I say they're froze up pretty good, so Johnny says we should go get more beers in me before the feeling comes back. So I agree, and on the way out we show the receptionist my stitches.

Holly's coming home, going to teach at Bishop Smith.

She is.

I know it.

• • •

The Trout River flows through our village, and then, a few miles later, spills out of the country. We had a damn psychic around town last century. I've mowed around her and everyone who's appeared in her visions—like the five kids who didn't come home one night. This woman told the kids' parents that she'd seen shadows leaving the river, rising from where the water poured through the milk-house dam. And when a group of fathers scraped pikes along the grates of the dam, they came up with driftwood and beaver sticks and young bodies tangled together. They hauled them to shore like that, all hollow-mouthed and some punctured from the pikes. So I'm glad we don't have any frigging psychics in town these days—no room for optimism or pessimism with those freaks around—always telling it like it will be and all.

Early in the spring, during sugar season, they got spigots and buck-ets on the maples in the cemetery, bleeding them for all they're worth. They probably drip five thousand gallons of sap out of there in a good year. My great-grandparents are dead there, on the New York side, contributing to the quality of the syrup. They had a farm just this side of the border and would share the warmth of their heifers with Chinese immigrants, letting families gather strength in their barn before pointing them toward the distant thread of St. Lawrence River that would guide them to Montreal. And probably on moonlit nights my great-grandfather would give them food and point north one last time before watching them move off carefully toward the border, melting into his fields. And people still sift through this town, leaving prison or the spinach fields, others hoping to slip out of the country to some other goddamn place, while the rest of us hold on— little stones in the flour, impossible to shake free, forever kicking around Burke, New York.

Maybe those fish do have mercury in them and maybe they did get Holly sick, but more likely it's one of Serge's conspiracy theories. He's always screaming about how satellites watch everybody, and why hos-pitals deliberately switch babies. So the fish around here might make you sick, but I know that there's medicine in this town, too. Here's why: I shot a bear that'd been tearing up Hesseltine's corn and after we got a bucket loader to haul it out, I went back and rummaged around in the gut-pile and sliced off the gall bladder from the liver. I wrapped some dental floss around it so the juice wouldn't leak, dried it by our wood stove, then hid it in my boot. At the border, they only asked Holly and me a couple of questions before waving us through. Then we picked up my brother from his lawn mowing and kept driving until we hit Chinatown in Montreal, where we stomped into this little medicinal shop that had glass urns of dried seahorses and elk horns stacked to the ceiling. When I took that bear part out of my boot and dropped it on the glass counter, the owner got so excited that he paid us enough to buy a case of Labatts and tickets to the Canadiens game.

That next morning Johnny bought me breakfast, and then we were back in the waiting room. I was thinking about the lights of Canadian towns and how the prison's floodlights make it impossible to see them anymore, when suddenly Serge was standing in front of me, looking down and saying something about how they're loading Holly onto a helicopter. Then we were walking through the hospital parking lot, Johnny wishing us the best and asking if we needed anything and Serge telling him thanks but we'll be fine and me getting behind the wheel and driving the old man toward Burlington. As we drove out of town, it reminded me how, in late summer, he and I would start out into the cornfields when the sun touches the tips of the trees and the air begins to cool—when the milking starts, carrying our stools and rifles, passing the cows as they lumber back to the barn, udders fat and swaying, heavy steps raising clouds of flies from their legs while we move toward the back fields, where the corn meets the woods, stepping around more and more piles of bear shit as we get farther from the barn. Serge will stop and kick at the fresher piles, full of ripe kernels and cherry pits, as I climb the stone walls and look out over the corn, trying to find where the bears are coming into the fields, studying the paths of broken stalks. Sometimes, when the bears wander out of the woods early, and the cows are late leaving the pastures, bear scent will drift between the herd and the barn and even with the pressure of milk welling up inside them, it's sweat and hell trying to push and beat them back through that wall of musk and dead air that separates them from where they need to be. But we slap their asses with broken hockey sticks, driving them back toward their stalls, swearing about how we should have been out sitting on our stools earlier, knowing that once a damn bear slips into the corn, he's impossible to get. But most nights the cows file down the rutted path without our prodding, and in the fields we see no stalks falling. So we hurry to the edge of the woods, flushing partridge from the chokecherries as we step along, slipping shells into our rifles, watching the birds glide away from us, into the woods. And it's on these nights that we sit, like we're doing now, full of quiet hope, ready for what is moving toward us, knowing that what'll be remembered is never the waiting.

Heather McGowan
Brown University

CHEMISTRY

They sniff glue. In the alley behind the tudor watch shop where the vegetable smells marry piss. Brickie *you stay away from him, Sophie said, you'll see that boy's a bastard* fumbling with the tube, squeezing airplane fixative into his father's handkerchief. Bringing the white square up to cover mouth and nose. Bastard eyes on her.

What? . . . kicking at a bottle on the cobbles . . . How can I hear you through that?

Taking it down, eyes watering . . . You're supposed to be looking out, not looking at me.

I told you not to bring her . . . Paul *him too stay away from both once he pushed my elbow up behind my back for no reason* waiting for the glue. Tips of fingers in trouser pockets just the nails. Scarf a concertina around his ears. Looking one way down the alley then the other . . . A yank . . . muttering . . . God help us.

Paul can be lookout.

And into the bright street. As if she needed Paul with his rattlesnake neck always saying Yank. Through the village green past the fountain of a rearing horse. Tea at five-thirty. Half past that is. A great mattress of bread to make up for the hot food. Jam sandwiches three times a day. Into the Chemist's. Lavender grannie soaps in crenulated wrappers, shelves of orthopedic devices and plasters. Pumping a solution for eczema. Never warm at Monstead, not like this at least. Never nearly hot. Crossing to linger at the lip display. Behind her a woman curses a child. Salmon to mud with something plummy in the middle range.

The word chutney. Why. Maybe ploughman's for Tea. In fifteen minutes she sees by the clock over the door. Late for chutney. In the mirror she tries Fire Fire. Hair chaotic, you could say. She never brought a brush to school and why would Father remember. Forgotten pencils, lost hairpins stick her when she lies down at night.

Sniffing epoxy vapor, what did that feel like? Pressing her lips to even the color. Was high like drunk which she had been slightly last Christmas when the tree ornaments overbled their edges when everything seemed funny even though Mother had cancer which was not really funny at all.

Form a comb with your fingers. Or use a palm to smooth it. Chutney Chutney. Could have seen it on the menu posted outside the dining hall. Placed there to temper your appetite. Gilbert never says anything about her wild hair among the jokes he makes. In class once he made fun of her American accent but when the boys from the back row joined in hollering, he looked sorry. Didn't stop his other jokes though. Calling attention to her hips when they studied calcium or saying *Perhaps Evans will follow the example set by Miss Monroe* when they did the hydrogen peroxide experiments. As if she didn't have enough problems with hair.

If she had the money in her belt, she would buy bubbles for the Wednesday night bath or a new sponge or oil to turn her legs brown.

I know things on you . . . Brickie leaning against the counter in torn sleeves . . . What's on your mouth?

How long have you been there?

Don't go thinking you're telling or—

Are you spying on me?

What do I care about this stupid girl crap. I'm warning you is all.

Why . . . wiping away Fire Fire . . . Would I tell?

Brickie picks up a silver tin from the display . . . What's this do?

Eyelashes. You have to wet the paint.

Move it . . . knocking her from the mirror spitting in the tin.

What is it you know?

Brickie, reflected . . . Something . . . mouth open in concentration, pinkie extended, painting an eyelash masterpiece . . . You'll find out soon enough.

Hastening over, the clerk, What blustering in misbuttoned smock, Do You Think as if they have personally degraded her commented on her exposed roots, You're Doing with rising indignance, With That? Brickie all the while unwavering in his careful application, Young Man?

Putting it on.

The clerk snatches for the tin but leftover glue has affixed it to Brickie's palm launching the blondish woman into an attack of You public school You think you're the Well I'll tell you Think you can Give it over and Brickie into a dramatically pained Ow You're hurting me That's skin Watch it. Until the woman rips free the mascara with a terrifying smile.

Calm yourself . . . Brickie rubbing his palm, batting thick eyelashes . . . You're hysterical.

Brickie's downturned mouth like that of his trouty father. The ambassador presented Caitlin with five dead fish saying *It's a pleasure to make your acquaintance* so she understood that it was a hand being offered. That she was to shake it.

Why are you smirking? . . . after they shook hands he gave Brickie his handkerchief. Politely indicated nose care.

You're a snob . . . Brickie and his eyelashes turning to hang elbows against the glass counter.

Look, lend me some money.

What for?

Just lend it to me.

If her hair were wet first she might get a comb through it. What could Brickie possibly know on her? How much did a comb cost? Gilbert was two days away. Bath night tomorrow. Enough time to shampoo. To control.

Thin walls separate the baths. Only four feet high or so. A milking shed down to the low stool. Sunk underwater deaf and weightless. Almost private. Until Maggot smacks open the door checking her way down the row of stalls.

Remember when Isabelle took her to the lake that time and the fun they had then how it was even after Isabelle stopped wanting to ride the treehorses after she said that part was over now that there was the point when you were just a kid and the point when you were a teenager and now even though they were both just twelve it was the time to start acting like girls and maybe even stop playing around in grubby shorts but when they went to the lake they could still play games in the water dive off the dock or at least until those boys came. That was the last time she swam in the lake. In London letters came from camp where Isabelle rode her first real horse and Long Island where Isabelle visited her father not Peter but the first one the one she hardly knew. In Bayville she played badminton with her father's friend only the friend told Isabelle she had nice legs so she decided never to play again. Maybe it was time for them to stop playing but they did have the lake that one last time at least.

Bringing her head out. A bath is not a lake.

Caitlin look . . . Sophie hangs her arms over the wall, head slumped to one side . . . I'm Jesus.

You're crazy . . . drawing knees up, arms around . . . Let me take my bath.

What are you hiding?

I'm washing my hair.

You should cut it all off like mine. Then it's easy to wash . . . Sophie drops back behind the wall with a splash muttering . . . Oh I was a sailor had a sheep oh and it was good to me.

And Mr. Brickman I can see has made steady progress on the copper oxide experiment from last week, in fact I sense you've been mulling it over these past seven days . . . Gilbert waist against his lab bench . . . That right Brick? Between meals been considering the subtle but not insignificant effect of oxygen on a copper wire? But perhaps you've been preoccupied with reactions upon addition of a catalyst, hum? On the way to prep at night undoubtedly considering elemental differences between fluorocarbons and hydrocarbons, or have we been more concerned with memorizing our periodic table?

Sir? . . . Brickie plays the fool, the boys laugh . . . Sorry sir?

But why is Gilbert paying all the attention to stupid—her hair is clean. Mostly straight. She arrived early to claim the newest the whitest lab smock. Why won't he notice?

I'm sure once again you will today display the workings of a mind blessed with genius . . . Gilbert smiling with one side of his mouth, lab coat propped open, waist cocked between thumb and forefinger . . . You will awe us with your intellect. That right Mr. Brickman?

Sir.

A game between the two of them and she with washed and smooth hair bleached smock leaning as Gilbert does against a scarred wooden lab bench waiting. Next to her, Henrietta tapes her leaking fountain pen. On her other side, an empty seat for Deborah still smoking her morning cigarette behind the pavilion. Next to Hen, Sophie has a finger dug in her ear. And on down the row. All of them waiting standing waiting for the lesson.

He is calling her name . . . What? Yes sir?

Was that a yawn?

Sir? I don't think so.

You don't know whether you were yawning?

I. I guess I was.

Guess. Yes Americans guess a lot don't they? What is it Evans? Too much bed and not enough sleep is that it?

The class laughs at her. He has made a remark again like the ones about her hips and teeth. Everyone is laughing even Sophie even Henrietta arranging the burettes. All of them.

I don't know . . . she answers finally . . . Sir.

Dropping his coat and waist, Gilbert has turned away from her, from her disgusting yawning, turned to the board with chalk, dismissing her clean hair her useless smock.

Henrietta licks a finger to turn a page in her exercise book. Sophie steps back to wink but she was laughing too only a moment ago.

Gilbert's white lab coat back right arm raised chalking out $2Cu+O_2 = $ *To see you oh.* Bleached collar defining the back of his neck. Hairline cropped close maybe even shaven.

At the bench in front of her, Brickie has turned to stare. Elbows hung.

Caitlin raises her eyebrows. Sneers. A catalyst but he won't react.

Won't balance the equation. She stares. He stares. Stubborn both. Brickie with his black hair his bastard hair in his eyes leaning as he did at the Chemist's. That upper lip up to no good.

Deborah slides in past Hen past Sophie holding the last and too small lab coat shedding wrappers gold twix and old tests reeking of cigarette smoke. Caitlin helps her with the coat. When she looks up again Brickie has turned away.

What did Brickie mean in the Chemist's that he knew something on her. She hasn't been in England long enough. Father and her moving into the London flat in July Father saying Remember this is just temporary because really I can always commute but you'll be away at school anyway and I thought it was important for you to see London first not only to see a city a city other than Portland but a European city. Soon you'll have seen Paris and Florence and Nice and maybe even speak Italian we already know how your French is. This is the kitchen here's the bathroom this is what they call a bidet you can wash your bottom in it no it isn't disgusting Caitlin it's French and this is the sitting room here's your room down that hall is mine. Now I know it's small and you're used to a house but you should realize we might not be able to manage what we had at the farm not for a while anyway and this is the dining area I don't know what's on that carpeting it appears somewhat suspect perhaps there were suspicious circumstances regarding the previous tenants out this window you can see our little garden no that one down there you can lie out in a chair and sunbathe if there's any sun to speak of. We'll go visit the school day after next but for now I'm off to investigate office space here's the map to the buses and one for the tube but I'd rather you didn't use either just yet I'll be back in an hour and a half can you manage until then see what's on the television make yourself something to eat. You're sure? Right then. After Father left and he was gone four hours not just one and a half she made toast. Someone had shopped for bread and milk. A pyramid of soup in the cupboards but also cans of string beans and carrots. Caitlin sat down then in a plastic chair in the tiny flat kitchen. Sat down and cried. But she had four hours to stop four hours to wash her face to look like she hadn't cried. When Father came home he took her to a place where they made burgers and milk shakes but the shake left her mouth powdery. Picking at the gray burger she thought they would always eat in restaurants now that they lived in a city and with Father hating to cook. All she could think was that she hoped she wasn't expected to learn not in that kitchen with the plastic chairs and cracked-up table.

Skipping stones across the dirty pond after school. Sophie and Henrietta come to the other side their four legs casting shadows two and two across her and the water.

Brickie stares at you . . . Sophie. Hands in blazer pockets thumbs out.

No he doesn't.

He does Caitlin, I've seen it as well . . . Henrietta like a little bell ding ding as well as well.

Do you speak to him?

Sometimes . . . throwing a rock into the pond to see how quickly it will sink . . . He lent me money.

Money? What for?

Sophie . . . Henrietta pulls . . . Let's go in to Tea.

Oh go on Hen, I don't want to.

Why not.

Go by yourself why can't you? . . . Sophie watching her try to skip a stone one not flat enough then back to Hen . . . I'll be there in a moment.

As Henrietta retreats toward School House, she stops once and turns. The sun low behind the girl, Caitlin can't see Henrie's face. Just the pause.

Did you have friends in America?

Of course.

What did Brickie lend you money for? Brickie hates everyone.

They all seem to like him.

That's not the same thing.

No.

They built this dirty hole when my brother was here . . . Sophie kneels down on the other side of the pond . . . People are always falling in trying to jump across.

It seems pretty wide to jump over.

Caitlin . . . Sophie folds the hem of her skirt under, watching her fingers do it . . . Someone told me your mother's dead.

Did they.

Is she?

Raking the dirt for flatter stones . . . You laughed at me in Chemistry.

What? Oh, it wasn't at you particularly. Gilbert's like that to everyone, you'll laugh when he does it to someone else.

Really? . . . *he's like that* taking in Sophie's earnest knees fingers *to everyone* worrying skirt boyish hair . . . To everyone?

At some point.

Another unrooted stone not flat enough to skip . . . I didn't realize.

Don't take it personally.

I don't . . . fingering off dirt off the stone.

Caitlin.

In March. She died in March.

Here I've found you flat ones.

You skip them.

I'm hopeless.

Hold it like this, like pinching . . . like a waist held between thumb and forefinger.

Caitlin, what did Brickie—

Why do you think he doesn't like anyone?

I've never thought about it . . . Sophie waddles for stones . . . He just doesn't.

Out the back gate lanes switch down around the school fields. One leads to the village the village where Brickie lent her money for a comb to straighten her hair for Chemistry for Gilbert for nothing. What are the names of these English plants in lanes banked by hedges hugging the neighboring farms and fields. Scattered with horse droppings the frozen ruts trip them as they concentrate on where they are going which is nowhere. Sophie's hands are big as a man's big as Brickie's father's and as she talks her hands chop the air.

Boys from town pass yelling NUNS for their uniforms but

whistling at them all the same. In one field grazing cows black and white like the watch shop where Brickie—what was it he had on her?

Sophie with those cobalt eyes . . . You seem to do as you're told. I'd never have thought you'd miss Tea.

I've skipped school before . . . and rolled a tire into traffic slinging a motorcycle . . . I'm not so good . . . a sudden red bird from the trees what kind why doesn't she know the names of birds . . . Isn't it funny that you thought that about me . . . watching the bird fly the man fly . . . That I was some kind of girl you thought you knew but you don't at all.

You probably think you know things about me. That I'm a certain type.

I think you're alright. You ask a lot of questions.

Do I?

See.

Well, you don't ask very many at all.

The light cold and orange edges down like it did that day she and Brickie were in the Chemist's when he put on makeup and was rude to the woman. Behind a dairy covered with vines beyond the mill-house and a thatched barn past pencils of silos they ramble on with no ideas of destination only the idea that they should not return. Not straightaway. Sophie knows how to sneak into school. They will be okay. They will be alright.

Midnight maybe at least a few hours since Lights Out. What has she woken to the stories of hauntings the white lady and the headless man breathing of the other eight a grunt here Mareka Holland talks in her sleep the nine beds the blue bobbled bedspread pulled up so cold she wears socks a hat beginning of November what awakened her? Moonlight through a slice in the curtains the windows reach up to the ceiling. Window beds are always snatched by London girls who arrive early on purpose. What book is it where a girl hides behind a curtain on a wide windowsill like that?

Pull your head under the covers to get it hot with breathing. Alone now. Not like in Maine because there was always Isabelle Daniel Joy but there was never herself so much as here.

Sophie.

Face deep in her pillow blankets tossed hands folded under stomach Sophie shifts in sleep.

Wake up . . . next to Sophie's bed working out a shoe wedged under her knee.

What are you doing? . . . Sophie suddenly awake.

Shh.

Go back to bed.

I have a question.

You'll get caught.

I don't care. Anyway, who's so good now?

What's wrong?

Can we go somewhere.

Tell me here what is it.

I'm freezing.

Get in.

In your bed?

Yes.   What is it?

There's ghosts.

You saw the—

I don't know.

Your mother?

No.

What then?

It was a ghost of me or something.

Did it have a head? Maybe it was the white lady, the—

No. Shove over.

Sophie tries to give her room under a fat and warm duvet brought from Hampstead not the thin wool blankets stitched in red *1922*.

Remember I was telling you about my friend in America my friend Isabelle?

Go on.

Once we skipped school . . . they had why had they had it been her idea she remembers it as her idea but maybe it was Isabelle now it seems more like something Isabelle would think up but she was sure somewhere that it had been her idea . . . And took a bus to a different town any town it didn't matter we just wanted to get out . . . with just enough room in the bed that she can lie on her back dropping off the edge a bit and Sophie can lie on her side watching her as she stares straight up at what would be the ceiling if there were light enough to see it . . . We walked up the curving road . . . curved like an ear . . . Into the woods and we talked but as we were leaving we found a tire . . . Sophie waits for her to tell it . . . In the dirt. So we dug it out and we could see the road down below us.

You pushed it down the hill.

We rolled it into the traffic and we knocked a man off his motorcycle.

Is he dead?

He could be . . . looking now at Sophie not caring that it's close and they can smell each other's breathing . . . I don't know.

You killed him.

Don't tell.

A man . . . Sophie's eyes can seem so big her hair so short . . . It's his ghost you're seeing.

I told you. It's mine.

Cold here the buildings the wind air seeping in crannies so many cracks swimming on Fridays in the unheated pool Chlorine dates blocked in tile 1917 clung to the edge fingers blue bitten with eczema why Father don't they believe in heat here why have you brought me here.

Why does Brickie stare at you? . . . Monday at breakfast Paul in his tight gray stinking like the cigarettes he smokes with Deborah . . . Brickie left me with glue stuck everywhere. Said he had something to tell you . . . leaning down close to Caitlin tipping his plate his boiled tomato slipping around the bacon . . . What was it? . . . grease leaking from his fried bread and eggs . . . What did he say . . . so close and even at this time in the morning smelling of cigarettes . . . You'll tell me what it was.

Why would I?

Everyone does.

Doesn't mean I will.

Oh yes . . . the plate right under her nose all she can bear is toast and . . . You will . . . cups from the pitchers of tea and coffee they put out alternating . . . Oh yes . . . tea coffee tea coffee . . . You will . . .

snarling sixteen at least if not seventeen Paul the smell of his grease tomatoes curdling her stomach . . . Yank.

Before she has thought not a good idea in fact a particularly bad idea don't do this just think it she has leaped from her chair to escape the rancid greasy smell but tipped the rank plate eggs bread bacon tomatoes down Paul down his tight cigarette saturating his chest with breakfast hearing as she runs the SMASH of plate his bearish roar the gasps the laughs the trouble she's in.

Out across the cricket field Do Not Step On the Pitch flying to the back lane *howzat* through the trees the shrubbery and out lurching on the furrowed earth. The clear air sings in her ears as she runs scrambling Paul will kill her he must be at least seventeen and no one can protect her from that. How should she know why Brickie stares his pretty mouth and black bastard hair why did they act like she should know when she couldn't even tell them what he had on her. Why did they want to know so much. As she tore from the dining hall she saw Sophie turn from Henrietta turn with surprise that said she probably couldn't save her now yes half a bed half a night under a duvet but no protection none from a seventeen-year-old.

The cold air hurts her chest. Walking down a different lane now, one to take her away from school. They will call Father in London to tell him she has flown. *Gone, sir, she's gone.* The teachers won't know why not even Gilbert. Gilbert who apparently shows the same attention to all of them even gobstruck old Deborah in her too-small smock.

Isabelle would know what to do. Whose idea had it been to roll the tire, she couldn't remember. Isabelle would protect her from Paul.

As she walks, the morning sun a cold ball above, grass at her feet stung with white, the world seems to curl up and away.

Leave the lane for the road to town to find a park or shop. Make friends with the butcher or a woman with cats. Forget sleeping nine to a room, Father would find her, *I expected more but I was wrong to.* A car passes then slows. *After all, I was nine when I went. Just a boy.* Brake lights redden. *It was eight years before I saw Da and then a world war between us.* Up ahead, the car pulls to the side. Men kill girls, Isabelle once said. Everyone knows that.

Crashing back into the lane squeezing through a hedge heart

thumping madly for the second time today. Then she hears him. The jouncing waist and dry almost high voice teasing Too much bed, now calling EVANS, hears him where the lane meets the road muttering Oh my shoes were not made for this.

What is he doing here why him driving by why now with her face red from running and the cold her nose running and red. Why now?

Yes . . . around the hedge this time picking leaves from her sweater . . . Mr. Gilbert?

What in heaven's . . . not smiling pointing at his head . . . Twigs in your hair. What are you up to?

Brings her hand up to pull them out . . . Aren't you at school? . . . well if you were noticing hair why not on Thursday.

Clearly not. And you? A particular dislike for Monday's lessons? Off to town for a change of pace?

Straightening her skirt adjusting stockings aware he watches her adjustment.

Dear girl, are you running away?

Why do you say that, Dear Girl . . . circumstances making her bold . . . Why do you talk as if you're about sixty?

Are you changing the subject?

Yes.

Well . . . smiling so she'll know know he doesn't pay that kind of attention to the whole class know that he wouldn't watch the adjustment of just anyone's stockings . . . Come on I'll run you back.

Where were you driving to?

Been up all weekend making sure one of you lot doesn't burn down the assembly hall. I was on my way home. I have one you see . . . he falters . . . I didn't mean anything by that, I was trying to be funny. I meant that I spend so much time at Monstead.

Too much. I mean I do—I feel like I spend too much time there.

Doesn't your family come to take you out? . . . opening the car door for her . . . Or are they in America?

No. Neither . . . inside the car warm the seats covered with cream wool . . . Is this sheep?

It's fake . . . revolving the key.

I can't go back, Mr. Gilbert . . . a hand nearly on his to stop it at the crest of the wheel . . . I'm in trouble.

He looks at her hand then her and she puts a plea in her eyes not too much not too dramatic but just enough just enough to say the jokes the class laughing a cup of tea not back to school not yet an hour or even half just a small favor. Gilbert harbors a small white scar under his nose.

What kind of trouble?

If he finds me Paul Gredville will kill me.

Now that can't be true. A young lady and American to boot. Gredville's a delinquent. Won't come anywhere near you.

Please Mr. Gilbert.

Turning into a driveway hidden from the road by hedges and a yew. Not what she would have imagined. If she had. A small lopsided house. Covered with ivy.

It's rotting the structure, the roots get in and undermine the mortar still I do love it . . . wild mess of a garden not the usual careful English . . . Well when I have the time I'll get round to weeding that . . . leading her through as he untoggles his duffel, into the heavy-beamed sitting room. Newspapers tented on the table cups a plate with crusts and jam dark paintings of streets. Books everywhere. On table speakers chairs yes on shelves but piled in corners and under the windows.

I should telephone the headmaster Caitlin or they'll have the hounds out.

He'll make you bring me back.

Perhaps that's the right thing hum? Oh god . . . Gilbert takes a sheet of newspaper kneels twisting sections placing one by one in the fireplace . . . I don't know. I'm not used to these situations. I'm a Chemistry master not some kind of psychologist. I should take you back, you must speak to Miss Maggone about this unpleasantness. She has experience in these matters.

Maggone doesn't like Americans.

I'm sure that's not true . . . Gilbert removes books from a stack of wood selects two logs replaces the books logs go in the fire . . . Actually that probably is true.

Do you . . . in the chair removing a book *Tropisms* from under her . . . Like Americans Mr. Gilbert?

I don't have anything against Americans . . . standing up peering into a toby mug on the mantel then a small box finding matches behind a framed photograph . . . When I mimicked you that time, I was trying to amuse myself, the class . . . kneeling again striking a match . . . Sometimes my jokes aren't so funny I realize that.

It's okay . . . crossing her legs then uncrossing finally settling on crossed . . . What city is that supposed to be?

Yes well actually those are a rather miserable attempt to capture Amsterdam . . . worrying the flames blowing lifting a corner of newspaper . . . Trip I took a year ago. Paintings don't do it justice.

The fire lit, the room seems to darken as if the light has been sucked up by the fire, as though the light were O_2.

My mother would have liked those.

Would have?

She died . . . turning to the window because it really does seem darker outside.

Gilbert pauses . . . I'm sorry . . . then continues fussing at the fire.

She liked dark paintings . . . back again . . . She called them democratic.

Well these aren't very good I'm afraid.

I like them okay.

Why is he puffing away at the fire when he could sit? She has removed the foliage from her hair she should be in a class, English or . . . Do you still paint, Mr. Gilbert?

You needn't sound quite so sad . . . finally leaving the fire crossing to sit on the sofa across from her with his scar . . . Surely they're not that awful. I paint on weekends sometimes when I'm not on duty.

Paint what?

Caitlin.

Sir.

You needn't call me sir in my house we're friends here.

Okay.

Well I'm glad you like my paintings, I'm glad your mother would have liked them, I can't say anyone from school has ever seen them but—

I like them a lot.

But. Are you warm enough, are you shivering?

I'm fine. But what?

I should put more paper on or another log—

But what?

I feel somewhat awkward that you're here. I feel the school wouldn't like it.

You haven't even asked what the problem is.

Well . . . down at the cushion next to him memorizing the brocade taking his time to say . . . What is it Caitlin?

Stretching out her legs they are long for nearly fourteen she is one of the tallest and that includes boys should she arrange stockings again carefully or just stretch and say . . . Like I told you before, Mr. Gilbert. Paul wants to kill me.

You know how boys are Caitlin they pretend to hate girls but really.

The dark sky and a white scar dancing in the firelight nose so fine and Does that include you? almost pinched is that why his voice comes out thin forced down through his nose . . . I don't think that's it. Anyway I spilled eggs on him. I embarrassed him in front of everyone and that's the worst thing you can—

Is that all it is I thought good god I thought it was something dreadful something—

It is dreadful.

Gilbert jumps up strides to the window squints out and yes takes waist between forefinger and thumb as he seems to do when thinking or pleased and inspects the sky . . . I think it's going to snow . . . smiling back at her then not smiling . . . You weren't even wearing a coat out there.

I do feel a little sick.

We must get you back.

Please . . . can't help that it comes out so forcefully, bite it down . . . Mr. Gilbert I haven't finished telling you.

But you're ill.

Shifting . . . Maybe I'm just hungry.

Releasing the sky the assessment of snow . . . Well hum I suppose Paul is wearing your breakfast . . . out into the passage . . . Let's go see what there is. How's toast?

Gilbert's kitchen warm with its Aga stove and old cowhand picture.

Yes I picked that up at a jumble sale does this bread seem alright to you or does that appear to be mold I also bought a complete set of medical dictionaries get yourself a plate from that cabinet published in the seventeen hundreds it's horrifying what they practiced in the name of science in those days.

Taking the plate, blue with a shepherdess on, nodding as he flips her the toast, to butter of course jam.

Back we go . . . she has the plate, he steers her by the shoulders to the sitting room.

And sitting . . . What's the upstairs like? . . . awkward toast jam on the corners of her mouth he watches her lick it off . . . Is the rest of the house as nice?

Caitlin I think we ought to call Headmaster it could snow and who knows what frenzy they're lathering themselves into over your disappearance—

Is it her leaf caught hair or that she is American why can't he let her be why can't he let her stay.

Can't you tell them I'm alright that I've fallen asleep in front of the fire that you think I should sleep for a while because I seem sick or exhausted or something?

Considering her, Gilbert seems fourteen or so with his white scar and his uncertain testing of a finger against the table his leaning forward to hear the sound of his voice making that telephone call looking at her with dubious eyebrows waiting to hear it. How a conversation like that would happen how it would go and who would say what.

Paul Gredville hum?

Sir?

But he is halfway from the room and she knows he is not *like that to everyone.*

Outside the light grows dimmer still. She moves to the window in homage to Gilbert's movement there, testing her hands on hips, waist between forefinger and thumb, looking out into the garden, wondering at the sky, whether it will bring the snow it warns of, exasperated at the weeds she never got around to pulling, marveling at mortar's submission to ivy, cataloguing repairs. In the recesses of the house the faint chime on noon yet dark enough for midnight.

Do we need a lamp on? . . . behind her somewhere, she can't turn . . . Caitlin?

What did Headmaster say?

Most disturbingly, they had no idea you were missing. He thanked me for my concern said as soon as you were awake I was to deliver you to the San . . . judging by the echo, Gilbert must be standing in the doorway she noticed the roof eaved in the hall . . . It's gross deception I'm taking part in Caitlin. It's a mistake.

I'll go back.

The click of a lamp a pool of light. And he crosses the room to the lamp next to her.

Wait . . . she touches his arm . . . Look at the snow.

Side by side they watch the white fall. Gilbert does not hold his waist but folds his arms. Snow. A marvel to the scarred and she cannot . . . Have you ever . . . what the hell is she saying when she doesn't know anything.

Hum?

Painted . . . again words again god will she run out of them *Painted* like that like she has any idea what she is trying. Something about the possibility of a lab coat draping itself so damn so elegantly so carved over a wrist at the end of which a hand whereon a thumb and fore-finger conspire to hold a waist . . . Well have you ever painted a person?

Finally he places one hand on his waist holds it turns and leans the other arm and his body against the fogged window behind which the snow floats before which they stand like two decent people in ordinary conversation and facing her he says . . . Have I ever painted a person? I can't say I have. I'm no artist, Caitlin. I'm simply amusing myself.

I'd like to see the others.

Hum.

You said you had other paintings.

Did I? Well I do so I suppose I must have.

He has forgotten that he has made a mistake that he has lied to the headmaster that she offered to go back to school. He could be thinking of her adjusting stockings he could be thinking of her licking jam she has felt him hold her waist between thumb and forefinger this man bouncing his grasped waist against the lab bench on his rounds so purposefully inserting his unclean but could it be shaven in the back hair before her nose to correct her failing experiment to discern what mistakes she has made retrieving a hair from her page to hold it up between that celebrated thumb and forefinger and ask *Yours?*

Pardon Mr. Gilbert?

The paintings . . . again he reaches for the lamp beside her, his hair within smelling distance . . . They're stored away somewhere.

Do you still paint? . . . breathing in his faint shampoo . . . What about Chittock Leigh?

As he draws back . . . I suppose I don't find it as glamorous to paint what surrounds me although it can be inspiring here at sunset or even sunrise . . . back to leaning against the window . . . But I can't think you're ever up that early.

No . . . remember too much bed and not enough sleep Mr. Iron Mr. Nickel Mr. Zinc.

Still I go driving sometimes, some weekends. Try to find something.

Look at the two of them leaning against the cold windows like old friends chatting about painting and snow and she tonguing her molars to find raspberry seeds from his jam. To review: He has leaned across her to offer up the scent of his hair. He has phoned the headmaster to ensure she will stay. She has eaten his toast and showed him her legs. Has stretched them languidly in front of her sitting in front of his fire.

Caitlin.

Yes.

Are you avoiding the subject of Mr. Gredville?

Oh . . . the snow quilting the unweeded lawn . . . It's not important.

Him killing you?

I can't think about it now.

Mr. Brickman seems to have taken a fancy to you . . . he watches her reaction she chooses to consider the whitening grass . . . Does he have designs on you?

I don't know . . . Brickie knows something on her is all it is.

You be careful of those lads.

At some point tea has been made he holds a cup where did it come from she could do with some tea. Standing in his small Master's

house Gilbert takes in the snow covering weeds the ivy thinking of—
what? Of the composition and behavior of matter? Water trans-
forming to snow. Freezing points both zero and thirty-two? Gilbert's
face changes. Something. A glow in the scar a deeper crease in the
crease by his mouth. Before he can wonder why she is standing in his
house leaning against the same window as he with her long for nearly
fourteen legs toast-licking tongue unruly hair he has not yet had
chance to ridicule but soon will no doubt Caitlin says, and it could be
true . . . Mr. Gilbert, sir I think I really do need to sleep I really think
I don't feel well maybe it was being out without a coat like you said.

Under striped sheets behind the wardrobe she finds the paintings.

Could it be nearly one o'clock the chimes again although it seems
as though they just heard them the unused room dusty . . . Sorry it's
a little—I'm just thinking I ought really run you back you ought really
go to the San it could be something serious . . . but all the while heft-
ing up the mattress to tuck under the sheet, running out to take a pillow from his own bed . . . I will get around to tidying one of these days
it's not often I have visitors . . . unfolding blankets drawing the shade.
A moment by the window . . . How dark . . . then back to fussing as
he did by the fire, wiping the bedside table with the sleeve of a robe
hanging from the door . . . You'll call for me when you awake, if you
need anything. Do you think—should I take you back?

I don't feel well enough . . . kicking off one shoe . . . I mean I just
need to sleep I'm homesick I'll be . . . now the other . . . Alright after
a nap I'll call you if I need anything besides . . . a little yawn . . . It's
snowing your car could get stuck. The roads around here aren't so
good.

Something about homesick, that was the trick, because he softens
. . . Some sleep will do wonders.

And she sits on the bed because to get under the covers she should
take off her skirt but should she do it here in front of him will her shirt
reach down to cover enough.

I'll fetch you a glass of water . . . Gilbert slips from the room.

Pull the skirt around so the zipper faces front then unzip it step
out. Sweater too? Yes and a few blouse buttons just for air. Pull back
the blanket slide under the covers in stockings and shirt head down
on the pillow no surprising pencils. His pillow smells of a nearly

shaven back of the neck recently shampooed but still a little musty hair smells of Argon Potassium smells of a draped lab coat at the wrist or when necessary folded back one two three times to mid forearm smells of Thursday mornings ten to eleven-thirty double Chemi smells of smells of smells of white scars a pinched waist pleated trousers smells of too much bed and not enough sleep.

Here we are . . . back with a glass of water placing it carefully on the robe-shined table next to her judging the distance. Supine, can she reach it easily if she wakes suddenly dry or parched or needing to sip water because she doesn't know what else to do in this Gilbert house in this Gilbert bed?

Thank you . . . up at him that look in her eyes that slightly sick but not sick enough to be taken to the San in the snow that slightly tired homesick look in her eye that girl oblivious to a toast-licking tongue or stockinged long for nearly fourteen legs . . . Mr. Gilbert.

Don't be homesick . . . looking down at her that noble crease that scar . . . We'll take care of you here.

Suddenly he is stooping is placing hands either side of her shoulders is leaning down is moving toward her so that the smell of him rising from the pillow and the smell of him floating down compresses her as he kisses.

Under striped sheets behind the wardrobe she finds the paintings.

She can't sleep how could she. Leaning. Four of them. She knows they will be of the woman and they are. Mr. Krypton flying through the air helmeted and hidden in the highway grass that dry grass that hides bottles and plastic bags and men ejected from speeding motorcycles.

All four paintings have a naked woman lying on a bed, her skin a mess of different blues. So Gilbert's understanding of color not limited to testing for the presence of acid. The woman sits, legs folded under voluminous thighs. The background dense ridges of paint. Her alone. No candle bottle or fruit. Considering his palette, did Gilbert think about valency, the capacity of colors to combine? Amsterdam was clearer. Next the woman lies on her side, face pressed into her arm. The behavior of her matter, a turquoise roil of shoulder ribs waist bottom. Mouth set caustic and impatient. The last painting shows her turned away, back a blue mass. The effect of heat.

It was just a kiss on the cheek but he should have known she wouldn't sleep if he was going to even just kiss her on the cheek and besides he is a man in a lab a Mr. Radium he knows chemistry. Not sure a man in a white coat even a toast-making weed-talking snow-watching man in a lab would usually give a good night kiss. Was that a usual thing.

Back in bed now. Well was it a usual thing? A student even a tall for nearly fourteen student of chemistry in your house about to sleep on your smelling pillow should you be kissing her in an as if it were usual way? Well what about the time Daniel kissed her right after Mother died when they were sitting in that tireless car in the junkyard the one they drove south. That was on the cheek too. She never even thought about why he kissed her when they wanted Florida, some relief from winter. Did it feel like this for Daniel in the mercury. This need to smell a pillow deeply.

Downstairs in adjusted stockings loosened blouse yes and skirt. It happened that she could sleep an hour or so even after being kissed and finding the blue woman paintings. After thinking about Daniel Isabelle the astronaut she could still sleep some. Down the stairs her hair a thicket the clock chiming it must tell the half hour too it rings all the god damned time.

Well hello . . . outside the day stays dark, inside he turns down a corner of his paper to locate her . . . How are you feeling?

Better . . . pulling her hair behind one ear that's new where did that come from? . . . What time is it?

Nearly Tea. We'd better get you back.

The snow gets on her hair and the coat he has lent. Not his duffel but a wool suit jacket because *I have nothing better.* How soft the cream notsheep fur how cold his car how quiet the white around them. In the parking lot behind the San he comes around to let her out saying . . . You can return it anytime what day is it today well perhaps I'll run into you before Thursday . . . hands on her shoulders . . . You shouldn't be homesick you're sure you're alright perhaps we should have left you in bed . . . holding her and looking into her as if—

Are you going to kiss me again?

He drops his hands. The white snow and scar. Behind him the school rises up through the weather. His eyes his scar jumping or is it only the snow falling between them. Why does he always look at her. What? In his eyes what?

You get some sleep . . . then he turns, slamming into his woolly car so, before she realizes, it is just her and the snow.

DONG Morning assembly in the great hall DONG waiting for masters black capes open DONG like crows eyes still slow still DONG puffy from sleep to file past the statues mustached Giles Duprés Raynes founder in bronze DONG Apollo a broken Cromwell and Queen Victoria that one just a bust DONG up the aisle between the rows of DONG students standing in carved pews to the first row DONG the row of velvet chairs. Headmaster stands to lead the prayer.

Our Father who.

Yesterday, after the nurse took Caitlin's temperature and informed her that there was hardly time for play acting what with students who were actually sick what with winter coming on them, she was sent to Tea.

Hallowed be.

Taking her tray, she received the benediction, the pink meat pie slice with a hard boiled egg staring from its center, some dull beans.

Thy name.

There were no empty chairs near Sophie or anyone so she had to sit with first years.

Thy kingdom come.

The younger girls wanted to know all about America and she told them. Mostly lies until Brickie passed by on his way to the bread giving her a look that made her quiet. She just hoped Paul was somewhere smoking with Deborah.

On earth as it is in heaven.

She doesn't try to locate the back of Gilbert's head but it seems to float wherever she looks.

After Tea Sophie brought her to an empty classroom saying that Paul was telling everyone Yank was in trouble and if anyone saw her they were to tell her it would happen the first time she was alone and he warned them all they should stay away from her or they might get some too.

Give us this day our daily bread.

Sophie drew circles on the board while Caitlin stamped grids on a desk with a dusty eraser. Sophie said I'm not afraid of Paul Gredville who has the intelligence of cow intestine. Caitlin stopped stamping to ask What do you think I should do?

And forgive us our trespasses.

Her fingers raining chalk Sophie circled some more before answering I don't know because it's not going to go away and he's not going to forget about it but something will turn up. Then she stopped drawing dusted off her hands looked at Caitlin. Don't go anywhere alone and I mean that.

As we forgive those who trespass against us.

On the telephone Father said Good news the realtor in Portland has a found a buyer he's been keeping me on my toes these past weeks but it seems like a goahead so I'll be up there in a few weeks to celebrate and we can start looking for a house we can get out of the flat in London. We'll ship the furniture over.   What? You sound like you don't want a beautiful house out in the country.   Well, you'll be there on holidays. We can try to find something before Christmas.   Why are you being like this Caitlin?   Yes I'll live there alone do you think I enjoy living in a cramped flat in this polluted city? I'll keep a bed in the office but we'll have a house again.

Headmaster stands . . . You may sit . . . spectacles fixed to the end of his nose by force of concentration, three dark strings plastered across his globe . . . Later this week we will be lucky enough to hear excerpts from Mr. Spenning's travels in Borneo but we will continue this morning with Dr. Thorpe's thoughts on Man's rise from the innocence of brutehood.

Sold the house in Maine? Father was moving so quickly.

Questions of morality arise when an alternative is offered of leading a better life.

She never considered a different house. Took the London flat plastic furniture lumpy

rise from a bestial to a moral plane of

linoleum for home.

Existence involves the apprehension of distinctions between good and evil.

Light through the stained glass above the altar plays on her hand.

A yellow circle in the design appears to be a fried egg but is in fact a sun.

Conscience and the hope of spiritual ascendance keeps us from wrongdoing.

Remember finding the bird's nest right as they were moving? With Mother's hair wound into the branches. No chance of finding something like that in any new house.

It is after all only after long ages of social discipline fraught with despair, hopelessness and grinding misery that

light stipples Gilbert's bowed head. If no one ever visits clearly the paintings are hidden from himself.

Moral law becomes dominant.

Across the courtyard with Sophie and Henrietta. Sophie singing Boring boring boring laddering a scale and the sun coloring everything sharply. The morning—

Yank . . . he moves in leaning down thin but man sized.

They have reached the door to School House. So close. One step up through the heavy oak door four steps down the short corridor to History.

Sophie stops singing . . . Leave her.

Look at me bitch.

You bore us . . . Sophie puts up a protective arm.

Look, I'm sorry . . . reaching past him for the door . . . I'm sorry about spilling on your sweater.

Sweaterrr? . . . knocking her hand away voice ugly so she will understand the mockery.

What is it you want?

Something. You don't get away with that.

A movement in the shadowed doorway. Paul turns. Brickie steps out.

Hello . . . Brickie doesn't look at Paul only at her his shifting bastard hair an old tired light in what she can see of his eyes.

Paul leans one shoulder slowly against the wall. The sun behind a cloud, a scream of laughter across the courtyard. Henrietta gives a little cough. Something has happened between Brickie and Paul.

Look man . . . Paul says finally coming off the wall . . . You saw what she did, now leave this.

Taller, maybe three years older, why does Paul have the disadvantage, his voice pleading like that.

Sophie's arm on her back. Once Isabelle now Sophie now Brickie in the shadows with his shadowed eyes shorter than Paul. When does she begin to protect herself?

You'll be late . . . Brickie one hand in pocket turns and pushes back through the door. What did Brickie have on her?

Watching the door ease closed Paul snorts . . . Safe for now . . . begins to walk away.

Hey . . . her voice louder than she expected . . . What did I ever do to you?

Paul turns strides backwards long legs stoking . . . You lived, Yank.

Walking back alone from prep in the damp night. How different the action of walking a long slow loop to School House, of offering herself as a target, of getting this over with, is from the idea of it. A sensible seeming idea in bed.

What will the house be like, the new one in the country, think about that. Depends how Father's new work is going. He said they might visit Wales at Christmas he might take her to the village where he was a boy. He said sorry he didn't have as much time to write as he thought he would but he hoped she was getting letters from Isabelle. Well she is. Pages decorated with sticky biro flourishes. And exclamation points. It is fountain pen only at Monstead including for mathematics. No flourishes. But Isabelle is free. Free to scribble in untidy ballpoint. When did she begin to think things untidy. Isabelle's r's are the American ones that look like staples. But here she has learned to curve r's like a horse head. In bed during the hour before Lights Out Mareka Holland loses her inhaler and she has to safeguard her blankets. So how can she concentrate? How can she imagine what Isabelle will think when she reads her r's? Or even what it's like back in Maine? When she tried to reply once, sitting in bed, ready with pen and paper, she could only stare at the blotchy cartoons of dogs and men with big noses. In the end she put away Isabelle's letter, the blank paper and pen and pulled on her ski hat because it all made her feel about a hundred years old.

Her footsteps in the quiet Monday night. Lights Out in an hour. Plenty of time for a seventeen-year-old boy to kill and stash a body.

Death loop around the classrooms chapel gymnasium boys' dorms headmaster's house swimming pool upper forms dining hall tennis courts. An orbit to attract Paul Gredville and get it all over with.

Isabelle's profile in the bus how she always took the cold seat how she wouldn't let anyone say a thing bad about Caitlin. The two of them standing at the top of that strange hill shoving the tire off watching their lives roll down a hill to send a man into the atmosphere.

Yank . . . out of the darkness like a cat like a life lived under a bush.

Now it will be done with . . . Yes . . . turning to see those skinny legs doesn't he eat? Well who can choke down the food here the pink slabs with eyes . . . What?

Thought I told you not to be alone. Thought I told you you had a problem.

I don't like being told what to do . . . Isabelle would call that voice prissy.

Can't say I didn't warn you . . . standing in her path shaking his head sorrowfully . . . Now it's just a matter of what damage I should inflict, what—

Leave me alone . . . that was even worse than prissy should she run? Fight? She could get a scratch in or punch at least. What was the plan again? . . . Get out of my way.

Yank . . . taking his time . . . Has anyone ever told you that you sound like you're chewing a brick?

Standing in a part of the path between two streetlamps a place so dark light outlines only one strip on his cheek. Running she could make it to the dorms in two minutes but he can make it in one.

Didn't you think I meant it when I told you what would happen? . . . he circles her. Down the path behind him two figures melt together in lamplight. Could they hear her if she screamed? But the couple moves away holding hands . . . What? . . . Paul does not turn . . . No one's going to save you, Yank. It's just you and me.

What do you want?

First let me explain about that little incident in breakfast . . . he reaches out his hand, the pressure on her arm so tight his fingers meet . . . Let's step off shall we? . . . says it almost kindly, pulling her into the darkness off the path under a tree pushing her against it . . . Stay like that . . . Paul shakes out a cigarette a cigarette here just off the path so close to School House . . . I didn't care for the disrespect you showed my country . . . meeting a match to it . . . English food not good enough for your American stomach? . . . packet back in his back pocket and one arm out. Hand on the tree above her shoulder so she can smell his underarm.

It wasn't that.

In that case . . . musing. A deep inhale. Fingers scissoring the cigarette . . . I can only believe it had something to do with me . . . raising his eyebrows exhaling.

Pinned against the tree in his bad breath exhale underarm so thin his chest curves the wrong way convex or concave cannot see his eyes can only smell him. And he. Can he smell her fear or hair washed for Chemistry does he know she has a father or what she ate for Tea.

If you hurt me Brickie will . . . for god's sake the whole point was to protect herself.

Brickie . . . Paul takes his hand down crossing it to support his other elbow cigarette hovering by his ear . . . Fuck. Brickie.

I thought he was your friend . . . watching the burning end wondering how to smash it in his eye.

Don't change the subject Yank . . . throwing down the cigarette. An odd smile . . . Our Brickie's being detained shall we say. So you can't be saved.

Even with his arm down she can smell him worse than that day in breakfast. The night so still that even without looking she knows there is no one. How can she protect herself? They took the tire dug it out from the worms and dirt held it between them then rolled it rolled it down the hill where it bounced once at the bottom before launching into the road into the motorcycle into the man flying the man into the bushes into the grass into the hospital.

We love our Brickie don't we? . . . Paul brings his head close whispers . . . But we have to teach our American friends some manners, that there's no throwing food down people's jumpers not in front of the whole fucking dining hall.

Against the tree feeling every nodule every bark bit grit biting her palms pressed against it her shoulders back of her head as she eases from his oily breath broken sticks rooted on the trunk pins and pencils jabbing her at night.

How would you like me to throw bacon on your jumper your *sweaterrr* . . . with two fingers Paul traces the V at her neck . . . Down here? Now would you like that? Food here and here . . . tracing along her shoulders now down and—

Stop it.

Stop what?

How could she not have realized that this is what it would be her with her stupid lab man with hands on bouncing waist with blue lady paintings a good night kiss the motorcycle jerked like it was attached to string the man flew in his helmet an astronaut but he must have wondered where it came from and why him.

I said stop it.

Stop this? . . . hands slipping under her sweater on her rib cage but moving up his eyes volatile the pressure of his knee between hers pushing up at her skirt with his knee her palms caught against the tree struggling to get them out to get his knee out to get his hands off his everywhere hands over her mouth she tries to bite his dirty cigarette palm as he grabs both wrists in one hand pulls so her head scrapes against the trunk pulls her down yelling now but there is no one as he drags her pulling her across rocks dirt pinecones branches soda can *Squirt* throwing her into a bush landing on top of her what kind of bush why doesn't she know the branches bending under their weight their mass the needles tearing her legs and hands even through layers of blazer and sweater with fifteen hands but she fights yes kicks Paul tries inhibiting the screams with one shoulder but she fights for air breathing hard surfacing for oxygen her skirt up around her his energy constant kinetic ripping her shirt then undershirt she spits up at him a fine mist not the blinding glob she hoped for but suddenly he pitches violently to the side as if he has been kicked.

And it is silent. Just their echo held in the trees. She looks. No one. Scrabbling up pulling down her shirt and sweater and thank god this morning she was cold enough for an undershirt. Paul lies on his side clutching his stomach. Half-life is what he is. Sounds like crying. Why did he stop what was it? She backs out of the bush.

The whites of his wet eyes shine in the darkness . . . Fuck Brickie.
What?

Fuck off.

And she runs. Her hands white enough to see by. Hurtling down
the path to School House. She almost said, are you okay, she has
never seen a boy that old cry. Up the marble stairs valleyed in the center from wear like the horsehair mattress old as the blankets. Same mat-
tresses as when Father was here. Think about that. How many years.

Caitlin.

Yes? . . . one flight up smoothing hair down behind her ears not
turning.

His voice from outside the Duty Office under the stairs . . . Why
the racket?

Not moving . . . Racket?

Come down here.

The office hardly bigger than the desk it contains. Hooking her
heels on the rung. Palms face down on the chair seat under her bottom. A crack in the plaster runs into the calendar and out the other
side. Like what. A graph or tributary.

Now . . . Gilbert folds his hands . . . Mind telling me what you've
been on the losing end of?

It's not the weekend. What are you doing here?

Caitlin?

I fell.

Or you can tell the Head first thing in the morning.

So dark I couldn't see where I—

The truth.

I'd rather not.

I insist . . . Gilbert picks up a pen lying on the desk.

You'll think I'm an idiot.

Right, first thing after breakfast—

So she tells.

He did what . . . standing up but no room to . . . Unbelievable . . .
so sitting again.

I don't know why he gave up.

It was time I did a walk around and I thought I'll just correct one
more. I should have—well.

We could forget it ever happened.

I'll have to tell Headmaster.

Please don't.

What if it happened again? What if it's happened before?

It hasn't. I'm sure it hasn't. It's just me spilling the eggs and that he hates Americans. He's. Patriotic.

Yes . . . assessing her . . . You're cut.

I'm alright.

Paul is a peculiar lad. A bad apple.

Is that what he is.

I'd feel better if you cried or something.

Would you?

Don't you want to?

I wanted to stab him in the eye with his cigarette.

I'm not surprised.

I wanted to beat him.

Well now we can leave that for the school, hum?

Whatever they do it won't be enough.

Come on, I'll drive you around to the San. You need to get those cuts looked at . . . Gilbert picks up his coat shaking it to hear the jingle of keys.

I saw your paintings . . . her face tight, the scratches swelling . . . The ones you hid.

We should get you to the San . . . leading her outside.

Why are you always trying to get rid of me?

You should have something put on those cuts.

Mr. Gilbert.

Come on now . . . and over to his car.

Looking for gloves in her blazer pocket . . . Eighty-year-old dried up nurses and their pinching fingers.

I'm taking you, that's final . . . opening her door then the back door to throw his duffel on the seat.

Running her hand on the notsheep next to her . . . It's funny how last time I thought this was real.

Slams the door pushes back the driver's seat then he waits. In the cold car together. She looks where he does at School House the top three floors lit classrooms below dark.

Caitlin.

What? . . . why does he say her name like that? . . . What Mr. Gilbert?

You must speak to someone.

I'm talking to you aren't I?

You're not crying.

I don't feel like crying.

Why do you act so old?

Why did you paint her blue?

You just turn everything back on me don't you?

I wish I had beaten him.

Still looking up at the school . . . Look, perhaps you're thinking that you're weak. You're stronger than you realize . . . now down at his hands ready on the steering wheel steering her . . . People might think you older than you are.

What does that mean?

Hum?

No . . . she won't let him . . . What does that mean?

Gilbert won't answer. After a moment Caitlin pushes her head into his shoulder his delicious sweater it seems so terribly sad the two of them like this in his woolly car looking out at the night and school this waist pinching chemist with hidden paintings and a nearly fourteen American who smells the lab man's warm sweater and through it feels the swallow high in his chest.

"Chemistry" is a chapter from a novel in progress.

Connie Barnes Rose
Concordia University

ESCAPE

The man I love has just walked into the visiting room. His hands are stuck in his pockets, his bald head shines under all the bright lights. You'd think he was wandering in the park by the way he looks around at the inmates sitting there, each with a number stamped on his breast pocket. Most of them sit across from women who stare into their eyes and hold their hands tightly across tabletops. Finally he stops at my table and, sitting down across from me, stares at the window.

"You've shaved it off again," I say, trying to catch his eyes.

I wish I hadn't said that. He ignores me when I say things that aren't all that important. I fiddle with a piece of gum wrapper that someone has left on the table, and wait for Tyler to come out of his meditation. Tyler can meditate anywhere. He has told me meditation is one of the two things that help him survive in here. The other is the excellent hashish.

Now he stands up. He raises his arms high above his head. "It feels so good to stretch," he finally says, smiling down at me. "It makes me feel like a cat."

I say, "I know what you mean. I've been doing a lot of yoga lately."

"That's good, Natasha. Yoga will keep you in touch with yourself."
Then he laughs. "You know what I find funny?" He jerks his thumb

back toward the guards in the observation booth behind him. "Them. They think that they have me locked up in here when I'm as free in here as I am anywhere. They're the ones in prison. Look at them there."

I look at the guards, knowing exactly what he means. They're there every time I come here, which is at least twice a week. They sit in the same chairs, wear the same uniforms, and don't look one bit freer than the men who live here all the time.

"Look at the fat one," says Tyler. "Is he looking this way?"

I look at the fat one who is reading a newspaper. The other guard is watching an inmate who stretches his arm across the table to stroke his girlfriend's hair. "It's okay," I say.

Tyler reaches down and slips his fingers into the side of his running shoe. Then he folds his hands in front of him and nods to the Styrofoam cup on the table. "Pass it over when it's clear."

I slide the empty cup over and he slips a rolled-up wad of money into it. I quickly look over at the guards before I pull the cup back to my side of the table. He smiles at me as I take out the roll and slip it down the front of my jeans.

"Ah, Natasha," he says. "It's good to see you."

Tyler likes to call me Natasha, even though my name is just Nancy. The summer before last, we ran into each other on the beach, out there on the hard red flats. It must have been fate that brought us out there on such a windy, cloudy day. He had just come out of prison after catching a five-year sentence for selling a couple of joints to some stupid university kid who got caught and got scared. Before he was put away, I'd only known Tyler from seeing him hanging around town. With his green leather jacket and long red hair, he'd reminded me of Robin Hood. But out there on the flats, I thought he just looked alone. We walked along the wet sand and he wanted to know all about the music I liked, whether I turned on to pot, if I had ever tried to meditate.

Back on the shore, my father watched us from the cottage we were renting for the week. My father is a town cop. The first time Tyler got busted, he'd said, "I'm glad they got him before he went and ruined some kid's life." I was only fifteen then, but I remember thinking that what my father said sounded pretty weird considering Tyler was the one going to prison for five years. So I guess it shouldn't have surprised me that he wasn't too happy to see me out there on the flats with Tyler after he'd just been paroled. I reminded him that there wasn't much he could do about it seeing as I was now eighteen. He told me that as long as I was living under his roof, I wasn't allowed to see him. The next night I met Tyler in a field. He spread out a blanket and we lay on our backs and just paid attention to the universe. After we smoked a joint, he pulled a timothy straw from its shaft and began to stroke my forehead with its fuzzy tip. He told me about the seven chakras contained within our bodies. Slowly he dragged the straw down over my chin, my shirt and my bare skin below it, stopping at each chakra to explain what it meant. Then he ran the straw down the zipper of my jeans to right between my legs. You'd think with all that denim separating me from a straw, that I wouldn't feel a thing, but when he stroked me with it, I just about went nuts.

"You see, we think of this as the lowliest of all the chakras," he said, smiling at me as I lay there trying not to squirm or laugh or cry, "but you see how powerful it can be?"

Until that night, I'd only been with guys who smelled like beer. That night I fell in love with Tyler with all my heart.

The visiting room is getting pretty noisy with all the laughing and talking and kids running around the tables. Tyler takes my hand. "Have any of the seeds come yet?"

"Not yet," I say, "but I only ordered them last week."

"How are they sending them?" he asks as he twists the little silver ring on my finger.

"By bus," I say.

"That's what I thought."

We have a big garden out behind the apartment we rent in town. A couple of weeks ago I brought in some organic seed catalogues and Tyler and I had the best time planning this year's garden. I even brought in some Crayola markers and we drew a blueprint. We got a little carried away with actually coloring in the corn and tomatoes, but it was fun. The guards kept coming over to see it, and then shaking their heads. Tyler liked the picture so much, he tacked it up in his cell. He won't be able to work in the garden since he's stuck in here, but he'll be out by harvesttime and I think by planning it with me, he can see the end in sight.

I say, "I figure as soon as this month is over, I'll borrow my uncle's rototiller. That is, if the snow ever leaves." My words trail off. I've lost Tyler again. He stares at something on the floor.

Tyler landed back in here because he broke his parole last September. He was out at the beach with Helmer McKay checking out Helm's cannabis crop. They didn't actually catch him with the plants but the RCMP turned down the road into the field just as Tyler and Helm were leaving it. Ty's parole officer said he couldn't buy the story that he'd only gone down that lane to go for a swim. So for that, he's back in for at least a year, even if they couldn't prove anything, and look at Helm, still strutting around town. "That's how the system works," Ty said to me the first time I went in to see him. "Once they get you, they got you for good. What if I'd just been down there for a picnic?"

When I reminded him that he'd broken his parole conditions by hanging around with Helmer, who everybody knows is a dealer, he got all pissed off, and said, "You're missing the whole point, Natasha. They don't want to see me free because they think I'm a threat to the whole of society. You should know how these people operate by now."

I couldn't believe he was getting so pissed at this. He stood up and I grabbed his arm.

"I can't be with someone who thinks the way *they* do," he'd said, walking away. Through the door, I saw him raise his arms to be frisked. He looked up at the ceiling as the guard ran his hands lightly along his sleeves. When the door shut him from my view, I stood there stunned for a minute before I could move. I cried all the way back to town. Maybe he couldn't escape from those prison walls, but he sure could escape from me.

When I got back to town, I drove straight to Alana and Danny's. Alana was hanging out a wash in the backyard. Even in winter she hangs out her wash. She says seeing it flapping in the wind makes her feel safe somehow. After she made us some tea, we went out on the back steps. "That Tyler," she said, "is chock-full of shit." Alana has known Tyler all her life. She says she loves him like a brother, but I should know by now that he works things to suit his own ideas of how things should be. "But, I understand how he must feel," she says, twisting her hair up into a bun. "I know I'd go nuts being locked up in there and knowing everybody else is running around free."

Maybe Alana knew him before, but I think that's what makes her blind to what he's really about, what we are about. Tyler and I are not like ordinary people who are controlled by primitive emotions. We don't even use the word "love" except when we're talking about all of humanity.

A lot of Tyler's old friends laugh at him behind his back. They knew him from before, when he was just like everybody else. They don't know how much he changed in prison. I'm the only one who believes him when he says that all he really wants to do is buy some land in the country where we can grow our own food and live quiet lives. I believe him because that is what is most honest about him. He wants to feel free in this world. And I do too.

I can understand why Alana and Danny are a little pissed at him though. Not long before he got sent back in, Tyler decided we should only breathe clean air, and since Danny and Alana weren't about to stop smoking cigarettes, we would have to stop going there. "Besides, they eat meat. Can't you smell it on them?" I couldn't, and I sure didn't want to stop seeing Alana, but Tyler was right about one thing. If I was going to try and live a healthier life, I should avoid temptation. Before I met Tyler I did stuff like smoke cigarettes and eat hot dogs. Tyler says that one day we won't want to smoke cannabis anymore either. But for now it's okay because of the way it sweeps the dirt out of the far corners of the mind.

Now Tyler raises his eyes to meet mine. He says, "Have you seen Jack lately?"

"Yesterday," I say. Jack is Tyler's cousin. He's one of the people who like to laugh at Tyler, especially behind his back. Everybody calls him Father Jack because he has a job cleaning the churches around town. And also because he jokes about being celibate seeing as his wife won't sleep with him, won't even talk to him half the time. He jokes around a lot, doing impressions of people around town. I have to admit he does a good one of Tyler. He closes his eyes and says something like, "Om. We are one with the universe. To achieve divine perfection we must cleanse our minds and bodies. We must drop our possessions and clothes and live as nature intended." Then Jack will open one eye and say, "Nancy, or, pardon me, Natasha, you may start by removing all of your clothes. Then you may sit yourself down upon my holiness so that I may explore your inner self."

Jack told me that he heard through the family that Tyler got raped soon after he went into prison that first time. "Tyler may have been fucked up before he went in, but that really fucked him fuckin' permanently," he told me, not long after Tyler and I rented the apartment down on Deacon Street. Jack was there helping me clean it up while Tyler was at work at the big farm out by the beach. His job was driving a big liquid-manure spreader over the fields all day. He said he took the job because humility is the way toward truth.

I asked Tyler about the rape once. He just shook his head and said, "All of prison is rape, Natasha." That's when he told me about Jeffrey, the inmate who changed his life. Tyler said he could look at anybody and make them feel blessed. He called himself Joss, and he was in for sailing up the bay with a hull full of hashish. He taught Tyler how to play chess. He let him read his books. Tyler says that after meeting Joss, he began to put his faith in fate.

"Give Jack a message," Tyler is telling me. "Tell him to throw the next bag over the fence behind the tool shed. Somebody on yard duty will pick it up. And this is important," he says, leaning closer, "don't forget to tell him to make sure the bag matches the ground. Like if there's snow that day, put it in a white bag, but if there isn't, make it brown, okay?"

"Okay," I sigh. "But I thought you said you weren't going to be doing this anymore."

Tyler nods. "It was supposed to be the last one, but, Natasha, the way I see it, we're providing hope. This way they get to escape, even for just a little while. And it's a hell of a lot better than booze. I wish you could see how peaceful it is in here since I've been back. Even the screws are starting to wonder."

"That's what I'm afraid of."

"What can they do, throw me in prison?" He puts his hands up to his face, looking at me over the tips of his fingers. "It takes courage to live like us, Natasha, whether we're taking risks, or just surviving. We've chosen a path that goes beyond ordinary life. At least I have. Sometimes I'm not so sure you're ready."

"I have to go to the bathroom," I say, because I can see in his eyes that he has shut me out like I'm no different from one of the screws over there. I go into the visitors' washroom and lock the door. I run the water in the sink and splash my face. I look at myself in the mirror. I have a very red pimple on the side of my nose.

I remember another time I was in this washroom looking in this mirror. I'd gotten up from the table and slipped in here to wait for Tyler to follow me in. As soon as he'd slid around the door, he locked it and turned me around so I was facing the sink. He pulled my long skirt up around my waist. I held on to the sink and stared at my face in the faucet chrome. It was all bent out of shape, my nose swollen to three times its size, my lips looking twice as wide. I almost laughed, until I looked up at myself in the mirror over the sink and saw that I really looked fucking scared. But it was exciting scared too, the way we hurried, all the danger we were in. After, Tyler smoothed down my skirt, kissed my neck, and I walked out of there, calm as any summer day. Tyler came out soon after and nodded to the inmate mopping the floor near the washroom door. After we sat down we couldn't stop laughing. The guards were looking at us, and every time we looked up at them we'd start laughing all over again.

When I come back from splashing my face, I half expect Tyler to be gone. But he's still there, sitting with his eyes closed, his head swaying just a little, like he's listening to music. When I sit down he says, "I'm sorry, Natasha." I'm wondering what he means by that, like if he's going to jump up any second and walk out again. I touch his sleeve and say, "Ty?"

"Life is full of contradictions," is all he says, just before he opens his eyes. Sometimes I think he can read my mind.

A bell rings in the end of visiting hour. Chairs scrape and the guards come out of their booths to make sure nobody gets carried away in their good-byes. Sometimes when I'm carrying the money I worry about spot checks. But like Tyler says, it's not illegal to carry money.

Tyler holds me close, nuzzling his face into my hair. "Sometimes I think you are the strongest person I know," he says, then pulls away and marches quickly to the door, leaving me standing there as usual, wondering what he meant.

Today the guards are in a good mood, and they joke with us as we sign out. They don't even bother to check any of our bags.

"See you ladies next week," says one, winking at his friend.

"And don't you worry," says the other. "The boys will still be right here when you come back."

The last sliding gate rattles shut behind me. I gulp at the cold air blowing up from the bay. I feel the eyes of the guard up in the tower as I walk to my car. Behind the wheel, my knees start shaking so much I can hardly keep my foot on the pedal.

I guess you could say I'm a prison widow. Alana told me I couldn't be luckier. "Look," she said, "here you get to be single and free, but you know you've got someone a short drive away who's jerking off just for you. When they're loose, who the hell knows what they're up to?" Maybe she needs a break from Danny. They've been together since they were seventeen. He drinks too much, but then again, she doesn't put up with much shit. He hit her once, slapped her face because she called him an asshole. But she just picked up a bread-board and slammed him so hard that we got a little worried later on when he started mumbling about being on some carnival ride. Maybe he is an asshole when he drinks, but when he's sober he and Alana sometimes disappear for hours until they come back, hanging off each other like it had been their very first time.

It was hard getting used to Tyler being gone at first. Mostly, I was just lonely. We'd shut ourselves off from the people in this town, and it got so we could pretend no one else existed when we walked through the streets in our long navy coats. There's no furniture in our apartment except for a mattress and a long Oriental rug that Tyler got from his grandmother when she died. On that carpet we read and meditated. We practiced our yoga and Tai Chi. The room was so long that I could do running handsprings. Sometimes I could hardly wait for him to leave the room so I could go flying through the air, then sit down again before he came back. He would say, "What was all that noise?" I'd just say a truck must have driven by or something. I don't know why I didn't want to do them around him. I guess I was worried he'd think I was being childish.

Jack is at the Jupiter Restaurant, sitting in his usual booth, the second from the door. He asks me how Tyler is. "Bald," I say, and then wish I hadn't.

Jack laughs into his coffee. "I bet he's a pretty sight. The great guru. When are you going to shave your hair off, Nance?"

I hand him the money. He counts it. "I'd say he did well in there that last time, wouldn't you?"

"I have no idea," I say. "I just want him to stop doing it."

"I thought you wanted this land-in-the-country thing too," he says, stuffing the money into his pocket. "I keep telling him we should be bringing in fucking cocaine. A kilo of that would speed things up real quick."

"I have to go," I say, getting up.

"Oh, by the way, Nance," he says, and for some reason, the way he says it makes me stop in my tracks. "There's a package coming in on the bus tomorrow and it has your name on it."

I sit back down. I know he doesn't mean any organic vegetable seeds. "What do you mean, my name?"

The waitress brings Jack his dinner. She puts it down and says, "Here you go, Father Jack. Oh, hi, Nancy, I haven't seen you in a while."

I know her. We used to jig geometry class together, but I just can't remember her name. "Hi." I smile quickly. "How's it going?"

"Can't complain," she says, heading back to the kitchen. "Enjoy your dinner, Father."

Jack watches her until she's gone through the door. He whispers, "Just what I said. You'd better pick it up, because I don't think it should sit around in the terminal too long, if you know what I mean."

I watch him dump ketchup on the burger. I watch him take a bite, then wipe the grease off his chin.

He says, "It's two pounds of hash, and it should be here by Monday."

• • •

Danny is getting drunk and cooking up some deer steaks that he has pulled out of the freezer. The whole kitchen is full of gamey smoke. I'm sitting at the table playing solitaire and waiting for Alana.

Danny says, "Hey, Nance. You can go tell Tyler that we had a totally natural dinner here. Yessiree, we've got your wild deer, and wild mushrooms, and lookee here, we've got your home-brewed beer too." He spears one of the steaks out of the frying pan and bringing it over to me, holds it under my nose. It smells like blood. I turn my head but all of a sudden I've got these juices flowing into my mouth.

"Come on, little Nancy, I won't tell," he says, trying to follow my nose with the steak.

Alana walks into the kitchen waving her hand at all the smoke and saves me by asking if I want to go for a walk. She throws on Danny's hunting jacket and we start out along the old marsh road. It's quiet and dark here on the salt marshes. The road is a bit muddy yet so we have to step carefully. When we get far enough out of town and the stars are easier to see, Alana lights a joint. As soon as we get off, she gets to talking about her UFOs again. Ever since they found one of those rings out here, she's been right into watching the sky. I went and saw the ring, everybody in town did. It was perfect, how it crushed the tall grass so that it lay like dominoes, all splayed out from the circle. I walked around that circle, right in the rut. It felt pretty weird to think that something might have been there. Most everybody says it was caused by a wind twist, but Alana is sure that whatever it was, it'll be coming back.

She stands with her face tipped up to the sky and her hair riding down her back. I start thinking about that package on the bus that'll be riding the highway over this marsh on Monday with my name stuck on it. There's no way around it. I have to pick it up. I start pacing along the grassy ridge rising up in the middle of the road. The more I pace, the more I feel like screaming. I want to shout at whoever is up there, or out there or inside here, that maybe it's true that I am too weak, maybe I do want a regular old life. I don't know anything except one thing. I sure don't want to go to prison to prove that I am free.

I must be pacing faster and faster, turning and circling, and a noise is coming out of my throat. Suddenly, Alana plants her hands hard on my shoulders. "What's wrong with you?" she says, her eyes wide and looking all around as if maybe something has actually landed somewhere near. I sniff, look up at the sky, and wipe my eyes. "Alana, do you think Tyler really loves me?"

I shiver there in the dark. I can tell that Alana is frowning. "You mean, you put up with all his shit and you don't even know if he loves you?"

My knees are knocking together like crazy. Maybe I'm being paranoid, but when I called to see if the bus had come in, the guy on the phone sounded kind of tense. For all I know, the narcs could be hiding somewhere in the building right now just waiting for me to pick up that parcel.

I walk into the Terminal Diner. My father sometimes comes here for lunch with some of the other town cops, but he's not at his usual spot where the counter snakes around by the window. He likes to keep an eye out for things going on around town. Except I notice that whenever I happen to walk by the window, his back is to the street.

None of the other cops are here either, which really spooks me now. Somebody waves to me from across the room and I wave back. It's just my old History teacher, who took a liking to me for some reason and tried to talk me out of quitting school. I walk into the bus terminal. The waiting room is empty too. I go straight past the ticket counter and into the women's washroom. I sit on a toilet and try to meditate. I close my eyes and concentrate on my mantra. I listen to it until I know I'm locked in there, where my eyes have trouble opening, where my head feels light and heavy too. For fifteen minutes I sit, until I start to feel like I've slept. I try to take a deep breath but the place stinks too much.

I open the door and calm as can be, march right up to the booth. "Is there a package for me? Nancy McKinnon?"

The guy looks through a bunch of packages. "No-o," he says slowly as he sorts through them, "I don't think so . . ."

"Or maybe it's Natasha McKinnon?" I say, standing on tiptoes trying to read the packages.

"Oh, wait a sec, here it is. Nancy McKinnon, that you?"

"That's me," I say, smiling at him as sweetly as I can.

"Heavy for such a small package," he says as he passes it over. "Must be gold, is it?"

"Must be," I say, and I walk right out the door toward the Baptist church.

Jack's down in the basement arranging all the little chairs for Sunday school. He opens his mouth when I throw the package at him. But I'm out of there before he gets a chance to say a single word.

I'm back in the visiting room. Tyler looks surprised when he comes through the door because this is not my usual visiting day.

"What's wrong?" he says

"What's wrong is the package on the bus. The one that wasn't seeds."

Tyler leans back in his chair and folds his arms. "So? Did anything happen?"

"No." I say, "I was lucky."

Tyler smiles. "Ah, you see? Nothing happened. You really should have more faith in your own fate, Natasha."

I tap my fingers on the table and stare at Tyler. He stares back, his eyes calm and patient.

"My own fate?" I say, my voice cracking. I tell myself I will not cry.

He shrugs and says, "I knew you'd be safe. You're Walter McKinnon's daughter. Nobody's going to touch you."

There's a kind of buzz in my ears. He starts going on about strength and weakness and who has it and who doesn't. Alana and Danny don't have strength—they're just the same as everybody else. Jack doesn't—he was too chicken to go up to Toronto to pick it up, and that's because he's scared of any city bigger than Moncton. But me, he knows I have courage. I let him go on and on. I think about the last night we were together before he went back inside. He fell asleep before I did, and I saw how his closed lashes rested so lightly on his face. I couldn't stand to think of someone so beautiful being locked up in a cage.

"It's only through suffering that one realizes one has nothing left to lose, Natasha," he says. "This is a basic truth."

"Tyler," I say, clearing the catch in my throat. "My name is Nancy."

He sits back in his chair and shakes his head ever so slightly. "They got to you, didn't they?" he says. His green eyes watch me calmly—the eyes that made me believe.

Wendy T. Button
Bennington College

CLIMBERS

The door swings open, bouncing an extra time because of my brother's size. I am in front of the porch planting impatiens. I can see the planks bend and then rise as he moves toward the rocking chair. The cuffs of his corduroy pants rub against each other; it is mid-June and in the nineties.

He coughs and sits. The wicker makes a ripping sound from his weight. He rocks. I hear the rattle of his medication—six plastic canisters he carries in his pockets. The chair stops. He lights a cigarette and the sour smoke passes over my head like a cold front.

I breathe through my mouth to avoid the sulfur smell while making a tight moat around the impatiens.

I say, "You're outside."

"A couple of quick cigarettes," he says.

Jeffrey is not kidding. It takes him thirty seconds to smoke one. Our younger brother, Alex, timed him. I don't like to watch Jeffrey smoke, the way his body shivers when he exhales. I keep planting.

He says, "What do you call a tuna fish scared of everything in the ocean?"

I press the cool dirt. Jeffrey tells jokes when he is having a bad day: when the voices call him "useless," when he thinks everyone wants to take away his jokes, or when he can't open his eyes more than a thin line and apologizes for throwing my toys out the window when I was eight.

"What do you call a tuna fish?" I ask.

"Chicken of the sea," he says.

I stretch my back and readjust my bikini top. I look up and Jeffrey gives me a small wrist wave. The tobacco is down to the filter, gripped tight between the yellow stains and brown burn marks on his fingers. His brown hair is wild as a pom-pom. Sweat shines around his temples and a few drops fall from the earpiece on his horn-rimmed glasses. He wears an oxford cloth shirt, the cuffs buttoned tight around his wrist. He never wears short sleeves.

His new "miracle pill," the Clozaril, the pill that makes him dehydrated so he drinks non-stop and the pill that knocks him out at night so that he doesn't wake to go to the bathroom, requires that he have a weekly blood test to check his white cell count. Jeffrey claims that people stare at his arms and call him a junkie. I've seen his arms: a couple of red marks small as blemishes. I think about Jeffrey in high school: his hair was cropped at perfect angles, his body fit and healthy from being a star baseball pitcher; my friends (I'm ten months younger) thought he was handsome and flirted with him.

I force a smile, pulling my sunburned face. "You make that joke up?"

"Yeah," he says and laughs. He sounds like a child imitating a machine gun.

"What do you call a person who eats a lot of cereal?"

"What?"

"A cereal-killer."

I plant. I stab the ground with the small spade. Jeffrey rocks and then I hear the ashtray wobble as he puts out his cigarette. I reach for the last impatiens. A southwest breeze makes the bikini string tickle my back. My skin tingles and then chills. I have been outside since I picked Jeffrey up from his halfway house at ten. It is the first time I've been able to garden in weeks since I had surgery on my ankles to prevent bone from growing over my Achilles tendon. Six months of surgery and I had to quit my job working as a production assistant and move back home. Yesterday the doctor sawed off my last cast and the sunburn on my scar, the withered skin around my calf, feels good. It is close to five, and I am fried.

"Why are psychiatrists so popular?" he asks, his voice deep from smoking three packs a day, his words slurred from his pills.

"Why?" I ask.

"Because they have a lot of patients," he says and flicks his lighter.

I work the dirt as though I'm kneading dough.

"Right," I say.

I turn and check on the dogs to make sure that they aren't wandering through my new annuals. Penny, our golden, sleeps on her back, the sun warms her light blond underbelly. Winston, our blind English mastiff, sits in front of the Oriental dogwood. Winston was hit by the laundry truck, smashed his head into the truck's headlight. The glass scratched his eyes. It was hard the first day, watching him stumble down stairs, into walls, lifting his leg at the air in the middle of the side dog-yard. Then Penny took care of him. She guided him and he followed, relearning his steps. Though he's still off sometimes. Like now, he sits by the dogwood, but he is positioned a little to the left. He likes to sit there, wag his tail, and move his ears to the hum on the white blossoms.

"How many psychiatrists does it take to change a lightbulb?" Jeffrey coughs and then I hear the tobacco snap and hiss.

"How many?" I say.

"Just one, but the lightbulb has to want to be changed."

"That's a good one."

"Thank you very much, Sidney."

I hear the ashtray wobble.

Even though I am finished planting and my ankle aches from the standing and bending, I keep kneeling and think about that word "change." I want the Jeffrey I know to return. The brother who taught me how to avoid eating my peas by spitting them into my milk, the brother who did one hundred sit-ups a day and ate junk food only on Sundays, the brother who was the relief pitcher on the high school team and could strike out three batters with nine straight curve balls, the Jeffrey who acted like the older brother after our father left when we were younger, and who brought my mother breakfast in bed because she had a hard time leaving her room. That's the Jeffrey I refuse to let go of and wait for some combination of drugs to return.

I don't want to know this "new" brother. The one whose hospitalizations prompted our father's ghostly return three years ago. The Jeffrey who tells jokes all the damn time. The Jeffrey who wants to be a TV weatherman and moves his arms as though he's pushing a cold front across the screen. The Jeffrey who tries to kill himself by tossing full bottles of pills, sometimes his own, sometimes my mother's, down his throat. The Jeffrey Alex and I often accompany to emergency rooms.

"What do you call a wheel on a Rolls-Royce?" he asks.

"What?"

"Wheel of fortune," he says. "Why does Santa Claus have three gardens?"

"I don't know."

"Because he likes to 'ho, ho, ho.' "

I laugh a little. "I like that one," I say.

Jeffrey laughs and rocks. His pills rattle.

I stand up and turn my ankle in a small circle. I see the swelling, the yellow and green bruising, and the scar, thin and puffy and red. I have painkillers and will need one tonight. I try to take them only when it's bad and then I'll only take a half or a quarter. I'm not good on prescription drugs. After the first surgery on my left ankle, on Demerol, liquid Valium, and some other stuff because they'd tried to do local anesthesia, but failed and knocked me out anyway, I woke up in the recovery room singing Ray Charles at the top of my lungs. A week later, on a Percocet after they'd patched up my spinal leak, I watched a talk show about botched home repairs; I sobbed because someone's kitchen was a mess.

Slow and steady, I climb. My hand grips the railing. It is cool on the porch. I sit next to Jeffrey. A cloud of smoke hovers above his head. I smell Jeffrey: ash, piss, and rotted onions.

"Did you shower today?" I ask, picking at the dirt in my nails.

"I just want to relax," he says.

Alex and I have both tried to help him take care of himself. We try to get Jeffrey to brush his teeth, do his laundry, clean his sheets, shave, trim his fingernails, cut his hair. But he doesn't want to. Doesn't really care and the halfway house director doesn't take the time to teach Jeffrey a routine, a habit like smoking a cigarette. My parents? They both say that as long as he's not hurting himself or others, Jeffrey's fine. And that's their business to think like that. I don't like it, but it's their way.

Jeffrey looks down the porch. "A front is coming through," he says, moving his arm in a semicircle. "See the thin cirrus clouds. See the cumulonimbus cloud rising and growing." He uses both hands like he's lifting a glass bowl. "And storm clouds just beyond will push the humid air out and pull the drier air in," he says, pushing his arms toward the front garden.

I look at the cloud growing like smoke from a smokestack. "You can tell all that from looking at one cloud?"

"Been watching the Weather Channel. They just issued a severe thunder storm warning. Possible tornadoes in Worcester," he says, and makes spirals with his hands.

"My ankles hurt," I say, and it's so soon for my right one to hurt, for it to feel the weather too.

"Take a Percocet. They're by the sink in the kitchen."

"They're weak," I say. "And don't help."

I know that I should run inside and hide the bottle. But he's seen them. He knows they are there and if I move them, he'll know I don't trust him.

"When's Mom coming back?" he asks, and his thick glasses slip to the tip of his nose, one of the temples duct-taped at the hinge.

She is away in Italy with her new boyfriend, the one who Jeffrey says is always calling him a junkie.

"Two weeks," I say.

"When's Alex coming back?"

I glance at my watch. "About half an hour. I hope he misses the storms."

"Remember when I taught him how to say, 'My nose is crying' instead of 'running'? And 'I'm barefoot all over'? I feel bad about that."

"Don't," I say, watching a drop of sweat drip down his left temple and then get sucked into his ear. "He's fine about that."

"He with Liz?"

"On the Cape," I say and wipe my dirty hands on my shorts.

Jeffrey lights another cigarette. He sucks hard like he's drinking a thick milk shake. He takes three strong drags, ashes once, and puts it out.

"I hope to meet a girl too. Have five kids after I get my job on the news. Then buy a nice house," he says. "You could garden."

I don't know what to say about his future talk, his talk about love and a family. I know that he had a girlfriend in high school, but I don't know if he's ever made love. Alex once said that because Jeffrey speaks about women in a way like he's missing something that he used to have, he's not a virgin. I don't know what to think and I pick more dirt from my nails.

I say, "That would be nice."

I watch Winston lick Penny's ears. The sun is dimming; milky clouds blow in with the wind.

"Storm should be here in thirty minutes," he says.

"I'm going to secure some stuff, clip some Altissimos, and then make dinner. How about a pasta salad and cold soup?"

"Nah." He stands. "I'll just have a bag of chips and a milk shake," he laughs. "Okay, one more joke."

"Jeffrey, please don't eat that for dinner."

"Why did the chicken cross the road?"

"Why?"

"To get away from the Kentucky Fried Chicken," he says, and then the porch door bounces shut.

My stomach falls the way it does when I miss a step walking down the stairs. Jeffrey's halfway house is in Brighton. Gateway always has a fresh coat of gray paint and the front porch is white, inviting, and homey. Behind Gateway is a low-income housing project for the elderly, rusted washing machines in the yard, to the left a mechanic shop with hollowed Pontiacs, to the right is Store 24, which Jeffrey calls, "Store Two-Four," and across the street is Kentucky Fried Chicken, the parking lot littered with red and white buckets. Gateway looks like a nice place to live, but inside it is a dump.

Whenever Alex and I pick up Jeffrey, he's outside on the front porch, his duffel bag tight in his hand, pockets bulging with canisters of pills. He smokes and stares at the restaurant until he notices the car or hears the weak honk. But Alex and I were early one day and Jeffrey wasn't waiting.

We walked inside and the first floor was clean from the residents' chores. Even though it is the rule not to go past the first floor (Gateway's privacy policy), it was quiet and so we went upstairs. It was just for a minute.

When I reached the second floor, I noticed moldy towels bunched in corners. The hallway was dark and smelled rotten. I heard muffled music and crying. Punch marks spotted the cheap Sheetrock and the chipped green paint looked like scales. As Alex and I climbed to the third floor, he whispered, "Thirty fucking grand for this?"

The railing was splintered, dust thick along the sides of the stairs. Jeffrey's room was at the end of the hall, his door close to falling off the hinge. The smell made me gag as Alex tugged the door open.

Jeffrey sat on his unmade bed, reading a meteorology book. I saw the stains, large ovals on his navy sheets and wet marks on his pillow. His room was a mess: a pile of old shoes in the corner, clothes and trash covering the floor, empty pill bottles on his bureau, a fan thick with soot, and ashtrays filled with flattened white butts.

At first Jeffrey had an excited expression, a smile of hello; his teeth yellow like the soft side of an orange peel. Then he knew what we saw, what we thought, and he looked at the floor.

Alex said a quiet, "Jesus."

I said, "Let's go."

That night over the phone our father said that Jeffrey had to learn. Alex yelled, "No one's showing him!"

After Jeffrey's weekend at home, we drove him back. We bought him a new bed and rubber mattress covers, and tossed the old bed in a Dumpster. We garbage-bagged the trash on the floor. We threw out two bags of shoes. Cleared out his closet. I showed Jeffrey how to dust along the baseboards. He told jokes: one about sky divers and how they always fall for it. Jeffrey vacuumed. We placed a clean ashtray on his desk and a new fan. He liked dusting his meteorology books and joke books. When we left, he said, "Thank you."

The ride home was quiet. The windshield wipers, the back one and the front, made alternating thumping sounds. I kept wanting them to be in synch. We couldn't take our brother out of Gateway. It wasn't as bad as the state hospitals and he wasn't living in a hospital for the first time in a couple of years. We didn't have any money to move him: I was just out of college and Alex was still in school, with a bartending job that wasn't going to pay for a new place. We couldn't walk up the stairs to his room, pack him up, move him to a place in the country with a pretty yard, rose-fresh deodorizers, and painted walls and expect that he'd get better. There wasn't a choice; Jeffrey had to stay.

I rub the wicker arms. To this day, I'm still not sure what was worse—having to leave my brother at Gateway, or his expression on that bed, the way he shut his book, slow as an iron cellar door. Jeffrey has lived at Gateway for close to two years, and every couple of months Alex and I clean his room.

The dogs rest on the dark grass. The wind blows their fur in the opposite direction of their coats. Jeffrey's music pounds, "Penny Lane" for the twelfth time. I look at the front garden. To the left, in the shady area, are hostas and bishop weeds, wilting lily of the valley, and Prima Donna red begonias blooming and full. Above, on the tall white fence, the clematis vines: the lavender flowers on the General Sikaskis and then the white Marie Boisselots, twist toward the sunny part. The vines point to the pink Carefree Wonder roses, which move toward the Sea Foam whites and then the bright red Altissimo rose. It has saucerlike blooms, bright red petals and, in the center, yellow stamens. They come like clockwork every year in June, then they rest and keep coming back, growing and climbing on the fence. The Altissimo is a great climber, on old and new wood, and keeps blooming until the frost puts it to sleep.

Below the roses are the rhododendrons, the Blue Peter and PJM pinks. The geraniums, Shasta daisies, and achillea border plants: the Pearls and brilliant Yellow Moonshines rest on the ground below the fence. I stare at my new mounds of snapdragons, petunias, and thick patches of white, pink, and fuchsia impatiens. The strong breeze shakes all of the petals; they ripple like a sea of miniature hand-held fans. The yard smells sweet and Jeffrey's music mixes nicely with the hum of bees.

I push the wheelbarrow around the yard, picking up plant holders and securing annuals. I leave the rose clippers on the porch. I open the side gate and move past the Oriental dogwood, still clutching its white blossoms. The tools clank and rattle as I nudge the wheelbarrow over the gravel driveway.

I hang up the tools. The shovel bangs against a rake and it sounds like a dull bell. The boxes from the nursery rest against the far wall with small specks of dirt and white fertilizer. I place the holders back on the cardboard so that the nursery can reuse them. The wheelbarrow slides into its spot by the door. The barn smells like dirt, flowers, and musk. My thumb presses the button and the barn door whines shut.

Four empty cans of Coke and a dirty ashtray are what I pick up from the back patio table. I hate it when Jeffrey's used ashtrays are left outside in the rain, the puddles of caramel-colored water.

Inside, "Penny Lane" plays again. But the music comes from the back bedroom above the kitchen. It has the best view of the backyard down onto the open golf course and the approaching storm. Jeffrey has moved his music so that he can watch the weather.

The stove clicks three times before the gas flame blooms, orange and blue, underneath the pot. I hope to boil the water and cook the pasta before I have to shut the kitchen windows. By the sink is an empty carton of ice cream and plastic bag of chips.

The house is dark. I close the windows in the living room, the room no one sits in because it is too neat, filled with antique vases, tables, chairs, and old pictures. It is the room I found Jeffrey in two years ago after he tried to kill himself with my mother's Valium. He was on the rug, clutching the picture of the three of us after the Blizzard of '78. Only our heads poke above the deep snow.

Everything is still. Even Jeffrey's music. I look out at the front yard: the dogs lounge, the grass ripples, and the petals fan, their colors dull and chalky from the hovering storm clouds. Standing in the front hall, I hear a deep thump. Perhaps Jeffrey has his headphones on and his foot is pounding to the rhythm. I hear him hacking and I walk in slow motion.

In the kitchen, I watch the ceiling shake. I look at the chip bag and ice cream carton. In between them, the empty pill canister and one Percocet perched on the white plastic top.

"Not again," I think.

So I turn off the stove.

I let the dogs in. Winston follows Penny; she guides him around the turn into the kitchen.

Then, I go outside. This is a first, going outside. But I know there is plenty of time.

The plastic grips on the clippers are smooth against my palm. The wind is strong and the leaves rustle. I look up and the sky is slate gray. Standing in front of the Altissimos, I hear a distant rumble.

I clip. The shears angled up. My arm shakes as I reach toward the flowers high along the fence. My ankles burn and stretch. It takes a quick minute and red blossoms fall, the small stems green and jagged.

As I scoop and push them into my arm, I make a soft arc the same way Jeffrey does when he shows warm air lifting up from the south. I cradle the flowers and walk toward the door. A gust of wind rips the loose dogwood blossoms and the chalk-white petals whip around the yard like the frenzied moths underneath the porch light at night.

I climb up onto the porch and remember the first joke Jeffrey told. It was the first weekend he was home from the hospital, a couple of months after his first attempt to down his bottle of Haldol. He was on the front porch, chain-smoking, and the moths above us kept bouncing off the lightbulb.

Jeffrey asked, "What are mountain climbers' favorite snack cakes?" I shrugged my shoulders. "Yodels," he said.

I didn't crack a smile, say "Right," or anything. I stood there, stunned by his slurred speech and the growing brown hair and the dirty gray skin on his cheeks. Jeffrey sounded and looked like a stranger. I was still, except for a few shivers from the moth-dust falling on my arms.

My arms are scratched. The scratches sting as I look at my watch. It is five-forty and I look at the gravel driveway, the border plants, the snapdragons bending toward the silent gray pebbles.

Inside, I put the flowers in water.

The outside air bangs so loud that the windows rattle and the floor shakes. The lightning flashes close by and the kitchen windows turn electric blue.

I fill the dogs' water bowl because I know that we will be gone a long time.

My hand clutches the railing. Gravel crunches on the driveway. A car door shuts. I turn and see Alex running, a magazine umbrellaed over his head.

Again, I climb. Slow and steady up the back stairs. As I move, I listen to the familiar weather pelting the windows and rattling the walls. In the hall, I turn. I move toward the bedroom door, toward Jeffrey, the one who tells jokes.

Adam Marshall Johnson
McNeese State University

WATERTABLES

"Get me a witness," he yells from downstairs.

I'm lying on top of the covers because Molly, God, she's an oven. She sleeps so hot it makes her look unhappy to sleep, pouty, with her skin puffy and red, mouth folded open against the pillow. "Go put him to bed," she says. "Lock his window. It's cool out." Cool, I think. It's July. Her eyes are closed. Her lips move against the pillow. Then she's quiet all over. I've a few more minutes till she's roused again. I stare at the ceiling, at the roof, and listen to the clamor of a hot South Dakota night beneath me. I don't like to see him at night. He gets confused at night. I listen to him rumble around, hear the floorboards under his feet and the soft thuds as he bumps into things. Something crashes below. Mol kicks me through the sheets. "Jim," she mumbles and pauses. Her hair sticks to her damp cheek. I think she's done, but then she adds, "go talk to him." But she's not really awake.

"He's not doing it again," I say. "He's just having a bad dream." I look to see if she'll answer but she just moans some, from the heat. I get up and cross the warm floor to the window and hear her roll up into the free covers on instinct. I look out. My face is in that layer of air that hangs just off the glass and I think it should be cool, I imagine I can see my breath in the pane. It looks like mist out there, looming above the fields, glowing in all the lights. But it's not. It's the dust of topsoil, earth once washed into the Missouri River valley, silt, loam, now leaving us, moving on in a light breeze. We need rain.

I stare into the bean fields and find myself almost looking for her, almost wondering what my father sees, a woman running the plow rows in a blue paper dress. I follow this corridor of dark green as it leads south to the Watertables State Mental Health Facility. It's bigger at night, too big, with the lights always on, shining through the tall hedge that hides the high fence. There's no one out there. She's not out there. I know it.

When I get downstairs I see a racquetball rolled up against the front door. He's yelling in his room, "She's here. She's here." Then I hear him whispering. The hall closet door is open and the light is on. My gear is lying on the floor, racquets, gloves, balls. He sticks his head into the hall. "She's back," he says. "She came back." And he's gone again, whispering.

In his room, I walk to his bedpost and feel for the string that's run to the overhead light. I rigged it that way so he won't have to get out of bed in the dark, so he won't fall. I chink on the light and we stand there squinting, me and my dad in our underwear. The bedcovers are on the floor. He has dreamed himself out of bed again and he is worked up. He walks to the open window saying, "See?" His white hair is standing up straight, unsure of its once worn part. I walk to him and pull up his sagging briefs and then shut the window. I say to him, "Dad, where's the sports bag?"

"I gave it to her," he says, pointing out the window, looking through the glass to the lights of Watertables across the field. "She said she needed it to carry her stuff. She's running away."

"Stop it, Dad," I say. "There's no lady. We've talked about this. You had a dream. You sleepwalked again. Just show me where the bag is and let's go to bed." Last week it was the silverware. I heard a jangle in the night and in the morning all the forks were gone. "The bag," I say. He looks around the room with me like he forgot he claims to have given it away. His shorts are slipping down again. I latch the window and try not to look into the dark, try not to encourage him. He thinks maybe I saw her and smiles. "We had a deal," I say. "You agreed to stop doing this. Now where did you hide my bag?"

"She come out of the bean field," he says, talking fast. His lips are pasty from sleep and they stick together as he talks. I bend to look under the bed. "She says they put her in there after her husband died. It's awful in there." He points again out the window.

He must have been looking for something in his sleep. He got confused maybe. He dumped the bag out and then couldn't get everything back in. So he hid the bag. It's hidden here somewhere. I turn to look in the hall again. My useless things are spread all over the floor, bright in hall lights. There's no racquetball courts in South Dakota. I start shuffling the remnants back into the closet with my foot. "Get back into bed, Dad," I yell toward his bedroom. "She's just a dream."

"Her name is Margaret," he says. He says this and I stop.

I walk into his room. I walk right up to him. "What?"

"She said her name is Margaret."

"There's no Margaret, Dad. There's no ghosts and no escapees and no lady in the beans and she doesn't have a name." I try to slow myself but I'm scaring him. "Tell me she doesn't have a name. Tell me you're making it up. Say it!" But it's night. He gets confused at night.

They're both up before me. I come downstairs to Molly listening to the crop reports and drinking coffee with two hands. She's mad again. Her eyes look swollen, like she's been exercising, sweating, in the sun. She feigns interest in July hogs. The AM radio is one thing Dad wouldn't sacrifice for new tenants. It's on all day. She sets the cup down and begins eating eggs with a spoon. That's all we have now, knives and spoons. "You wore that tie yesterday," she says and twists open a jar of instant.

I take the kettle from the kitchen and sit to fill our cups. We all drink instant now. "You two had quite a night," she says, blowing on her coffee. "He doesn't deserve that, you know." See, she's mad. Molly watches him during the day. She makes glossaries for schoolbooks on the computer. But he's fine during the day. It happens at night, when it's my turn.

I undo my tie—it's reversible, brown and blue—and I look around the room for him. It's not good to talk about this around him.

"He walked to the road for the paper."

"He's doing this on purpose," I say sharply. "He's making it up. When we make him understand he's not going in there, this will all stop." I don't like talking to her this way, but she doesn't see this like I do. She says she's practical. I think she wants to believe. The first night he saw this woman, after Molly and I had just moved in, we were desperate. Mol walked the property looking for footprints with a flashlight. She said maybe we could draw a picture of her from his description. I called Watertables from the dark of the kitchen. I told them their mental patients were crossing the field and terrorizing my father. They said no way.

I decided he would sleep upstairs; Dad climbs stairs just fine. I said if he slept upstairs he couldn't claim this woman came to his window. Mol wouldn't budge. What if he should slip? she said. What if he fell? Jim, she told me, your grandfather went and now your father is going. Deal with it.

I sip my coffee. It tastes salty. The well water always tastes salty during a dry spell. The announcer is running off lists of numbers, soy and pork bellies, steer futures. The prices seem low, though I am unsure. It's my job to know the cost of things. I try to remember back when I lived here as a boy, what Dad got a bushel then, which makes the numbers seem high. "He's just scared," I say. "That's all. He thinks we might put him in there."

She looks at me. "I talked to Litner," she says.

"No doctors, Mol. I'm serious." My father needs me, and that's okay. But I didn't come here for him. I came here for us. Mol says we have time, but we don't. We don't have any time for this.

Dad's up the landing with his head in the door. He's slumped in overalls and wearing the cap I gave him: Farmers Do It in the Dirt. "Paper's here," he says.

"Look like rain?" I ask. He looks at me like I'm foolish to have to ask someone else.

"Eggs?" Molly asks.

"Eggs are for birds," he says and walks out into the yard to read. Every morning she says eggs and he says birds. They have this together, her and him, these little jokes.

It's quiet after he's gone, just the radio. Out the window, I see him sit on a bucket under the tree. Near him, the rose leaves are coming in red, and past those are summer beans running downhill to the shade trees of No Show Creek. The beans look waxy. "Look," I say. "When I was a kid, there was only one rule: Don't go near the Watertables. Dale and I could jump off the barn, run the reaper, shoot the Damascus, anything. But stay clear of Watertables. He's always been afraid of it. Always."

"I'm just saying someone for him to talk to. It's not getting any better. What if it gets worse? What if you don't figure this out?"

"No doctors, Mol. He's never going in there. He's going to get old and read his paper and tell his stories and then he's going to die. Grandpa Jim dropped dead picking apples from that tree." I point out the window, but she won't look, especially with Dad sitting there. I don't want to argue. The coffee is getting cold. I drink my salty coffee and watch through the window the wind clipping his hair, his cuffs. It tries to take the paper from his hands. "Grandpa Jim started going when we were young. He told stories that didn't make sense. He always gave Dale bad advice and showed me how to do things wrong. But Dad helped us understand, made it okay, made us see it was just part of the deal."

"But that's not what you're doing, Jim," she says earnestly, softly. "You were yelling at him last night."

It's quiet again. Paul Harvey comes on the radio to tell us exactly how the world works. Mole-A-Way can rid our garden of pesky rodents through the use of undetectable sound waves he tells us. Our turnips will be protected by modern technology. It worked for a woman in Lincoln he says. I trust Paul Harvey and I really want to believe he's right about a simple box saving my garden, about mysterious waves fixing my problems.

We both jump as Dad knocks on the window. It scares Molly for a second, him looking in like that, waving the newspaper.

I unlatch and open the window. "Je-sus," he says, handing me the article. "He paid his friend to cut his foot off to fool the insurance. Anybody ever try that on you?"

I look at the article. "No, Dad. I sell crop insurance. Remember?"

"Go ahead. Read it," he says, walking back to his bucket. "They ought to take those crazy birds out in the middle of nowhere and push 'em off a hill."

Molly laughs. She leans forward and whispers with her diluted Boston accent, "Where do you suppose he thinks the middle of nowhere is?" I miss her laugh. She has an honest laugh and it fades too soon.

I have been preaching pestilence for a full year and now it's all coming true. I've been talking men into banking on doom while I bet against it. But honestly I don't know the first thing about the weather. So I'm reading the almanac when Gene Allen comes into my office. He's wearing a short-sleeved collared shirt with jeans and dirty penny loafers and coming into my office in July means he's on his last leg.

The meteorologists in Omaha tell me forecasting's an art, at best. But my father could smell a cloud a week in coming. He'd step out into the blue sky wearing an open white shirt and black boots laced with leather tails, jeans half buttoned, a bachelor eating a drumstick and squinting in the line-to-line arcing blue. He'd toss that bone and stand licking his fingers before buttoning his pants, squinting in the morning sun, a man about measuring. Then he'd tarp the hay. He'd shed the tractor and put up Grandpa's old mules, Miggs and Jenny. And Dale and I would leave our bicycles in the dirt approach, wheels spinning, to enter the fields and wait under a blue sun for a rain that must be coming.

That's how I remember him now as Gene takes a seat, my father seen from the broad-leafed beans below, a man on his property deciding, while I waited in the rows next to my brother for the first big drops to come out of nowhere to bend the dusty plants. Dad would say it was coming but Grandpa Jim could still tell you how much. Grandpa Jim got to where he couldn't figure out his shoes, but he'd clod onto the porch and say seven-tenths. Me, I'm betting. I lick my fingers and stare at the sky and see nothing. I see a crop-beating sun and dust. I hurry the book into a drawer; it's not something for me to be seen reading, not what I should be subscribing to.

Farmers today are like Gene, like me, guessing. Gene knows I'm from the big city. He thinks I have mysterious technologies at my beck and call. Farmers want to know what satellites see and computers tell, but they're leery, too. They want me to be someone like them, someone they can trust. At the same time they want me to be a distant expert with a clipboard and a phone link to Skylab. So I wear blue jeans and a cheap tie across a crisp white shirt. I drive a brand-new Chevy, but always with bale or a barrel in back, sometimes planking. I sit in a rolled leather chair and watch Gene track dirt onto my carpet and I decide I'll leave that dirt there for a week, or longer, as a sign of that certain mix of hard work and prosperity that people want to believe in. We shake hands. He sets a bag of dirt on my desk. I test their soil in Dad's basement for free. I read a library book on how to do it, but my answer is always the same: fertilize, nitrates nitrates nitrates. Anything to ensure a yield.

"I got browntops all across and I can't keep the dirt on the ground for all this wind," he says and points toward my wall, toward the wind we both know is out there. "They say we're going to come up low on water this season, Jim. They say the rains aren't coming."

"A well's always the best bet," I say, and I start my monologue: the cost of drilling and irrigation, numbers and statistics, fast mathematics and calculations, and I'm losing him, dazzling him into a slight stupor, which I want. I turn the computer screen to him and start running charts and graphs in the iridescent green. He holds his chair arms and watches my hands move. His father's land's his now. His father, who never once sought help and never took it, who Gene probably never once saw fearful of the future, of something that couldn't be helped, and now Gene's in my office pricing an easy way out, pricing safety. I add wind and hail and flood and tornadoes, my hands swirling above the desk. I talk of Chinese moths and cotton weevils. There's blight and black root and hydrosemitis and I'm talking as if there are too many dangers to list when Molly calls. She tries to sound sincere as she asks me if fifth graders would know what magma was.

"Molly, I'm working on a policy here. I don't have time."

"I talked with Litner," she says. "Go see him today, he wants to speak with you about your father."

I don't say anything. I watch Gene read an article I cut out of the paper and taped to the wall. It's about the plains drought; the headline reads, "Farmers Lose Everything."

"I made an appointment for you."

I still don't speak.

"Jim?" she says. Then she gets this talking-to-herself tone. "I'm trying to be understanding here. I'm trying to be wifelike about this."

"No way, Mol. You know how I feel. We talked about it. We're not seeing him. Dad's going to live with us and then he's going to teach his future grandkids how to whittle wrong and they're going to cut their fingers off, okay. One big happy thumbless family. No doctors."

Now she's quiet. Gene has turned from the article and is looking at me. In his pale eyes he seems lost and confused, like me. He doesn't want insurance but he's reached a point where he's prepared to pay. He eyes the headline again and I understand him for a moment here, someone gotten to a place he doesn't know. I don't want to sell him a policy. I want to talk him out of it, to tell him to go home, to quit praying for rain. Quit praying, I think.

"Look," I say to her. "I can't see anyone today. After lunch I have to drive to Omaha to pick up the new trends. I have to have this month's rates out Monday."

"Come home for lunch."

I'm quiet. I tap my pencil on the desk so she can hear. Gene wants to leave so I mouth at him to sit, sit.

"I'm working too. Just come home and we'll talk."

"Okay," I say, quieter. "You're right."

I can hear them talking on the other end. "Your father wants you to get him a beer on the way home. Any kind," she says. "No, it's a Coors now."

Gene has my father's difficult eyes. They are gray and set in with lowering lids, searching eyes that roam the room for guidance. Troubled eyes lighten with age. Dad's are almost white. Gene shifts some and then stands, looking at his bag of dry dirt on my desk, looking for a sign as to whether he should take his dust with him or not, and I can only think that someday soon I will have those eyes.

"Did you look for the bag?"

"Yeah," she says. "I looked."

"Look again, okay?"

"It's not the bag," she says, and I tell her eleven and hang up.

• • •

Inside the No Show Tavern, I order three tenderloins, slaw, a six of Coors and a draft. Willert's youngest, Winston, sets the beer before me and I suck the cool foam. The glasses have gotten smaller. I rent Dad's land to Willert for a third of the futures and Winston rolls up once in a while in a million-dollar Steiger to watch game shows in a climate-controlled cab as he cultivates the rows. He has walked into the cooler and I can see him looking out into the bar through frosted glass. I put a handful of plastic forks in my shirt pocket and I can see him stare at me through rows of brown bottles. He wipes the white from the glass with his hand, to see what else I may take. Sweat drips from my nose onto the bar. Even the beer tastes salty in this heat.

I set to thinking in the hot room. The windows are painted black. Fans move fast and out of balance. On the wall is a picture of a penguin pointing to blue icicles hanging under the words Air Conditioning. I don't think about all the policies I'll have to pay or the underwriters or Gene, a customer I was probably lucky to lose. I think about Molly, the way she's trying to humor Dad, like he was one of those kids in her textbooks. There's no humor in this. I know my dad. He's just got to be shown there's nothing to fear. He sees that and this whole thing stops. I show him and it's over.

I call for another draft and Winston comes out of the cooler. His hair is frosted and his lips are pale, but he's still sweating. The tavern doors open bright as two, three, five men enter, a full crew dressed in brown with tan name tags, all with large key rings hooked in cracked belts. I look at my watch. Ten-thirty. It's the third shift getting off from Watertables.

The end one has to take the stool next to me, an idea he doesn't seem to like, and he bumps me as he hunkers down. I look at his round face, at his buzzed hair under a brown baseball cap. He's a guy I might have gone to school with. But then I see his boots; they're steel-toed with the leather roughed at the tips, the metal showing. Winston starts pouring beers, lots of them, as they pass the dice cup in turn, shaking and spilling them onto the bar to see who'll pay. The end one begins clanking his steel toe against the brass rail like he's comforted by the sound. He turns to look at me. His name tag reads Shick, and Shick takes his time looking at my tie, the folders of papers on the bar, the bundle of plastic forks in my pocket. He catches me looking at those steel toes, clanking away at the rail. He scratches the scruff on his neck until he's taken things in and turns to talk Dakotadome football with the guy next to him. ". . . but the main problem with astro—"

"You work out there?"

Shick slowly rolls his head to me, mouth open. "Yeah," he says and swings back to the other guy, "—turf is that there's too much traction."

"You guys guards?"

Shick stops again. The guy on the other side of him shakes the dice cup and watches in the dark heat of the bar. His name tag says Lem and he has a deep-grooved face, like a misironed shirt, which seems to crease and uncrease as he considers my question. His boots are similar except they're pointed. "We're monitors," Shick says in the direction of Lem.

"Monitors?"

"Monitors make sure things go smooth."

I want to let this go, but I can't. "Then why the boots? They look all—"

"Oh, that," he says and smiles. "That comes from kicking old people in the head." Then there's a quiet as he shakes the captain's cup and spills dice on the bar.

Lem laughs. The grooves loose, then bind. "Tell him to piss off," he says to me. "Shick's just being an asshole. We use our boots to slow the tires on the wheelchairs. Like brakes. You know, it rubs the leather."

I smile a little easier now, relax some. I sip my beer and I feel the joke, the way you want to trust a man who can put you off. I drink deeper than I normally would, a true gulp. "You got a woman in there named Margaret?" I ask Lem.

Shick has rolled triple twos. His big face studies the dice on the bar. Lem has to pay, he decides, and Shick calls out for another round.

"I don't know names," Lem says in a voice that you wouldn't know from his face. "Go to the Divisions desk. There's a form you fill out."

"She's probably older, with longer hair maybe."

Suddenly Shick turns to me, as if he's noticed me for the first time.

He eyes the forks in my pocket. "Look, you got someone in there or not?"

I pause. I can feel the fans whirring overhead. I open my mouth but there's nothing there. I'm sitting here and everything I can think to say feels unfamiliar. My eye catches Winston in the cooler again, looking scared and angry through yellow glass the way my father did last night. "No. No, I guess I don't."

"Then what the hell do you care?"

The bar is quiet and I want my food, I want to leave, now. Three empty beer glasses sit on the bar before us. The dice are still. Then Shick shakes his head. Facing the bar, he starts to laugh, at first a low snorting sound through his nose. Lem starts to smile too and soon they're both laughing. Shick turns and laughs right at me, but it seems as if he's saying none of this counts and I start to smile. "I can't take it," he says. "That's a good one. Slows the wheelchairs. You kill me with that, Lem." I laugh with them for a moment until different punch lines begin to surface.

"Kick 'em in the head," Lem says, and soon they are dying.

"Like brakes," Shick howls, and now they're laughing so hard they forget where they are, babies, just the two of them, laughing and laughing.

I'm tired on the way home. Driving past the Watertables I feel the cool mist through the windows of their sprinklers running that long green lawn, bright water running in the middle of the day. I don't care about Omaha or the trends or my rates. Every policy I sell now is doom and I know it. I just want to lie down and turn on the air conditioner. Up the approach my fenders rumble and one of the empty barrels bounces out. I drive on, faster. Coming up the way, I see the windows are open with the curtains blowing off of the screens. A big white house in a hot wind against a green field and blue sky. I don't want to fight.

When I park, I see Molly doing something I've never seen before. I grab the food off the seat and walk over. She is picking apples from Grandpa Jim's tree. She's set up a sort of picnic, a card table and chairs and iced tea in the shade of the tree. Mol has on sandals and a white cotton dress. She is using the front of her skirt as a catch for the fruit, and I sit and watch as she shows me the backs of her legs when she reaches. I pour a glass of iced tea and enjoy looking at her. I haven't looked at her this way in a while.

"The picnic looks nice," I say. "It was a nice idea."

She turns and says thanks and continues picking. "I think I'll make a pie. I've never made an apple pie before."

She comes over and lets the apples roll from her skirt onto the table. They make a pleasant sound, like bare feet on old floors. I lean back in the chair and decide I won't tell her they're crab apples. I decide right now I'll eat that pie. I pour her some tea. "Look, Molly. I know I've been a pain lately. I know it. I haven't been myself. The insurance, this thing with Dad. Maybe it's the weather. You know me. I get an idea in my head and it builds and builds, you know. I just want to say this is a nice thing you did for us. I want to—" I stop. I stop and I count. "Who's the fourth chair for?"

Molly's quiet. She pulls her hair back and exhales. She shakes her head. "It's just a social call, Jim."

"Who's the chair for?" I'm standing now.

"He's doing us a favor. He's just coming by to—"

"Jesus Christ, Molly."

"There'll be no office or bill. He just wants to come by and see you two."

"Jesus." I shake my head. "I can't believe this."

"You're down there every other night, yelling. It's driving me crazy."

"It's driving you crazy?" I say, trying to lower my voice.

"Why not let him hear? You think he likes being yelled at less than being whispered about?"

"He doesn't even know what's going on."

She turns her head and looks at something far off. "You really believe that?"

"No doctors, Molly. That's final." I point across the field. "It's just that place."

"No, it's not, Jim," she says, slowly, looking at me. "It's you. He's fine with me all day. Something is happening with you two."

"There she is," I hear him yell, and I spin toward the house looking for my father. "I got her," he says, and suddenly I see his boots dangling off the roof. I see his hand lifted toward the Watertables.

I open the attic window to the sun off the shakes and there he is, sitting at the edge of the pitch, looking at Watertables with his long field glasses. A light mist of dust has settled over him. I step out into the light. The shingles are shrinking, drying up, becoming loose. They shift and crack under me. My clothes rattle as a cornice of dust runs over the gable and turns at my feet. "Dad," I say, trying to speak calmly, trying not to frighten him. "You need to come off the roof."

He turns, his white hair flips in the wind. "Call your old dad a liar, will you. You'll see."

I step toward him. The silt is slick on the roof and I leave long footprints. His skin is pink. He has stopped sweating. "How long have you been up here?"

"As long as it takes." He lifts the binoculars again. "You bring the beer?"

"Yeah. It's downstairs. Let's go have a beer, okay?"

"Is it Coors?" he asks, squinting into the glass. I can see he's got them all out of focus.

I sit on the eaves next to him. "You have to come down with me."

"She's coming. You'll see."

"Dad, you can't do this to me." My eyes are hot and I rub them until they throb. My collar pops up. "Not in the daytime. You can't do this to me during the day."

"Do what?"

"This." I put my hands out. "This."

He shrugs. "My roof."

No matter what, I decide. I'm not going to get mad. No matter what.

"I think they're dancing," he says and passes the glasses to me. He puts them in my hands and explains, pointing. "See how they got them gardens set? Don't have that damn hedge in the way. That's where they've got 'em. In circles, dancing around. It's crazy, isn't it? You wouldn't catch me dancing with those birds. Go on, look."

I don't even want to touch the glasses. I force them back into his determined fingers.

"Are they dancing?" he asks, looking at the binoculars. "Tell me if they're dancing."

"No. We're going to get off the roof. It's not safe up here."

"Oh, no. No way." He loops the binocular strap around my neck and they fall against my stomach.

I kick at the edge of the roof and a shingle falls and turns in the wind to snap on the rider mower. "See, Dad, they're so dry they're falling out. There isn't any rain."

"Gonna rain tomorrow."

I wave my hand at the sky above us. I'm so frustrated I can't even seem to shake words out.

"I know," he says.

"No, you don't know, Dad," I yell. "You don't know."

"You read the barometer? Mostly I use that," he says, and I want to just pick him up and carry him in. The barometer hasn't changed in weeks. "See them heifers over at the fence, eyeing that alfalfa?" he says, pointing. "Those are Willert's cows. Ain't seen them in a couple of weeks, have you? They're four miles from the tank. It's a good sign. You check your gauge. It'll change."

"That's it, that's your answer? You watch the cows?"

"Your Grandpa Jim did. Like I said, I prefer the barometer." He stops and looks into the air.

"This isn't cows, Dad. This is serious. I mean, this is really serious." I look up in the sky, into the encompassing blue. Not a cloud. Below I see Molly gazing up with me, her hand over her eyes.

"Boy, she's hot," he says, and for a minute I think he means Molly, who I'm thinking of. Molly, who I'm watching back slowly into the bean field to get a better view of us, and I think, God, if he sees her, if he sees her out there, it's over.

Dad wipes the dirt from his forehead and I motion with my hand to flag her out of the field. She waves back, a small movement at her waist, as if she were afraid of being seen as encouraging and suddenly I am afraid of her. But he won't let up. "You look in those glasses and tell me what you see. You look and we'll go."

I lift the rims to my brow, but I can't look.

"Are they dancing?"

"Yeah," I tell him, my eyes closed. "It looks like they're dancing."

Dad squints at me in disbelief. "You're lying, aren't you?"

I pause. "No."

He opens his mouth. "You, you did it again, didn't you?"

This is funny to him. He gets the craziest look on his face. His pale eyes widen with surprise. No, I say, but he's laughing now, I mean, he's really funny. I start to smile, I almost can't help it because I haven't seen him smile in so long, but I look into his failing eyes and it is not funny.

"You did. You lied," he says, shaking his head, shifting his hip to stand. "Three times." And before I know it, he's walking toward the window with his head listing, laughing softly in the wind, and I feel I've . . . I feel as I look from my father to my wife in the rustling green that some unseen force holds me just beyond them.

I help him across the pitch and guide his unsteady foot over the sill. I stop at the window though, and stand with my clothes buffeting. There is a glimmer in the beans that catches my eye, a quick flash, and I start to lift those glasses. I don't know anymore. The scary thing is, I truly don't know what I'll see. It could be my forks in a bean row or Litner dusting up my drive. It could be rain clouds on the horizon. I stand on the roof gripping those black frames and I honestly can't tell you if I'm searching for a woman in blue paper dancing with my bag or for a boy crouched in the beans, a boy who's been told the future and still believes.

Caroline Cheng
Columbia University

CONSOLATION

I didn't think much of Ninfa when she first came to the house, but my employer, Mrs. Garcia, said to me: "Mila, give her a chance." I took it she didn't cost much. The girl was supposed to help me out in the kitchen, but the first time I had her set the table, she put the soup spoons in the middle of the plates. And she was dirty. Her hair hung past her tailbone, ragged at the edges. It smelled. I don't know why I expected more. She had been left by her mother to grow up with strangers, wild in the province. Nor had she known her father; he had run away long ago.

What her mother hadn't taught her, I did. It wasn't easy. The girl didn't start out speaking Tagalog very well. The other maids poked fun at her, saying that it sounded as if she had rocks in her mouth. But I stuck by the child. Mainly I did so as a favor to her mother, Soledad, who had once been my friend. She used to be the cook for Dr. Garcia's father when the old man was still alive.

The thing I insisted on was that the girl be clean. Knocking against her in the kitchen one day, I felt a hard crust scrape me where her elbow should have been.

"Ninfa," I said. "You really must start cleaning yourself better."

"Yes," she answered, addressing me *Manang* out of respect for my age.

The more I pondered the matter, however, the more I became convinced no ordinary treatment was going to get rid of that dried-up sediment.

"Your elbows," I said. "You need to soften them first."

Her gaze darted over to the bottle of cooking grease.

"Not that way," I laughed, catching her drift. I told her about the cream that I used, and my volcanic stone. "Come," I said, motioning, "I'll show you how."

She followed me to the room where I slept with the Garcias' youngest, and she just stood there waiting outside the door. "It's all right," I said. "Leave your rubber thongs in the hall; you can come in."

But there must have been a breeze coming through the screen when she did, or maybe the girl walked by me a hair too close, because I caught the scent of her then, and she smelled foul, like long-curdled milk.

"Do you wash?" I said, about to scold her some more, when I felt her stiffen, like a snail recoiling back in its shell. The girl couldn't lie.

"In this house," I tried instructing her gently, "all of us, we wash ourselves every day." Everyone did in Manila, I told her; even in my sister's house, where they had to pump their water from a well.

"You're not in the province anymore," I added, but as soon as the words left my mouth, I started thinking about those old country ways.

"Is it that time of the month?" I asked her. There was this saying that a woman should never wet her head when the moon was full, or else.

"Don't worry," I said, reaching in the medicine cabinet for my cream, "you won't go crazy. At least, not from wetting your hair."

I laughed, and turned around to face her. But she wasn't laughing. She was pasted to the wall outside the bathroom, crossing herself and repeating her prayers, as if she had been visited by a ghost.

"For Heaven's sake!" I said.

And then I knew what I wanted. I wanted her to look in the mirror, and get a grip on herself.

I put my hand on her arm—I only meant to touch Ninfa lightly at first—but I found myself dragging the whole weight of her, like a sack of rice, into the bathroom. I held her face in front of the mirror, locking her head in my hands. It was like trying to put a bridle on a horse,

I could see the white bouncing off the tops of her eyes. "Look at yourself!" I said.

Her neck snapped to meet her reflection in the mirror. And then she broke down, laughing and crying—with relief, I realized.

She started coughing up a story. Apparently, someone had told her that a sure sign of insanity was if you looked in the mirror, and couldn't see your image. The girl really had been afraid of going crazy.

But there had to be a reason she would be worried in the first place.

Something about a sister, or was it a cousin, who'd died.

I wasn't going to force her to tell me more than what she was willing. A house might look fine until you started poking around, and then you discovered the termites had left only the crumbling facade. If there was nothing you could do, though, what good was it to know? "We all have sad stories," I ended up telling her. "There are people who make it, and those who don't. It's a choice."

But I began looking out for the girl after that, taking her under my wing, teaching her things she would need to stand solid on her own. I showed her how to open the vegetables by the neck to check that they weren't too white, too fibrous. I trained her to choose the fruit depending on when we planned for them to be eaten, to get the ones that were about to become golden for today and the ones that were still a little bit hard for later in the week.

And Soledad's daughter learned fast. After I brought Ninfa to the market a few times, she was able to go through the stalls by herself. In the meanwhile, I visited with my *suki*, the pork dealer, and my other connection, the fish vendor; this way, we could do the job in half the time. I still had to do the bargaining, but Ninfa's cooking had improved to the point that I allowed her to prepare the meals of the maids. She became very good at this, cooking a fish so tasty that you forgot it was cheap—frying the *galungong* over a hot fire and flipping it over so both sides became crispy, then covering the fish and leaving it to simmer under a low flame, so it would also be soft in the middle.

And I admit, I had plans for this one.

The child was obedient, which is more than I could say for the others. She walked to church every Sunday, and she sent her salary to her mother once a month. I knew that because I kept the money locked in my closet for her, in an empty can of coffee.

The others teased that Ninfa was fast becoming my favorite. They had heard me say to her, "When I get too old, you can take my place." I paid them no mind. I saved the best food for her: the meat near the bones, and the black stomach of the fish. I let her take the head of the pig to her mother, to use for a stew, and she didn't even have to ask. With all this attention, the girl started filling out, and I wasn't the only one who noticed.

Sweeping the dead leaves off the sidewalk one day, I saw Boy, the security guard of our neighbor across the street, giving Ninfa an eyeful. I knew him well. He was always whistling and clucking at other people's maids, trying to get them to talk to him. I did not trust him. Later, as I was gutting the fish for the evening's dinner, Ninfa asked me what I thought of this Boy.

"You know," I said, after a moment, "he's *pabling.*"—A player. This guard was always reporting to us in detail the latest news on his "sweethearts," though I suppose many of them were only pen pals from provinces far away, whose names he had obtained from the *Komiks,* a local newspaper. I had even met the girlfriend he really had his heart set on. She lived in Hong Kong, working as a maid for a young foreign couple. She was earning a good salary—a hundred fifty U.S. a month, at least five times his—and he had found himself hard-pressed to convince her to come back.

"Have you heard about a Marietta?" I asked, looking squarely across the work table at my young charge.

"The one from Hong Kong," Ninfa said. Her knife was raised midair. "They've broken things off."

"Go on," I said. I meant, with the chopping.

The girl nodded. "The mother of Marietta didn't approve of Boy."

"But she's never met him . . . ?" I could only guess that the mother had read her daughter's letters.

Then Ninfa told me the whole story. Boy had been straight with his girlfriend right from the start. He had confessed to her he was employed as a security guard; that's what the mother objected to. "She wants her daughter to find a Hong Kong Chinese. Better yet, an American."

Though I didn't approve of Boy either, I felt bad hearing this. "You never have to be ashamed if you make your living the honest way," I said to the girl at last.

I threw the fish in the pan and we left it at that. Other worries sprung up that I had to take care of. The rainy season had started, and the Garcias' roof was leaking. A few years back, all Ma'am would have had to do was make a call, and some construction workers would have come right over to fix it. With the Garcias no longer what they once were, we had to make do with a few buckets, taking turns to empty them out by the hour.

And it rained, one day into the next, in sheets that unwound endlessly from the skies like a bolt of a cloth. Thundered to the point the dog didn't lift an ear. My mind filled to think there would be another six months of rain. The laundry took three, maybe four days to dry. Even then, it was half damp when Nene, the girl who worked as our *lavandera,* ironed it. By ironing, Nene sealed the odors into our clothes, and we walked around smelling like sour washcloths. She used to be able to dry the clothes during rainy season by laying them on top of the centralized air-conditioning unit beside the garage; it had big fans.

When it stormed like that, there wasn't much we could do. After dinner, when we finished wiping down the tables and washing the dishes, our entertainment was to talk, or to watch TV, or both. Sometimes I would get one of the maids to pluck the gray out of my hair. None of us felt much like going out in the rain; even the cockroaches came scuttling into the house.

I took up crocheting again, and started making some covers for the living room sofa. Ma'am hadn't changed it in years, and the material had yellowed in places. I liked to do this in the library, where I had my sewing machine in one corner and I could be by myself. That's where I was, the night Ninfa came to me. She stood in the doorway, her shadow wavering like candlelight, until I could no longer ignore her.

"Come now," I said, motioning at her with my hooks. "If you have something to say, don't let it fester inside you."

"*Manang,*" she blurted, settling at my knees. "Why did you never get married?"

"That was a long time ago!" I said as a joke.

She didn't laugh. "Please," she said, "tell me."

I put down my crocheting. I looked at her, a white uniform at my feet. With my doing, the girl had now become quite presentable: clean, and slender like a young tree. Come to think of it, she didn't completely have the features of a maid. Her mother was dark; that left her father. He must have been *Tisoy*—American looking—very handsome. Put a little shine in her hair, and she might even have been competition for the girls I saw posing in the commercials. But that would have been another life.

"*Siempre,*" I said, "*dalaga ba . . .*"—Of course, when you're a young lady, you have many suitors . . .

She waited, picking at her nail.

I sighed. "After my sister died," I began again, "my brother-in-law asked me to be his wife. The war ended *na*. He wanted me to take care of his children, but I didn't like him. So my mama said, 'If you want to go away, go away to where he can't find you.' That's when I became a *yaya*. From that time on, I always took care of children."

I had come knocking at the Garcias' door over twelve years ago, and Ma'am had hired me to care for Bing, the youngest daughter. Only when Bing had gotten to be older, did I become the cook. Before the Garcias, I had worked for another family, until the last of their children had left for college.

All this was true, but somewhere in the telling, my voice box had rusted.

Ninfa didn't say anything. Her face twisted.

"*Wala na.*"—There's no more to the story. I meant for them to come out slowly, but I strangled on the words. Maybe because they were things I hadn't told anyone for God knows how long, things no one had since cared to ask.

We sat in the green light, not talking. The air sparked, thick with electricity. I shifted in the chair; a bone in my back cracked. Rain dripped from the gutter. It rang hollow, loud, steady as a pulse. A lizard clucked, and I saw it, liver-colored, snaking up the wall.

Finally, I understood. "This isn't about me," I said.

She shook her head.

It had to be Boy. I reminded her of Marietta. "Don't accept to be second best."

The girl kept looking at the floor.

"Don't repeat the mistakes of your mother," I warned. Ninfa's mother had children by three different men.

"How would you know?" she sobbed, letting loose a torrent of tears.

I bit my lip, and kept my quiet. "You're how old now?" I asked, after a while. "Sixteen?"

I tried to explain our options. Above all, I was realistic. I thought it best for those in our station to find a position as a *yaya* or a cook. Anyone could wash clothes or sweep the floor, but if you had a special skill that added to your value, your employers would find it harder to let you go. And for a girl like Ninfa, there were added complications. Some employers (the wives I was thinking of) didn't like having their servants too pretty. I knew she didn't like hearing what I had to tell her, but this was the extent of our possibilities.

I tried softening the blow. "You may not realize, but we are treated very well here. Especially in Manila, a lot of families don't believe in being 'too good' to the maids. Well, the Garcias aren't like that."

I told the girl a story about our driver. How he could always be found sleeping in the car, mouth hanging loose, fists over his eyes, the front seat reclined the whole way back. How he seemed to be perpetually tired, which was a great mystery to us all, considering that the only duty required of him was to make circles—to and from the hospital, the supermarket, the beauty parlor, and school! And how it was only after he got the car in an accident, that Rico confessed he was also moonlighting six hours a night: delivering vegetables from Bulacan to the market here in Manila.

"And you know what Dr. Garcia said, after he found out?" I asked the girl.

She shook her head.

"That he would rather pay the driver a little more, so he wouldn't have to work two jobs!"

I sensed Ninfa grow calm, even heartened. "Thank you, *Manang*," she said, kissing me on the cheek before leaving me alone again.

I felt I'd done the best I could have for her, considering the circumstances. The next thing I knew? The girl had flown. I was still in bed early that morning, wedged up against the wall, when I felt a tugging, urgent on my shoulder.

"*Manang*," whispered a low voice. "*Manang Mila . . .*"

It was the housegirl, Inday. She hadn't yet dressed. "Come quick!" she said.

I glanced at Bing, oblivious to everything on the other side of our room, and followed Inday noiselessly through the hall to the maids' room downstairs. She pointed to Ninfa's closet, completely barren, save for two white uniforms which she'd left behind for the next girl to use, like an insect's discarded shells.

The dawn hadn't yet broken; the sky was still purple, clotted with dark clouds. We rapped, in spite of the hour, on the gate of our neighbors across the street. No matter. Their maids were already buzzing; they were also missing one of their party. We figured out then that Ninfa and her security guard had run away together.

I unraveled the whole truth soon enough, while brewing coffee for everyone in the kitchen. They were going to get married. Ninfa had stolen away in the middle of the night, leaving only an explanation and an apology, scribbled on the back of a crumpled grocery receipt. She was already three months pregnant. When I told Ma'am about Ninfa later in the morning, she only said, "Foolish girl!" at first; then crumpling the scrap of paper, "*Pacienca*"—What can you do?

But it was hard on the ones left behind. I kept chewing over the things I'd said to Ninfa, the things I'd told her about myself. And now she was out there, somewhere in the gray distance, lost to my knowledge. I felt the piece of me missing, like a phantom limb, or a hole in my heart.

So for a while, we all did our work, cooking and cleaning, in silence. Inday polished the furniture so hard, we could see our faces reflected in the wood. I thought the others dreamed of Ninfa speeding away with her boyfriend in the front seat of an old Jeep, leaving a great plume of dust in their trail, though I would have bet that was far from the truth.

At length, we heard rumblings of the two, through my connections in the market. Not surprisingly, it was my *suki*, the pork dealer, who broke the early news.

"Your *alaga* . . ."—Your ward—said Aling Felicing, waving excitedly at me to hurry over to her stand. "She's been spotted, all over Manila!"

I listened quietly as she spoke, staring meanwhile at the rubbery pork head hanging on the steel hook, not knowing quite what to make of its crinkle-eyed leer.

Boy and Ninfa had approached several households, trying to get hired together, but the realities were just as I suspected. People were willing to take in Boy, but not his wife and future child. They ended up having to move to the *esteros*, the canals, a strip of land unwanted by most—though in the Philippines, there were still numbers who would claim it. I knew the location, in Pasay, but it was the kind of place you passed every day without seeing, like a sewer.

I thought of Ninfa's new life, out in the slums. All of us maids knew well those houses: a single room built on top of hollow cement blocks to raise it up from the ground, splintery boards for a floor, and aluminum sheets weighed down by tires for a roof. Scavenged pieces of junk; the kind of house that could blow away like a leaf in a storm. I was certain they slept on the floor, cushioned not by beds but by sheaves of *banig*, mats woven from the dried leaves of coconut trees. Surely they became cold; then I remembered, plywood kept a floor warm.

It had been a long time since I'd lived like that. Maybe I forgot, maybe I'd grown soft. I liked being in a house with enough room to walk. I only took my showers hot now, and I found myself growing impatient if the water pressure was too low and I had to chase things down the toilet by throwing a pail of water in the tank.

And I worried, the whole car ride home and afterwards. When it rained and their house flooded to the knees, where would they put their baby? Would it catch cold? Have enough to eat? Would they be able to send it to school? Or would their child have to support them early on?

I didn't know; the girl wasn't mine. And even if she were! You could give your children all the love in the world, but when they left, maybe the most you could do was hope they'd be all right.

At the market the next time, though, I left word with the pork dealer that Ninfa or Boy should pass by the house. They could inherit some of our old garden furniture which Ma'am was getting rid of anyway, the chairs with the flowered plastic cushions that leaked air when anyone sat on them. I collected the things Ninfa had forgotten to take in a plain paper bag—a flattened toothbrush, the can of money I had kept for her—and the sack stood inside my closet, waiting, until her mother finally came by the house to claim it.

I was upstairs in the kitchen listening to the radio and peeling some garlic that afternoon, when I heard the dog bark. I looked out the window onto the street and saw a thin old woman. The only reason I recognized Ninfa's mother was because we had been expecting her.

"You look happy enough," Soledad said, as I showed her in the back way.

"*Ay!*" I said. "Well-fed." I had put on some weight in the last few years.

Her skin was deeply cracked, dried from the inside like a plant starving for water. She had let her hair go gray, and it was as dull as our drains. No doubt she was worn, tired by her life. But Soledad had never been happy: she was a woman who had been left by men.

We sat downstairs in the open air of the terrace. The leaves were singing in the trees like chimes, and we watched the colors bleed across the sky, slow, like a spreading stain.

"And you," I said. "Are you happy?"

"Yes," she said.

That surprised me. I knew how she had suffered in her life. We had been close some ten years before.

"What changed?" I asked.

"Nothing," Soledad said, shrugging her shoulders. "I'm still cooking. I don't see my children much. And when I do see them, all they want is money."

Then she smiled. Her teeth were brown. "But now I have grandchildren, and they make me happy."

"And this makes a difference?" I was curious.

"Oh, yes," she said. "When I get old, I know I'll be taken care of. I won't be alone."

I said, "I have nieces and nephews who will take care of me, too."

Our eyes grazed. I bit into a slice of green mango that Inday had picked earlier that afternoon in the garden. It was much too sour, and the sting brought sudden tears.

"Maybe when you look back on your life," Soledad said, "you end up thinking that it's nice." She laughed. "Even when it wasn't so nice when you were living it."

I wasn't like that at all. Most days of the year, if anyone had asked, I would have said I was happy—and meant it. If I never married, maybe it's because I was always working. I'd worked hard all my life; hard enough so I could support many of my brothers and sisters, and their families. I had done nothing to be ashamed about.

Yet, I found myself lingering on about Soledad and her daughter long after they were gone. For the first time, I understood why nothing the priests and the nuns said ever prevented the young people from running off and getting pregnant: because the very thing that ruined your life was also the gift that could end up saving you.

It made me wonder what I'd been missing. Once I allowed myself, it wasn't so hard to see. The band that I wore, for example, a diamond like the head of a pin on the ring finger of my left hand, to stave off too many questions. I found myself face to face with the life I might have had: she was a woman who had grandchildren she could call her own.

The knowledge caused me to act in strange ways. For example, I wasn't officially Bing's *yaya* anymore, yet I found myself yearning again for that old life. One morning, a Saturday, Bing was just too lazy to get out of bed. At eleven o'clock, I poked my head in our room and saw her, a lumpy shape under the comforter. She hadn't moved since I woke up that morning at five to go to the market.

"Okay, we'll let her sleep one more hour," I told Ma'am.

At noon, I marched back in the room and yanked open the heavy drapes saying, "Get up, get up, it's time to get up!"

I was greeted by a grumble.

I returned again an hour later. I sat on the edge of Bing's bed and said, "Baby, what do you want me to prepare you for lunch?"

"No-thing," she said, from under the covers.

At two, I touched her forehead with the back of my hand. It felt cool. "Are you sick?" I asked.

"No-o."

At three, I asked if she didn't think it was time to take a bath.

"No."

I tried again. "How about if I give you one?"

She said, "Okay."

So I filled a basin with warm water mixed in with a splash of perfume, brought it over to the bed, dipped a towel in it and started wiping the sleep out of Bing's face, just like in the beginning when she was a baby and I used to be her *yaya*.

"*Naku*," I said. "When will you ever grow up?"

"Ne-ver," she said, eyes still closed.

I studied her, her long hair fanned on the pillow like the tail of a peacock, the arm I'd been sponging stretched out toward me as if I should kiss it; she was every inch the pampered princess. I felt proud.

"Look at me," I clucked. "I'm so old *na* and still I'm taking care of you. What about when I'm really old, will you be the one to take care of me?"

"Yeah, yeah, yeah."

It dawned on me, I might never see that day. Maybe I'd gone through life with blinders on—one almost had to—but I suddenly saw myself walking a dirt road that was leading nowhere. I was past fifty, and I saw no out. The thought disheartened me so. I found myself bumping into walls, cutting my finger deep with a knife, then blistering my arm from splattering hot oil, yet I hardly noticed. And for a while, I kept eating without ever feeling full.

I never believed in looking back, but I started doing so, skipping through the milestones of my life, unable to find any comfort—that is, until the day Julio, the eldest grandson of my sister, dropped by the house to visit. He stood before me, handsome and tall, in a clean polo shirt and carefully pressed jeans. If I hadn't known better, I could have sworn he was solid: strictly middle class.

"What are you doing with yourself these days?" I asked him, to mask my amazement.

"I work for the telephone company," he said, smiling cheerily at me.

Then I remembered. This was the child I'd helped put through Polytechnic. I had heard he was smart. "You graduated *na?*"

Looking at him, I found that I had made a big mistake. The mistake lay in confusing what I saw in Soledad with the life I thought I might have had. That comparison was too easy. The real one to consider was, if I hadn't worked in two homes nearly thirty years as a maid, I probably would not have had enough money to help my family.

I was the youngest of thirteen children from two mothers. My father died soon after I was born. My oldest brothers from the first wife of my father helped support us when we were little. I was glad to be able to return the favor when they grew old. I helped send some of my brothers' and sisters' children to school, and a number of their children as well. I asked Julio about all of them then.

"Chit, you remember her? She's an accountant, working for Central Bank. Yeye, she's finished nursing and they want to get her for a big hospital in the States..."

Maybe it was just the way he told it, but they all sounded smart. I felt wonder. This new generation seemed a complete stranger to suffering.

As I caught up with the family, a thought suddenly occurred to me; it had to do with reincarnation. No one ever convinced me one way or another, but it was almost beside the point, for I could see the next life in front of me right here. And I could say with pride that none of the younger generation in our family have had to become maids.

Then my grandnephew said, "*Lola Mila,* I wanted to give you this." I noticed he addressed me "grandmother." And he put a thick letter-sized brown envelope in my hands.

"What's this?" I asked, my throat tightening to find it full of money.

"My first earnings," he said, the smile going crooked on his face.

I took the packet from him then; it seemed fitting.

I thought again about my life, late that night. Bing was asleep and I took my basket of needlework out again. So maybe there were things I would have rathered. I couldn't quite decide which, and I'll tell you why. It's not like knitting a sweater; how could you unravel a life in this way—not to mention all the others your life had touched —and then hope to see what it would look like "if only" one thing or another had or had not happened?

I pulled the comforter up over Bing's shoulders before I finally lowered the lights; somehow the covers had slipped. Nothing ever seemed to bother this child, one way or another. Only a couple of years separating Ninfa and her, but what a world of difference. This one, with her slight downy fur, not a worry on her face! But that's the way I liked it.

I thought of Bing, how I continued to spoil her, and I realized that every day, in little ways, I was faced with a choice, and that every day, knowing everything I knew, I ended up making exactly the same choice. That looking back at my life, I would have done the same at every turn, with no regrets. And that is why I never complained.

I'm a lucky person. Although we were raised in Manila, my mother came originally from the south; that's why in general I'm as happy-go-lucky as they get. I was always entering the lottery, or betting on basketball games. This time, it was the jai alai match. "Manang," the driver said, handing me the money, "you won again." He was shaking his head, a bemused look clouding his face, because he hadn't.

I used a part of my winnings to buy Kentucky Fried Chicken, sticky rice cake, and beer. I threw a party. I held it downstairs, in the covered portion of the garden. There was enough food for our maids and our driver, the maids and the security guards and the drivers next door, and of course Ma'am and Sir. We ate with our fingers, just like in the province, and somehow the food tasted better that way.

Ma'am and I were standing together in the corner, surveying the scene, when she told me: "Mila, I always said to the Mister, you're not like the others. You share."

She half turned away to leave us alone to enjoy. And then she added: "You and me, *we're* more like each other."

Ma'am laughed then, and I laughed too. Because, of course, in many ways we weren't.

I did this a lot; throw parties, that is. But now that I think of it, maybe I shared because something in me knew all along that things are not fair, that I was luckier than most. It was my way of evening things out.

Long ago, I had accepted the fate that I'd been born into. The day I stopped reviewing the events of my past—the day my sister's grandson came by to greet me—I made my peace again. But here's the funny thing about life: sometimes you mourn that you've taken one road and not the other, and then you find the two of them meet up again.

That's what happened the day Ninfa sent her husband over to the house. He asked me if I would be the godmother to their baby. In the Philippines, this is the biggest honor. "Really?" I asked. He smiled. He made me shy. I said, did he want to enter the gate. It was the first time anyone had asked me. I mean, I had many nieces and nephews, but someone inviting you to be a godmother meant you were their *choice.*

"Have you already thought of names?" I asked.

"Jesus," he said, laying a hand to the back of his bare head. "Or Elvis."

Both good names, I thought. "And if it's a girl?"

"We'll try again!"

I wasn't used to thinking of Boy in such a good light, settled down and responsible.

"*Sosmariosep!*"—Jesus, Mary, Joseph!—he said. "If we ever need a baby-sitter, we know who we can count on."

The rainy season was slowing to a trickle when we got word of Ninfa's new baby, a five-and-a-half-pound girl. She told us she was thrilled when the baby's birthday coincided with Bing's: a lucky day.

They named her Consolacion; Baby, for short. I attended the baptism at their place, a couple of weeks later. I put on a dress that I had sewn special for the occasion, being the *ninang* after all, the godmother. Boy looked happy to see me, and even happier to see the gifts I offered—a pair of booties and a blanket I had crocheted, and five hundred pesos, the equivalent of twenty U.S., which buys a decent amount here—all wrapped in clean newspaper.

The festivities were held outside, in the common areas of the squatter colony, as the house was too small to accommodate the outpouring of well-wishers. The guests had brought food, mountains of it, and all the menudo, sweet-and-sour fish, pansit, fried chicken, lumpia Shanghai, leche flan, and beer glittering on top of three tables promised days of continued celebration, though the afternoon sky had already clouded up. I felt strange, kin to these people and at the same time not, as I looked around me—at the clutter of houses like thrown-away shoe boxes, and at all the happy, smiling faces, most of them squatters, wearing a dignity befitting that of saints.

As for Consolacion herself, she was such a good child. Quiet in my arms, her eyes were large like olives, trusting and alert, as she calmly watched the priest pour water over her head. I held her carefully, more precious than a vase that might break. It surprised me, how much I could feel for something that was not my own. She seemed so light, lighter than any of the babies, including Bing, that I had cared for; I wondered then if her bones were hollow, like a flute made out of reed, and if music ran through them instead of marrow. A shock of hair sprouted wildly from her head, and I did not think she looked much like her mother until a clap of thunder surprised us, and she cried, stretching her mouth wider than a baby sparrow's, gulping air in shuddering breaths, laying her greedy claim on life.

Like in a dream, I felt people scatter around me, gathering away the food, dragging the tables back in the houses. Her mother took Consolacion away from me; I just stood my ground.

Finally, a voice at my arm said: "*Manang*, come inside. What are you doing?"

I stayed there looking at the sky. It was pearly gray, cracked in streaks like a giant eggshell. The air smelled stiff, fertile. Any minute now, it would start pouring.

"Nothing," I said, and made the move at last to go indoors.

But really, I'd been thinking of the baby. I had been hoping that, in spite of everything I knew, the world would break wide open for her.

Marjorie Priceman

Pennsylvania State University

A FEW FISH AND ANONYMOUS SPANIARDS

Kelly spent nine summers in the bungalow on the North Fork of the Island, though she can only remember two; the summer she was eleven, and all the others merged into a single snapshot where the sun was always just breaking through the clouds and a green Studebaker was always coming up the drive and a screen door banged three times and her father was always reading *Exodus* by Leon Uris (a long book, maybe it did take several summers). And the plays they staged in front of the honeysuckle trellis were always "Mary Poppins" or "The Revenge of Fu Manchu." And a fat, salty bug flew into her open mouth and into her open mouth again and the neighbor's Frisbee was always floating over the fence into their yard and every afternoon her mother tried to capture, in watercolor, the quality of the light coming through the leaves of the crab apple tree ("A melancholy light, there's *longing* in it"). And a dog named Mister Repair or Mystery Bear always ignored his owner's calls and a garter snake sat eternally coiled beneath the redwood table and the smell of charcoal and lighter fluid filled the air and a hurricane with a lady's name (Angela? Beatrice? Caroline?) was coming their way. And the air tasted like salt and seaweed and it was always four in the afternoon with the shadows going long unless it was eight at night, dusk-dark, and a kick ball game was assembling in the cul-de-sac. And every night she was sent off to sleep by the muffled ticktock theme of the ten o'clock news from the TV in her parents' room and everyone was tucked away in their beds and safe.

And then there was that other summer, the one between fifth and sixth grades, when none of these things happened. That was 1968. It comes back to her sometimes without warning

That summer her mother went insane, but temporarily. Addicted to painkillers and tranquilizers prescribed for her migraines, she haunted the bungalow like a beneficent ghost. Pale and delicate, her face, once faintly mapped with lines of expression, turned smoothly placid, untouched by worry. Her eyes childlike, clear blue as the sky. Hair hanging down in loose ringlets, a straw hat on her head. She took on a vaguely Victorian aspect. There was talk of hospitals, "rest homes." The aunts, her mother's sisters, would convene and speak in feathery voices punctuated with lots of clucking and sighing. "Faraway," one said. "In a fog," said the other. Kelly put these two things together in her mind and arrived at England, a place both foggy and far away. Even the words on the pill bottles, Darvon and Miltown, sounded like the names of charming English villages. And for her mother, it was a foreign excursion, a cruise to strange shores. When it was over she said, "If I could remember, I'd write it all down. 'How I Spent My Soma Vacation.' "

Afloat on this mixture, she glided through days and nights. Waltzing into rooms to straighten a picture or plump a pillow, stepping back to smile and assess, as if she were expecting company to arrive any minute. Sometimes clutching a little amber-colored pill bottle which she would now and then shake like a shaman's rattle. And all the time humming, or softly singing, a sound track whose cues only she responded to.

Kelly's father, it seemed to her, hardly came home anymore. He retreated to his laboratory and lost himself in the utility of molecular biology, of atoms and electrons. Quantifiable things. Things you could see through a high-powered microscope. Her brother Steven dedicated his life to breaking the record for consecutive hours jumping on a pogo stick and everyone believed he was headed for serious neurological trouble. They spun out into their separate orbits. Father in his lab. Mother in her England. Steven on a blind quest. And Kelly with more freedom than she knew what to do with.

※　　※　　※

It's the memory of a memory, several steps removed. The film seen in negative. *Or infrared—a photograph not of light but heat. In places the picture disintegrates. Shot through with h o l e s. The silver worn thin. A woman in a straw hat. A woman stirring something on the stove—a woman like bell songs and gemstones and dark perfumed blossoms. Orchid, cat's claw, Saint John the Conqueror root. Swamp moss, tuber rose, shepherd's purse, rue. A strand of hair tied with string. A square of linen folded in thirds. She turns three times in a circle. She holds a footprint in her hand.*

※　　※　　※

They lived in the city then, about two and a half hours away by car, but it seemed much farther. Driving east from New York, past the industrial sprawl, past the succession of overlapping suburbs and shopping centers to where everything thinned out—the traffic, the air (freed of the soot and debris of the city)—towns sprouted smaller and farther apart, the oaks and maples that lined the parkway were replaced by scrubby pines, reeds, cattails—whatever the sandy soil would sustain. There the gods of Industry, Light, Communication, and Transport hurled their tentacles to the outer reaches. But their power strained and faltered in the extremities farthest from the heart.

The town had only the most tentative grasp on electricity. A healthy breeze rustling the wires could interrupt service for hours. TV was an indefinite proposition, subject to shifting winds, with at best two channels to choose from. Trains ran or didn't as if the posted timetable were only a suggestion. Approaching Orient Point, where the land on either side of the road was sometimes no wider than the road itself, one had the feeling of riding a unicycle on a tightrope. On the left, close-set cottages in pastel paint vied for views of Long Island Sound. On the right, potato farms and vineyards formed margins along the Great South Bay. And at the very end, at the tip of the upper fin that forms the fish that is Long Island, also called the North Fork, standing among the rocks and rubble deposited by a glacier in the last ice age, this sign: Welcome to New England. For there you could catch the ferry to Connecticut or Block Island. But really, as far as Kelly was concerned, it was the end of the world.

Her father stayed in the city, joining the family only on weekends except for the two-week vacation he took at the end of August. He arrived on Friday night, the second weekend of June, to find the car missing its front fender, tire tracks on the lawn, a week's worth of newspapers still lying on the drive. There was a lamp perched on the edge of the bathtub, blue paint on the cat's tail, and his wife was serving cupcakes for dinner. There was an interrogation along the lines of, "Is this what you consider to be a proper supper for two growing children? Is this your idea of a nutritionally balanced meal?" which she answered by looking first at Kelly, and then at her brother. "But they're homemade," she cried, "from scratch."

She was puzzled by his anger. She tried to leave the room. He grabbed her elbow and reeled her back. He pushed her down in the chair. She hugged herself and squinted at him sideways, from behind a curtain of hair. "What in God's name happened to the car?" he yelled. She put her head in the bend of her elbow. "This is going to stop," he said. "Right here. Right now." He slammed his open palm down on the kitchen table. Her mother jerked and pressed herself against the chair back. Her father winced and brought his hand up to rub it. Then he got a hell-bent look and started tearing the kitchen apart. He flung the pantry doors open in succession so they ricocheted back on each other. He pulled a drawer out with too much force and its contents spilled to the floor. A heap of tangled scrap metal. Forks and knives poised at perilous angles. He stood holding the drawer by its handle like a briefcase. Her mother held her hands over her mouth. Her father kept saying, "Where are they, Margaret? Give them to me." Steven ran up to his room. "Give them to me now." Kelly slid off her chair and walked out on the beach, where the slapping of the water and cries of the gulls cloaked the sounds coming from the house. She dug in the wet sand for crabs or buried treasure or loose change. She was open to anything. Then the screen door banged not three but four or more times against its frame and her father marched from the house to the edge of the water and, uncapping a bottle of pills, emptied them into the ocean where they bobbed on the surface like little pearls from a broken necklace.

Kelly was glad of this. Glad that her father was finally going to fix things. But at the same time she worried that some fish might eat the pills and become all dreamy and sleepy and forget to feed their children. And maybe they'd eventually just lose track of their children altogether in the vast, dark ocean. She slept little that night as even worse fates edged out her earlier fears. What if, she wondered, the pills made their way across the sea to Spain where Spanish people might succumb to their power?

Other summers, her mother, her brother, and Kelly wrote messages in the wet sand at the water's edge and when the high tide erased their words her mother said not to worry, that they would float across the ocean and land on another sandy beach. She called them "letters to Spain," and showed them on the globe how New York was directly west from Spain. In a straight line from Vigo or La Coruna. On the exact same meridian. And sometimes she'd run into the house and gather up Kelly and Steven saying, "Hurry, hurry. A reply from Spain." And they'd race to the water and there they'd find some words. In Spanish. And they'd get out the Spanish/English dictionary and look them up. Sometimes they were spelled wrong but their mother said that was because the letters got a little jumbled being tossed around by the waves for three or four thousand miles. So far that summer, there had been no mail from Spain.

Kelly considered these things till dusk fell and the ocean turned to liquid pewter and a cold wind came off the water, then she plowed through the sand to the house and put herself to bed. And while the rest of the household paced, tossed, and monitored the ticking of the clock, Kelly spent the night agonizing over the fate of a few fish and anonymous Spaniards.

The next day her parents drove into town to consult with a doctor about Mother's "condition." They returned a few hours later with Claudette Parfait. She wore a white uniform so Kelly believed she was a nurse. She was hired to provide home-help, to monitor and mete out her mother's medication. It was decided that the best course was to ease her off the pills gradually. In addition, Claudette would help with cooking, cleaning and grocery shopping, as well as generally keep an eye on Kelly and Steven. What can be said about Claudette Parfait? First, Kelly had no reason to believe that was not her real name. Though sometimes she thinks she just plain invented her. Kelly's brother recalls her only vaguely. Oh, he says, she was a little strange. The funny songs and her *cooking*.

⟨ ⟨ ⟨

In the last light of day in the darkening kitchen a woman stirring something on the stove. Fromherfingertipsfall flo w e r p e t a l s. A handful of grass. Steam clouds of vapor and incense. Echo of bells ringing. A hat floats by the window. The wind whipping up. A storm cloud of tarragon and rose hips rises from the pot. Violet, sassafras, yohimbe, squill root, senna leaves, slippery elm. Poke root, passionflower, lodestone and scorpion d u s t.

⟨ ⟨ ⟨

At first, Claudette scared Kelly. Maybe it was her long fingers and pointy red nails, the way she jangled like wind chimes when she moved, the quicksand of her eyes. She was from Aruba or Antigua which she referred to only as "The Island." She spoke in a lilting singsong rhythm and smelled of something mysterious and dark like a blossom from deep in the impenetrable rain forest. She chewed licorice root and smoked herb cigarettes, which she rolled herself with one hand while eating an apple with the other hand. She often had her head in a little book, worn, tattered, the corners of the pages turned down, its yellow cover spattered with stains like Mother's copy of *Joy of Cooking*. After the first week Claudette gave up the white uniform for sundresses in bold florals and Bermuda shorts with canopy stripes of turquoise and salmon. Through her ears she wore gold hoops the size of bracelets, which caught the morning sun slanting through the kitchen window and cast blinding reflections around the walls that the cat would chase.

Claudette was serving one of her weird breakfasts (spiced fruit, coconut milk, fish) when Kelly's mother, or rather the top of her hat, passed by the window for the third time as she dreamily circled the house. Claudette motioned with her thumb. "I've been thinking . . . that maybe your mama she been conjured,"

"What?" Kelly shifted in her chair.

"You know, cursed. Like somebody put the fix on her."

Kelly looked out the window as her mother circled a fourth time.

"She got any enemies?" Claudette nodded her head toward the passing hat.

"No. I don't know. Of course not," Kelly said, and pushed away from the table. "It's just the *pills*."

"Maybe yes and maybe not so yes," said Claudette, shaking her head, earrings tinkling like chimes, the sun igniting amber flames in her brown eyes.

In general, Kelly thought it best to avoid her. She often left after breakfast, said she was going to the neighbors' to play, but really she just wandered the beach. Or else she rode her bicycle the three miles to the point and peered through the mist for a glimpse of New England. Sometimes a fishing boat or trawler came by and she'd wave to the people on board.

She walked the beach the whole afternoon, hunting smooth stones and sea glass. Mostly she found the rounded-down remains of broken Coke or beer bottles but she had a few rare blue- and rose-colored gems in her collection. These she stored in a glass jar on a mirror on her dresser top along with an assortment of other treasures, including three foreign coins, a crab claw, a book of matches from a place called The Crow's Nest which featured "Topless Entertainment Nitely," a starfish, a bullet, and a red die.

She came back to the house for meals but otherwise kept to her own schedule, usually making the rounds to the point, the jetty, the dunes, sometimes into town for an ice cream or a magazine. Living most of the day outdoors, she took on the look of a shipwreck victim, her skin brown and freckled, her sandy hair bleached white from the salt water and sun. She had gone native.

On Friday nights, her father arrived but he was distracted, tired, carrying a briefcase full of paperwork from the office. He held long, weary conversations with her mother which usually ended with him disappearing for long walks or to sit out on the rocks of the jetty and stare at the surf. When he left on Sundays, it was with great fanfare, hugs, reminders to be good, to look after Mother, to call in case of emergency. And Kelly's mother would look up from what she was doing, turning the pages of a book or weeding the same row of the garden for the third time, and wave in a ceremonious way. Like the homecoming queen on a parade float whose job it is to smile and wave, wave and smile, at people she doesn't know but who, nevertheless, seem to know her.

Kelly took to running with a fast crowd, a rough crowd, which included the Johnson twins, Timmy and Teddy, fourteen, who had a reputation for loitering (train station, 7-Eleven, high school parking lot) and vandalism (stealing a stop sign), among other crimes. And Sally Finneran who was thirteen and wore white frosted lipstick and thick black eyeliner and dirty white Keds without shoelaces and smoked Kools that she sneaked from her mother's purse.

Sally became Kelly's role model and teacher. She showed her how to make a halter top out of a bandana, and how to fringe the bottoms of her cutoffs. How to smoke cigarettes. How to curse. How to steal. How to nonchalantly pick up one-gallon milk bottles from the back of the Dairy Barn and return them for the twenty-five-cent deposit. (The stupid Dairy Barn people never caught on.) How to prowl the aisles of Grant's five-and-ten and slip sunglasses or barrettes up her jacket sleeve. Once as she was browsing the stationery aisle for a pen to steal she passed Steven and his friends. They nodded to each other like casual acquaintances. Like people who used to know each other. He looked taller. Older.

Sally Finneran taught her how to kiss, first demonstrating on her knee, then the back of her hand. She moved her head from side to side and made smacking and moaning noises. Kelly suspected she had learned the criminal arts from the Johnson twins and kissing from the movies. After the demonstration she said, "Are you ready to be tested?" She placed her hands on Kelly's shoulders, said, "Close your eyes," then pressed her frosted lips against Kelly's. Kelly wasn't sure if she liked it or not but thought it was useful information that would come in handy later. When Sally said to meet her at the jetty the next night at nine-thirty, Kelly nodded her head yes.

She waited until Steven had fallen asleep in front of the TV and

Claudette had finished the dinner dishes and retired to her room. Then Kelly stepped slowly down the front staircase, fearful the creaking boards would give her away.

Passing Claudette's room she smelled perfume filling the hallway. A glow, a golden flickering light, illumined the rectangle around the door. Claudette was crying. Kelly stopped, listened. No, she was chanting or singing. A song in another language. Kelly held her ear to the door and listened. She leaned against the door, laying her ear flat against the wood, but couldn't make out the words, only vibrations. She pressed closer to the door. There was a *click* and the door gave way and Kelly sprawled headlong onto the floor.

"What have we got here?" Claudette said, her eyebrows forming great arches above her shining eyes. Her mouth turned up slightly at the corners and she shook her head back and forth. Over her shoulder, a dozen candles in little pots flickered on the dresser top. The air was heavy with wax and incense. Kelly stood, took a few steps toward the strange altar. Taped to the mirror were pictures of the pope, of St. Sebastian, of Fabian. Books were stacked pyramid style holding little jars filled with colored oils, shimmering like liquid jewels in the candlelight. On a saucer sat strands of what looked like human hair, some dried leaves, metal shavings. The little book with the yellow cover lay open on the dresser. Circled in pen were instructions for "how to keep a man/woman away from your woman/man."

"Now you've found me out," Claudette said. "All my secrets."

"Is it magic?" Kelly asked, her eyes mirroring the flickering firepots.

"No, child," she said. "Not magic, *Bizango*. Religion."

ᘓ   ᘓ   ᘓ

On the tape loop of memory, it is black-and-white. It is Kodacolor. It is overexposed. It is mirror image and upside down. The audio from another film has somehow been dubbed onto this one. Like something glimpsed in a rearview mirror. It is provisional, half-remembered, cut and spliced. A song in a foreign language. French? Spanish? Bells ringing and strange smells from the kitchen. Heat and flames. A woman stirring something on the stove. Scent of coltsfoot and fennel. Anise, nettle, silver weed. Orangeflower, trillium, vandal root, yarrow. The wind whipping up. Flames. Tall flames. Glass in her hair. A woman jangling as she walks. Another woman, in a big straw hat, comes into the house and goes out. And comes into the house again. The smell of seaweed. Glass in her hair. "Kelly, Kelly, Kelly." Someone is saying her name. "Here, drink this." Saying it over and over. "Kelly. That's right. That's a good girl. Bottoms up."

ॐ   ॐ   ॐ

Kelly never made it to the jetty that night but the next day wandered over and found Sally and the Johnson twins smoking cigarettes. One of the twins was digging in the sand, the other was throwing stones into the waves. They wore matching T-shirts that said "Have a Nice Day" only instead of the smiley face there was a skull and crossbones. Sally was in a tie-dyed two-piece, peeling the flaking skin off her sunburnt shoulder. "We have a proposition for you," she said. Since the Johnsons' uncle was visiting and he was a policeman it wasn't safe for them to keep the stop sign in their house and they wanted Kelly to take it to her house until their uncle left. She didn't think she could refuse so she took the stop sign plus a half pack of Camels ("Better not smoke them") and a pair of binoculars that Tim had stolen right off someone's beach blanket. She hid these things in her closet under a pile of dirty laundry. At first it was thrilling, being an outlaw, a criminal. A person with secrets. But worry invaded her days. She begged the Johnsons to take the stuff back but they flatly refused. They laughed.

They said, "What sign? What binoculars?"

"Cut it out, you know exactly what I'm talking about," Kelly said.

"I don't know," said Tim. "Maybe she's imagining things." He made eyes at his brother.

"Yeah." Ted nodded. "I heard that kind of thing is hereditary."

"Like mother, like daughter?" said Tim.

"That's not . . ." Kelly said, but they were gone. Riding away on their matching Stingray bicycles laughing their stupid matching laughs.

That night she buried the loot in the sand. While she was at it, she buried the stolen sunglasses, barrettes, and costume jewelry she'd never had the courage to wear. She thought her problem was solved until two days later when a nor'easter churned up the ocean and the tide swelled and spilled over half the beach and washed away buckets of sand. When the policeman knocked on the door, Kelly hid in the kitchen and listened. Claudette told the policeman she had no idea how those things came to be washed up on their beach. He folded his arms, tried to look over Claudette's shoulder into the house. She stepped outside, pulling the door closed behind her. He said that those items, the stop sign and the binoculars, had been reported *stolen*. "Be on your way now," Claudette told the policeman. "Nobody here knows nothing about it." She found Kelly cowering, said not to worry, "There's more than one way to fix a cop."

Claudette flipped through the yellow book. She made a list. She pulled a box out of her closet and sorted through envelopes and jars. She unwrapped a Court Case candle and burned it for ten minutes at noon and ten minutes at midnight. Together they mopped the floors with Law Stay Away Oil. They sprinkled iron filings over the doorstep, made a brew of dulce, broom tops, mugwort, and aloe, threw a footprint in the ocean, wrapped a chicken bone in a handkerchief tied with a strand of Kelly's hair and buried it in the front yard. Mother passed by in her straw hat and smiled at them. Steven raced by on his bicycle, barely aware, on the way to a baseball game or a soccer game or a game of jacks. They patted the ground around the chicken bone, Claudette recited the Lord's Prayer, walked three times in a circle and said, "I think we got you covered."

"Really?" Kelly said, still anxious.

Claudette shrugged. "Sometimes works. Sometimes doesn't. Belief is main ingredient."

Kelly tried to believe but she couldn't sit still. She watched at the window. Waited for the worst. Waited for the police to come and take her away. She couldn't just sit anymore so when Claudette went out for groceries, Kelly sneaked into her room and got the Court Case Candle and the Law Stay Away Oil, and, for extra protection, washed her floors again and burned the candle on her night table. She only left her room for a minute to get something to eat. The house was quiet. Steven was off somewhere, Claudette at the market, Mother a distant speck on the sand. Her skirt whipping in the breeze. Her head down. Her hand holding the brim of her hat, steering it into the wind. A storm was coming on. The curtains blew sideways into the kitchen. A plant spilled on the windowsill. Outside, a lawn chair tipped and skidded across the patio. The lights flickered, then died. People called in their pets. Kelly ran from room to room shutting windows and doors.

Through the kitchen window she saw her mother walk into the ocean. Waist high in the dark gray sea. And something else out there in the water, riding up and over the roiling waves—her hat. Kelly flung open the window again and yelled to her mother but her voice carried straight up on the wind. The wind that rushed through the house blowing newspapers and toppling glasses.

The wind that blew the candle off her nightstand, igniting the oiled floor, traveling up the bedspread to the curtains, to the ceiling. By the time Kelly smelled smoke the room was in flames; a box of fire. She ran tripping down the stairs through the living room, chased by black smoke. She could see the tiny figure of her mother through the sliding doors to the patio. She yelled and swallowed mouthfuls of black air. She could see her mother through the smoke. Out there. She held her arm over her face and ran toward her. Straight through the sliding door. As she crashed through the glass, her mother, standing shoulder-deep in water, turned and saw her. Kelly collapsed on the sand. She was aware, coming to, of feeling cold and wet on her face, knees, forearms. Her scalp stung and her left arm lay twisted under her. She gasped and coughed. Her throat and chest seared from the hot smoke.

Someone was saying her name. Chanting her name. "Kelly, Kelly, Kelly." Her mother's voice. "Look what the tide washed in," she said, smiling, but her eyes were scared, sharply focused. Then she ran to the pump and filled a pail with water. "Drink this," she said. "Bottoms up." She never even glanced at the house. She looked straight at Kelly. And Kelly felt she was seeing her mother for the first time in months. Someone, the neighbors, must have called the fire department because in minutes there were sirens.

The house burned down. Not exactly the whole house but enough to call out the fire departments from two towns. Enough of a disaster to merit front-page headlines in the *Greenport Daily Tribune*, plus photographs, plus an interview with the chief of police who called the fire "suspicious." The investigators determined it started in the second-floor bedroom. But in the guest room, off the kitchen, they found candles, matchsticks, and other flammables. They collected as evidence whatever wasn't destroyed: a few votives, some beads, a copper crucifix, a partly charred book with a worn yellow cover called *King Solomon's Alleged Guide to Success? Power!* The newspapers reported, "Voodoo Cult Infiltrates East End." "Witchcraft Alive and Well on Long Island."

Claudette disappeared. But she must have seen what happened. There were two bags of groceries sitting at the end of the driveway. She must have returned to see the fire engines and the house in flames and so she left the groceries by the curb and then just drove away. Claudette Parfait must have known a bad omen when she saw one. She drove away and never came back. Kelly kept a low profile.

Kelly's mother changed after that, came back to herself. Came back to them. Maybe she had just eased herself off the medication but Kelly believed she was shocked, shaken back to her senses. She wouldn't take her eyes off Kelly that entire night at the White Sands Motel. She washed the glass out of her hair, bandaged all the little cuts. (Remarkably, she didn't have any serious injuries.) When she spoke for hours on the phone to their father, Kelly and Steven lay on their backs and let the Magic Fingers of the motel bed soothe them to sleep.

By next spring, the carport and porch and two bedrooms on the east side had been rebuilt, the bungalow freshly painted cornflower blue. Her mother's easel stood once again in its corner of the patio. Once again, telegrams from Europe landed on their shore, though they communicated less with Spain and more with France. This due to shifting ocean currents, Mother said. So they bought a French/English dictionary and translated the words they found in the sand and didn't even mention the occasional misspellings. Kelly hardly ever saw the Johnsons or Sally Finneran anymore, though she eventually got to put some of what Sally had taught her to good use.

And the house settled back to its old routine, and the furniture breathed a sigh of relief as neighbors and cousins and casual drop-ins fell into its pillowed softness and the barbecue sizzled on Saturday nights and the sun rose and set at the usual time and her father picked up *Exodus* on page 284 and resumed reading and her mother was this close to defining the light filtering through the leaves of the crab apple tree. And the ten o'clock news once again came on at ten o'clock and Kelly lulled herself to sleep at night counting Frisbees skimming silently over a fence. And she was surprised to find out that the dog who never came when called was *two* dogs, one named Mister and one named Ebert. And the plays they staged in front of the honeysuckle trellis were either "Gone With the Wind" or "Cleopatra." And the breeze smelled like salt and seaweed and it was always four in the afternoon with the shadows stretched long unless it was eight at night and the thwack and shout of a kick ball game was starting. And the garter snake returned to its post beneath the redwood table and the fat green bug flew into her mouth and out again and a hurricane with a lady's name (Deborah? Eleanor? Felicia?) was spotted off the coast of South Carolina and like every summer before that as far back as she could recall, they made X's with tape on the plate glass windows and gathered inside to wait out the rain.

Andrew Foster Altschul
University of California, Irvine

THE ONE LIFE

The only time I leave the apartment is in the early morning, to get coffee or cotton balls or Kraft macaroni and cheese. I love it when it's so quiet, I can leave Jill lying on the couch, wrapped in that old knit blanket, and take the dog out onto the streets of the Mission, which, around six-thirty, are dirty and bright, smell of oil and flowers. The red and brown apartment buildings grow out of the hills, over their forbidding black swing-up garage doors, and the little pebbles of asphalt crumble and crunch under my shoes. The cars are few and the dog knows to look both ways before she crosses the street, so I don't need a leash and can just walk anywhere and she'll be there, I don't have to worry.

These mornings, when I go out, I feel again like everybody else and sometimes that scares me, but sometimes I like it and maybe I'll stay out awhile and buy a newspaper and drink coffee at a sidewalk table while I try to remember what the world is like. I look at the paper, but I can't really read it, there's so much going on that I don't know about and don't care about. I can check to see if the Warriors won. Maybe there's a science story, some newly discovered vaccine that you don't need background to read about. The dog will sit patiently next to the table, turn her nose toward anyone who walks by, wag her tail and follow them away with her eyes. I suppose she would like to go with them.

I used to take her to the park a lot. We'd take the car over to the Panhandle and I'd throw a Frisbee to her for an hour or so. She's fantastic at Frisbee, at her peak I could throw it with my whole arm and if there was enough air, she would be there to bring it down, probably sixty yards or so. People would watch us, maybe even clap or whistle when she got a tough one, and they would think, "There's a normal, happy guy with a dog."

Tuesdays and Saturdays we'd go. Every other day of the week I had classes or labs and Sundays I set aside to read and do work. That was when I wanted to be a doctor and I was so pleased with my natural aptitudes that I floated through classes like Clinical Pathology and Cardiovascular Systems as if I already had my M.D. and was just attending lectures to lend them my stamp of approval.

And I was good, really good. I tested like a genius, aced my MCATs, did my whole premed in a year and a half and they accepted me at every school I applied to. I could have gone to Cornell or Virginia or Davis, anywhere I wanted. But I chose to stay in San Francisco, to stay with Jill. I said I was comfortable here, that I wanted to be near my mother, that a new city would pose too many distractions. At home, I said, I could focus.

Now, though, I'm not in school and the dog rarely, if ever, gets to go to the park. I'm too busy now, in the apartment with the shades drawn, sleeping and eating with Jill, smoking cigarettes and sucking brown rapture through a needle. The last time I saw my mother, I told her it was just a rash from the heat that made my arms look like they were eating themselves.

My father died last summer of cancer and left me $50,000. I didn't know him all that well—I grew up in San Francisco with my mother—but I spent a lot of that summer sitting with him and his wife in the hospital in New York, watching him grow thin and ashy while they prodded him with needles and catheters, blasted his body with radiation and chemical cocktails that hadn't even saved the mice. He asked a lot about me then, seemed proud of the things I'd done, told me he was glad I was there. I was really surprised when his lawyer called me a week after he died. My mother was angry about it, said it wasn't fair that my father should use his own death as a trump card.

I wake up in the mornings and the flat sun is slipping between the slats and the dog is sniffing around the table, sticking her nose in the pot full of macaroni. She doesn't go near the spoons or needles or cotton balls, they don't interest her very much. The stereo is on, maybe still playing something we put on *repeat* when it seemed to us to be the most intense song ever written, when we let it play over and over while we fucked on the hardwood floor, stretching our skin against each other and moving slowly, loving the rhythm more than the sex, neither one of us comes anymore.

She'll be asleep for hours, I know, she's never lost her teenage ability to sleep past noon, she's blessed that way. But I'll throw on my jeans and a sweatshirt, splash water on my face without looking in the mirror, and take the dog out. It's our quiet time together. Once Jill wakes up, the dog will lie in the kitchen or by the front door as if she hates to see what I do to myself.

Then I go to get a cup of coffee or read the newspaper while the dog sits next to me on the lumpy, patched sidewalk, sniffing at the clean people who walk by. Sometimes they look familiar to me, but I don't want to recognize anyone.

This morning I walk to the market at the corner of Valencia, one of those classic San Francisco shops that look like the cover of a cigar box. The proprietor knows me, opens the door even though it's five minutes before seven and he was still cranking out his awning. Marlboros and applesauce and tuna fish and maybe some soda, but I decide on orange juice instead.

"Morning, Angelo," I say to the proprietor as he rings it up. I always try to be very friendly to him, I feel like he takes one look at me and can see the reflection of my apartment, Jill naked and thinning on the couch.

"You up early again, my friend," he says, putting the cash tray into the register. "You want coffee? French vanilla this morning, you can smell it?"

"Sure, I'll take a cup. Black."

He hands me the cup and my change and I ask him, "The Warriors win last night?"

"They didn't play."

"Oh."

I take a copy of the *Chronicle* and go sit outside, pull the baseball cap low over my eyes and feel my back crack as I lean into the metal chair. The dog sees that there will be no Frisbee today and lies at my feet, sniffing at my shoes as I open the paper.

There is an article about the "legacy of Randy Shilts." I know all about Randy Shilts from the HIV lectures in premed. We read his book in an ethics class my first year of med school. Also, he's just a hero around here, you'd have to be totally shut off not to know. But I didn't know he was dead, apparently for a couple months now. It makes me sad and I think about it for a minute. I guess I'm less sad about the tragedy of it—after all I didn't know him—than about the lost opportunity. If he had just *lived* it would have been better. A better story. But knowing as much as he knew couldn't even save the one life that was the most important to him.

Jill used to ask me, "Why do you want to be a doctor?"

You don't get asked that very often except in admissions interviews when they already know the answer. When everyday people hear you're in med school, they are instantly impressed, ask you about your specialty, tell you about their daughter who is roughly your age. But they don't ask why. I always thought it was strange that Jill asked me that.

She wanted to be a singer. She used to be pretty good, sang with a band called Viscous that would get opening slots at the Last Day Saloon or the Elbo Room. They almost got to open for Big Head Todd and the Monsters once at the Fillmore, but some L.A. band got picked at the last minute instead. Viscous is still together, but Jill rarely hangs out with them these days. She sings in the shower sometimes, tells me that a rock singer is the only career she's ever imagined for herself. I never ask her why.

Heroin used to scare the shit out of me. You see the movies, hear all the songs, it's like this big fucking thing that might kill you just for thinking about it, or leave you crawling on the sidewalk, dying of frostbite in the middle of summer. It's like an equation: good life plus smack equals death and ruination.

But it isn't anything like that. I've tried telling that to some of my friends, the ones who get edgy if I even mention it. I want them to know that I'm not some drooling addict, that I wouldn't steal their cars for a fix, that I'm not sharing needles with homeless hemophiliacs from the Castro. It's so mellow, I tell them. You can't imagine. Just the best feeling you've ever had in your life. Or never had in your life. Mostly, though, they don't want to hear about it. We don't talk that much these days.

The dog is walking around on the sidewalk now, people stop to pat her on the head or they shy away even though there never was a less threatening dog. I tell Jill to take the dog with her when she walks alone at night, for protection. But the dog isn't a very good watchdog. Jill says if anybody ever attacked her, the only thing the dog might do is slap at the rapist's feet with the Frisbee.

Someone is standing near me on the sidewalk, I can feel him looking at me, petting the dog, and for a moment I feel panicked. I look up. It's just Brad Pelter, I had a few premed classes with him at State. One time Jill and I met him at the 500 Club and played pool until 1:30 A.M., but the conversation never really went past the stock subjects.

When I look at him, he is still not totally sure it's me, says, "Martin?"

"Hey, Brad, how've you been?"

"Hey, I thought that was you!" he says, sitting down across from me. "What's going on, man? I haven't seen you in like a year or so, right?"

"Yeah, about that. How are you, Brad?"

"Good, good. I'm in the nursing program at State. First year."

"Nursing?"

"We can't all be naturals," he says. "How's UCSF? It's your second year, right?"

I tell him that I'm taking some time off. I tell him it's because of money problems and when he looks confused I tell him it's really complicated and look down at the table or across the street so that he gets the idea that I don't really want to talk about it. When he asks what I do with all my time, I mumble about how you never really know where it all goes and make it sound like I'm doing odd jobs or something, saving up money, without really lying about it.

"Hey, Martin, guess what?" Brad says. "I'm getting married."

"You're kidding."

"Can you guess who?" He's got this enormous grin on and I already know who.

"Not Laurie?"

"Yup!" His head is nodding like a toy clown. I went out with Laurie a couple of times, back in the first semester of premed; she's very pretty, but we didn't have that much to say to each other either. She started dating Brad when I met Jill.

I congratulate him, tell him they're a good couple. He promises to send me an invitation and I promise to come. Soon enough, he walks off after petting the dog again and suggesting the four of us get together sometime. I watch him fade away, the streets and sidewalks are getting a little bit more crowded and I lose him at a corner when a group of people comes the other way.

I can't imagine Jill and me at his wedding, at anyone's wedding. I feel bad about lying to him, but I can't tell him the way things really are. I feel like it would scare him. It scares me sometimes.

But most of the time I don't think about it. It's easier to just go with the momentum of it, let the undertow sweep me along and all I really have to do is take care of the dog and go out for supplies every once in a while.

It's been this way since December. It's almost May now. We've gone through half of the money and if one of us doesn't get work or if I don't go back to school, we'll be dry by midsummer. But we don't think about that.

Before, the days of the week were like tightly packed sardines, crammed side by side into a tin can with a key, the little chunks would slip by one after another and into the next week and month leaving a salt-oily residue and vague dissatisfaction.

But now the days and weeks are like a glucose solution, dripping lazily down through a clear plastic IV tube, and you only feel them crawl sweetly through your veins and you can't really tell if there are more or less than when you started.

Jill is waking up when the dog and I come back in. She is sitting on the couch facing straight ahead, eyes wide open. This is how she wakes up—she has to sit like this for about ten minutes before she really knows what's going on. It reminds me of *The Exorcist.*

I throw in some Velvet Underground, the banana album, because "Sunday Morning" is such a funny song to wake up to, and put the bag down on the table, unwrap a Marlboro pack.

"You remember Brad Pelter?"

She doesn't hear me. As I lean against the table smoking, she is staring right at me but I know she isn't awake yet. I wonder if she's still dreaming. Maybe she's onstage somewhere, singing with Big Brother and the Holding Company or Sonic Youth. Maybe she's climbing the Alps or burying her father. I have no idea what she dreams about. I don't ask.

I used to dream of space, of hurtling through the black void on some important mission, I had a crew to command but it wasn't like *Star Trek* or anything. And then sometimes I would dream about hospitals. I would be the doctor performing life-saving surgery, standing confidently over the opened body, suddenly gripped with terror that I had forgotten some crucial step, misplaced the necessary instrument.

But ever since November, since the night at the emergency room, I don't dream about being a doctor anymore. I don't even remember my dreams these days, but I know I have them because a lot of the time I wake up with my heart racing and lost words in my mouth and I have to smoke a cigarette and watch Jill, sleeping blissfully, before I can fall back to sleep.

Now she's awake and she smiles as the song ends. I take out the disc because "Waiting for the Man" gets me jumpy and I'm rummaging through the pile on the floor for something more soothing.

"God, I'm so stiff," she says.

"You should take a walk. It really helps."

"Maybe we should go somewhere today."

"You want to take the dog to the park?"

"Maybe. I'm gonna take a bath."

She grabs the cigarettes and walks into the bedroom, wrapping the red knit blanket around herself as it trails along the floor. The dog is sitting under the window and looking over at me and I'm hoping we don't let her down again.

I hear the water running in the bathtub and then Jill comes out again without the blanket, standing naked in the doorway.

"We have to be back by two if we go anywhere. Z-Man is coming by. Do you have money for him?"

"Oh, right, I almost forgot," I say as I slip in an Elvis Costello CD. "How much?"

"I think $75. We could do $125 if you want."

"If we go to the park, we can stop at my bank on the way back."

While she is in the tub I drink the whole quart of orange juice. I imagine that I can feel it spreading inside of me, brightening the dark crevices of my interior, balancing my electrolytes as I sit on the couch.

I had just finished my fifth cup of coffee and left the lounge when Dr. Feller brushed quickly past me and turned to say, "Come on, Martin. You might learn something."

His white coat fluttered behind him and I could feel his adrenaline triggering my own and the coffee and the bright white halls and it had to be almost four in the morning but I broke into a trot, caught up with him in the receiving area.

The paramedics were wheeling in a stretcher, but I couldn't see who was on it because a nurse was sitting on top of it, her back to me, I could see her shoulders working like pistons as she gave CPR. It's strange—when I remember that moment, it was very quiet.

But everyone was shouting. I can see their mouths moving and their neck muscles protruding and I know what they said. It's just that there's no noise in my memory. And all the whiteness.

I was aware that two people ran in behind the stretcher and were stopped by one of the paramedics, but I didn't pay much attention to them, knew they would be shepherded into the waiting area.

I stood against a wall and tried to see what was happening, I was only supposed to be observing, understood only some of what was being shouted, things about the young man on the table, the ambulance ride, an uninterrupted stream of specifics, and I didn't know if one person was talking or many. Then Dr. Feller started speaking loudly, above the others. I felt a small lull of calm as he took control, barking to doctors and nurses the names of drugs and doses and procedures. Feller was shining a pen light in the unconscious man's eyes as they all trotted beside the stretcher into one of the trauma rooms; people came from out of nowhere with carts and tubes and long shiny needles that squirted tiny sprays of crystal magic into the whiteness. The nurse got off the stretcher and I could see, finally, the man's face, pale and peaceful, and I winced as Feller slid the needle into the flesh beneath his left nipple and watched the monitor for a few seconds before he yelled *Fuck!* and started pumping the man's chest again, the moment of calm clattered to the sterile floor, while another doctor rubbed together the paddles of the defibber. He yelled *Clear!* just like they do on television and then the man's whole chest seemed to arch upwards to meet the paddles, his back bending maniacally and the monitor blip jumping, I was jumping, the breaths held, needles suspended, but it quickly stopped, flattened out, tracing a needle across the screen until they hit him again and Feller motioned to me *Get in here* and put my hands on the man's chest and told me to do the CPR in between shocks and I pushed so fucking hard I probably cracked ribs.

I remember thinking maybe I would save him if I just wanted to enough, maybe there was magic in your first life and death situation, maybe I could just pump my will through my arms, mainline it into his dying heart. Feller told me to get back and they hit him again, jump and flatten again, and everyone knew that it was over, that no shock or needle was going to bring him back, he was dead on the table, dead on arrival, sign the certificate, 4:07 A.M.

I stood there and looked at him, he was young, a couple years younger than me. His eyes were closed, his face showed nothing of the ravishment he had just endured. People drifted away and someone turned off the monitors, leaving a scalpel-sharp, bone-dry silence.

"Shit. Second one this week," Feller said.

Without taking my eyes from the stretcher I asked, "Second what?"

After a moment, Feller answered me in a weary voice. "Look at his arms, Martin," he said.

I followed him into the waiting room where the man's two friends were sitting. I didn't know them but I easily could have, they looked like everyone else who lives in the Mission, or North Beach, or the lower Haight, and they knew right away when they looked at us, one of them leaned all the way back and rested his head against the white wall, the other rocked forward, head in hands.

"We should have called right away," one of them said, and I couldn't immediately tell which one had said it. "I told you we should have called, Sam."

Then I knew that the one leaning forward had said it, because the other one, with his head against the wall, stood up on the navy blue carpet and glared down at his friend. Sam stared at the seated figure and then over at us, I couldn't read his face, divine his thoughts, his eyes were wide and his jaw muscles working without sound, he looked as if he might lash out or break down. He wasn't an unusual looking man, but I can remember vividly his dark eyebrows and slightly bent nose, the hair tucked behind his ears, and every time I go out I think I see him sitting at a bar or buying cigarettes or stuck in traffic.

"It wouldn't have made a difference," Sam said, to all of us.

Feller and I just stood there, waiting for something. I think I remember hearing the tick of the clock on the wall, wondering if I would tell Jill about this. We stood and looked at the two of them, waiting for them to do something, Sam just stood in the middle of the floor, hands clasped behind his neck. He looked at Feller, then at me. "It wouldn't have made a difference," he said again. Then he shoved his hands in his pockets and walked out beneath the red glow of the Exit sign.

The other one started to cry.

"He wouldn't let me call," he said through his hands, and I looked at Feller, wondering what to do, but Feller stood there expressionless. "He said we'd get busted. I wanted to call, but he wouldn't let me. He just let him *lie* there . . ."

And after Feller left the room and told me to get the deceased man's information from his friend, I stood in the same place and tried to picture it—the works on a table somewhere, Hendrix on the stereo, body on the floor, and what were they doing? Did Sam physically stop the other one?—listened to him sob and sputter, "I *wanted* to call. I *wanted* to."

I thought of Jill and the dog and how they'd be waiting for me when I came home. I thought of the needle, pushing into the vein, the plunger sinks down, the body hardens and disappears.

Jill is in a good mood when she gets out of the bath. Her face has a healthy glow from the steam and as she is tying her shoes, bending over with no shirt on, I feel for a second that little twist in my guts that I always used to, like the days when I first knew her, when everything was a dare, when our bodies seemed to attract like electromagnets. For a second I want to walk over and touch her, but instead I go and roll a joint on the table while the dog paces nervously.

"You ready?" Jill says, pulling a sweatshirt over her clean blond hair.

"Let's do a skin shot first," I tell her. "It's a tough world out there."

She smiles and walks over while I'm drawing what's left of our stash into the syringe and I ask her where she wants it and she says wherever I want to give it to her, so I slide it into the back of her hand, in the baby fat behind her thumb, and I take mine in the side, pinching a little flab with my free hand.

It's not much, just enough to know it's there, to feel the *thrrummm* of the car's motor leap up through the stick shift and into my muscles, tickling my insides with its vibrant warmth, enough to make the stoplights on Steiner twinkle with a ruby glow and give the cool air rushing through the windows the thrilling taste of fresh baked bread. The dog rides with her nose out the back window and I wonder if she can smell it too.

The Panhandle is crowded, it's one of the first nice spring days we've had and everybody is out having picnic lunches and playing with their kids. We smoke our joint and lie in a sunny spot while the dog roams from family to family and the new leaves are moist and juicy green, the lawn seems to stretch long and thin forever to where it joins the rest of the park, stolid houses on either side like railroad tracks, and the noise of children and cars and wind weaves into a slippery warm quilt that runs through our hair and fills our bellies.

Jill is holding my hand and humming something to herself, the melody wraps itself around the branches of the trees, seems to come from everywhere at once, seems to cushion my head as I lie back and stare up into the sunlight.

I remember one time that my mother and I drove down to Malibu, took the Coast Highway the whole way. I was seven years old and we alternated between singing TV songs and silence while the road crawled past the cliffs. Somewhere near San Luis Obispo, she told me that my father would not be coming home from his business trip. Later, she held my hand as we walked along a beach that seemed endless to me, and suddenly I looked up and she was crying, biting her lip and staring at the ocean, and I asked her why Daddy had left.

"I don't know, Marty," she said, shaking her head. "I think he was scared."

When I asked why he was scared she told me that it was because he had a good job and a lot of money and a beautiful family and everybody thought he had it made. I said that didn't sound very scary and she just smiled a sad smile and squeezed my hand a little.

We lie there, Jill and I, for a long time, at one point I look around and see her sitting up, watching some children playing a game, and I realize I've been sleeping. I spot the dog way down near the other end of the Panhandle and hoist myself to my feet, ruffle Jill's hair, and start walking toward the dog, feeling the damp spring of the grass massaging my knees. I'm a little light-headed until the fluid roar in my ears balances out.

The dog is playing with a little Asian girl of maybe three, her father and mother are sitting on a blanket a few feet away and the mother is taking pictures. The dog is nervous around small children, she stands very still while the girl giggles and slaps at her and finally falls backwards with a light grunt and the mother and father laugh and smile at me.

I smile back and say something about it being a nice day and for a second I want to sit down with them, it almost makes me cry to watch them laugh, but I know it's just the pot and the smack so I get the dog and start walking back toward Jill.

The dog is trotting next to me, looking up expectantly though she can see I don't have a Frisbee, I'm barely looking where I am going, just staring up through the branches to where the bright, cotton candy blue is sewn into the brown and green canopy, the edges of the leaves form the glowing, vivid border, and I can almost hear how it all comes together, the maternal birdsong of the sky, the breezy, milky solo.

Jill is just ahead, she sits on our blanket leaning back on her hands and I know she is seeing the same things I am, if we were very much alike before, we've become exquisitely calibrated to each other after all this time. Sometimes I feel like I am inside her tingly skin, she is my projection or I am hers.

The dog runs to her and I am walking up, almost ready to sit down next to her, when I see a man and woman walking arm in arm the other way and I know, more by the sudden clench of my stomach than by sight, that it is Sam. Sam.

Really, this time, it is him, not just a pair of eyebrows or a head of longish hair that panics me into thinking it is him. All of those times I thought he was there, times I've ducked into stores to avoid total strangers or turned up unknown side streets. Sam is really here now, walking with a pretty redhead in a sundress, and the brass symphony in my head has turned to deep cellos, I am cold, and he is smiling.

He doesn't recognize me, scans past me without a hitch. I wouldn't expect him to recognize me, after all he only saw me for maybe a minute, but it is the moment I have feared, the moment when I could say something, maybe should say something, I've even thought about just walking up to him and belting him, knocking him down and spitting on him, but I'm frozen with shock and sadness and fury and he walks right past and I don't stop him.

I don't tell him that his friend should still be alive. I don't tell him that he's a murderer and that because of him another person has to live with the horror of watching someone die. I don't ask him how he can walk outside, how he can make love to his girlfriend or even hold her hand. I say nothing, just like I knew I would all along.

Now I'm sitting next to Jill watching Sam and the woman in the sundress walk away into my warm landscape, cutting across it like a streak of sour charcoal. Her arm is through his, they are laughing, I wonder if they are on, even now, and does she know? She can't know. She can't.

• • •

Jill is saying, "Are you okay? What's the matter, Mart?" She is rubbing the back of my neck. "What's up?"

And I say, "Nothing. I'm fine. You ready to go?"

All the way back I am quiet. Jill knows enough to leave it alone, these kinds of swings happen to both of us, they're to be expected, you know. But the air has turned colder and its sharpness makes my nostrils sting. The orange lights seem to shout something at me and when we pass the old Castro Theater, the dark entryway feels empty, sagging with a hollow resonance, and my breath comes short and gray.

Every time it starts to get dark outside, later and later as spring moves on, I look out the window to where all the lights are, in the buildings across the street and the lights of our living room whose reflections gain clarity in the evening. It's a calm time, but a little lonely, even if Jill comes and stands next to me and I put my arm around her.

These times, I feel the separation, sense that we have barricaded ourselves in here, in our comfortable apartment with the old couch and the ashtrays and the hardwood floors that slip and echo, and it feels like I haven't been outside in far too long. Maybe I'll flip on the TV, see if there's a basketball game or a rerun of *Cheers*. The dog is curled up on the couch, she sleeps on and off, when I walk by she'll twitch her tail lazily to tell me she still loves me.

The Z-Man has come and gone and traded us a little paper pouch for $125 that I don't even know how my father earned. He says this stuff came from Laos, it'll make me feel like I'm swimming through feathers and custard, but when I open it up it looks just like Mexican black tar to me. Jill is munching a tuna fish sandwich, putting all the CDs back into alphabetical order while I clean our works.

"You know that's just gonna come right back up," I tell her, hunched over the table like a kid with a model airplane.

"I'm just so sick of macaroni and cheese."

There's always this moment of awkwardness, when everything is ready to go and we just look at each other, suddenly shy, waiting for someone to say "now," and tonight I get up and turn off the TV and the overhead lights, the room is lit only by a lamp that sits on the floor near the window.

"Come here, baby," I say, checking for air bubbles one last time.

She tosses her hair as she walks over and gives me a long French kiss, sinking to her knees in front of my chair, and I tie her off and slap her arm until the big vein comes up, she's got such beautiful veins, and there is a look of satisfied ecstasy in her eyes, she stares at me and I know I'm the greatest love of her life as I slowly push it into her, empty it slow and tender, and when it's gone I lay it back on the table and kneel down with her, kiss her shoulder as I untie the tourniquet, and I can feel her stiffen and give as the first rush comes.

She has just enough time to shoot me up before she runs from the room and I can hear her puking in the bathroom. I spit up a little into the kitchen sink and go back to the window to watch the rainbowed lights spread through the cool soft glass, I press my fingertips against it and hear how it hums

we sit and smoke cigarettes, change the music a hundred times when a song has suddenly blanched and gone flat, the air of the apartment becomes a warm haze of smoke and light and voice, on the couch we are entwined, she and I, there is nobody and nothing but the soft brown cushion, she is my cushion, I run my eyes along the polished hardwood floor and it gives me delicious chills, my goose bumps, she loves me, there's only tonight, this moment, second, instant, eternity sticks in my throat and fills my head with the smell of new rain and peppermint

later we rise from the couch, the dog peers at us from where she is lying next to the front door, I change the disc, put on the cocteau twins, their sinuous and elusive lullabies, and jill goes to the kitchen and comes back with the big jar of applesauce, no spoons, and we open it and scoop it with our fingers, pour it into each other's hands and let the thrilling cold mash glide over our tongues, our throats, feel it all the way down, hear its little infant's murmur, and jill has a little blob of applesauce sitting on her chin and I lick it off and she dabs some on my ear and licks it out of my ear

she is taking off her clothes and she rubs the applesauce over her breasts and I kiss it off, pull her nipples erect with my chilled lips, and then she pours some into one hand and smears it between her legs, slathers it over herself like a stone mason, and as the clouds of music swirl above us, she lies back on the hardwood, her back arches sharply as I suck the applesauce from her thighs and her belly button and her body opens to me like a mother's arms or the gates of heaven or the wheel of fortune, the cool, lumpy sweetness hits my tongue and behind it is the dry, wiry darkness of her hair, the combination of the two is like a hot tub or a jump shot or a late-night car ride, head out the window over the golden gate bridge

and I pour more applesauce all over her, the yellowish stuff catches little sparkles of the lamplight, she is letting out little sighs as I eat her taut flesh, arms raised over her head, I can see the texture of the applesauce, feel it just by looking at it, the back of my throat ripples with its ridges, and I run my eyes along the undersides of her arms, feel my mind slide along her skin

and then I am entering her, I'm inside her, fucking, we ride together on a morphine cloud, slip along the swells of the music, clutch hands when it surges, the coolness of the applesauce is like a high note of melody over the rolling bass line, she is my siren, she is my magic carpet, she is my life preserver and I am hers and we heave and dip, twist and milk, the glow from the window blurred to a ghostly halo like northern lights in the distance and I want to get there, bring her there, that blanket harbor that's just beyond us, if we can hold on and sing, breathe deep and suck all the air in between, just go, hold on, baby, hold on

    hold on

    it's not so far

    hold on

    don't be scared

    only

I don't know if I've been sleeping, only that the disc is over, we are lying cool and naked and flat, the apartment feels like the velvet insides of a jewelry box.

The dog is nearby, licking the mouth of the applesauce jar, and Jill lies quietly, arms over her head, her face is turned to the side and I can see her nostrils flare slightly when she takes a breath, her hair fans around her and whispers against the wood. It's so quiet and I feel sticky and sweet and I don't want to move, take my body from hers, don't want her to be suddenly cold, or shocked.

Sometimes I look at her sleeping and I can't tell if she is breathing, suddenly my heart will jump, I'll lay a hand between her breasts and wait to feel the slow rise.

It's always there, the evil grin of the chance event, the careless mistake, death in the tiniest bubble or drop, and to lose Jill would be my ultimate defeat, failing at my failure, perfection itself.

Because I love her, I know that I love her. I would rip out the veins in my neck with my fingernails to save her. I would kill a man, kill myself. I would carry her on my back and crawl inside of her, don her flesh and let my organs work for hers, my heart pump her blood, my lungs drink her air.

And I would make that fucking phone call. I swear to God, I swear on my father's grave, on the Hippocratic oath I never took, I would make that call, save us both.

Marlais Olmstead
SUNY at Stony Brook

MRS. SARAH QUASH

Faint whorls of reddish brown hair line the child's spine. The hair is thicker at the base; near her tailbone it is like fur. Behind her bent knees there are hairs too. Golden shoots are unfurling from hundreds of follicles on the knuckles of her clenched toes, as well as from the backs of her curled tiny perfect fingers. They are impossible to see, because she has burrowed head first into the musty debris of old newspaper, lint and rags, but soft hairs also sweep up her cheeks, only slightly darkening her rosy skin. Behind her ears, on her neck, the hair curls down and under her chin. Her little earlobes are downy. The effect is kittenish. Far from behaving like a kitten, when she is discovered and cornered in the dilapidated fishing camp, the child hisses and spits and howls like the most nocturnal, the wildest, of cats.

Within months of the child's becoming a ward of the state, the profusion of body hair falls away.

The child's parents are never found. Her story never reaches any papers. The little girl passes from the state orphanage to a transitional care center, the Bean Home for Little Wanderers. At the

Bean Home an elderly caretaker, Imogene, calls the girl Sarah. During her nine months there, the entire staff comes to call her Sarah. Eventually she is quietly adopted by a childless couple in their thirties. When Alba and Ned Blanc meet their daughter-to-be they make no attempt to alter the pattern; they simply call her Sarah.

So Sarah goes home with Alba and Ned. Sarah, who must be somewhere over three years old, does not cry when they take her from Imogene's arms, although Imogene does. The transaction occurs on the long Victorian gallery that spans the length of the white clapboard edifice of the Bean Home. Imogene's sniffing and dabbing echoes and her square face is raw and florid in the early morning dead flat light of mid-March. Sarah's feet do not touch the highly polished wooden floorboards as she passes from body to body. As the Blancs begin to move away, Ned nods his round head at Imogene and the woman suddenly sobs loudly, *It's just her cryin', that cryin' in the middle of the night, always . . .* And Alba turns, *Didn't it stop, didn't it?* And Imogene just nods and tries to smile behind her big knuckles and crumpled tissue.

For one year Sarah sits silently, nearly motionless, through TV dinners and game shows. She allows her long hair to be combed and braided. She never fusses. She does not run or play or throw temper tantrums or speak. Alba and Ned are unsure about her placidness but they do not know any other children, aside from TV children, and those children are for the most part very well behaved.

Sarah is fed well. She sleeps in her own little pink room. She has dolls. She is read to, given a remote kind of love. But she never gives any love back, never hugs unless hugged, and even then her affection is a stiffer mimic of an already stiff and unwieldy expression.

Alba and Ned take Sarah to see the circus at the Shriners Center. When they are almost there, Alba points out the big statue of Paul Bunyan at the foot of the hill. Alba turns in her seat, smiles back at Sarah as she points again. Sarah just stares at the red and black checks of his gigantic buffalo plaid chest. Ned laughs back over the seat as he turns into the parking lot, *Boy, could he swing that ax,* and the large red and silver blade appears just behind his left ear.

Once inside they buy her a giant pink cotton candy, and when that fails to make an impression they buy her a blue one. They sit in the bleachers and watch the clowns; Ned and Alba laugh nervously. Ned moves Sarah to his lap and bounces her a little; Sarah's head just wobbles like a daisy on a withered stem. The lights dim and cymbals crash from the hanging speakers. A man in black tails runs into the spotlight. His white-gloved hands fly. A voice booms from the speakers; it announces the elephants. Ned points to a far corner where the first pachyderm is loping in; he half shouts into Sarah's ear, *Could she say, EL-IF-ANT?* Sarah's lips do not move. She inhales sharply; her spine becomes straight as an arrow and her eyes widen.

Alba is bothered by the little girl's resignation. *Is it supposed to be so easy to have a little girl? Is it all right to be so, so quiet?*

Ned looks over the top of *Reader's Digest,* a brief glance at the little mite sitting so still in the middle of the hooked rug. She only fingers the design and stares into the empty fireplace. *Give 'er time.* And he places his hand on the crocheted doily covering the arm of his chair.

In the afternoon light, Ned's gold wedding band glows dully against his pink flesh and the white doily; breaking her fixed stare from the band, Alba sighs and rises from her place on the couch. As she walks to the kitchen she touches her hair and gives it a pat. She does not look down at the little girl, does not bend to touch the little girl's hair. For some reason, as she walks by the girl she is keenly aware of the nakedness of her own ankles. Her legs are clad only in sheer hose. Her ankles appear bony above the rims of her soft black comfort oxfords. Alba seems to feel the breeze there, against her bones.

Eventually Sarah speaks, but not until the summer before she will start kindergarten, on the day her hair is cut.

At least six inches are cut. Her reddish brown hair, always changing in the sun, ranging from chestnut to blond-gold, slips through the hairdresser's fingers. The small woman sighs as her scissors flash against the glowing tresses. *Oh, she can almost feel it!* A small theatrical wince, a rise of the shoulders, but the snip bites and the tresses fall to the tile floor in suddenly lifeless, snaking, damp loops. Sarah is given a pert bob with too-short little-girl bangs. The hairdresser looks at Sarah in the mirror. *How did she like that?* And assuming that Sarah will be her mute self, Alba inhales sharply, as if to commence to answer for her daughter with an *I'm sure she likes that just fine.* But Sarah turns in the high vinyl chair and raises her black eyes to Alba, *Mine?* and she points down to the severed tresses on the dull gray floor.

Sarah talks, if prompted, throughout the summer and Alba, who quietly pushes the notion that Sarah must be almost five, convinces the school to let her start.

Sarah remains rather shy, but after a while she plays with a few of the other children. No great period of adjustment. No acting out. Sarah simply becomes a rather ordinary, if nondescript, little girl. She receives a modest number of gold stars, but most are silver. Without fuss, she wears the nubby hand-knit sweaters, mufflers and mittens that Alba knits. She says nothing if peanut butter and runny homemade jelly sandwiches populate her not-quite-right cartoon character lunch box for four days in a row. Only rarely does she skin her knees. She keeps her black eyes trained on her Mary Janes. At first her teachers may fail to place her face in their minds when they set out to write report card comments, but they feel mild satisfaction as they recall that *No, she was never any trouble, quiet little thing.* Those teachers never hug Sarah, never experience spontaneous rushes of joy in her presence. She does not make them smile, as other children might.

Sarah keeps her bob through grammar school and on into high school. Other girls wear their hair long and lanky; their hips sway in frayed blue jeans. They go nearly barefoot in warmer months, dusty toes exposed in slapping sandals. Those girls string beads and feathers around their necks, hang them in their ears. They stare at big glassy mood rings on their thin fingers. They call to boys in the hall. They smoke cigarettes in the back of the bus, and maybe worse.

Sarah walks through four years of high school in stiff dark blue jeans. She never wears blue eyeshadow. Her earlobes are not pierced and Alba's clip-ons hurt too much. One tiny gold cross sits just between her collarbones. She wears white socks and brown oxfords, tennis shoes for gym. She tucks in her shirts. She does not call to boys in the hall. She does not dally at her locker and she never smokes anything. Sarah plays the clarinet, practices daily, even performs in the band, but no one notices; Sarah barely even notices.

In her senior year Sarah meets Bob. Bob does not play sports or any instrument; he works for his father at the lumber mill. He works before school in the morning and then goes back to the mill in the afternoon. He is one of the only seniors with a car, but he only drives the red Chevy truck to and from the mill.

After eating a box dinner at the mill, Bob returns to the tight white yellow-shuttered house at night with his father, Ralph, and his younger brothers, Ed and Gabe. They walk into the bright kitchen where his mother, Emily, is just finishing packing tomorrow night's box dinner. She ladles doughnuts out of a copper kettle, stacks them up on paper towels and loads the silver coffeepot for tomorrow morning. As her boys remove their coats and boots and bang in and out of the bathroom, she rolls the fresh doughnuts in cinnamon. Ralph sits at the Formica table and slides his suspenders off his square shoulders. She takes a can of beer from the refrigerator, opens it and sets it on the Formica table before her husband. She takes a glass from the cupboard and sets it before him. He does not tell her how delicious the doughnuts smell, because after years neither one of them can smell them anymore. She wipes the countertop and sets four clean coffee mugs on it. Ralph stands and groans. She walks to the table and bends to pick up can and glass and as she does this Ralph kisses her temple, just where her wiry gray hair begins. Emily smiles vaguely and turns to place the can in the trash, to rinse the glass. Ralph walks heavily up the stairs. Emily calls the dog in, turns off all the lights. By the time she sits down on her side of the bed, removes her pink fuzzy slippers and maneuvers her small barrel-shaped body between the pressed sheets, Ralph is snoring, beginning to saw his way through the night.

Up until his senior year, Bob had attended only one school dance, and he wore his work boots to that. His skinny freckled date looked at his feet and giggle-snorted, wagged her frizzed head. *He couldn't wear those!* One fingertip with chipped pink polish on the nail snagged the corner of her sticky glossy mouth, *Gawd, he couldn't!*

But Bob attended a second dance in his senior year. On a Thursday morning in May, 11:15 A.M., Bob Quash looks up from his hot lunch. A familiar figure, Sarah, sits with crippled Kelly Bean, talking about band practice. Bob Quash clears his throat before speaking.

Sarah becomes Mrs. Sarah Quash almost a year after the senior dance. Alba cuts down her own wedding dress for Sarah. Under the long yellowed veil, she wears her hair, which she has allowed to grow longer, in a chignon at the nape of her neck, instead of the long perfect braid she has come to wear daily. When Sarah smiles for the camera she wonders if her eyes will glow red in the picture.

Sarah means to go to secretarial school, but somehow that falls through. In their first year of marriage, she starts to help manage the mill's accounts. Ralph gets older and more responsibility falls to his eldest son, and his daughter-in-law too. Secretarial school slips away, seems pointless and frivolous.

She comes to do the books at home, the mill is just too noisy and they have the space in their new little white house with black shutters. Bob rises early in the morning. Sarah packs his lunch and dinner the night before. Bob comes home late at night, walks through the kitchen, past the neat brown bags and waiting thermos on the counter, removes his gloves, his coat and his boots. He climbs the short flight of stairs and slips quietly into bed beside his wife.

Bob is a good man; when he can, he comes home for dinner. On Saturdays in spring and summer they work side by side in the garden as the sun sets. Maybe on Sundays they get in the truck and drive to Long Pond and fish all day together. Sometimes, in late summer, they even take the dog, Rusty, and go blueberry picking and Bob kisses Sarah out in the open air and she laughs quietly as she glances edgily over the bushes into the surrounding woods.

Time passes and Bob's brothers graduate from school and work full-time in the mill. Ralph talks more often of retirement, although they all doubt that he will ever stop working—the Quashes are hard workers, honest hard workers. Ralph and his oldest begin to go hunting or fishing together more often. Sarah feels that it is wrong to attend these outings, as father and son will most likely discuss the future of the mill. Bob protests, *No, he wants her to come along,* but Sarah still declines. Bob stops protesting. Husband and wife begin to spend fewer weekends together, Bob is often absent from dinner, but now it is not because he is at the mill.

The fishing and hunting balloon to expedition proportions. Whole weekends are devoted to the pursuit of trout, deer, and eventually bear. Then the moose hunt.

The men win a lottery license to shoot moose. Little chunks are taken out of the young couple's savings to purchase gear. A rifle mount is installed in the cab of the pickup. Camouflage clothing, hats and insulated jackets, clog the hall closet. Sarah works on the books during the weekends too. She bends over the ledgers when she cannot sleep. She and the dog go blueberry picking and she looks uneasily into the woods, imagines a stray bullet flying out and making a startling impact with her skull. She thinks about the moose, lumbering through thick forest or grazing in open meadows, the dark hulking form, naked to chance.

Bob never brings his kills home in any recognizable form. He and Ralph butcher everything out there. What come into the house are neat plastic packages, pinkish contents, freezer-ready. Bob even spares Sarah the birds, little plucked and naked bodies, as innocuous and removed from reality as the yellow chickens under cellophane in the A&P. Sarah is grateful that Bob cleans everything before it enters the house, but only for practical reasons; he is sparing her the fuss.

No unclean thing ever blemishes the white linoleum of the kitchen floor, mildew never gains any strength, dog hair does not mottle the blue couch. But this is not because Sarah is a stickler for cleanliness.

The uncomplicated clean spreads uninterrupted through time because the house is so quiet. Few feet walk across the floors, the rugs. Toilet paper never runs out unnoticed. The dog does not shed. The doors to the outside world open very little and so dust does not filter and fall. Surfaces are free of film. Sarah can hear the kitchen clock tick as she sits in the spare room upstairs because there is nothing to diffuse or absorb the noise. As the clock ticks, her mind flows to every corner of the house and finds no gaps, nothing is wanted, all is sealed. She might look out of the upstairs window to the convoluted twist of bramble and Africanish sumac beyond the squared, mowed lawn, but her mind does not travel into it. Where the manicured, defined lawn ends her curiosity seems to stop. Squirrels or chipmunks might run through the square and she watches them avidly. She is sparked by their jerky, nervous movements. As they peer anxiously around she feels their anxiety. So open, so unprotected. But when they disappear, darting into the undergrowth, she returns to the ledger and all she sees are numbers on a green grid.

Bob brings home his first moose kill. He has been hunting alone not far from their house.

Incredibly, very early on a Saturday morning while the light is still gray and dim, Sarah looks up from the ledgers she has been working over, without the aid of lamplight, and sees her husband emerge from the partly frosted sumac and bramble. First one leg, and then the rest of his form parts the tall grass and appears on the mowed lawn. His rifle is slung over his shoulder and when he removes his orange cap he wipes at his forehead, as if he is sweating. He does not look around him but walks straight toward the back door, replacing the cap. His strides are long and swift. She cannot see his eyes under the bill of the cap, but as he approaches the house she sees that the corners of his slightly open mouth are turned up, his front teeth are visible. Sarah looks around the room. She stands up from the desk, her knee knocks one of the legs and upsets her cup of black coffee. She begins to sweat, anticipating the sound of the back door opening and closing behind him.

Sarah does not go downstairs to greet Bob. Instead, she quickly walks away from the spilt coffee to the bedroom and shuts the door. She lies down on the bed and listens. She can hear him walking through the living room and taking the stairs; she feels that he is looking. He pauses at the door of the spare room before entering the bedroom. He opens the door and finds her lying there with her eyes wide open and he knows that she has been working on the books. He must think that she is trying to hide this fact. Sarah's heart beats like crazy when he stands over her grinning, his big sure teeth glowing in the early morning gloom. She did not go into the bedroom and shut the door to make him think that she had not been up and working. In fact, she is fully clothed, having risen just after Bob left the house at four. He sets his gun down against the bed. The barrel nearly touches her leg.

Bob and his brothers drag the body nearly a mile through the woods. Ralph arrives and the men stand in a ring around the big body, exclaiming over its proportions, rubbing their chins, grinning. *Yup, his first kill, a big sucker.*

When Sarah finishes tucking four napkins under each fork at each place, she covers the bacon and eggs and wipes her hands on a fresh white towel. She walks out into the yard to stand next to her husband and gaze at the creature and the men stop talking. Bob slips his arm around her waist, *What did she think? His first kill . . .*

It is a female. The long, odd, horse-like head is cranked around at an angle from the neck and one ear flops up against gravity, as if listening. And as the sun breaks over the top of the house and spills across the body, Sarah can see the eyelashes. They are delicate and dark, but shine gold and feathery in the sunlight. The ears appear velvety, but she realizes that they must in fact feel coarse to the touch. The gangly legs sprawl out into the short grass. The knees are scabbed in places. The strange, pale, soft-looking undersides of the hooves can be seen. Her tail, now a mute inexpressive thing, is ridiculous. The bullet entered her chest, must have exploded her big purplish smooth heart muscle. The entry wound is dark and oozy, a poor record of the power responsible for bringing down such a large animal. Only a trickle escapes over the matted hair. Sarah barely breathes, conscious that she is resisting smelling. Sarah looks into her eyes, looks for some sign or record there. Was the image of the killer frozen upside down in the warm liquid black eye?

They do not know it, but she watches them butcher the animal from the window of the spare room. At the bite of the chain saw, coarse hairy hide gives way to pink flesh. Steam rises from the innards as they are tossed on the grass. The head is severed. Hooves and tail leave the body. The span of ribs lies bare. Her blood leaves her veins and stains the hands of the men. Sarah watches as she is drawn and quartered, made into understandable cuts of meat. But the head remains, staring off into the woods with cloudy eyes. Sarah's nostrils widen and flare, seeking the scent and it is there, the heavy scent of the blood and hair has made its way into the house. Sarah looks beyond the squared yard, to the woods.

The head of the moose, the first kill, will never be mounted; being female, she lacks the great rack of antlers. But her meat is eaten.

Sarah draws a plastic packet of the pink meat from the refrigerator. It is only a few hours since the men butchered the moose but she is surprised to find that the packet, weighty in her palms, is still warm. She lays it on the tidy white counter. She stares at it, wondering what she will do with it. She opens the seal of the plastic and the scent of the meat floods out into the air. It floats around her face, heady and rich; it strikes her nostrils and she inhales it timidly at first, and then with vigor. She lays the sinuous fillet on a wooden chopping board. The blood runs around her thumb, coats the skin, fills the whorled print of her finger. It is not cold. She lifts her thumb from the board and raises it to her eyes. She examines the way that it clings to her. She sniffs at it and then sticks the tip of her tongue out. Carefully she touches her tongue to her thumb. It is salty.

That evening, after venison stew, Bob announces that he will not go hunting for anything for a while. He will stay home more so that they can start on a family.

They'd never talked about children before; they made love shyly and infrequently. Now, after Bob's announcement, children still seem as remote as the woods beyond the lawn. How could her body bear another being? The idea is bizarre, it defies her adult knowledge. Logically she understands, but Alba never had a baby and so never told her what it was like. Bob's mother hardly speaks at all, let alone about childbirth. Sarah is not stupid. She was a virgin on her wedding night, but she was careful to use birth control; she knew what she had to do. Birth control is a systematic choice now, like wiping down the countertops or making entries in the business ledgers—you don't want to not do these things. Untidiness is the consequence of not doing these things. But Sarah never really finds herself thinking these things out, contemplating consequences, she just sort of follows a path. What you are supposed to do presents itself sooner or later, no one really tells you, your surroundings tell you.

But the clean white countertops, the washed dishes, and the laundry neatly folded on the bed do not tell her. She adds columns of figures and sips coffee and stares out the window into the dark and still she cannot summon the image of a human child emerging from her body. She looks down at her belly, puts one hand on her right thigh, and then, self-conscious, she laughs a little at herself and picks up her pen.

Before bed Sarah opens the gray plastic case, but she does not pop the tiny smooth yellow pill from its plastic bubble. She looks at it. It is a wonder that a tiny yellow pill can make that difference. She closes the case and tucks it away in her sock drawer.

Bob comes home and they eat dinner and later, after TV or the paper, they go upstairs and make love in the dark. Bob is careful with his body, with her body, careful how he uses his big callused hands. Sarah, in turn, is tentative and accommodating. She moves her tall frame to fit with Bob's body, to make him less self-conscious. They are quiet. Sometimes Bob cries out a little and his voice is shocking in the still dark, as if a bird cries over them, calling attention to their lovemaking.

After it is over Sarah cannot sleep. The scent of damp earth and other wild things drifts through the house. Fecundity blossoms invisibly in the air above their bed. It is not the scent of human bodies, of lovemaking. She can smell that. It is the mixture of many smells riding the night wind and seeping through the house.

Sarah cannot sleep. Dry grass rustles, a branch snaps under the weight of something. Bob's breathing rakes in and out. His mouth is slack. There is a trickle of warm saliva and she can smell that too. The moonlight tickles her forehead. She sits up. She yearns to open a window, to let in the cool night air. A twinge, a twist in her belly. She places her palm over her small abdomen. Through her cotton nightgown she feels the round warmth. And her pulse is quick. She feels flushed, confined.

She wrestles the knotted sheets and tumorous comforter away from her body. Bob's ragged breathing keeps time. She looks to the window, it holds nearly the same view of the yard, the square patch that she gazes out at from her ledgers in the spare room. She wants to tear away the twisted nightgown; there is a feverish effort to remove the cumbersome garment. What is stirring beyond the cut grass, in the dark? What parts the tall grass and maybe crosses the lawn in the moonlight? Were animals sniffing at the place where blood stained the grass, as their dog had done, rolling in it, savoring it? Would another moose come? Would it moan? Would it stamp and scrape at the grass? Would other things come loping along with feverish intent to hunt down the scent? She throws the nightgown to the floor and strides to the window. A lone coy-dog stands in the naked yard. He is not rolling on the spot where they butchered the moose, instead he is tearing open a sack of garbage that he has hauled there. But the animal suddenly stops and looks up to the window. The eyes lock on Sarah and the animal is gone.

Sarah races through the woods. Her eyes tear a little from the cold and the dazzling sun that now fills the sky above a clearing into which she emerges. Her nose burns a little, the smell of pine sap is so strong. Rusty leaps up against her and his pink tongue flaps out of his black mouth. His breath is like mist against her face and heavy with Alpo. She is elated by a sense of knowing this other animal, smelling him, hearing his throaty barks, feeling his pulse as a tremor that passes through his paws to her. They have startled a rabbit and a pheasant. Sarah cannot remember the last time she felt so happy.

By now, she has been up for hours. She feels invigorated despite the fact that she barely slept after seeing the night visitor. She and Rusty sit in a clearing, under the mid-morning sun. The long grass is no longer hoary with frost, it is damp. Rusty sniffs at the wind and Sarah closes her eyes. She feels the skin of her face buffeted by the wind. A branch whines and a flock of Canada geese pass east to southwest. Her fingers twine in the long, brittle, damp grass.

She remembers that early in the morning, after creeping around the house, she lay on the sofa for scarcely an hour, her brain, dreaming, awoke her. She smiles at the picture in her head, remembers how her body jerked her into consciousness. She was dreaming of walking in a forest. The dream was so vivid that, like a dog whose legs twitch in a dream of the hunt, her own moving limbs roused her. There was no transition and the effect was startling. One moment she was pushing branches from her face and the next she was lying on the blue couch and the furniture in the room was foreign. She climbed the stairs, still naked except for the afghan she had wrapped around her body, and made her way into the spare room. She sat before the window until it was almost time for Bob to get up.

Then she fried bacon and sausage for Bob. She scrambled fresh eggs. Bob was surprised when she lowered her own heaping plate to the table too. Usually Sarah had black coffee and perhaps some toast. She filled her mouth with buttery eggs. A trickle of bacon grease even ran down her chin. Bob smiled briefly and blushed. *He guessed they'd worked up an appetite.*

As Bob drained his second cup of coffee, Sarah placed the last dish in the drying rack. As he rose from the kitchen table, Sarah stepped into the hall, beginning to call for Rusty,

"C'mon, Rus, let's go for a walk!"

Her voice was robust and frankly loud, or louder than usual. Bob watched as Sarah swept past him, clapping her hands for the dog and laughing with the animal's excited barks. The screen door banged shut behind his wife. She had left a dishcloth where it fell on the floor and the inner door was wide open. He shivered as he watched her traipse out into the dim gray morning. She turned, and her long braid whipped against her shoulder. She called back to him, looked right into his eyes, knowing that he was watching. Her breath plumed,

"See ya tonight!"

When she followed the dog into the frosted sumac, it was only 5:30 A.M.

Sarah rolls onto her side, opens her eyes, now it is nearly 10:30. Rusty is rooting into a groundhog hole on the other side of the meadow. He pushes clods of dirt with his muzzle. Sarah inhales the scent of grass and half-frozen dirt, she feels the dirt wedge beneath her fingernails as she kneads the earth.

"Rus, Rus, c'mon, boy!"

The dog turns to her voice and runs, four feet pounding the ground, a rhythm she can feel. Sarah smiles.

She bends to pick up a stray tin can; a scrap of oily tuna fish still clings to the bottom. She throws it into a new garbage bag. The garbage bag is now slightly full of reclaimed debris. The rest of the household garbage, not pilfered by the hungry coy-dog, lies scattered across the backyard. The tattered old garbage bag, caught by a bare finger of sumac, blows in the October wind. Sarah straightens up and tilts her head back to take in the sky, then she reaches for a torn potato chip bag. A few broken crumbs shift in the husk of bag. Her stomach leaps. A terrific hunger wells up in her, making her sweat a little.

Not until she and Rusty return does she realize they have been in the woods for hours. Her clothes are muddied and she has torn a corner of Bob's flannel shirt. A bright scrape from a thorny brier stands on her neck like a thin necklace stretching out in tiny crimson dots. The morning was invigorating, never has she felt such strength in her limbs. And now it is not a realization of hunger, like a pang, but a drive to consume for her body's sake that grips her.

Her hand juts into the crumpled bag and a fistful of salty, oily crumbs reappears and she crams it to her lips. Shards of stale chips fall all over her shirt front. Salt finds a spot where a splinter pierces her flesh, between the first and second fingers, but she does not care. She is all mouth. Next an apple core, surprisingly sweet and giving. The relic of a chop. Rusty has appeared, fairly dancing; he nuzzles into a smear of spaghetti noodles. Then, beneath a crumple of paper napkin, she can smell it, Sarah finds a morsel of fat and gristle trimmed from the chops before she fried them. Her heart surges. She flicks away a cucumber shaving and seizes her find. The smell is sweet, sweet and heady; the fat melds to a sinuous bit of meat which still retains some blood. Without question, this is irresistible. Rusty snaps at it as Sarah pops it in her mouth. Her saliva runs thick in her mouth, working to dissolve the piece as she masticates, and swallows.

As she slides the shower curtain aside and steps over the low wall of the tub, Sarah is keenly aware of her body. Her breasts bob heavily against her chest. She turns to close the curtain and feels her flesh crease when her torso twists. She runs her fingers beneath her breasts and notices that there too is a crease, flesh meets flesh and for the first time in her life her breasts sit pendulous and round against her ribs. It is miraculous. Her fingers move to her abdomen.

Instead of smooth skin, her fingers meet a sweep of whorled hair, and looking down she sees that this reddish hair, flecked with gold, sweeps up toward her belly button, far exceeding the limits of the normal triangle in the crux of her thighs. She gasps, struggling to recall yesterday. It is dizzying to realize the speed of her body, its rush to manifest the mystery deep inside.

Usually only mildly aware of her body, Sarah is now stunned by her findings and begins to examine herself. She finds reddish hairs curling under her arms and she wonders how she could have neglected to use the razor for so long. She begins to see the dissolution of her fastidious custody of her body. Her body's life seems to veer away from her, obeying another control. She discerns fine hairs beginning to protrude from the darker knobs of her nipples. And the fine hairs line the backs of her hands, on her fingers, above and below the knuckles. The nails, no longer white-rosy, appear to have a slight cast of yellow, the delicate crescents are fading. The same is true of her toes. She spreads lotion over her body and finds that hair is winding, just perceptibly, up from between her buttocks, spreading out across the small of her back.

She swings her legs over the side of the bed and walks to the window. Bob lies gasping on the bed; he grabs and wrenches the sheets that wind hotly around his limbs. Sarah turns back and looks over her shoulder. He looks like a turtle floundering on its back. No smile crosses Sarah's lips. She turns back to the window, aware of something on the lawn. She leans forward, craning to see, and her right breast swings against the cold pane, but she does not flinch. The heat of her skin clouds the glass. Out there a deer flashes under the moonlight, white tail disappearing into the tall grass. The scent of her perspiration radiates around her head, flowering in her nostrils. Behind her Bob groans. She withdraws from the window and momentarily places the flat of her palm to the glass, obliterating the thin haze her body left; the glass still holds the warmth of her body. She turns away and swings through the open door, her long hair catches the moonlight and she passes into darkness.

Bob strains to hear his wife's step. Down the stairs. Through the living room. Now in the kitchen. The tap turns on and is jerked off abruptly. Nothing. For some time, nothing. The sweat dries on his chest. He rubs at the little patch of hair there, suddenly intensely itchy. Then he stops, realizing he cannot make out any other noise while so engaged. He lies absolutely still. Then a sudden burst of noise. A chair screeches across linoleum and crashes into a table leg. Fumbling with the bolt. The screen door bangs. Thumps down the wooden steps and then nothing. Exhausted, he rolls to see the red numbers of the clock, but they blur. His vision cannot fix them and sleep closes over his head, drags his limbs down; he feels the immense weight of the bedclothes.

The previous night's dishes lie in shallow orange-scummed dishwater. Crumbs of garlic bread range around the lip of the sink; a crusty half-eaten husk of it poised at the table's edge. A smeared and sodden-dry dishtowel is twisted on the floor below. Bob rubs his eyes and staggers to the window above the sink. Brilliant blue sky makes the flaming maples prick his eyes. He feels like crying. A stiff breeze blows through the screen door and playfully ruffles his rumpled, sleep-teased hair. He slaps the errant hair back against his head with a broad palm. Goose bumps rise on his arms and his nipples pinch to attention. Sarah is nowhere. Bob walks to the sink, ignoring the open door, and slips his hand into the clammy foul water. He worms his fingers beneath a slimy plate and pulls up the plug. Utensils crowd into the drain, clotting it. With disgust he slams his other hand into the basin and pulls the knife blades, fork tines and spoon necks up and out, deposits them on the crummy counter. The orange sauce scum clings to the sparse hairs on his forearms. A bloated soggy bit of something sits on his thumbnail.

The wind abates and the snow ceases to blow. The sun rises. The sky is a hard square of blue above the cold white land. Sunlit and soundless, drifts roll and ripple across the broad pasture below the old Scaman place. The wind rises once again and skins the sunken roof of the falling barn, revealing a bit of old tar paper shingle. The wind then whistles through the few protruding rusted teeth of a dead thresher and falls down into the pasture only to fly up the far hill. It tosses a spray of snow from the crest of the hill and pushes up through the stand of old white pine that rises into the blue square. The wind agitates the needles of the stand; they rub together, murmuring, then roaring and spitting snow. The wind drops. One crow flaps up from the stand into the blue expanse like a swiveling black triangle. Another saws the air with its cry and flaps up to join the first. The birds dip back down.

The crows alight in the hollow of an uprooted pine. An animal bedded down here for the night, to weather the storm. Now the animal is gone and the birds pick at bits staining the packed snow. They quarrel over a slippery piece of something. There is no fur to indicate mouse, rabbit, or weasel. A few deep red dots sink into the snow. Delicate tracings of crimson show where the crows have dragged the lacy dregs, as ephemeral as afterbirth licked from a newborn calf, out of the hollow, over the lip of the drift. The animal, or animals, are long gone. Outside of the hollow, on the broad crest of the hill, the wind pushes the snow; drifts obscure the tracks.

One crow blinks, cries and beats up into the blue square. It wheels away from the stand and flaps low across the next pasture. The wind drops and so does the bird. The crow alights on the top of a drowning fence post. One rusted length of barbed wire stretches tautly away from the fence post and eventually disappears into a drift of snow. A long tuft of auburn hair, snagged by a barb, ripples in a gust of wind. The wind shrieks and the tuft briefly stretches from the wire, flicks like a little fish and then is pulled away, up into the blue hard air. The strands begin to slip away from each other and mingle with tiny grains of snow. The strands dance across the white back of the pasture, tumble, and disappear.

Bob follows his brothers and their father into the tight little white house with yellow shutters. They pass through the bright kitchen where Emily is ladling doughnuts out of a copper kettle. They remove their heavy leather gloves, wool caps and insulated coats in the hallway and hang them on the appropriate pegs. Gabe and Ed climb the stairs and bang in and out of the bathroom. Ralph and Bob return to the kitchen. Emily puts a container of cinnamon back in its place on the spice shelf and then sets a fresh dishtowel, white with yellow butterflies, on the countertop. Ralph washes his hands and dries them with the dishtowel. Before Bob washes his hands, he sets a black leather-bound ledger on the counter next to the sink. After washing his hands, Bob picks up the ledger, holding it carefully, just touching the edges, as if it is a photograph. He moves to the kitchen table where his father has taken a seat. The metal leg of the chair stutters against the floor as Bob pulls it out from the table. The red vinyl pad of the chair sighs as he sits. He places the ledger on the table. Emily pulls two cans of beer from the

Frigidaire and Ralph eases his suspenders off his square shoulders. Emily places two glasses on the Formica table next to the black ledger. The surface of the ledger is covered with a thin film of fine dust; fingerprints, four ghostly smears and an odd thumb print, trail through the dust. Emily sighs, turns and reaches for the dishtowel. She steps back to the table, bends beneath the low metal ceiling lamp, over the ledger, and efficiently wipes the dust away.

Lindsay Fleming
Johns Hopkins University

LADY SLIPPER

Young Drew Rutledge was six months married when he and his bride bought a black Lab pup, a bitch out of champion stock. They were living in their first home at the time, a four-bedroom Cape an hour's commute by train from New York, where young Drew worked as an investment banker in the firm his father had started thirty years before. Young Drew was a hunting enthusiast and, as his father's only son, had inherited the family's second home at the exclusive Pennsylvania hunting and fishing club known as Deerwood. The pup would be sent away to hunting school when she came of age, and Drew looked forward to crisp fall days in the duck blind at Deerwood with his Lab.

Drew senior had always said if you give a pet half a chance it will name itself, and there had been a long line of self-naming animals in the Rutledge family, including four Labs—two yellow and two black, and a couple of clever cats. The puppy hadn't been in the house two hours before she'd honed in on one of Drew's old sheepskin slippers and reduced it to pulp; they decided to call her Slipper.

Two weeks later the pup earned a title, and proved the aptness of her choice, when she blundered into Kit Campbell's prize bed of lady slippers on her first trip to Deerwood. Lady Slipper was a fine name for a fine pup of rare breeding and the young Rutledge Jr.'s soon had polished the tale of how their pup had named herself, desiring a title, disgracing herself forever in the eyes of Mrs. Campbell, and so on.

Slipper went on to destroy a pair of Drew's moccasins, one of Jennifer's custom-made riding boots, and a pair of $150 Italian sandals. Often, coming upon a pool of pee on the kitchen floor, or surprised by a pile of well-camouflaged poop on an Oriental carpet, one or the other of them would say, as they set about cleaning up the mess, "Honestly, it's like having a child!"

The dog wasn't particularly smart, though she was a great adventurer, and a water enthusiast from early on—she scouted out every puddle and kiddie pool in the neighborhood. She had some bad puppy habits, a taste for fine leather, but she was a beautiful pup and everywhere Drew and Jennifer went people stopped them to fuss over Slipper. More often than not young Mr. and Mrs. Rutledge would wind up telling complete strangers the tale of how their puppy had named herself, hell-bent on having a title, interrupting each other affectionately to add choice details along the way. The story always got a hearty laugh.

Drew's bride, Jennifer Collins, had spent her first two years out of college working as a rep for one of the better fashion houses in New York, but had gladly retired to spend a full year planning the wedding and reception, a gala event that included a sit-down leg of lamb dinner for four hundred guests, a lavish raw bar, and a twelve-piece band out of New York. The reception was held at the country club, and everyone said it was a pity Drew senior couldn't have been there, he would have been pleased to preside over the merger of two of New Canaan's finest families. He'd dropped dead of a stroke on the golf course one particularly hot summer day not quite a year before. Many of the guests were friends of both families. Drew junior made a poignant toast to his father at the reception, and there were tears in the eyes of more than one of the wedding guests who'd been close to Drew senior. His son favored him in appearance, and the boy was still young, of course, and time would tell, but Drew senior's memory loomed large. There were whispers, here and there among the blue hairs in the wedding crowd, that the boy was a bit of a disappointment, and wasn't that often the case, that greatness skipped a generation.

Jennifer had been keen on the idea of a puppy, though definite about not wanting children for several years. She was young, just twenty-six, and enjoying her newlywed status; too, she'd always been vigilant about her figure and was fearful of losing her size six forever. Young Drew, on the other hand, was less than fussy about his appearance. He'd been cultivating a paunch since his college days and, at thirty-two, with a receding hairline and a face overly red from the elements and high blood pressure, he could easily have passed for forty.

Jennifer assumed responsibility for his health. They made it a habit to have a nice bottle of red wine with their dinner most evenings, for medicinal purposes. She enjoyed fussing over his diet and learned to make several kinds of heart-healthy pasta as well as her mother's famous low-fat vinaigrette. They had friends over often. Young Drew was a grill maestro, just as his father had been. His friends all said no one could grill up a better porterhouse, but Jennifer started substituting tuna steaks in deference to the high blood pressure. The puppy would lie nearby, watching her master at the grill, head cocked and tethered to the flagstone by a thread of drool.

The couple's first home, more than seventy years old, needed work—a new kitchen, renovations to the bathrooms. While they were at it, they decided to add a family room off the kitchen, with French doors leading out to a terrace suitable for entertaining. Jennifer had her hands full supervising the renovations, choosing colors, ordering window treatments, and finding places for all of the wedding gifts— the china and crystal, the silver and candlesticks, the casseroles and linens. Then there were all of those thank-you notes to be written. It took her a full six months to acknowledge the gifts, and still they kept trickling in. She thought she'd never be through with her thank-yous. There was furniture to be slipcovered, the puppy to be walked and fed—her life had never been fuller or busier.

Drew spent time working with the puppy evenings when he got home from work, teaching her to sit and stay and lie down. Jennifer tried to get him to take up jogging, it would be good for both Drew and Slipper, but he had no energy for it after the commute and working all day. Instead he'd pop a lite beer and go out on the terrace with the puppy trailing along behind. From the kitchen, where she'd be making her mother's vinaigrette for the tossed salad, she'd hear him schooling Slipper in a firm, sometimes fierce voice, "Sit! Stay, Slipper! Down!" She'd feel happy to have her husband home and proud of their little family and the lovely home she'd fashioned for them.

On weekends, they loaded Slipper, the Playmate cooler, and a couple of canvas duffels into Drew's Jeep and made the four-hour trip to Deerwood. The club had a lively social calendar, particularly in the summer months, and they tried to participate in most club events. They spent almost every other week at Deerwood, from early May through the first snow, and the cottage had recently been winterized so that they might begin to spend winter weekends there in the future. In addition to hunting and fishing, Deerwood offered four clay tennis courts, a prime croquet lawn, a lake for canoeing and rowboats (motorboats disallowed in the interest of tranquility), and a clubhouse with Ping-Pong and pool tables

Fourth of July weekend was one of the biggest at the club, with most of its thirty-five member families in attendance, and every cottage filled to capacity with reunited families and their guests. There was a club tennis tournament every year, and Drew and his good friend Doug Perkins had held the men's doubles title two years running. The weekend culminated in a lavish barbecue with a raw bar, T-bones, corn on the cob, sliced tomatoes, and an impressive array of cold salads and rich desserts. Drew had never missed a Fourth of July weekend at Deerwood in all the years that he could remember, and Jennifer had attended the last three with him. This year they'd invited friends to join them—Jennifer's roommate from college who'd been maid of honor at their wedding, and her new boyfriend, whom neither Drew nor Jennifer had yet met, but of whom Jennifer had heard but plenty.

The boyfriend, an artist, supported himself by working as a gondolier on the Hudson. He especially liked painting landscapes, Terry told Jennifer, and the scenery at Deerwood was sure to stimulate his creative juices. And so it was decided. Terry and David would take the train out to New Canaan with Drew on Thursday evening of Fourth of July weekend. They'd drive to Deerwood together that night and return late Sunday evening.

Jennifer spent the whole day making the house perfect for Terry's inspection. She finally got around to putting photos in some of the sterling frames they'd received for wedding gifts—one of the wedding party out on the ninth green at the club with the foliage aflame in the background, a favorable photo of herself and Drew on their honeymoon in Italy, and another photo of Slipper making a full sweep of Jennifer's cheek with her soft pink tongue. Jennifer got carried away with making everything just so and forgot to take Slipper out for a walk in the afternoon. When Drew, Terry, and David got home, Jennifer took them in to show off the new family room and found a pile of dog poop in the middle of the white carpet.

She was mortified, and ran to get paper towels to clean up the mess. Drew explained that the puppy still had accidents now and then. He pulled Slipper over to the scene of the crime by the loose skin of her neck and he pushed her head close to it, but not in it. He said, in a loud, stern voice, "Bad girl, Slipper. No!" He took her chin in one hand and with the other hand he rapped her nose smartly. The puppy yelped and ran for the French doors.

"Ouch," David said.

Drew let Slipper out. She slunk to the terrace wall and lay down beside it, her chin on her paws, casting guilty eyes in the direction of the house. Jennifer came back with a roll of paper towels and a bucket. "I swear," she said, shaking her head. "It's like having a child."

They set out for Deerwood with Slipper sitting in the back between David and Terry. "Sorry you're stuck with the dog back there," Drew said.

"She's adorable," Terry said. "I don't mind." Slipper lay with her head in Terry's lap; Terry stroked her head.

"We usually stop at a diner about halfway for a bite to eat. Good food, and quick," Jennifer said.

"Jenn," Drew said, "hand them back the case and let them choose a tape."

Jennifer handed a large tape case over her shoulder to David. He looked over the titles for a few minutes, then handed it back to her. "That's okay," he said. "Whatever you guys want is fine."

"Give me a beer, doll," Drew said. Jennifer fished a lite beer out of the small cooler at her feet and popped the top.

"Just one," she said, handing it to him. "Anyone else?"

"So," Drew said, "how much does a gondolier make in a good night?"

"Enough," David said.

"He sold a painting for a thousand last week," Terry said.

"Oh, yeah?" Drew said. "What of?"

"Abstract," David said.

Terry went on about his accomplishments—his career as a gondolier would likely be short-lived because his work had been taken up by a respected, if small, gallery, which had right away sold a couple of his paintings. The gallery seemed keen to have as much of his work as they could get their hands on. David reached across the seat and stroked her hair. She rearranged Slipper so that she might sit right next to him on the seat, tucked under his arm.

"Great," Drew said. "I'd like to find someone to do a good portrait of the pup."

"She's growing up so fast," Jennifer said.

"Don't do dogs," David said.

Every time Drew looked in the rearview mirror there was some embarrassing public display of affection going on in the backseat. They couldn't keep their hands off each other.

They got to Deerwood around midnight and the caretaker, responsible for opening and closing the cottages, had left the porch light on. Drew showed his guests to their room, the room that had been his as a boy, the green room, with twin beds and pointing hunting dog bedspreads. He walked in and turned on the duck decoy lamp on the stand between the beds. The walls and ceilings were knotty pine and there was a green and blue shag carpet on the floor; a bookshelf filled with thrillers and dated best-sellers; and a little pine dresser over which was mounted a stag's head, not a big one, Drew's first trophy, bagged at age thirteen.

"Wild," David said, glancing around the room.

The next day it was rainy, gray, and unseasonably cold, and they all slept late. The lake was choppy, and the rain held steady through the morning. Drew built a fire in the fieldstone fireplace in the living room. Jennifer and Terry made a late breakfast, scrambled eggs and bacon, and they ate it at the card table in front of the fireplace. "Hope it clears up this afternoon," Drew said. "The courts will be pea soup."

After breakfast David sat on the screened porch that looked out over the lake. Drew came out and stood beside him, looking out at the rain. "What a bitch," Drew said. "Can't even see the far end of the lake."

Drew took the dog out out for a walk and came back dripping. After the girls cleaned up from breakfast they started a jigsaw puzzle on the card table. By 2:00 that afternoon they'd finished the edge and were into the second round of Bloody Marys. The rain still drummed the roof. David suggested he and Terry turn in for a nap. Terry yawned widely and agreed. "That fire's making me sleepy," she said.

Jennifer and Drew stayed on in the living room. She read a fashion magazine while Drew threw a tennis ball for Slipper from the living room and out the door that opened onto the screened porch. Slipper retrieved the ball, dropped it at his feet. He threw it again.

"Did you hear all that last night?" Drew said.

"What?"

"Going at it half the night."

"I didn't hear anything. I was out like a light."

Drew threw the ball out toward the porch with particular force but it hit the doorjamb and ricocheted back into the living room, hitting Jennifer in the knee.

"Oww!" she said. "You're going to break a lamp."

Slipper galloped out onto the porch, and looked around for the ball, confused. "Shit for brains," Drew said.

"What? What did you say?" Jennifer looked up sharply from her magazine.

"I was talking to the dog."

By late afternoon the rain had stopped and when David and Terry got up from their nap, showered and fresh, Jennifer suggested they all take a walk around the lake. Drew went to change out of his moccasins for the walk, and as he passed by his old room he looked in and saw they'd taken the liberty of rearranging. The twin beds had been pushed together. One of the bedspreads was on the floor, and the rest of the bedding was balled up at the foot of the beds.

The bedside stand had been moved over in front of one of the windows. The duck decoy lamp was on the floor with a bandana thrown over it so that it gave off a subdued, golden light. The shades were drawn and clothes were strewn all over the shag carpet—underwear, jeans and wet towels. When Drew and Jenn had been dating, and came to Deerwood with his parents, she'd slept down the hall in the pink room that used to be his sister's room before she got married and moved to Atlanta.

Over the dresser in the master bedroom, which had been his parents' room up until a year ago, there was a framed needlepoint: *The hostess must be like the duck, calm on the surface but paddling like hell underneath.* Under the adage a duck floated on blue, rippled stitching. Drew sat on his father's bed and slipped out of his moccasins. He tucked them neatly under the bed, where they were hidden by the dust ruffle. He put on his sneakers, still damp from his morning walk. He glanced around the room and his eyes lit on the half-empty water glass on the bedside stand. When he picked it up he saw a ghostly ring had marked the wood. He carried the glass out to the kitchen where the others were sitting around the table, snacking on a can of mixed nuts and making plans for dinner.

He said to Jennifer, "Haven't I told you about using a coaster? There's a ring on the bedside stand."

"I'm sorry, hon. I didn't even think—"

"Everyone ready?" David said. "For our walk?" Slipper jumped up, ready to go.

She ran ahead of them, flushing out squirrels, and an occasional pheasant, splashing through the puddles that riddled the dirt road that circled the lake. They passed by the Whitings' camp, and the Bucknells' and the Perkinses'; by the Atwells' and the William Martins' and the Frederick Martins'. It was cocktail hour and Independence Day, and from every house came the sound of laughter, clinking glasses, and animated voices. As they approached the Campbells' camp, Drew whistled for Slipper. She came running and he fastened the leash to her collar. As they walked by, Drew said, "The famous flower bed," and pointed toward the stone retaining wall that ran along the east edge of the Campbells' lot. When they reached the far end of the lake, they found a party in progress at the Webbs' camp, and some of Drew's buddies out on the porch, including Drew's tennis partner, Doug Perkins.

"Hey, Rut!" Doug called out. "Doesn't look too good for tomorrow."

Indeed, it didn't. When they passed by the tennis courts, Drew tested the surface with the toe of his shoe. They stopped at the clubhouse and shot two games of pool. Back at the cottage, David and Terry started making dinner, their penance for losing at pool, while Drew made drinks, standing at the little bar in the living room, cracking ice for whiskey sours. They had a couple of bottles of red wine with dinner and stayed up late working the puzzle. Slipper lay under the card table, sleeping with her head atop Jennifer's feet.

The tennis tournament was canceled but the day dawned bright and sunny, and they spent most of it out by the lake. Jenn and Drew swam out to the dock in the middle of the lake and Slipper paddled along beside them. They hauled her up on the raft and sunned there, while David and Terry drifted in the rowboat.

The barbecue was scheduled for late afternoon out on the lawn by the clubhouse. Jenn and Terry held a picnic table while Drew and David made a trip to the raw bar. Slipper was on a leash, lying at Jenn's feet, but kids kept coming over to play with her, and Jenn let the little Maddox boy go off with the dog. For a time, busy with their oysters and shrimp, they forgot about her. Drew was in a dark mood, his face and chest burned from sleeping too long on the raft, and Doug Perkins had just beat him four games out of five in Ping-Pong. He couldn't remember the tennis tournament ever being rained out. David fed Terry an oyster, and Drew tossed off the last of his gin and tonic. Jenn and Terry went to get the next round.

Kit Campbell came over and asked about Bette Rutledge, a conciliatory gesture, the first move she'd made to be friendly since Slipper had plundered her flower bed. Drew reported that his mother was off on an educational cruise in the Mediterranean and doing well. Kit asked Drew to give his mom her best, said she hoped to see her Labor Day weekend. There was a cry from over by the big stone barbecue pit, "Stop, thief!" Drew looked up to see Slipper slinking across the wide swath of lawn with a raw steak in her jaws, the leash trailing along behind.

"They ought to get that dog out of here," somebody said.

"Or tie it up."

"Hey, Rut," Doug Perkins shouted. "Get your mutt under control." This drew hearty laughter from every table.

Drew got up and stalked across the grass after Slipper, who'd stopped long enough to gulp the steak. She saw him coming, dropped what remained of the meat, turned tail, and started to trot off, but Drew caught the end of the leash and yanked it hard, pulling her up short. The dog rolled over onto her back and thumped the ground with her tail. "Sit up!" he said. She lay looking up at him, wriggling in the grass. He grabbed her collar and pulled her up into a sitting position. She tried to twist out of her collar but he held it tight.

A piece of deadwood lay on the ground nearby, blown off an oak in the rainstorm, and holding her collar tight in one hand, he reached for the stick with the other. He raised the stick and struck her hard on the back, just above her tail. The members and their guests looked on, perfectly silent. He hit her seven times, gaining force with each blow. The puppy yelped and cried most tragically.

Drew left the picnic, dragging his dog along behind him. Back at the camp he took out a bottle of twelve-year-old Scotch and started drinking in earnest. Slipper went out to her dog bed on the screened porch and fell asleep, an active, twitching sleep punctuated by soft, fitful yips. Firecrackers went off here and there in the dusk, and the creak of oars and a rowdy chorus of the national anthem filtered up through the trees to where Drew sat brooding on the porch overlooking the lake.

Deerwood's governing board met the next day, as they did each year, to discuss club business. Discussion revolved around the barbecue debacle. All other business—the stocking of the lake, the new roof for the clubhouse, the Labor Day Dinner-Dance Committee nominations—was put on the back burner. Mrs. Frederick Maddox had been so sickened by the incident she'd had to leave the barbecue. Her husband, acting president of the club, reported she became physically ill at home, and had passed a dreadful night. They had never, he said, witnessed anything so upsetting in all their forty years at Deerwood.

Everyone agreed that some sort of swift disciplinary action was called for. At length the board made the unanimous decision to preclude the young Drew Rutledges from participating in any club functions for the balance of the summer, including the Labor Day tennis tournament and dinner-dance. Tom Campbell, club secretary, drafted a letter to that effect, and the six board members signed it then and there. Bill Webb volunteered to drop it by the Rutledge cottage on his way home from the meeting. He and Drew senior had been close, and though he too had been sickened by the sight of young Drew beating his dog, he felt a paternal responsibility in the matter.

Jennifer met Mr. Webb at the door.

"Drew's in the shower," she said. "Would you like to wait?"

Terry and David were out for a walk around the lake with the dog. Jennifer had been tidying up the kitchen, getting ready for their late afternoon departure.

"This is difficult for me—" Webb said. He gravely handed over the letter. "If you'd tell Drew—well, I'll be at the cottage through tomorrow if he needs to speak with me."

"Are you sure you won't come in? He should be right out."

"No, no. I can't stay."

In fact, Drew was lying on his father's bed, with a cold washcloth over his eyes, and a pounding headache. Jennifer brought the letter in and laid it over the water mark on the bedside stand. She left the room.

By three o'clock they were nearly ready to go. Jennifer had cleaned out the refrigerator and washed the towels while David and Terry went out for a final spin in the rowboat. Drew had stayed in bed all day. When she went in to pack her things, she saw the letter had been opened. She read it.

"Are you happy now?" she said.

"Fuck those assholes."

"Are you going to be ready by four? They want to get back in time to catch the train in."

"I'll be ready."

"We're going up to the clubhouse to shoot some pool. Why don't you just drive up when you're ready, we'll leave from there."

"Sure. Where's the dog?"

"We'll take her up with us."

"Leave her here."

"Are you sure?"

"Leave her."

Drew stuffed his things in the duffel and took it out to the Jeep. In the master bedroom, on a high shelf in the closet, next to the Monopoly game, the Chinese Checkers and the Dominoes, there were a couple of boxes of ammo. He slid one into his pocket.

In the living room he took a rifle from the gun rack hanging over the bar. He picked up the tennis ball, wet with saliva, that was lying under the card table. With the gun resting on the crook of his arm, he went out onto the screened-in porch where Slipper lay on her bed.

"Come on, girl," he said, and held up the ball. Slipper rose and followed him out the back door, prancing and wiggling with excitement. He threw the ball into the woods and she ran to retrieve it. They walked out into the woods, Drew pushing his way through the undergrowth, heading in the direction of the duck blind. Slipper ran ahead, forging a path with the ball in her jaws.

PARTICIPATING WORKSHOPS

UNITED STATES

American University
MFA Program in Creative
 Writing
Department of Literature
4400 Massachusetts Avenue
 N.W.
Washington, D.C. 20016-8037
202/885-2972

Bennington College
Writing Seminars
Bennington, VT 05201
802/442-5401 (ext. 160)

Boston University
Creative Writing Program
236 Bay State Road
Boston, MA 02215
617/353-2510

Bowling Green State
 University
Creative Writing Program
Department of English
Bowling Green, OH 43403
419/372-8370

Brooklyn College
MFA Program in Creative
 Writing
Department of English
2900 Bedford Avenue
Brooklyn, NY 11210
718/951-5195

Brown University
Program in Creative Writing
Box 1852
Providence, RI 02912
401/863-3260

California State University,
 Fresno
Creative Writing Program
Department of English
5245 North Backer Avenue
MS#98
Fresno, CA 93740-8001
209/278-3919

California State University,
 Sacramento
Department of English
6000 J Street
Sacramento, CA 95819-6075
916/278-6586

Chapman University
Department of English and
 Comparative Literature
333 North Glassell
Orange, CA 92866
714/997-6750

City College of the City
 University of New York
138th Street at Convent
 Avenue
New York, NY 10031
212/650-5408

Colorado State University
Department of English
Fort Collins, CO 80523-1773
970/491-6428

Columbia College Chicago
Fiction Writing Department
600 South Michigan Avenue
Chicago, IL 60605
312/663-1600 (ext. 5611)

Columbia University
Writing Division
School of the Arts
Dodge Hall 415
2960 Broadway, Room 400
New York, NY 10027-6902
212/854-4391

Cornell University
MFA Program
Department of English
250 Goldwin Smith Hall
Ithaca, NY 14853
607/255-7989

DePaul University
M.A. in Writing Program
Department of English
802 West Belden Avenue
Chicago, IL 60614-3214
312/325-7485

Eastern Michigan University
Department of English
 Language
 and Literature
Ypsilanti, MI 48197
313/487-4220

Eastern Washington
 University
Creative Writing Program
705 West First Avenue
MS # 1
Spokane, WA 99204
509/623-4221

Emerson College
Graduate Admissions
Writing, Literature, and
    Publishing
100 Beacon Street
Boston, MA 02116
617/824-8750

Florida International
    University
Creative Writing Program
English Department
North Miami Campus
North Miami, FL 33181
305/919-5857

Florida State University
Department of English
Tallahassee, FL 32306-1036
904/644-4230

George Mason University
Creative Writing Program
MS 3E4
Fairfax, VA 22030
703/993-1185

Georgia State University
Department of English
University Plaza
Atlanta, GA 30303
404/651-2900

Hollins College
Department of English
P.O. Box 9677
Roanoke, VA 24020-1677
540/362-6317

Illinois State University
Department of English
Normal, IL 61790-4240
309/438-3667

Indiana University
MFA Program
English Department
Ballantine Hall 442
Bloomington, IN 47405-6601
812/855-8224

Johns Hopkins University
The Writing Seminars
Baltimore, MD 21218-2690
410/516-7563

Long Island University
Brooklyn Campus
University Plaza
Brooklyn, NY 11201
718/488-1000

Louisiana State University
English Department
213 Allen
Baton Rouge, LA 70803
504/388-2236

Manhattanville College
Office of Adult and Special
    Programs
2900 Purchase Street
Purchase, NY 10577
914/694-3425

Mankato State University
English Department
Box 53, Mankato State
    University
Mankato, MN 56002-8400
507/389-2117

McNeese State University
Program in Creative Writing
Department of Languages
P.O. Box 92655
Lake Charles, LA 70609
318/475-5326

Miami University
Graduate Admissions,
    Creative Writing
Department of English
Oxford, OH 45056
513/529-5221

Michigan State University
Department of English
201 Morrill Hall
East Lansing, MI 48824-1036
517/355-7570

Mills College
5000 MacArthur Boulevard
Oakland, CA 94613
510/430-2217

Mississippi State University
Drawer E
Department of English
Mississippi State, MS 39762
601/325-3644

Naropa Institute
2130 Arapahoe Avenue
Boulder, CO 80302-6697
303/546-3540

New York University
Creative Writing Program
19 University Place
New York, NY 10003
212/998-8800

Northeastern University
Department of English
406 Holmes Hall
Boston, MA 02115
617/373-2512

Old Dominion University
Norfolk, VA 23529
804/683-3000

Pennsylvania State University
Graduate Admissions
MFA Program in Writing
Department of English
University Park, PA 16802
814/863-3069

Purdue University
Office of Admissions
1080 Schleman Hall
West Lafayette, IN 47907-1080
317/494-1776

Rutgers University
Department of English
University Heights
360 Dr. Martin Luther King
    Jr. Blvd.
Newark, NJ 07102
201/648-5279

Saint Mary's College of
California
MFA in Creative Writing
P.O. Box 4686
Moraga, CA 94575-4686
510/631-4088

San Diego State University
MFA Program
Department of English and
Comparative Literature
San Diego, CA 92182-8140
619/594-5443

San Francisco State
University
Department of Creative
Writing
College of Humanities
1600 Holloway Avenue
San Francisco, CA 94132
415/338-1891

Sonoma State University
English Department
1801 East Cotati Avenue
Rohnert Park, CA 94928
707/664-2140

Southwest Texas State
University
MFA Program in Creative
Writing
Department of English
601 University Drive
San Marcos, TX 78666-4616
512/245-2163

SUNY at Stony Brook
Creative Writing Program
Department of English
Stony Brook, NY 11794-5350
516/632-7373

Syracuse University
Program in Creative Writing
Department of English
Syracuse, NY 13244-0003
315/443-9469

Temple University
Graduate Creative Writing
Program
English Department
Philadelphia, PA 19122
215/204-1796

University at Albany, SUNY
Writing Program
Department of English
Humanities Building 333
Albany, NY 12222
518/442-4055

University of Alabama
Program in Creative Writing
Department of English
P.O. Box 870244
Tuscaloosa, AL 35487-0244
205/348-0766

University of Alaska,
Anchorage
Program in Creative Writing
3211 Providence Drive
Anchorage, AK 99508
907/786-4356

University of Alaska,
Fairbanks
Creative Writing Program
Department of English
P.O. Box 755720
Fairbanks, AK 99775-5720
907/474-7193

University of Arizona
Creative Writing Program
Department of English
Modern Languages Bldg. #67
P.O. Box 210067
Tucson, AZ 85721-0067
520/621-3880

University of Arkansas
Department of English
333 Kimpel Hall
Fayetteville, AR 72701
501/575-4301

University of California,
Davis
Graduate Creative Writing
Program
Department of English
Davis, CA 95616
916/752-2281

University of California,
Irvine
Program in Writing-Fiction
Department of English and
Comparative Literature
Irvine, CA 92697-2650
714/824-6718

University of Central Florida
Department of English
P.O. Box 161346
Orlando, FL 32816-1346
407/823-5254

University of Colorado at
Boulder
Creative Writing Program
Department of English
Campus Box 226
Boulder, CO 80309-0226
303/492-6434

University of Houston
Creative Writing Program
Department of English
Houston, TX 77204-3012
713/743-3013

University of Iowa
Program in Creative Writing
Department of English
436 English Philosophy Bldg.
Iowa City, IA 52242-1492
319/335-0416

University of Maine
English Department,
    Room 304
5752 Neville Hall
Orono, ME 04469-5752
207/581-3839

University of Maryland
Creative Writing
Department of English
3101 Susquehanna Hall
College Park, MD 20742
301/405-3820

University of Massachusetts,
    Amherst
MFA in English
Bartlett Hall
Box 30515
Amherst, MA 01003-0515
413/545-5497

University of Michigan
Hopwood Room
1176 Angell Hall
Ann Arbor, MI 48109-1003
313/763-4139

University of Montana
Creative Writing Program
Department of English
Missoula, MT 59812-1013
406/243-5231

University of New Orleans
Creative Writing Workshop
College of Liberal Arts
Lakefront
New Orleans, LA 70148
504/280-7454

University of North Carolina,
    Greensboro
MFA Writing Program
Department of English
Greensboro, NC 27412-5001
910/334-5459

University of Oregon
Program in Creative Writing
144 Columbia Hall
Eugene, OR 97403-1286
541/346-3944

University of San Francisco
M.A. in Writing Program
Program Office, Lone
    Mountain 340
2130 Fulton Street
San Francisco, CA 94117-1080
415/422-2382

University of South Carolina
English Department
Office of Graduate Studies
Humanities Building
Columbia, SC 29208
803/777-5063

University of Southern
    California
Professional Writing Program
Waite Phillips Hall, Room
    404
Los Angeles, CA 90089-4034
213/740-3252

University of Southern
    Mississippi
Center for Writers and
    Mississippi Review
Box 5144
Hattiesburg, MS 39406-5144
601/266-4321

University of Southwestern
    Louisiana
Wendell Mayo, Director
Creative Writing Program
Department of English
P.O. Box 44691
Layfayette, LA 70504-4691
318/482-6906

University of Texas at Austin
English Department
PAR 108
Austin, TX 78712-1164
512/471-5132

University of Texas at Austin
Texas Center for Writers
FDH
702 East 26th Street
Austin, TX 78705
512/471-1601

University of Texas at El Paso
MFA Program in Creative
    Writing
English Department,
    Hudspeth Hall
El Paso, TX 79968-0526
915/747-5529

University of Virginia
Creative Writing Program
Department of English
Bryan Hall
Charlottesville, VA 22903
804/924-6675

Vermont College
Master of Fine Arts in
    Writing
Montpelier, VT 05602
802/828-8840

Virginia Commonwealth
    University
MFA in Creative Writing
    Program
Department of English
P.O. Box 842005
Richmond, VA 23284-2005
804/828-1329

Warren Wilson College
MFA Program for Writers
P.O. Box 9000
Asheville, NC 28815-9000
704/298-3325 (ext. 380)

Washington University
Writing Program
Department of English
Campus Box 1122
One Brookings Drive
St. Louis, MO 63130-4899
314/935-5190

Wayne State University
Department of English
Detroit, MI 48202
313/577-2450

Western Illinois University
Department of English and
  Journalism
Macomb, IL 61455-1390
309/298-1103

Western Michigan University
Program in Creative Writing
Department of English
Kalamazoo, MI 49008-5092
616/387-2572

Wichita State University
Department of English
Box 14
Wichita, KS 67260-0014
316/978-3130

CANADA

Concordia University
Department of English
Creative Writing Program
LB 501
Montreal, PQ H3G 1M8
514/848-2340

University of Alberta
Department of English
3-5 Humanities Center
Edmonton, Alberta T6G 2E5
403/492-3258

The University of British
  Columbia
Department of Theatre, Film
  and Creative Writing
Creative Writing Program
Buchanan E462 - 1866 Main
  Mall
Vancouver, BC V6T 1Z1
604/822-2712

University of Calgary
Department of English
Graduate Office
2500 University Drive N.W.
Calgary, Alberta T2N 1N4
403/220-5482

The University of Guelph
The Department of English
Guelph, Ontario N1G 2W1
519/824-4120

University of New Brunswick
Department of English
Box 4400
Fredericton, NB E3B 5A3
506/453-4676